SM

P9-DNO-163

EVERY
DEEP
DESIRE

SHARON
WRAY

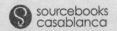

sourcebooks
casablanca

Copyright © 2018 by Sharon Wray
Cover and internal design © 2018 by Sourcebooks, Inc.
Cover design by Eileen Carey/No Fuss Design
Cover images © Westend61/Getty Images, Cloudniners/Getty Images,
Ysbrand Cosijn/Shutterstock, CURAphotography/Shutterstock

Sourcebooks and the colophon are registered trademarks of Sourcebooks,
Inc.

All rights reserved. No part of this book may be reproduced in any form
or by any electronic or mechanical means including information storage
and retrieval systems—except in the case of brief quotations embodied
in critical articles or reviews—without permission in writing from its
publisher, Sourcebooks, Inc.

The characters and events portrayed in this book are fictitious or are
used fictitiously. Any similarity to real persons, living or dead, is purely
coincidental and not intended by the author.

All brand names and product names used in this book are trademarks,
registered trademarks, or trade names of their respective holders.
Sourcebooks, Inc., is not associated with any product or vendor in this
book.

Published by Sourcebooks Casablanca, an imprint of Sourcebooks, Inc.
P.O. Box 4410, Naperville, Illinois 60567-4410
(630) 961-3900
Fax: (630) 961-2168
sourcebooks.com

Printed and bound in the United States of America.
OPM 10 9 8 7 6 5 4 3 2 1

In loving memory
of
Karen E. M. Johnston
Best friend and critique partner
Be brave. Be strong. Be dauntless.

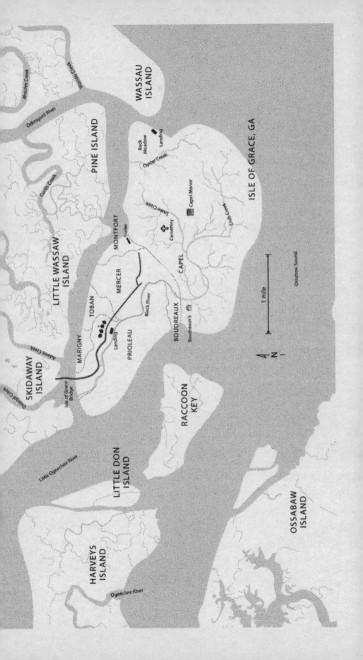

PROLOGUE

JULIET'S DADDY HAD ALWAYS TOLD HER TO STAY AWAY FROM men who bowed. But tonight, as she struggled with her groceries in the snow, she almost asked the stranger in the shadows across the street for help. He bowed as she walked by and, as creepy as that seemed, she was reconsidering her daddy's warning. It was still Valentine's Day, after all.

She blinked against the freezing wind, and the man had disappeared. She made it to her apartment and almost stepped on the ivory envelope. Balancing her bags in one arm, she picked it up. From its weight and polished paper, a letter instead of a bill.

A valentine, maybe? From Rafe?

Flurries blew as she unlocked the door. Five months apart. Five months since their argument. Five months and he'd finally sent her an apology. The ache in her heart loosened, and she went inside. Frigid, mildew-tinged air blasted at her, and her breath came out in cold, white gusts. The heat was off. Again.

She placed the bags on the kitchen counter and turned the envelope over. The linen stationery felt thick and expensive. Someone had sealed it with a wax stamp of a sword piercing a heart and written her name in script on the other side. It wasn't Rafe's familiar, irregular printing.

After trading her coat for her favorite sweater, she curled up on the couch. Her husband was undercover with his A-team. Had someone else sent the letter on his behalf? It wouldn't be the first time he'd broken the rules. Still, five months wasn't the longest they'd gone without contact. Last year he'd been away for eight. Except this goodbye had been different. They'd argued, said things she prayed they hadn't meant, and hadn't made love before he left.

Something that had never happened before.

She held the letter to her heart and looked at the unpacked boxes stacked around her. Rafe had left the week they'd moved from Fort Bragg's temporary housing into this apartment, days after his mother's funeral, and she'd refused to unpack completely. Without him, it didn't feel like home.

Worry and lack of sleep had left her exhausted. Nightmares plagued her nights. Dreams she'd had since childhood that only Rafe's touch could heal. For the past few weeks, she'd been obsessed with a heavy feeling in her heart she could only define as doom.

She broke the seal and read. The back of her throat burned. Her sweaty hands gripped the edges of the stationery, tearing it. And she read the letter again. It wasn't a valentine.

No. No. No. She fell off the couch and crawled to the bathroom. She barely made it before the eruption hit. Minutes later, she rinsed her mouth and leaned her forehead against the window. The room smelled like vomit, bleach, and mold. It reeked of betrayal.

Outside, the moon hung full, like on the night he'd left. Another wave of nausea drove her to her knees. She rolled into a ball, her arms tucked in close. He wasn't dead. He just wasn't coming home. *Ever.*

The doorbell rang, and she ignored it. She lay there for minutes or hours or days. When even the moon turned in, she shifted onto her back and stared at the stained ceiling. The brown concentric circles reminded her of constellations. The star patterns she and Rafe identified together out on the Isle when they were kids.

"Pegasus." She raised one arm to reach the sky. The winged horse constellation had been her favorite, only visible a few weeks of every year. She'd always dreamed of flying away from the Isle, her father, her poverty. But instead of reaching the stars, she'd married the man she'd adored since she was four and he was eight.

When the doorbell rang again and again and again, she got up, determined to send whoever the hell it was away. She flung the door open to find two Army MPs in full uniform, wearing pistols, standing side by side. Their grim faces shared identical hard angles. Cold air burst into the room, chilling her even more.

"Mrs. Montfort?" the first MP asked.

"Yes?"

"Ma'am." The second MP held out a pair of handcuffs. "You'll need to come with us."

CHAPTER 1

JULIET'S HOUSE HAD DISAPPEARED.

Rafe Montfort scrubbed a hand over his face. A strangling ache invaded his chest, filling the empty space that once held his heart. He shifted the Army duffel he'd shouldered for the past six miles, moving the burn from one arm to the other. Why had he assumed her father's trailer would still be standing? That she'd be living there? Waiting for him?

Because he wasn't only a bastard who made assumptions. He was a fool who once believed the Prince's brutal goals justified Rafe's ruthless actions.

Or, as Escalus used to say, "*a fool whose violent delights have violent ends.*"

Summer cicadas hummed in the Isle of Grace's surrounding woods, their mournful drone filling Rafe's head with rhythmic disapproval. Sweat soaked his T-shirt, pooling low in his back above his waistband. Where he used to keep his gun.

He wasn't just a bastard. He wasn't just a fool. He just wasn't the man he'd once hoped to become. With a nod to his broken past, he left the overgrown property and headed home.

Keep it moving, Montfort. That's right. One boot in front of the other.

He kicked an empty beer bottle into a ditch, shattering the brown glass, and marched toward Pops's trailer tucked between the towering Georgia pines a half mile down the

Isle's dirt road. He'd given up his honor, his wife, his men. Thank God his mother had died before he betrayed everyone he loved. In the years he'd been away, he hadn't just cut out his heart; he'd sold his soul.

Despite the breeze, questions about Juliet's departure burned his blood.

Why had she left? He climbed the pine steps to the deck alongside the double-wide.

Where'd she go? He jumped the last two steps to avoid the missing planks.

Did she ever think of him? The Capels had arrived on the Isle long before the American Revolution. It'd never occurred to him that her family would leave. For eight long years, he'd been counting on that.

His duffel landed with a thud next to an outboard motor and buckets of fishing gear. He rubbed the knotted muscles in his shoulder and faced the broken screen door. His vision faded until all he could see was the blurry mesh.

What the hell was he doing? Why had he even come home? Because he'd had no choice. Everything depended on him remembering that. With renewed determination, he raised his fist and hit the metal door.

No answer. He closed his eyes, took another breath, and knocked again.

Juliet's family was gone. Had his left as well?

He heard a banging around back, pulled out his leather jacket, and covered the tattoos on his arms. He'd rather die of heat stroke than start an argument. Then he jumped over the deck rail. His combat boots made it easier to walk through the tall weeds to the red barn a hundred yards behind the trailer. Three times larger than the home, the barn and surrounding yard held remnants of every American classic car ever made.

Everything stood as if he'd never left, except for the cell boost antenna on the barn's roof. From the height and distance, it probably provided a cell signal the width and depth of Pops's property. Pops had joined the twenty-first century? Maybe miracles were possible.

He drew closer and saw his daddy's gray head bobbing up and down beneath the hood of a black 1958 Chevy Impala. He stopped on the other side of the car and exhaled until his lungs ached. "Pops?"

His dad raised his head, his eyes squinting. "Who's there?"

"It's me. Rafe."

A man, shorter than he remembered, stood. In a stained red T-shirt and overalls with one strap hanging down, his father waited a few moments before nodding. At least he wasn't holding a beer. Or his shotgun.

Rafe waved at the car. "She's a real beauty. She yours?"

"No." Pops wiped his dirty hands on an oily rag, and Rafe focused on the remaining finger on his father's right hand. He'd given the other four to the Marines. "She belongs to your brother."

"Good for him."

Pops tossed the rag onto the engine and gripped the side of the Chevy's frame. His hard stare took in Rafe's leather jacket in what had to be triple-digit heat. "What you doin' here, boy?"

He held out his hand. A hug would only be an invitation to an ass-kicking. "The Army released me from prison."

"Released?" His father picked up a dirty wrench, his face brown beneath a haircut the Corps would salute. "What the hell for? Good behavior?"

"No, sir." He dropped his hand. If disapproval were a color, it would be the dark, muddy brown in his father's grim gaze. "I don't know why."

Since he'd spent two years in a Russian jail and then the last nine months locked in isolation in Leavenworth, he wasn't sure what to think. "I was told to return to Savannah and wait for a call."

While it went against every one of his hard-earned instincts urging him to run, he'd come home to find out what the hell was going on. Besides, it wasn't like he had anyplace else to go.

"You still a sergeant?"

A sharp ache hit Rafe's back molars, and he eased off the teeth grinding. On his left, he noticed a band of magnolia trees surrounding a white glory cross. He shoved his hands into his jacket pockets and forced himself to meet his father's reproach. "I don't know what I am." Sergeant? Prisoner 061486? The Prince's warrior? Hell if he knew.

"I know what you are," Pops said. "Damn traitor. Not to mention adulterer, liar, thief."

Rafe's exhale sounded more like a hiss. While he wasn't all of those things, he'd done other things—worse things. "I was also dishonorably discharged."

His father snorted and rocked back on his heels, watching, waiting. Probably for an apology. So like Pops.

Without a word, Pops ducked back under the hood and collected his tools. A torque wrench, the old spark plugs, another rag. "What reason would the U.S. Army have for letting a dishonorably discharged ex-Green Beret out of prison?"

Rafe gripped the frame with both hands. "They dropped the case against me."

"That makes no sense. You ditched your men. Then got caught working as a mercenary or somethin'. Ain't no way to walk that back, Son. Ain't no chance."

"I know." There'd been extenuating circumstances, the

kind of circumstances beyond any soldier's control. Five thousand one hundred and eleven reasons, to be exact.

Pops straightened and they shut the hood of the car together. The click-bang echoed around the yard littered with wounded vehicles, followed by the hollow clatter of tools being tossed into a metal toolbox.

Pops wiped the sweat off his brow with his arm. "You want to stay here until you get that call?"

"Until I figure out what's going on. But I need something from you. Information."

His father's eyes thinned, looking like slits in a wrinkled potato. "Juliet *est partie*."

Pops spoke in French—the language of Rafe's momma—and that meant no more questions unless you wanted to see the buckle end of his belt. Except Rafe was taller and stronger than his father. Had been for a long time.

"*Où est-elle?*" Rafe kept his tone casual, but when Pops didn't answer, he tried again. "Where'd she go?"

Pops headed for the trailer. "You can't undo what you did, Son. And what you did to Juliet was bad. Real bad."

Rafe followed, inhaling the humid air until his chest burned. "I need to know she's okay." Although there weren't enough sorries to make up for what he'd done, protecting Juliet was his priority. Always had been. He was done with war and its ever-changing rules. Once assured of her safety, he'd ditch Savannah and start his life over again. Alone.

Only problem was he had to disappear before the Prince found out about his release. And it had to be forever.

"What about your brother?" Pops said. "You worried about him, too?"

"*No.*"

"Still damn stubborn." Pops shook his head. "You two have things to work out. Bad history. But family's important."

"Which is why I need to check on Juliet."

Pops faced him. "Do you know what St. Peter uses to polish his heavenly gates?"

Rafe crossed his arms. Some things never changed. "Not a clue, sir."

"Humility." Pops poked Rafe in the chest with the only finger on his right hand. "Considering the shit you're standing in, you'd do well to shut down your pride and hold your temper."

Rafe wasn't the only man in the family with anger issues, but he answered, "Yes, sir."

Pops pulled a humming cell phone out of his back pocket. He tossed it to Rafe. "Is this what you're waitin' for?"

He caught the phone and read the text from a blocked ID.

Welcome home, Romeo. Tis Escalus.

Rafe went for the weapon in his back waistband, except it wasn't there. He scanned the tree line of the surrounding pine forest. If Escalus was near, so was his sniper rifle. "Maybe."

Pops harrumphed and left Rafe standing in the weeds.

Once Pops went inside, Rafe pounded the phone's keyboard.

Did the Prince buy my freedom?
*No. And the Prince will doom thee to death
if thou speak.*

Considering the Prince had thrown Rafe's ass into a Russian prison, his former boss wouldn't be high-fiving the change in status. But what would the Prince and his warriors—including Escalus—do about it?

> How did you find me?
> *We've never lost a kinsman. You belong to us, Romeo. Remember thy vow, such as lovers used to swear?*

Rafe stretched out his right arm covered in leather, ruined from wrist to shoulder. He more than remembered his vow to the Prince. His damn tithe. The life he'd given up to save those he loved. Nothing less than everything.

> What do you want?
> *Come back to us. Unless you no longer love Lady Juliet?*

Rafe typed, You hurt my wife and I'll kill you but deleted the message before hitting send. Starting a war with Escalus would only make things worse. Rafe had only been out for three days, and already his past was fucking with his present. Fantastic.

Thunder rolled in the distance, storm clouds approached, and the air hummed with static. He studied the dense veil of kudzu a half mile from the trailer. The border between Capel land and Montfort property. Close enough for a well-trained sniper. *A Fianna sniper.*

"Rafe?" Pops called from the back deck. "You coming, Son?"

"Yes." Rafe wanted to pray that his deal with the devil hadn't followed him home. Except he no longer believed in prayers, and the churning in his gut told him the devil hadn't just hitched a ride. The devil was driving. "I'm coming."

୨

Juliet stopped in the middle of her store, pressed the phone against her ear, and stared at the marble archangel's smug face. Gabriel stood in the corner, over six feet tall, with his wings folded behind his back. He held a sword against his muscled thigh, and he was naked. "Are you sure, Detective?"

"I am," Detective Garza said with an accent she guessed was from New York or Connecticut or someplace else up north. "I reviewed the security footage. Yesterday's vandalism attack on your shop—"

"The sixth in nine months."

"Wasn't captured on your cameras."

"How's that possible?" Her shop's doorbell jingled, and her friend Philip came in with a sympathetic smile and two takeaway cups. She nodded as he handed her a coffee, hot and sweet, just as she liked it.

"We're looking into that," Detective Garza said. "According to the security company, your cameras have been turned off before each event and turned back on after."

"The security company has no idea how their system was breached, and then fixed, six times?"

Philip raised an eyebrow, and she shook her head in exasperation. She had little faith in the SPD and less in Detective Garza, the new detective who wasn't even from Savannah.

"No, ma'am. But I'll call back when I have more information."

"Thank you." Once she hung up, she sipped her coffee, listening to the sounds of her foreman, Bob, and the men who worked with him outside fixing her broken windows.

"I got your message," Philip said. "Why are they changing the terms of your business loan?"

Once the warmth hit her stomach, she sighed. Time to

move on to her next problem. "My lawyer says my bank—including my loan—was sold to a bigger bank that wants more collateral and a higher interest rate."

"And they can do that?"

She shrugged. "Apparently."

Philip took her free hand and squeezed. "I'm sorry." The morning sun backlit the impeccable tailoring of his gray wool suit and white silk shirt, which matched his perfectly cut blond hair and Italian leather loafers. He reminded her of a Ken doll. With her own pink linen sleeveless shift and long hair twisted into a complicated knot, she had to admit to a vintage Barbie vibe. So different from the children they'd been on the Isle.

She dropped his hand and inhaled. Lavender was the signature scent of the store, but today the smell made her queasy. "I own a landscape architecture firm with a storefront catering to high-end clients, and I always pay on time." Something about this didn't make any sense.

"You can still design without a store."

"My clients—from people renovating mansions, to family members planning elaborate funerals, to brides getting married in the city's squares—like to come for consultations where they can peruse my design books in a beautiful, air-conditioned space, look at the statuary I keep outside in the courtyard, and even have a glass of champagne while I sketch their ideas. My store sets me apart from the other design firms in the city that just drive around in a van dropping off reference sheets and photocopies of previous projects."

She moved behind the gothic altar she used as her counter and shut the cash drawer of her antique register. After everything she'd worked for, the years struggling alone, she was about to lose her dream because of a bank decision?

No. Which meant she needed a plan. Now.

Philip steadied a silver bowl that threatened to fall off a stack of horticulture books on the counter. "Could this have anything to do with Senator Wilkins's death on Capel land?"

"I doubt it. That happened months ago."

A loud *dirrrg, dirrrg, dirrrg* made her switch problems, and her foreman came in the front door. "What's wrong, Bob?"

"Sorry about the racket, ma'am." Bob took off his Georgia Tech baseball cap and scratched his head. "The vandals broke the window frame this time. I need to use a masonry bit. Damn kids."

Philip moved behind her and held her shoulders. "Have the police caught them yet?"

"Not yet," Bob said. "That's why we're installing bulletproof glass and hand-painting Miss Juliet's gold lily logo."

"It's all outrageously expensive." She pulled away from Philip as thunder rolled. Another storm, for the fifth day in a row, during the hottest summer in years.

"Don't worry, ma'am," Bob said. "We'll have your shop tight and dry before it rains." With a nod, he headed outside to his white tool van and extension ladders.

She grabbed the loan folder and opened it on the altar.

"How much do you need?" Philip asked.

"At least twenty thousand." The numbers and legalese blurred. She reached for her mechanical pencil and her glasses. Tears were not an option. Lord knew she'd cried enough for all the women in Savannah. "I'm barely staying open now."

"How about your antiques? Can you sell them?"

"I've already sold a few." Besides the twelfth-century altar that had been transformed into her counter, a fifteenth-century round table sat in the center of the room. She'd pushed her worktable from Provence against one of the broken windows. The rest of the shop was filled with horticulture and gardening books, fresh floral arrangements, photos of her current projects, and the botanical prints she sold on commission. The back room held her workspace and floral refrigerators. Sometimes, to make her rent, she subcontracted large, freestanding arrangements for special events.

It'd taken her five years before she'd saved enough to make a down payment on a business loan to open the store. That didn't include the school loans she was still paying off.

Philip nodded toward the angel in the corner. "You could sell Gabriel."

"Gabriel and I have a long history together. He stays." Not to mention he was the only man who'd never left her. "I'd like to sell Capel land, but it's tied up in centuries-old real estate trusts." Unfortunately, old, boring, and complicated legal matters meant one thing: expensive billable hours. "Because my daddy put Rafe's name on the deeds, I can't use the property as collateral for the new loan."

Philip rested a hip against the altar and crossed his arms. "I'd love to know what Gerald was thinking when he added Rafe's name to the Capel land deeds."

She would too. Especially since, at the time her daddy had made the changes, Rafe had just been transferred from a prison in St. Petersburg to Leavenworth. She threw her pencil and it bounced off a book and onto the floor. "Hell."

Philip picked up her pencil and handed it to her. "Where are you going to get the money? And with Senator Prioleau's birthday event coming up? You have a huge up-front cost for her party."

"No idea." Which wasn't quite true. She could call Deke. She swallowed, the disgusting thought burning her throat. After all, Deke was how she'd managed to survive while in school and save for the original business loan.

Being homeless and without any family left a young woman with few options. Which was why she couldn't lose her business. She didn't want to be dependent on anyone ever again. Philip knew that. She'd told him enough times, anyway. The steel-reinforced employee entrance at the back of the hallway opened, and a woman with long, reddish-blond curls came in, letting the door slam shut behind her.

"Rain's coming." Samantha's voice rang out as she appeared in a floral dress, combat boots, and black tulle petticoat. She was all emo all the time. After placing her white bakery bag on the counter, she handed her purse to Juliet.

Juliet locked it in her desk drawer. There'd been too much vandalism to take any chances. Even Juliet's antique iron doorknocker, wrought into a lily, had been stolen the first night her windows had been broken. There was also the new heroin epidemic to worry about. All this violence in the city she loved made her sad.

Bob came inside and handed her a folded paper. Philip read over her shoulder while she proofed the work order sketch of the store's logo, Juliet's Lily, she wanted painted on her new windows. The unusual eight-petaled lily formed the apostrophe between the *t* and the *s*.

Philip changed the subject. "What about that new client buying Prideaux House?"

"Mr. Delacroix is *hot, hot, hot*." Samantha took a bite of her bagel, using a tissue as a napkin.

"Mr. Delacroix is a *potential* client, if he can make a deal with the Habersham sisters to sell him the house." Juliet signed off on the work order. "I'm hoping he'll hire me for a complete garden redesign."

Philip headed for the door. "You'll figure this out, Juliet."

"You could get a second job." Samantha threw out her bakery bag and headed for the back room. "I have three."

Juliet wished she could fix that. She'd met Samantha while dancing for Deke at Rage of Angels nightclub. Samantha still worked there as a waitress, but Juliet left after opening her store. It'd been the happiest day of her life since returning to Savannah. "I'm meeting Mr. Delacroix later. And Calum agreed to install a new alarm system."

On his way out, Philip said, "How about asking him for a loan? Calum Prioleau isn't only the richest man in town, he's your landlord, and he adores you."

"I'll think about it."

The door closed as Samantha brought in a vase of yellow roses and white hydrangeas and placed it on the table in the center of the store. "Juliet, you shouldn't lead Philip on or lie to him."

"I'm not."

"Not intentionally, but it's clear he'd like more from you."

"Philip knows how I feel. He'd never ask for more than I'm willing to give." Juliet went to the pile of paperwork on her desk in the hallway between her shop and the back room. Her head pounded with the promise of another stress headache. She had to figure out this loan mess. And she had to do it quickly.

She found her cell and left a message for Calum. She hoped he'd call soon because her only other choice was Deke.

Her phone hummed with a text from a blocked ID.

Juliet of the lily? Remember me?

She reread the message from the man who texted in odd language. The man who'd been her last link with the ex-husband who'd lied to her, betrayed her, and left her penniless.

What do u want?
Take heed, my lady. Thou art wedded to calamity.

She'd always hated these cryptic messages.

Meaning?
Your husband has returned.

CHAPTER 2

WATER POUNDED RAFE'S BACK, AND HE RAN HIS HANDS OVER his face, feeling three days' worth of stubble. He couldn't remember the last time he'd had such privacy or unlimited hot water. For the first time in eight years, he allowed himself to believe the lie that he hadn't ruined his life.

He soaped his body, letting the rivulets run over the hard muscles that hadn't been there when he'd left home. Five years training with the Prince's men and three years in prison had left him stronger than he'd ever been in his adult life. *What would Juliet think of me now?*

With his guard down, memories slipped in. Juliet curling against his back on a winter's night, her hair trailing over her naked breasts, her hands reaching for what made him a man.

His body responded, and he washed his lower half, letting the pressure of the hot water take some of the tension away. But he welcomed the deep contractions in his lower stomach. He could almost smell her lavender scent, feel the softness of her skin when his fingers skimmed over her breasts, across her stomach, down her thighs. His rough skin would catch on hers like sand over silk. When she straddled him, her hair fell down her back while his mouth found the rosy tips of her breasts.

What wouldn't I give to taste her again?

His chest hurt, and his body tightened. He punched the shower wall and leaned his forehead against the tile while the water eased from hot to cold. Visions of Juliet were a pleasure he'd forbidden himself since he'd joined the Prince. From the moment he tithed, all he'd done was survive. And memories of Juliet only led to two things: longing and self-disgust. Living without her had become a pain he'd learned to endure. Just another form of self-mortification. Escalus would be proud.

Rafe turned the shower off. After realizing there was no escape from the Prince's Fianna army, he'd had no choice but to become like Escalus. If Rafe broke his vows to the Prince, Juliet would be killed. Not in triumph or as a sign of power but as a message: once you tithe, you belong to the Prince. Forever and always.

Her life meant nothing to the soulless men Rafe had worked with, the type of man he'd become. Now he had to find out who'd paid for his freedom, figure out what was going on, and come up with a plan to protect Juliet. Before Escalus acted.

After drying and shaving, Rafe pulled on jeans and socks he'd dug out of his duffel, boots, and a black T-shirt he'd found in the bedroom he'd shared with his younger brother. When he shoved the dresser drawer in, something shiny shifted beneath the clothes. A blue satin ribbon.

The silky fabric slid through his fingers. He didn't know how it'd gotten there, but he knew to whom it belonged. Memories of the night he'd tied Juliet's hands with the satin made sweat bead on his forehead. He wrapped the ribbon around his left wrist and tightened it. Then threw on his leather jacket. Once ready, he followed the sounds of his father's cooking in the kitchen.

Would he stay? Would he go? That decision, like all his others, would be determined by what was best for Juliet. Since he hadn't heard from his contact, lack of a plan left him hot and restless. A familiar ache he used to work off with intense physical training and pounding rounds at the range. The pain fueled his aggression, the aggression caused more suffering, and the sick cycle of punishment helped dull the reality of the man he'd become.

Helped him forget the people—his father, his A-team, his woman—he'd left behind.

Pops turned, a knife in his good hand, an iron fry pan on the stove. "You up for eating?" He dropped a battered catfish into the pan of hot oil. "Went fishin' this morning."

Rafe's stomach growled. Eight years was a long time to go without lots of things, and his father's fried fish was one of them. "Sounds great."

"Got something for you." Pops pointed the spatula toward the kitchen table.

Rafe remembered the chipped gray Formica that once held his momma's brownies. Except now, on top, lay his father's cell phone, an iron key chain, and a Glock 19.

He held the gun, testing the weight, feeling the cold metal. "It's military issue. Special Forces." He turned over the weapon he remembered well. "You knew I was coming home."

"Heard you were free. Didn't know if you were coming home." Pops went back to battering. "Ammo is in the Walmart bag on the counter."

Rafe aimed the weapon out the window, testing the sight. "You bought this at Walmart?"

"Just the ammo," Pops said over the splattering sizzle of more cold fish hitting the hot grease. "The nine-mil showed up a day ago with a note saying you were out and the weapon was yours. No idea who sent it. But whoever got you released has a hell of a lot of pull." Pops flipped the fish in the pan. "He'll want something in return."

No kidding. Rafe's stomach roared at the smell of fried catfish. He grabbed the bag, sat at the table, and dug out the ammo. When he'd been with the Prince, they'd carried H&K nine-mils. He hadn't held a Glock since leaving his unit. But the heft felt familiar. "Question is, did the same person who got me out of jail send me the weapon?"

With a flourish, Pops dressed the fish with his special blend of spices. "You'll find out soon enough."

Pops's phone on the table buzzed with another blocked ID text from Escalus, and Rafe read it.

Heaven is here where Juliet lives.

"Pops? When did you last see Juliet?"

His father placed the plates on the table. "A week ago."

"Does she still live in Savannah?"

Pops didn't say anything and sat across from him.

So Rafe pushed the limits. "Her trailer's gone. Is her daddy living at Capel Manor?"

"Her daddy's dead."

Rafe took a bite, and then another, savoring the flavor and processing the news. He'd had no idea that Gerald had died, and Rafe was surprised he felt…sad. Gerald had been a troubled man known for his temper and strike-first mentality. The only things Rafe and Gerald had ever had in common were Juliet's happiness and the fact that they'd both failed her miserably. "Does Juliet live at the manor?"

"No. *Ça suffit.* Enough."

He had a ton of Q's that needed A's, but he kept quiet and went for the pepper. His heart hurt on his wife's behalf. Although she and her daddy had had a strained relationship, his death meant she was even more alone in the world. If she wasn't living at the manor, she wouldn't have gone far. Rafe picked up the iron loop that held the keys to crypts in the old cemetery on Capel land. She was tied to her people as surely as he was bound to her. "Why do you have the keys to the Cemetery of Lost Children?"

"Juliet gave them to me after her daddy died. Grady and I've been hunting on Capel land, keeping down the wild boars in the back meadow. In return for hunting rights, we're maintaining the property. Roads, docks, and such. It's why I got the boost cell tower. Gives us reach to the cemetery. Less than one-twentieth of her land, but better than nothing."

Rafe nodded. Pops and Grady Mercer had been hunting buddies since receiving their first rifles when they were twelve. "Are boars still a problem in the back meadow?"

"Worse than ever since the fire," Pops said around a mouthful of food. "You're not eating."

Fire? Rafe wanted to ask more questions, but his father's glare warned him off. With a loud sigh, he took another bite, enjoying the taste he'd missed more than he'd realized.

Pops checked his phone. "What does this mean?"

Rafe hated lying, but Pops's safety beat the fourth and eighth commandments. "Not sure." That, at least, was the truth. While Rafe had once been able to communicate easily in Shakespearean verse, like all of the Prince's men, prison had destroyed his literary side.

"Son?" Pops handed over the buzzing phone.

Rafe read the new message: an address for Juliet's Lily in Savannah's historic district. He tossed the phone onto the table and stood. "What's *Juliet's Lily*?"

"Your wife's landscaping boutique." Pops's eyes widened. "What the hell's goin' on?"

"Don't worry. I'm taking the truck." Rafe grabbed his sidearm and ammo and slammed the screen door so hard the frame broke. He'd apologize later. First he had to find Juliet.

CHAPTER 3

Major Nate Walker screamed out in darkness. His arms flailed, words dried in his parched throat. A loud crash jerked him up, soaked and shaking. *Where am I?* He opened his eyes. Right. His shitty motel room.

Stale air burned his nose. The nightmare receded while his body convulsed in the aftermath. He swung his legs off the bed and ran his hands through his damp hair. Unable to remember. Desperate to forget.

The shadowed room offered no answers, nor did the slivers of light slashing through the closed plantation shutters on the doors leading to the balcony. The clock radio lay upside down on the floor. His beat-up bike stood against the far wall. He inhaled, orienting himself between the present in this motel room and his recent past, and reached for the medal around his neck. Except it wasn't there. His head pounded in that oh-so-fucking-familiar way. Like an ax had been jammed into his skull.

Get your shit together, Walker.

He stumbled to the dingy bathroom and stepped into the shower to scrub himself raw with generic soap under the hot water. Why had he taken this assignment? Right. To get half of his men out of jail and keep the other half from going to jail.

Groaning, he shut off the water, dried off with the world's thinnest towel, and left the room, slamming his forehead on the lintel. Welcome back, full throttle headache.

The ringing phone snapped him to attention. He found

his cell beneath the bed. Next to his weapon. What happened while he slept? Grabbing both, he answered, "Walker."

"You're up," Pete said. "Good. I'm on my way."

Naked, sweating, and standing to the side of the plantation shutter, Nate opened a slat with his gun's barrel. Not enough to show his assets but enough to scan his perimeter and let in some sunlight. From the third floor, he saw a barge inching up the Savannah River, a heroin addict sleeping in the no-man's land between the riverbank and railroad tracks, and four CSX train cars overfilled with coal stopped at the track switch. His CO's earlier warning circled around him, igniting sparks in the moldy air. *Always beware the not unusual.*

His hands jerked, his blood hummed, and he gripped his weapon until his fingers ached. "Bring coffee. And something to eat."

"Got it. And I have a guest. He may have intel. I want you to meet him."

Nate reached for his jeans and shoved one leg through, and then the other, phone tucked between ear and shoulder. "If he can't help us, I'm not interested. I've no friends and more enemies than I can count." He shrugged his jeans up over his hips and zipped. He reached for a black T-shirt. Clean? Hopefully a harbinger of a better day.

"I'm your friend. Even if you're my boss."

Nate pulled the T-shirt over his head and shoved the white handkerchief in his back pocket. "Not your executive officer anymore, bro." The truth was he'd once had many friends and an A-team under his command. Now he had Pete, a bullshit mission, and a time limit he wouldn't meet.

"Once an XO, always an XO. I'll be by in a few."

Nate headed to the bathroom. He hated having hair hang to his shoulders. But he'd been ordered to grow it years ago, and until he was ordered to cut it, it stayed long. He reached for a brush. The fact that he even owned a brush made him feel like a girl. *Fucking pansy.*

By the time he pulled his wet hair back in a rubber band, knocks pounded. He palmed his gun against his thigh, the weight easing the tension in his lower stomach.

He opened the door with no ceremony or greeting.

"Hey." Pete White Horse, shorter than Nate but wide as a Humvee, carried in a drink holder with two large cups and a bag from the coffee shop.

Despite Pete's long black hair plaited down his back until it hit his ass, a black tee barely covering the Mohawk tribal tattoos on his biceps, black commando pants, and combat boots, he managed to walk around without being stopped by the cops. Nate just hoped his buddy had a ready answer for why he looked like a rogue Mossad agent who—Nate knew—carried five concealed weapons: one nine-mil on his left leg, a forty-five on the right, and three knives tucked into his many pockets.

Except with the level-ten frown on his friend's face, Nate doubted anyone, even the police, would have the balls to go near him today.

Pete handed him a coffee. "We're screwed."

Nate took the cup and shoved his gun in his back waistband. "More than usual?"

"Oh yeah." Pete threw a nod toward the man outside the door and deposited everything on the table in the corner.

The stranger in a seersucker suit refused to cross the threshold. Instead, he collected and stored everything within his field of vision.

Sweat pricked the back of Nate's neck, and he fought the urge to shut the door. But the contempt in the stranger's blue gaze stopped him. He'd never backed down from a fight and wouldn't start today. But that didn't mean he had to be polite. "You are?"

The man tilted his head and crossed his arms, his fingers tapping his bicep. Instead of showing his pearlies, he kept his lips sealed and secured. His starched white shirt and blue silk tie worked into a complicated knot screamed trust fund. A Southern gentleman from his Italian leather shoes to his gold signet ring.

Nate squared his shoulders, but he couldn't stop watching the man's fingers keep time to some unknown beat. "Are you deaf?"

The man exhaled in a long hiss.

Nate flexed his fingers until Pete clapped him on the shoulder.

"Give Calum a chance, Nate. You want to hear what he has to say."

Nate scowled, but he trusted Pete. So, despite the fact that Calum's eyes were too bright and his blond hair too neat, Nate stepped back, Calum entered, and Pete shut the door.

Calum moved into the room and unfastened the shutters and the French doors.

Nate inhaled the fresh air, tasting both mold and sulfur, and blinked. Nothing primed his headaches like the smells of ruin and decay. "What's going on?"

Pete opened the bakery bag on the table and parked his ass in the only chair, guarding the only exit. "According to Calum, we're screwed and he's the one person who can help."

Since Pete was the optimistic man in their unit of two, Nate drank his coffee and embraced the scorch.

Calum leaned against the jamb, backlit by the morning sun. "With the muscle you and Mr. White Horse bring to the club, it's not surprising you were hired without background checks."

Nate put his cup on the table and shifted his weight to his heels. He'd been well trained in diversionary tactics. "Not our problem if the club doesn't do its job."

"Fair enough, Major Walker."

Nate's head filled with a loud rush. "How do you know my rank?"

"I know everything about you and Captain White Horse."

Nate threw Calum up against the wall with a loud *umph* and bared his teeth.

"Don't hurt him, Nate." Pete took another drink of coffee and sighed. "I should've told you before. Calum *owns* the club. And we need those jobs."

Nate dropped him like a hot shell casing but stayed in his personal space.

Calum straightened his jacket. "I also own many of the buildings in this city. And my twin sister is a Georgia senator."

Well, la-di-fucking-da.

"So not only do I know your names and ranks, I know what you and Pete were, what you are, and what you're looking for."

Nate ran his hands over his head, stretching his biceps. "No idea what you're talking about."

Pete looked up from his precious coffee. "Actually, Calum does."

In no reality was that possible.

"You," Calum said to Nate, "are a dishonorably discharged ex-Green Beret looking for evidence to exonerate his men—most of whom are in prison—before the rest of his unit, including Pete, goes to trial. You have two weeks to succeed, or you'll return to prison where the rest of your men are waiting. Or, depending on the state of your migraines, back to the Army's prison hospital in Maine. I know what you're looking for, and I know someone who can help." Calum took a note from his jacket pocket. "But since nothing's free, you'll do me a favor."

Nate shrugged. "Why would I do you a favor? Hell, why would I trust you?"

"I also own this hotel. The only hotel in the city that takes cash."

The tic above Nate's eye kicked in. Since he'd been discharged and had no money, and Pete and the rest of the unit had had their pay suspended and bank accounts frozen until the trials, they lived a cash-only life. Even their burner phones were paid for with twenties. "If we don't help you, we're jobless, homeless, and on the streets with all those heroin addicts."

"Yes."

"See?" Pete shook his head and took another sip. "Screwed."

Nate settled his hands on his hips. "What do you want?" Did defeat always sound so bitter? Or maybe it wasn't the situation. Maybe it was him.

Calum handed Nate a business card and a throwaway cell phone. "This is your info if someone wants to meet you. When this phone rings and someone asks you if you're a parole officer, say yes. Do that, and you can keep your jobs and your home."

Nate shoved the card and phone into Calum's jacket chest pocket. "No deal." He didn't work blind anymore. Last time he had, there'd been explosions, downed helos, and men in pieces. That was before the prison camps.

Calum handed the phone and card to Pete.

"Come on." Pete tossed Nate the cell phone. "We can do this."

Nate breathed deeply to fight off the light-headedness.

"Not you, Mr. White Horse. It must be Major—I mean Mr. Walker. Except you'll go by the name Nathan Wall."

Now they'd entered the land of the absurd. "And whose PO am I supposed to be?"

"A former teammate and friend of yours."

Nate weighed the phone in his palm. "I don't have friends."

"You did. Once. Sergeant Rafe Montfort."

Nate stumbled back, and Pete's eyes widened into black moons. Nate made it to the edge of the bed and sat down, leaning forward with his elbows digging into his thighs. "Are you telling us Rafe Montfort, that lying, betraying, AWOLing sack of shit, is out of prison?"

"Rafe needs your help. In return, he'll help you," Calum said. "And from your reactions, Rafe's release is a detail your boss decided wasn't important enough to tell you. Unless Colonel Kells Torridan doesn't know?"

"Rafe Montfort is a traitor," Pete said.

Nate stood, keeping his hands fisted. "Rafe abandoned his A-team. *My* A-team."

Calum slipped his hands into the pressed jacket pockets. "Are you giving up on this mission because of your pride?"

"This has nothing to do with my pride."

"Maybe you'd just like to avoid Juliet Capel."

Pete moved until his shoulder touched Nate's. A brother protecting a brother. "I don't know what you're talking about."

"No?" Calum's sneer carved lines in his patrician features. "Unfortunately for you, Juliet is my friend."

Nate's heart pounded so fast it chafed his ribs. If Calum knew what'd happened between him and Juliet in a windowless shipping container eight years ago, it would explain the hatred. But not the offer of help. "You sure Rafe will help us?"

"After what you did to the woman he loves? I doubt it. But since he's your only chance to finish this mission and save your men, I suggest you make sure he doesn't find out. You can't help your men if you're dead."

CHAPTER 4

JULIET FOUND SHADE NEAR THE TABLE OUTSIDE HER WORK trailer in Liberty Square, took off her hard hat, and grabbed a water bottle from a cooler. Men in coveralls with *City of Savannah Public Works* insignias drove backhoes while Bob's workers hauled pink and white impatiens. The thunder rolling in the distance, threatening another storm coming in from the Isle, didn't help her mood.

She still hadn't heard from Calum. That meant if she wanted to save her business, her only other choice was Deke.

She took a drink, needing the water to soothe her hoarse throat. Then she pressed the bottle against her forehead and closed her eyes, letting the condensation drip down her hot cheeks and neck. Despite the stress about her loan and Deke, she couldn't stop worrying about Rafe. He'd come home. But would he come see her?

Then again, did it matter? She'd spent the past eight years grieving him and moving on with her life, doing whatever was necessary to survive. She was over him. As much as a woman could be after discovering true love didn't exist. That *forever and always* meant *never and not at all*.

A popping sound made her jump, and she opened her eyes. The fountain pump had stalled. *How much would a new pump cost her?*

She took another drink and wiped water off her chin with her fist. Bob was with a water inspector near the fountain when a man shaped like a stack of three marshmallows tip-toed through construction debris. Once he reached the plank walkway that wound through the site, he yanked on his blue vest and straightened his white jacket over pleated pants.

Henry Portnoy, a.k.a. Senator Carina Prioleau's campaign manager, headed Juliet's way.

She hoped he had a check because Carina still owed her forty thousand dollars.

Henry reached her table and shook each shoe. "Juliet." He waved to the fountain's three-foot-tall round brick—and still dry—basin. "Senator Prioleau's party is in six days."

"The square will be finished when I get paid."

"And the landscaping?" He picked up a cardboard rendition of the garden alley and fanned his face. "The senator expects perfection."

"Did you see the expensive live oaks?" She pointed to forty eighteen-foot trees lining the square's perimeter. "Once the crews finish the electrical work, we'll plant fifty Crepe Myrtles, dozens of azaleas, and flowering shrubs. Then we'll add annuals and mulch. It'll be done on time as long as I'm paid."

"And those heroin addicts who lived here. Won't they come back?"

"The police assured me they're doing everything they can to combat this heroin epidemic. Including taking addicts off the street and offering them treatment." She tossed her water bottle into a nearby trash can. "The city is desperate to keep the epidemic contained."

"But—"

"Liberty Square will be *the* square to rent for weddings and other celebrations. The city needs this revenue. The balance is due Wednesday. I have union workers to pay."

"Except"—Henry's teeth clacked like they often did—"the senator doesn't want to be seen as throwing her wealth around. She wants to seem as one with the people."

Juliet exhaled, lowering her shoulders. Carina could never be *one with the people*. And everyone knew it. "Her husband, Senator Wilkins, turned a parking garage back into an original garden square. Now that he's dead, it's his memorial."

Henry shook his head. "The senator can't pay until after the election."

Juliet inhaled sharply. In November? By then she'd be bankrupt and living on the streets. Again. "We have a contract. I expect to be paid on Wednesday. If not, all work will be halted. There'll be no party." Playing chicken with a U. S. senator hadn't been on her to-do list today, but neither had worrying about her ex-husband.

Henry pursed his lips, and she wanted to clamp them together with a binder clip. "I'll be in touch."

"Wednesday, Henry." She took the rendition out of his hand and tossed it onto the table covered in engineering drawings. "Or I shut the project down." Extreme? Maybe. But if she didn't come up with payroll by Wednesday night, the city would have something to say about it. And the city wouldn't care about Carina's desire to seem as one with the people.

Although Juliet sounded tough, she prayed such extreme measures wouldn't be necessary. Vulnerability wasn't a quality she could afford.

Rafe—and Nate Walker—had taught her that.

Henry left, and she rubbed the back of her neck. A jasmine-scented breeze lifted damp tendrils. She needed this job to be a success. Her future—as well as the jobs of her crew—depended on it.

Once Henry disappeared behind the orange-netted privacy fence hiding the construction from the tourists, she grabbed her hard hat and found Bob with the water inspector. Ten minutes later, after discussing how to run copper wire into a ten-foot-tall bronze winged horse, she went back to her worktable. Samantha had sent a text.

> *Someone's looking for you. Tall. Hot. Eerie walk. Cool tats. Did I mention hot?*

A jackhammer snagged bedrock, groaned, and backfired.

She gritted her teeth against the rising panic. She met with male clients all the time. And while Rafe might still be tall and handsome, he didn't have an eerie walk. Whatever that meant.

> What did he want?

While she waited for a reply, a workman passed with oleander bushes. She sent him to the west garden room. They couldn't be planted near the doggy fountain. They were poisonous.

Samantha texted back.

> *To see you. No idea why. Told him you were at the work site. Hope that's ok?*

Juliet swallowed, only to taste the bitter dryness of concrete dust and mulch grit. She should've mentioned Rafe's return to Samantha but was avoiding questions she had no answers to.

> Ok. After this going to Prideaux House to meet Delacroix. Will stop at store then go set up for funeral. Want lunch?
> *Thanks but Pete is dropping off lunch. SYS.*

Juliet sighed. Pete, Samantha's newest boyfriend, worked at Rage of Angels club with Deke and probably sold this new heroin fueling the city's epidemic on the side. Juliet didn't like being judgy, but the guy carried serious muscle and, with his long black plaited hair, tribal tats, and gunmetal lip piercings, looked like he could bench-press her mulch truck.

Juliet took off her hard hat and threw it onto a newly installed iron bench. The man looking for her could've been anyone. That hot, panicky sensation returned, making her hands and legs tingle. Despite the sunshine, thunder clapped in the distance again. She gripped the edge of the table and stared at an invoice until the image blurred. She didn't hate Rafe, she just had no reason to see him again. Their marriage had been a youthful mistake she'd put behind her.

Voices sounded from near the fountain, and she looked up. Bob and the water inspector were arguing again. Sighing, she slipped her phone in her pocket and went toward them…and stopped.

A man over six feet tall had come through the privacy fence and strode toward the fountain. She paused not just because he wore combat boots, low-riding jeans, and a black T-shirt that outlined his ridged stomach, wide shoulders, and tattooed arms. Not just because he reminded her of Michelangelo's marble male studies exhibit that'd left her with pudding knees. Not just because he carried the aura of carved masculine perfection with ease.

She paused because his gait stole her breath. Elegant, even graceful, he moved with a determined purpose wrapped in fluid weightlessness. She wouldn't call it eerie so much as powerful. It had to take enormous strength and self-control to move a body as large and muscular as his so…beautifully.

He spoke to Bob, who pointed toward her. The man nodded, shrugged on the leather biker jacket he carried, and turned. *Oh God.* His long stride ate up the plank walkway while she wiped her palms on her dress and inhaled deeply. In the space of her exhale, he stopped a few feet away. His brown-eyed gaze clasped onto hers with a longing that kept her still. His sheer size and the yearning in his eyes flooded her with the kind of heat that pooled low.

He was larger than she remembered. And the way he studied her, like she was the only thing in this world worth noticing, reminded her of everything they'd been to each other. Everything they'd once had in that forever-and-always kind of way. Which ended up being a total lie.

She had to remember that.

She swallowed. "Hello, Rafe."

Seriously? The man had abandoned and betrayed her, and that's all she could say? She couldn't even keep the tremor out of her voice.

"*Juliet.*" It sounded like a prayer, and her breath hitched in the back of her throat. After eight years, she still remembered how her name resonated on his lips, how the word ended with his soft drawl instead of a sharp consonant.

She blinked while he took her hands and moved in. He brushed a kiss on her cheek, and his familiar musky scent teased her nose. She closed her eyes, and her eyelids burned. It was like the anger and sadness and disappointment that had lived inside her for so long were so deeply buried they couldn't find their way out. She could only stand there, feel his lips on her face, and remember what used to be. Part of her—the traitorous part that exhaled when the kiss ended—was even relieved that he was still alive. For a few of the eight years he'd been away, she hadn't been sure.

Could she be more pathetic? Probably not. Because she

considered the possibility that if she kept her eyes shut, time wouldn't only stop, it would swing back to the last hours they'd spent together. The last moment they'd been happy.

What is wrong with me?

She opened her eyes and used her fingers to wipe her cheeks. Her gaze darted around—to her worktable, the fountain over his shoulder, his dusty boots—until landing on the blue ribbon wrapped around his wrist under his jacket's sleeve. She was over him. So why was this so hard? What was it about him that made her tremble, made her limbs feel heavy? She should be angry and dismissive, yet all she could do was ask, "What are you doing here?"

There were so many other questions loaded into that one: *Why did you leave me? Where did you go? What were you doing? Do your tattoos mean what you said they mean?* That prickly feeling rushed through her again, and she fisted her hands until her nails cut her palms.

His relentless gaze shone with unapologetic determination. A trait she remembered. "The army released me from prison."

"For God's sake, why?" She hadn't meant to screech— and had, in fact, never screeched before—yet his flinch testified to her pitch and tone. She tucked a stray hair behind her ear and shook her head. Embarrassment sent a flush from her neck to her face.

"The army dropped the charges and let me go." His voice was low and melodic. He even reached out to touch the strand that wouldn't stay put and hung over her forehead. Except she turned until he lowered his hand. "I know seeing me must be…unsettling."

Unsettling. Yes. That was a word she could support. She took two deep breaths before meeting the heat in his eyes. "I thought you had a life sentence."

Or was that a lie too?

He shoved his hands in his front pockets. Despite his jacket, the movement only emphasized the width of his muscled chest. He was so much bigger than when he'd left. "One day I was in solitary confinement, the next I was free."

She frowned. The whole thing sounded sketchy. "Do you know why? Or who orchestrated it?"

"No."

She studied the handsome face she used to cup with her hands and caress at will. Square jaw framed by firm cheekbones and deep-brown eyes. Shorn hair with slashes for eyebrows. Lips that protected white teeth, one with a small chip from the time he fell out of the tree next to her balcony. The same face she'd once loved now had tiny lines around the eyes, a jagged scar on the forehead, and a darkness in its eyes. "So you came home?"

He stayed still under her visual assault, as if daring her to look at *all of him*. As if daring her to see the man who had supposedly gone AWOL to work as a gunrunning mercenary. As if daring her to ask the question they both knew she wanted to ask but was too afraid to.

"Yes." He spoke softly, his words edged with steel. "I came home."

With his obvious physical strength and don't-screw-with-me-or-I'll-kill-you attitude, he seemed capable of working for an arms dealer. Heck, he could even *be* an arms dealer. Yet he kept a polite distance between them and moved slightly so the shadow he cast kept the sun out of her eyes. Then there was his upper body, which shook as if the act of standing still in a garden, talking to her, required a tremendous amount of self-control.

Frustrated with her all-over-the-place emotions, she tucked back that damn stray hair again and walked toward the fountain. He fell into step next to her. "When are you leaving?"

"*Depends*." The way that word rolled off his tongue, heavy and intense, loaded it with all sorts of meanings.

"On what?"

"On you."

She stopped near Bob and faced Rafe. "You nuked my life, yet your decision depends on me?"

"Yes." For the first time, his attention shifted from her to the horse rising out of the fountain four feet away. "Pegasus?" Memories of their childhood were evident in his half smile. "Our winged horse?"

She shrugged. If he wanted to play the deflection game, she would too. Because no matter what he said or did, she wasn't going to allow him to mess up her life again. She was no longer the wounded bird he'd married. "Classical architecture is still around. Timeless beauty always trumps dead war heroes."

When he turned to her again, his stare took in her clunky, steel-toed garden clogs and pink linen dress up to her hard hat–mussed hair. "It does indeed."

She pressed her palms against her skirt. "What do you want." No question mark. A direct statement requiring a direct answer.

His eyes narrowed. "To see you."

"*Why?*" Her question sounded desperate, but she didn't care. "It's been *eight years*."

He ran a hand over his head and glanced away. "Because it's been eight years, and I need to make sure you're okay."

"I sent our divorce papers to you in Leavenworth." She grabbed his leather-clad arm and forced him to look at her. "We're not married anymore. I'm not your wife."

"Juliet." His voice was so broken she almost couldn't

hear the words. "No matter what the world says, and regardless of what you believe, you'll always be my wife. Your safety always trumps everything."

Thunder hit hard, much closer this time, and she wrapped her arms around herself. "What does that mean?"

"I'm here to protect you. And I'm not leaving until I do."

CHAPTER 5

RAFE'S VISION NARROWED ON HIS WIFE IN A PINK DRESS AND adorable clogs, her hair twisted up with tendrils framing her face. Even with her arms crossed and her spitfire, brown-eyed glare, she appeared delicate, graceful, perfect. Everything he remembered.

Was this what it felt like to die from regret? His heart burning from the inside out. An ache in his arms from staying still when all he wanted was to pull her against his chest. And he had a hard-on, like an iron dumbbell in his pants, that he prayed she hadn't noticed.

"What do you mean by protecting me?" she demanded.

Since he'd left Pops's trailer with no plan or thoughts about what he was going to say or do, all he could offer was, "I was worried."

"Why?"

"I thought…" He ran a hand over his head again, grateful that none of his Fianna brothers—or any of his buddies from his ex-A-team—were watching. He could barely put two words together. "You might be in trouble."

"I've built a life for myself without you, and I can take care of myself." She waved an arm to indicate the garden square that he remembered as a parking garage. "I'm okay."

"More than okay. You're beautiful." *Fuuuuuuck.* Could he be more lame?

A flush turned her cheeks pink, and she pursed her lips. A sure sign of her rising anger and eventual retreat.

Hell. This wasn't going well. Which was probably why the Prince had forbidden Rafe from ever seeing her again.

He felt a raindrop and glanced up at the darkening sky. He'd missed the storms that rolled in from the Isle. The ionized air that cleared out the humidity, the city's moldy stench eclipsed by the tang of wet pavement, the static-charged breeze.

Since they had at least fifteen minutes before the storm hit, and Juliet stared at him like he had horns on his head, he motioned to the iron bench wrapped in plastic beneath an oak tree. "Can we sit?"

She turned toward the fountain.

He followed her gaze, and the warmth of hope loosened the tightness in his gut.

Yes, he'd screwed up his life beyond repair. Yes, he may have broken his tithe and put her in more danger by coming here for no good reason. Yes, she had every reason to hate him and not speak to him. But from the moment he'd seen Pegasus, the winged horse from the constellation they used to follow in the Isle's summer skies, he'd wondered if maybe there was a way to repair what he'd destroyed.

And if not fix, then atone for. Maybe that would bring them both some closure.

Maybe that would bring them both some peace.

Her rapid breathing, raising her breasts in a rhythmic pattern, proved she wasn't as immune to him as she pretended. While he stood there with his heart pumping wildly, his desire out and about for all to see, Juliet finally nodded.

After he used his hand to wipe her seat clean, she sat with her hands clasped in her lap, looking at everything other than him while he lowered himself next to her. Her lavender scent slammed into him, and he held back a groan. Not happy with the way his lower half responded, he leaned forward until his forearms cut into his thighs. "Has anything weird happened lately?"

"Weird how?"

"Has anyone been following you? Or harassed you in any way?"

"No." She blew away the strand of hair that kept falling forward. "I've had some vandalism at my shop, but the city is seeing an uptick in low-level crimes and drug use."

"Has anyone broken into your apartment?" From the pots of gardenias, lavender, and roses he'd seen on a balcony over her shop, he figured she lived above her store. She'd always loved those flowers. She'd even carried them in her wedding bouquet.

"No." She glanced at him with a furrowed brow and questioning eyes. "Have you seen Pops yet?"

"Yes. I'm staying with him for a while."

"Good." She slipped her hands between her clenched knees, the action pulling down the fabric of her dress and lowering the neckline a quarter of an inch. It wasn't much, but it was enough to make his sweat burn his skin. "I hope he was happy to see you."

As opposed to her? Rafe studied her face, with her downcast gaze, tight lips that were turning white, and high cheek bones that seemed more prominent. Probably due to her weight loss. Yes, he'd noticed that too. She'd lost at least ten pounds since he'd left her. "He didn't throw me out."

She nodded. "So why do you think you have to save me? Because, as I'm sure you've noticed, I can take care of myself."

Yes, she'd said that a few times now. He also knew it wasn't completely true. Hell, he understood her better than anyone. When faced with conflict, she retreated inside herself, afraid to rely on another. Her fear of trusting anyone—especially him—with her heart had been the greatest source of conflict in their marriage.

Then again, she had good reasons not to trust people. Her mother had died in childbirth. Her father had neglected her. The Isle had turned against her. Rafe had abandoned and betrayed her. The rationalization that he'd destroyed her to save her only worked on mornings when a bullet through the head seemed more inviting than the morning sun.

"I believe someone I worked for is following you. Or at least keeping track of you."

She squinted at him. "The arms dealer you left your A-team for?"

That was the rumor she believed? Although it wasn't true, it'd work for now. "Where'd you hear that?"

"It doesn't matter." She sighed, and her shoulders slumped forward. "Why would this person care about me?"

"Because he believes you're important to me."

"Am I?" she asked softly, her eyes filled with other questions he knew he couldn't answer. "Important to you?"

"Always and forever."

She stood suddenly, her hands tucking hair behind both ears. "How long has this *keeping track of me* been going on?"

He stood and made sure to keep at least a foot of space between them. He didn't trust himself any closer. "I don't know."

"Does it have anything to do with your release?"

"Maybe."

"Is there anything you can tell me for sure? Like why you left? What you've been doing for the past eight years? Why you came back?" The pain in her voice sent an ache deep into his heart. All of this hurt was his fault, and he had no idea how to fix it. The only thing he did know was that telling her the truth would get them both killed.

"I'm sorry, Juliet. I can't give you the answers you need. All I can do is ask you to trust me. And watch out for anything unusual."

Her laugh sounded hoarse, like she was holding back tears. "You should go. I'd appreciate it if you'd leave town as soon as possible—" A phone buzzed, and she took her cell out of her dress pocket to read the message. "When you said unusual, did you mean like this?"

She handed him the phone with a text. From Escalus.

What you've done? Tis forbidden.

"Rafe? What does this message mean?"

"It means I was right about you being in danger." Rafe texted back.

Where are you?
*Let us withdraw unto some private place and
reason coldly of your grievances. The site of
Lord Capel's demise, perhaps?*

Rafe deleted the messages and handed the phone back. "Where did your father die?"

She paused for a long moment before saying, "Capel Manor."

He wished he didn't have to do this, but since his wishes were never granted, he said, "I have to leave, but please go back to your apartment and lock the door."

"I don't understand. What's forbidden?"

"I can't tell you."

"Why do I have to hide?"

"Because I can't protect you right now. I'll come to your apartment later and explain as much as I can." He kissed her on the cheek—for the second time that day—and left the square.

It was time to kill Escalus.

⌇

Juliet pressed one hand against her cheek and watched Rafe walk away. How could she have forgotten that being with Rafe was like standing in the middle of a tornado? While the center was a quiet vacuum, the wind outside howled, lightning sparked, and debris brought down everything in the funnel's path. When the storm passed, it left behind destruction.

A few raindrops kicked her out of her Rafe-is-back stupor, and she moved everything from the work table into the construction trailer. She wasn't sure what to think of Rafe's return, the strange text message, or anything else. He had no right to come back and demand things of her. Especially since the few answers he'd given her only led to more questions. And as far as her being in danger? She'd been in far worse situations since he'd left, and she'd learned a lot about survival from her time with Nate Walker, not to mention Deke.

Besides, she had other things to worry about, like Carina's no-show check, the loan disaster, and winning the Prideaux House job.

Thunder and lightning rocked overhead, and she cleared the work site. Once the men were ensconced in the coffee shop across the street, she went back to the trailer to get her camera and workbag. She still had time to walk to Prideaux House before getting soaked.

As she left, she noticed a couple embracing at the end of the street. With his legs spread apart, his hands against her back, the man held the woman so close a knife couldn't slide between them. Her smaller hands, with fingers spread on his biceps, gripped shoulders double her width.

Memories slammed into Juliet, and her chest tightened. She knew what it felt like to be pulled against a body larger and harder than her own. To be so thoroughly kissed, held so close with such gentleness until they both melted away. She also remembered the lies, heartache, and betrayal. The ultimate disappointment that comes from being vulnerable.

Sighing, she turned the other way and pulled out her phone.

Three rings later, Deke answered, "*Damn*, Jade. I hope I have something you need."

"I have to see you."

"I've missed you too. Ready to come back, baby?"

It'd taken eight grueling years to rebuild her life, doing things she wasn't proud of, things she'd had to do to survive. And while she wished she didn't have to strip tonight, the heavy raindrops only strengthened her resolve. "Yes, Deke. I'm ready."

An hour later on the Isle of Grace, Rafe slammed the truck's door and wiped the sweat off his forehead with his arm. He'd ground gears until he hit the Cemetery of Lost Children and couldn't drive any further. The hum of cicadas filled the air, tombs shimmered in the humidity, and the scent of honeysuckle burned his nose.

Deep inside Capel land property borders, he stood halfway between Pops's trailer and Capel Manor. The woods had reclaimed the bush roads, and the path ahead was impenetrable. No different than his relationship with Juliet.

Hell. He never should have gone to see her. He'd known the danger and had essentially given the middle finger to the Prince. Yet his heart had decided before his head, which, come to think of it, was why he was in this situation to begin with. Despite his training as a Green Beret and then as a Fianna warrior, he'd always given in to his greatest weakness: his love for Juliet. It'd driven every life decision he'd ever made.

He hated leaving her in town, but he had to fix what he'd screwed up before the Prince found out.

Rafe took off his jacket and checked his watch. He'd have to walk the rest of the way and had two options: fight his way through the woods filled with gnarled yews and prickly ash or hump it through the cemetery where his mother had died eight years ago. The knot in his lower stomach tightened. Definitely the forest.

In the truck, he found a hunting knife and his gun. Hot, sweaty, and pissed off, he loaded up and headed for the trees. This morning he'd felt repentant, even humbled, but Escalus's threat changed that. Back to the way it should be. Back to the way it'd been while working for the Prince. Strange how easily he fell into routines of scanning his surroundings and carrying deadly weapons. It made him feel whole, strong, and dangerous. Like the predator he'd been in the Fianna.

Thirty minutes later, he used his T-shirt to wipe the sweat off his face. A hedgerow of thistles protected an expanse of pluff mud surrounding the vine-covered manor. Balconies sagged. Chimneys on both ends of the house held up the caved-in roof. The collapsed upper floor reminded him of a broken hammock. While he'd figured things would be different, he'd never expected ruin.

A branch cracked, and a deer bounded by. He reached for his gun. The brush on one side and the forest on his other left him with one option. He followed the deer.

CHAPTER 6

THIRTY MINUTES LATER, THE VEGETATION SPAT RAFE OUT onto what had once been the front lawn. Storm clouds hovered as he moved toward the eight-foot-wide mud flats separating him from the house. Ragged police tape swung from the columns. The double-wide front door had been blown open, like the house had died mid-scream. *Like it is still screaming*.

"Welcome, Romeo." A man's voice came from behind Rafe.

Chills traced his spine. He half turned, palming the gun against his hip. "Escalus."

The warrior appeared in jeans, boots, and a black T-shirt stretched across a solid chest. His black knife hung off his belt loop, resting against his hip.

Rafe rubbed his thumb against the gun's grip ridges.

At six-two, with shorn brown hair and brown eyes, Escalus blocked the exit into the woods. Which meant Rafe was stuck between the mud, thicker-than-hell vegetation, and a highly trained assassin. While he'd been skimming the memory playbook, he'd been trapped.

Escalus dropped his backpack and advanced. The man Rafe had loved like a brother moved with the predatory silence and grace all of the Prince's warriors worked to achieve. Rafe had even walked that way once. Some might say he still did.

Escalus hit his chest with a fist and bowed his head. "The Prince's heart is wondrous-light at the news of your release."

"Drop the verse."

"Speak no treason, Romeo. The Prince doth grieve at the loss of his beloved soldier."

Escalus's elegant speech contrasted with his kill-or-be-killed appearance. The warrior could take out a grown man with a pencil yet spoke with more eloquence than most world leaders. And wasn't that contradiction one of the reasons the Prince's warriors were so feared? Why even trained armies stayed out of their way? And Rafe had once spoken this way, walked this way, killed this way. Except now that life felt like a dream. Correction: *nightmare.* "We weren't beloved anything. We were slaves."

"You've been at odds for so long, you don't see we led lives of honorable reckoning."

Hell, Rafe had been fighting everything and everyone since he was ten. His right arm muscles contracted as if trying to scrub off the tattoos from the inside. "'Twas nothing honorable about what we did." He hit his chest with a fist, hating the fact that he had slipped into verse but unable to stop himself. "We were bound by penalty, strapped by fear, our pain only lessened by another's anguish."

His life with the Prince and the Fianna brotherhood had been a sadistic blood-fest of emotional enabling, codependency, and intense training with one purpose: to prolong their mental and physical suffering so they'd have enough aggression for the next kill.

Escalus waved his hand with the scarred thumb that had almost been cut off in a fight in Istanbul. "If one man's sadness is cured by another's burning, can you deny your will would have died by the rank poison of love if the Prince hadn't saved you?"

"You justify our existence because we fought *against* love instead of *for* love?"

"You knew the rules when you tithed."

Rafe circled, keeping Escalus to his left. "Why are you here?"

Escalus followed, matching Rafe step for step. "Once you return, seek forgiveness, grievances will be forgotten."

Forgiveness. Rafe had a back full of scars from the Prince's forgiveness. "And Juliet?"

"You've contacted her—"

"To ensure her safety."

"Against the rules of your tithe. Now a debt's owed. Who's to pay? Your lady?"

"*No.*" Rafe aimed the gun at Escalus's heart. "She's already paid, remember?"

Escalus nodded toward Rafe's tattooed arm. "That was *your* tithe. Not hers."

"My payment to the Prince destroyed her life as well."

Thunder rolled, pushing the black clouds closer.

"You broke the rules, and there's a new debt." Escalus strode forward despite the gun pointed at his chest. "You cause your own misery, Brother. You always have."

"Now you sound like Pops." And every commanding officer Rafe had ever had. Including Nate, his team leader. Colonel Kells Torridan, their CO. And the Prince.

"Juliet's life is forfeit." Escalus stopped inches from the end of Rafe's gun barrel. "There's no other way to set the world at ease."

Escalus pushed down the barrel, and Rafe let him. Since the men of the Fianna lived side by side in extreme circumstances, everything they did blurred personal lines. Death was no exception. If Rafe wanted to protect Juliet, he had to kill Escalus in hand-to-hand combat.

The wind increased as he focused on Escalus's brown eyes. And, again, brown was the color of disappointment. Rafe was surprised? Maybe he should buy a box of brown crayons and write out the rest of his life. A life filled with the disappointment of others. A life lived below the expectations of others. A life he'd never have a chance to redeem. A life alone. "I'm not letting you touch my wife. That means we have to fight."

And someone has to die.

Escalus wrapped one arm around his waist and bowed low, his head near the ground. A mannerism the Prince's warriors performed before they killed. "As you wish."

Rafe growled. After eight years, he was in the exact same place he'd been when he disobeyed Nate's last order. Desperate and screwed.

Rafe tossed his gun near Escalus's backpack. He'd only been free for a few days, yet here he was about to kill again. What kind of man did that make him? The kind that survived. The kind that would do anything to protect his wife. He pulled out his knife. "Each life I've taken weighs on my heart. Yet, if Juliet dies, I'll lose my soul."

Silence settled between them until the only sounds were the heavy rhythm of their breathing and the rolling thunder. Escalus came around Rafe's back. But he wasn't worried. He and Escalus were equal in strength, skill, and speed. And Fianna warriors never attacked from behind.

"What wouldn't you do to protect your beloved?" Escalus asked. "To save your tomorrow?"

"There's *nothing* I wouldn't do to save her. She's *everything* to me." Her death was an impossibility Rafe couldn't process. While his own would be a welcome relief.

"Violent passions have violent ends." Escalus ran a finger up Rafe's right arm, tracing the tattoos that reached from wrist to shoulder. At the top, he gripped Rafe's neck and drew him close until they were separated by a whisper. "If you win today, she'll still be in danger. To protect her, would you betray her again? Could you *leave* her again?"

The words tore through Rafe's mind until he felt dizzy. Three cracks of thunder made the ground tremble. A nearby tree splintered. Could he leave her again?

Another clap of thunder rang out, and he had his answer. *Yes.*

If it meant saving her life, he could lie to her again.

If it meant saving her life, he could betray her again.

If it meant saving her life, he could leave her again.

"I'll do whatever's necessary to protect her. Even if it means destroying her."

Escalus released him and came around front. A half smile broke up the vertical lines of the soldier's war-weary face. "A man must do what he will—"

Thunder rocked again.

"For the woman he loves." Rafe finished. The rain hit hard. His fingers cramped around the knife handle. Escalus lunged first, slicing Rafe's left shoulder. Pain ripped through his dominant arm. He grunted and moved the knife to his other hand. Then he met Escalus's triumphant gaze. Would Rafe be able to kill him? Hell, yes.

A surge of power raced through Rafe. He slammed an uppercut into Escalus's sternum. Heat rocketed through his arm, and Escalus stepped aside. Rafe followed up with a left hook into Escalus's jaw that snapped his teeth together and knocked his head back. Escalus made stuttering noises, his eyes blinked, he leaned left. What was he protecting?

Rafe shook his burning hand, the swollen knuckles already bruising, and swung a turnaround kick into Escalus's side. Escalus expelled a breath and fell to his knees. Rafe brought the knife down. Escalus blocked the hit and tossed Rafe onto his back. The stench of swamp replaced the air in his lungs. The rain blinded him. The tables hadn't just turned. They were upside down.

Escalus's knife came down fast. Rafe rolled so the blade hit the ground next to his head.

Escalus fell forward but quickly righted himself and swung again. The knife whistled. Mud spewed. Rafe grabbed Escalus by the legs. They fell with loud *ooomphs*. After two rolls, Rafe landed on top and rammed his fist into Escalus's face. Escalus grunted and slashed Rafe's left bicep before dropping his blade.

"Dammit!" Rafe stood. Blood ran down his wounded arm, which felt tingly and weak. For a moment, he saw a glimmer of regret—maybe even sadness—in his enemy's eyes. Rafe picked up the knife and threw it onto Escalus's stomach. If Rafe were to win, it'd be with whatever honor a disgraced Green Beret could muster. Which wasn't much.

So what was he trying to prove?

Escalus clutched his blade and rose. "Dost thou remember why you came to the Prince?"

"Yes." Rafe appreciated the pause to take three rib-wrenching inhales. His arm felt numb from the bicep and shoulder wounds, and he tightened his hold on his knife. "Why?"

Like Rafe, water plastered Escalus's T-shirt to his hard body. His boots stood in an inch of swamp sludge. "The past seeks to change the present. It can do nothing else."

"I don't understand."

Two shocks of lightning hit, followed by thunder and Escalus's fierce growl. His upper cut threw Rafe onto his back. His breath shot out with a moan, and he lost his knife. He sweep-kicked Escalus's legs out from under him, and the warrior fell near Rafe's feet. He kicked Escalus in the face one, two, three times. *Take that, and that, and that.*

Petty, maybe. But after years of abuse by the Prince and his warriors, he didn't care.

Escalus rolled away, and Rafe found his knife. Since his dominant arm wasn't cooperating, he had only one move.

Escalus crouched, knife pointed, teeth bared. His eyes dark and dangerous, showing no mercy, sadness, or regret. He launched himself and Rafe slammed the knife into Escalus's chest, then pulled it out.

Escalus fell to his knees, blinking rapidly. The rain smeared the dirt and blood on Escalus's face, the light in his eyes shifting like bulbs flickering during a brownout. Rafe had once loved and trusted Escalus more than any other.

What kind of man kills a brother?

Rafe took both knives and shoved them in his boots. He rubbed his eyes to clear his vision. Except he saw the past instead of the present. His mother's death. An undercover op gone bad. A missing buddy from his A-team. An order from Nate that changed everything.

Escalus's ragged breaths ended with a hiss. "The man who freed you requires payment."

Rafe knelt and gripped Escalus's T-shirt. "Who—"

A blast threw Escalus into Rafe's arms.

They hit the ground hard. Reverb rang in Rafe's ears. He smelled the tang of gunpowder and gagged on the blood dripping down his face. Escalus had been shot through the head. By a sniper. From the other side of the manor.

Rafe crawled from beneath the body and grabbed his gun, digging himself into the mud. That's when the rain began to fall like glass sheets, offering cover yet scraping the skin off his arms. Once he realized no other shots had been fired, he took Escalus's backpack. He ran to the woods while Escalus's words echoed: *The past seeks to change the present.*

Rafe's racing heart threatened to crack a rib. He spat out blood and kept going.

What the fuck had followed him home?

⁓

Thirty minutes later, Rafe slammed into the cemetery gates and collapsed against a moldy pilaster. His breath roared in his ears. *What have I done?*

He squeezed between the railings that hung like broken arms from limestone columns. His leg muscles contracted as he stumbled toward the protection of ancient oaks embracing his fucked-up past and ruined present.

When he reached the old well, he tossed in both knives. After hearing the water splash, he headed deeper into the graveyard. It'd stopped raining by the time he paused against the twelve-foot statue of the headless archangel Michael on a four-foot plinth. A sniper had killed Escalus. But whose? And why? He sank against the naked archangel, pulled up his knees, and scrubbed his face with his hands.

A flock of startled blackbirds flew away. He tracked their path to freedom, wishing he could follow. Instead, he dug a shell out of the crushed oyster-shell pathway and chucked it at the nearest mausoleum. ANNE CAPEL 1652–1713 was carved in the lintel block, and eight-petaled lilies—Juliet's lilies—were engraved down the edges of the iron doors.

Since sitting on his ass wasn't going to fix his situation, he dragged himself up. His arm ached, and he took off his T-shirt to hold it against the biggest cut on his shoulder. The pressure helped the pain. The rain had washed most of the blood away and turned the mud on his jeans to a grimy shell.

Once at the truck, he threw his T-shirt and Escalus's pack onto the front seat. Then he hid his gun behind the spare tire and found a bandana in the glove box. Although dirty, it allowed him to tie off his shoulder to stop the bleeding.

He drove to where his father-in-law's trailer had stood

and shut off the ignition. His wounded arm felt dead, and his head hurt. A breeze blew through the open windows. His dry mouth throbbed like it'd been scraped out with sandpaper.

He needed water. With a series of grunts, he rummaged through Escalus's backpack, praying for a bottle. Instead, he found something else: Escalus's cell phone.

Rafe typed in the passcode and smiled. Because Escalus hadn't bothered to change the sequence, Rafe was able to discover two unfortunate things. The first was a live camera feed of Juliet's Lily, the Liberty Square site, and another building he didn't recognize. *Escalus has been stalking Juliet.* The second was the most recent incoming text.

Where art thou, Escalus?

Fuck. The Prince's men—Fianna warriors—never hunted alone.

He'd never hunted alone.

He pressed the first speed-dial number.

A male voice answered. "Is all well, Escalus?"

The Prince. Rafe closed his eyes. "Escalus is dead. 'Twas a true reckoning. His dark heart met with my treacherous revolt."

Although a sniper had taken the final shot, Rafe's strike had been fatal. Escalus, like all men, deserved to have his murderer named.

"*Romeo.*" The Prince spoke the name like a curse. "What hast thou done?"

"What I had to do. To protect my beloved."

"You gave away your heart when you tithed to me. You belong to *me.*"

Although Rafe's arm spasmed, the pain was nothing compared to the tattoos that ran the length of his other arm. They were eight years old yet caused him more pain than a shot to the gut.

"I speak no treason, my lord. Only offer a sad truth. I broke my tithe by seeing Juliet. Escalus claimed her life was forfeit, and now our brother is dead."

"You didn't kill Escalus. He met a rogue's death."

The Prince had ordered Escalus's execution? Rafe opened his eyes. "I don't understand."

"Escalus and his partner were in town to retrieve something when Escalus decided to sell it to someone else. I discovered his treachery, and now he's dead. He had no right to pass a judgment on your tithe. If you find what he sought, you may return to me and your wife will remain safe."

The Prince was speaking contemporary English? "And Escalus's partner?"

"Since I don't know if Balthasar knew about Escalus's betrayal, I'll offer him the same deal."

"A contest between me and Balthasar?" The sadistic bastard who'd trained him? "You can't be serious."

"Whoever returns first receives a full pardon. The loser faces the Gauntlet."

Fuck. "What am I looking for?"

"A seventeenth-century glass vial."

Another obscure artifact. *Peachy.* "Filled with what?"

"Does it matter?"

"No." And if the Prince wanted it, it was bad.

"The vial was last seen in Savannah. And you're not the only one who seeks it."

"Do you know these seekers?"

"Yes."

Rafe waited, and then realized that was all the intel he'd get. Sometimes the Prince reminded him of Colonel Kells Torridan, Rafe's last CO, who was always tight with the info.

Rafe got out of the truck and leaned his ass against the metal. "You want me to find a vial before Balthasar and these other men do and return it to you?"

"Yes."

"Are these other men to be eliminated?"

"Do whatever's necessary to complete your mission and protect the brotherhood."

Meaning, if these men got in his way or found out what Rafe was, kill them.

A doe watched him from the edge of the woods. With delicate legs poised to run and wary brown eyes, the deer reminded him of Juliet. "Any clue where I should start?"

"Juliet may be of help."

The doe took off. "How?"

"The vial was once owned by her ancestor Anne Capel."

One of the Isle's accused witches, hanged in the seventeenth century, held the key to his future? *Super peachy*.

"Romeo?" Hints of the Prince's Boston accent cut the edges off his cultured voice. "Find the vial, return to me, and your wife will remain unharmed."

This was insane. But since Rafe's heart always decided before his head, he said, "Yes."

"If you fail, it's on your word to return and face the Gauntlet. Don't disappoint me."

Like he'd disappointed so many others. His laugh came out in gasps. He'd just remembered the Prince had brown eyes. "How do I contact you?"

"Keep Escalus's cell phone. Do you need money? Weapons?"

"No." The less he took from the Prince, the less he'd owe.

"I want my vial by Sunday. Seven days."

"Six and a half."

"'Tis an act of peace you're committing. An act of redemption and honor. Good luck."

Rafe tossed the phone through the truck's open window onto the seat and pressed his good arm against his eyes. Escalus had been right. The Prince had never lost a man except to death. So why had Rafe thought he'd be lucky?

"Hands up!" a man shouted. "Or I'll shoot."

Two hunters came out from the forest dressed in camo gear, orange vests, and rifles.

Dammit. Rafe held up his hands. "Grady, I'm not armed."

"On your knees, you fucking coward," Grady ordered. "Hands over your head."

Rafe knelt, his hands up, while Grady Mercer and Tommy Boudreaux cornered him. Although Grady was Pops's age, Tommy had changed from a spindly teenager into a full-grown man. "Grady—"

"Shut your traitorous mouth. We just found a body at your woman's manor."

Tommy swung his fist. A *whoomph* hit Rafe's ear, and he fell against the truck. Stars and stripes exploded in his head. Tommy grabbed his arms. A sharp pain speared Rafe's shoulder, and he fought until Grady's rifle barrel found his forehead. A sickening pain shattered Rafe's vision, and his stomach heaved. They threw him down. The gun against his head forced him to eat mud.

"One more move, you die," Grady said. "Got it?"

"Yeah." Rafe spat out vomit, dirt, and blood. "Got it."

CHAPTER 7

Juliet had to win this job. And she had to stop thinking about Rafe and his drama.

She left the fourth floor of the Prideaux House, hung her camera around her neck, and avoided the staircase's soft spots caused by termites and water damage. Like everything else in the antebellum mansion, the stairs needed to be replaced or the place would end up like her manor.

She gripped the railing. She could almost hear her father's boots on the wood floors, Rafe's laugh from the tree he climbed outside her balcony, and her kittens mewing. It hadn't been the easiest childhood, but there'd been some joy.

Mr. Delacroix stood in the foyer. His gray suit fit his trim body like it'd been painted on. His short brown hair was even more styled than Calum's. "What do you think?"

She'd gone upstairs to get aerial photographs of the two-acre backyard that claimed a city block. "The garden can be lovely again." And this job would keep her solvent for another six months.

He guided her through French doors leading to the garden. "I'm awaiting a guest and have some lemonade outside. I'd love to hear your ideas. And any history you know about the house."

"I know it was built by the Prideaux family before they changed their name to Prioleau. There was another structure on the property from the early seventeen hundreds, but that burned down during the Revolution and was rebuilt by a Prioleau after the war ended. He decided to keep the original name to honor his ancestors."

"I've heard that the eighteenth-century Prideauxs were notorious pirates." He whispered as if that story was forbidden gossip.

But she knew the truth. Despite the fact that Calum was one of her oldest friends, his family's pirate history was far worse than the history books suggested. Then again, hers probably was as well.

"That's what people say." She followed him onto the patio covered by a rotted pergola. The rain had stopped, and she raised her face to the sun. "How long until you close on the mansion?"

He poured from the decanter on an iron table. "A week if the inspection goes well."

She snorted and took the glass he offered. "I'm sorry. That was rude."

He swept his arm toward the four-story antebellum mansion with eight bowed balconies and four chipped chimneys. "The house needs attention."

And money. "The hard part is dealing with the Habersham sisters."

"That's why I made them an offer they can't refuse."

"Why this house? There are other historic homes for sale in better condition. And this one's on the edge of the not-so-nice part of town." *Near the center of the heroin epidemic slowly taking down the city.* But she didn't say that. She needed him to buy this house so she could renovate the garden.

"It's the second biggest."

She hid her smile behind her drink. "And Calum Prioleau, who owns the largest, wouldn't sell?"

Delacroix shrugged. "This one will have a bigger garden. So, what are your thoughts?"

"Keep the dependencies." She pointed to the brick buildings on the east side. "They're nineteenth-century but will make nice sheds and a gardener's office."

"And the fountain?"

She put down her drink, and they followed the boxwood-lined path to the raised pond. A cherub lay in pieces on the bottom of the round basin, leaving a rusted spout in the center.

She raised her camera. "My foreman says the plumbing works. You'll need to pick a fountain style. Nymphs are popular, and so are Pans and sprays."

"What do you prefer?"

She tucked a stray hair behind her ear. "Ariadne. Williams Ironworks in Charleston has one in iron, but they can cast one in bronze. That's what I'd recommend."

"The demigoddess who protects the secrets of her labyrinth." A crack between his lips broke up hard facial lines. It was as if he didn't know how to smile. "An unusual choice."

"There's no Ariadne in Savannah, Charleston, or New Orleans. It would be unique."

"A betrayed woman who knows her own mind and doesn't rely on others for help. Is she a favorite of yours?"

"Kind of." She photographed the broken stone benches.

"We've a lot in common, Miss Capel. We've both been hurt by love. We've both decided never to risk our hearts again."

She lowered her camera to meet his gaze. "What do you mean?"

"I did a background check on you, like I do with all those I hire, and do you know what I found?"

"No."

"It takes a strong woman to put herself through school

and open her own business." He spoke in a low tone that promised that secrets would be kept.

She studied the crushed oyster shell pathway.

"It takes a strong woman to move on from a difficult past and do things people look down on. To recover from a brutally broken heart. And I admire people who survive. I'm a wealthy man who scraped and clawed until someone gave me a chance. I believe in offering those opportunities to people like me."

"Thank you." He deserved a better answer, but it was all she could manage.

"You are your greatest strength. Relying on others will leave you wounded and alone."

Something she needed to remember if she was going to get in that cage tonight.

"Juliet?" Carina Prioleau's high-pitched voice rang out. "What are you doing here?" Carina moved through the garden, her short-sleeved black suit impeccably tailored. Her spiky heels caught in the patio's uneven bricks. Her driver guarded the garden entrance.

"Viewing the garden," Juliet said. "You?"

Carina smiled at Mr. Delacroix and held out her hand. "Fund-raising."

Mr. Delacroix kissed her palm. "Welcome, Senator."

Juliet's phone buzzed with a text, this time from her lawyer, John Sinclair. He wanted her to call him ASAP. "If you'll excuse me, I have to make a call, and then I'll take more photos before I leave. I'll have your estimate done by the end of next week."

"Thank you, Miss Capel."

"Wait," Carina said. "What's this talk about my square not being ready for my party?"

"What party?" Delacroix asked.

"My birthday party. My late husband—" Carina pressed a hand against her breast. "You know I'm recently widowed?" She played the rich, grieving widow-turned-senator to perfection.

"I do," Delacroix said. "I'm sorry. I also heard you took over his Senate seat."

"Yes, well, Eugene and I paid to tear down a parking garage and rebuild one of the city's original public squares. I'm throwing a birthday party in my honor and a memorial in his in the new Liberty Square. It's on Sunday, and the whole city is invited." Carina glared at Juliet. "But it's Monday, and the square's not done yet."

Juliet loved Carina's *I*s and *my*s. As if Carina had planted the trees and dug the paths. As if the renovation had been her idea and not her late husband's. "I told Henry we'll finish once we get paid. Final payment is due Wednesday."

Carina frowned until Mr. Delacroix led her away. "I'm sure Miss Capel will make your day a success."

Carina sent her a backward glare. "I hope so. For her sake."

Juliet almost threw out a witty comeback, but she'd experienced Carina's vindictiveness. Turning away, Juliet dialed her lawyer. "Hi, John. I got your text."

"Juliet, I wanted to let you know that I heard your husband has returned."

Good grief, that was fast. "Ex-husband."

"Have you spoken to him yet?"

"About?"

"Juliet." Exasperation threaded through his voice. "You own over two thousand acres on the Isle of Grace, acquired three-and-a-half centuries ago, marked in twenty deeds. Before your father died, he added Rafe's name to those deeds. Remember? You need Rafe's signature before you can sell."

"I'll let Rafe know." She'd get Pops to do it for her. "Now tell me about these King's Grants I need to find."

"The titles to your land date to the sixteen hundreds when the property was given to your family through a series of King's Grants signed by King Charles I and issued by the Lords Proprietors in Charleston between 1670 and 1682.

"Since the land was never sold or divided among heirs, the State of Georgia has always assessed the property as one piece without needing a clean title. South Carolina has dealt with sales like this before, but there's no precedent in Georgia. I can't give you a clean title to the land without seeing the original grants and getting your husband's signature."

"If I find the grants and Rafe signs, how long before I can sell?"

"It depends on the grant stipulations and finding the right buyer. Probably a few months."

Which meant she had to dance tonight. She rubbed her forehead with her fist. "I'll look for the grants. And get Rafe's signature."

"I'll have the paperwork ready. He'll need to bring a witness that's not you."

"I'll let Rafe know." Which meant she really did have to speak to Rafe again. When John put her on hold, she moved into the shade to study the house. The eleven boarded-up attic windows—black with mold—reminded her of rotted teeth. She'd tried to get into the attic, but it'd been locked. Using her free hand, she raised her camera and focused on the last visible window. The sun's angle and glare exposed the design. Worked into the center of the stained glass was an image of a skeleton hand gripping the blade of a vertical cutlass. Blood dripped down from the fist to the tip, and the drips formed red words beneath the image. *Sans pitié.*

No mercy. The Prioleau family crest.

"One other thing," John said, coming back to the phone. "Isn't there an investigation of Senator Wilkins's death on your land nine months ago?"

"The case was closed. The senator's death was deemed an accident from the wildfire he got caught in."

"We'll need affidavits. I'll look into that. I'm also sending you an email with a list of supplemental research items to find that could increase the price of the property. If you do the work, you can cut my legal fees."

"What do I need to find?"

"Besides the King's Grants, any documents dating to the mid–sixteen hundreds, including Anne Capel's will."

She shouldn't be surprised. With everything going on, why wouldn't she be asked to research a woman accused of killing forty-four children with witchcraft in 1677?

Because it was just that kind of day.

"Thanks, John. I'll be in touch." As she hung up, another text buzzed.

Beware, fair Juliet.

Now she was getting annoyed.

"I'm looking for Miss Capel." Detective Garza, in jeans, blue blazer, white shirt, and green tie strode into the garden.

She hurried over. She'd deal with the text later. "What's wrong?"

Garza took her arm. "Samantha Barclay, your employee, told me you were here. I didn't want to call."

After saying her goodbyes and collecting her work bag, Juliet followed Garza. "Is this about the vandalism?"

"No." Garza opened the unmarked patrol car door and settled her in the front seat. Then he slid behind the wheel. "We're going to the Isle of Grace."

"*Why?*"

"Sheriff Jimmy Boudreaux called." Garza pulled into traffic, his face all brown sharp edges and black stubbled shadows. "A body was found on your property."

"Excuse me?"

"A man was murdered…" Garza glanced over with his bullets-for-eyes. "That happens often on your property."

"Not often. Just occasionally." She stared out the side window before he noticed her lack of enthusiasm for visiting the Isle. "I wasn't aware the SPD did business with the Isle."

Garza changed lanes like a man on a mission. "The Isle doesn't have the staff to deal with a murder."

That was a snort-worthy understatement. "Why do I need to go?"

"The suspect." Garza turned on his flashing police lights. "He'll only talk to you."

ತಿ

"*Where's my wife?*" Rafe gritted his teeth, driving them into his skull. He sat, handcuffed, on a chair in the church rectory/sheriff's office in the Isle's center of town. If five buildings in the woods on a barely paved street with no cell service was a town.

"You'll see her when I get answers." Jimmy Boudreaux, who for some reason had been made sheriff of the Isle, rested on the corner of his desk. He'd pulled his hat down low.

Rafe grunted while the local EMT and Deputy Sheriff Tommy Boudreaux—a.k.a. the sheriff's brother—stitched up his shoulder. "I want to see her now."

Jimmy's fist hit the desk. "Then answer my damn questions."

Tommy disinfected the wound, and a sickening ache shot from Rafe's shoulder to his gut. He spread his legs wide and forced his feet against the floor to even out the pain.

"Jeez, Rafe," Tommy said. "Have you been doing 'roids? What do you bench-press?"

"Between three and four hundred pounds. And a lot of prison pull-ups."

"Can we continue?" Jimmy asked.

How many times did Rafe have to answer the same damn questions? He hissed when Tommy pulled the last stitch through, cut the thread off, and slapped on a bandage. "I don't know anything."

"You expect us"—Jimmy pointed to the other men in the room including Pops and Grady Mercer—"to believe you were released from Leavenworth—"

"Where you were serving time for going AWOL and treason." Grady rubbed the Marine tattoo on his arm. The same one Pops wore. *Third Force Recon, Alpha Company.*

Pops's face tightened until Rafe worried it would sink in on itself.

"Believe what you want." They would anyway.

Jimmy shot Grady a shut-the-hell-up glare. "The day you return you're found on Capel land, covered in blood—"

"My blood."

"And you know nothing about the man who was shot before you were found bleeding near your father-in-law's old trailer site?"

Rafe shrugged. He'd nothing else to say.

Tommy worked on the gash on Rafe's left arm. "What's this?"

Shit. It had been a long time since Rafe had worried about that. "A tattoo."

"Why?" Tommy smirked. "Your right arm full up?"

Pops stomped out, his boots echoing on the steps.

That's right. Rafe's right arm was covered in inked names. Believe the rumors.

Tommy, either too stupid to take Rafe's silence as a warning or too mean to care, said, "When Juliet learned about them, did she cry?"

Heat rushed through Rafe, and he rose until Tommy shoved a needle into his deltoid and hit the plunger. The sting burned, and Rafe fell into his seat. "Ow!" He tried to rub the site, but his hands were cuffed. "*Shit*."

Tommy smiled like he'd just won the girl. "Antibiotic."

Rafe leaned back until the front chair legs lifted, balancing the weight with his legs. There'd be time later for a reckoning on his wife's behalf. He'd make damn sure of it. Instead of responding to Tommy's taunt now, Rafe pointed to the *real* tattoo. The only one on his body that meant something. "It's a heart with a sword through the center." Along with a word underneath, which Escalus had sliced. A parting gift Rafe appreciated.

Tommy used a wet towel to clean the mud and reveal the intricate ink work. "The sword hilt is lilies."

Rafe flinched when the towel cleaned the cut. "The hilt is a cross fitchy. It's from the Crusades." The design was older, but he didn't want to discuss it. "Does it need stitches?"

"Nah. Just butterflies and a bandage."

"Great." *Then cover the damn thing up.* "And I'll take some ibuprofen."

Jimmy snapped his fingers in Rafe's face. "Can we get back to the questioning?"

"What do you want me to say?"

A man came to the door in a gray jumpsuit with an embroidered nametag: *SPD Medical Examiner.* "Sheriff, can we talk?"

Calum Prioleau appeared next to the ME.

"Shit," Jimmy said.

"Pleasure to see you again too, Sheriff." Calum, wearing a cool-and-collected smile, sat in the only other chair in the room. Behind the sheriff's desk. A knight in pressed seersucker.

Tommy stood, closed his first aid kit, and threw a disgusted glare at Calum. "I'll talk to the ME for you, bro."

"Thanks." Jimmy kept his gaze on Calum. "You here for a reason, Mr. Prioleau?"

Calum nodded at Rafe. "To see a friend."

"Your *friend* is going to be here a while."

Rafe stood, knocking the chair over. The cuffs cut his wrists. "You've no proof I was near the manor."

Jimmy got in his face. His hat's brim hit Rafe's chin. "The vic was shot by a sniper."

Calum stood. "As his defense lawyer, I suggest you drop this line of questioning."

Jimmy took off his hat and slammed it against his thigh. "You have to be shittin' me."

"I'm not. Unless you have a weapon, a bullet, or a track…" Calum glanced at Grady.

"The rain." Grady spat. "Pops and I couldn't find a thing. But if Gerald Capel was still here, he'd find something to put Rafe away until Judgment Day."

"No doubt," Calum said. "But you didn't find Rafe anywhere near the crime scene. You don't have enough evidence to get a search warrant for his truck. It's time to let him go."

"There's a gunman on the loose," Jimmy said.

"Your problem, not ours. And considering the Isle's police force consists of you and Deputy Tommy, I suggest you make nice with the SPD. Maybe they'll help."

While Calum and Jimmy argued about warrants and injunctions, Rafe moved to the window. He needed to get this damn show on the damn road before he committed a damn felony.

A stocky man stood in the dirt lot near the white church. He wore jeans with a badge on his belt, a white shirt, and a green tie. One hand on his hip, near his weapon, the other on Juliet's arm.

"Calum. We need to go. *Now*."

"You're not going anywhere," Jimmy said. "Not until I talk to your parole officer."

Rafe's head ached like he'd been bitch-slapped, and he craved water, a pain pill, and freedom. With his wrists in cuffs, he ran both hands over his shorn head. *I have a parole officer?*

Before Jimmy could ask for the parole officer's name, Calum handed him a card. "There's his name, rank, and phone number. Now free my client."

Jimmy opened a desk drawer, threw a tan uniform T-shirt at Rafe, and uncuffed him.

"Get dressed and stay here. Grady, come with me."

The moment Jimmy and Grady left, Rafe followed.

Except Calum barred the door. Although not as tall or wide, Calum put up a formidable defense. "You're not meeting Juliet looking like a reject from a gladiator movie."

Rafe held up the T-shirt that would barely fit. "Do you have clothes I can borrow?"

"After you shower." Calum checked his watch. "We'll go to one of my apartments—"

Rafe rushed his friend until Calum put both palms against his chest with enough strength to stop him.

"No." Hard eyes and straight lips replaced Calum's easy demeanor. "My game. My rules. We have a few minutes until Jimmy returns, and there are details to discuss."

"Like my parole officer?"

Calum's face flushed. "Like why I got you out of prison."

CHAPTER 8

JULIET LEANED AGAINST GARZA'S CAR IN THE DIRT PARKING lot, between the church and the rectory/ sheriff's office. Insects buzzed, and her peripheral vision clouded, like the humidity had smoothed the edges with Vaseline. Jimmy Boudreaux and Detective Garza completed the triangle. "What happened?"

"All I know," Jimmy said, "is Grady found Rafe near your daddy's trailer site."

"Did Rafe kill that man?"

"No," Garza said. "The sniper shot came from the river. Between the time Grady heard the shot to when they found Rafe, there's no way he could've run from the river to that side of the property. The vegetation is impenetrable."

"Juliet." Jimmy's voice dropped. "Rafe wants to see you. He's...agitated."

She tasted the dusty tang of the Isle. Like crushed dandelions and swamp sludge. She knew what Rafe was like when he was worked up, and everyone on the Isle knew she was the only one who could calm him down. As much as she didn't want to talk to Rafe again, she didn't want Pops or Grady to take the brunt of Rafe's temper. "Alright."

"While you're with Rafe," Jimmy said, "see if you can get more information."

"Like what?"

Jimmy pulled his hat lower. "I couldn't get a search warrant for his truck but I'd like to know if he had a weapon And why was he out there?"

"Isn't that your job?"

"Rafe and I have never gotten along," Jimmy said. "You know that better than anyone."

Because Jimmy and his brother Tommy used to torture her when they were kids. But there was no reason to say what they were both thinking.

Detective Garza added, "It's a delicate situation with your ex-husband's reputation."

"You mean because he went AWOL and ended up in prison?" she asked.

"Most of the men of the Isle have served. They consider Rafe a traitor." Jimmy turned his head toward the church where a group of men stood. "Are you okay with us going to your property? It may be a two- or three-day search."

"Yes," she said. "And the body?"

"The SPD is taking care of it," Garza said. "The ME will escort the body into town."

"Does anyone know who the victim is?" she asked.

"Some stranger." Jimmy handed her his phone, which displayed a photo.

The man had half his scalp and part of his face blown off. Mud and blood soaked his body. She looked away, her stomach regretting her earlier coffee.

Jimmy closed the photo. "There are rumors you're selling your land. Any chance he's a possible buyer scoping out the property?"

"I've never seen him before. And no one was visiting the property. According to Pops, it's impossible to get there now."

"If you think of any reason someone would go out there, let me know. I have to get the search parties going." Jimmy touched her arm, but she backed up. "You going to be okay?"

She nodded. "I'll deal with Rafe."

With a nod, Jimmy headed toward the twenty men standing in the shade of an oak tree preparing to search her land for a rogue sniper. She almost laughed at the irony of the men of the Isle near the church. If justice existed, the men would be blasted by lightning. Angels didn't appreciate hypocrisy. And neither did she.

"Do you know them?" Garza asked.

"Yes." Their family names intertwined with hers in every Bible on the Isle: Marigny, Prioleau, Toban, Montfort, Mercer, and Habersham. Except none of them had ever offered her a moment of kindness during her poverty-stricken childhood, after Rafe went AWOL, or the night her father died. The only one besides her father who'd ever cared for her, protected her from their taunts and scurrilous words, had been Rafe.

She smoothed down her dress. "The people of the Isle hate me."

Garza shoved his hands in his front pockets. "I doubt that."

"It's not personal."

"Hate is always personal."

"The people of the Isle have disliked the Capels since Anne Capel was accused of witchcraft in the seventeenth century. They think the land is cursed. It's not a big deal."

He smirked. "It's a good thing Sheriff Boudreaux doesn't need me for the search party."

She caught the dismissive tone in his voice and added, "People on the Isle have been caring for themselves for three centuries. And the SPD has a reputation for botching murder investigations on the Isle."

"You mean Senator Wilkins's death?"

She nodded. "Did you know the SPD detective on that

case was also murdered? I believe he was the detective you replaced." At his nod, she said, "Jimmy dislikes the SPD."

"Makes sense." Thunder cracked above their heads. "Ready?"

She nodded, and Garza led her to the white building that held the church rectory and sheriff's office. Rain started as she went in.

Calum stood with his back to her, hands on his hips. "We don't have time for this."

Rafe, covered in mud, muscles, and tattoos, held Tommy Boudreaux up against the far wall. Tommy's feet dangled, and he had a bloody nose. Rafe's fingers gripped Tommy's neck, his other hand was pulled back in a fist ready to fly again.

Tommy kicked the wall while he clawed the hand at his neck. "It was a joke."

Rafe raised Tommy higher, his back muscles contracting beneath a khaki-colored T-shirt three sizes too small. "Apologize."

Garza came in next to her. "Let go. Or I start arresting."

Rafe ignored Garza and ordered, "Say it."

Calum glanced at Garza. But Calum's eyes widened when he saw Juliet.

She ignored her oldest friend and focused her frustration on the men against the wall. This didn't surprise her at all. Rafe and Tommy had always been at odds. Actually, Rafe and the world had always been at odds. The only person he'd never been against had been her.

"I'm sorry." Tommy's words were garbled. When Rafe let Tommy go, he dropped to the ground. "You're crazy."

Garza went to Tommy and helped him up. "What's going on?"

"Nothing," Calum said. "Excitement's over."

"Bullshit." Tommy pointed at her. "Your man's an animal."

Rafe spun around. His jeans were encrusted with dirt, and the tight tan T-shirt outlined his stomach muscles and wide shoulders. Bandages covered his arm, and streaks of blood ran down to the blue satin ribbon still tied on his wrist. His knuckles were bruised, and his other arm was tattooed from wrist to shoulder.

Not images. *Names.*

"Rafe?" Philip stood in the doorway behind her, staring at his brother.

"Philip." Rafe's voice sounded sharp and low. "What are you doing here?"

"Pops called me." Philip reached to take Juliet's hand, but she pulled away.

She needed space to breathe. "I'd like to speak with Rafe alone."

Philip stormed away. Garza took Tommy by the arm and led him out. Calum hovered.

"Please, Calum. I'll only take a few minutes. Is there bail?"

"No. Jimmy has no evidence to hold Rafe. Once I sign the paperwork, Rafe is free."

"Then do it so we can leave this godforsaken Isle."

Calum paused in the doorway, one hand on the jamb. "Don't take too long. Rafe and I have things to do."

When he was gone, she used her arm to brush the stray hair out of her eyes and faced Rafe. "What happened after you left me at the square?"

"Nothing."

She sighed heavily. Why was she even helping him? Because she needed his signature on her deeds. That was all. "You get a strange text, drive out to the Isle, lose your

T-shirt"—she pointed to the bandage on his arm—"get hurt, and end up arrested for murder. Yet nothing happened."

"Shit," Rafe muttered under his breath. Then he leaned his backside against the desk, both hands gripping the edge while his body fell forward. The pose reeked of strength, power, and...defeat. "I came out here to protect you."

When she found herself focused on his fully tattooed right arm, trying to read the elegant script, she retreated to the window overlooking the church. Jimmy was talking to the men of the Isle, hands on his hips, probably giving orders. "Somehow these things that are all about me end up all about you. Why is that?"

She glanced back at him and realized his face was splattered with mud...and blood? If he hadn't killed that man, what had he been doing? Because it hadn't been *nothing*.

"I don't know. I never meant to hurt you."

The statement rippled through her. "When? Today? Or eight years ago? Because your letter said otherwise. Not to mention those." She nodded to his arm covered with ink.

"All of the above." He ran a hand over his head and stood to his full height. His physical presence filled the room with masculine heat and his oh-so-familiar musky scent. "I know I've made a mess of things, but I can fix it. I just need your help."

She laughed. A back-throated, this-is-crazy kind of laugh. "You can't be serious."

"I am. Deadly serious."

She crossed her arms over her chest and used the calmest voice she could muster. "I can't do this again, Rafe. Do you have any idea how hard I fought to reclaim my life? To build a safe, secure world for myself? I worked and studied for eight years to get my bachelor's and master's degrees, start my business, be financially and emotionally

independent. And now you come back into town, surrounded by half-truths and violence, and you expect me
to help you?"

"Yes." The tic in his jaw quivered. A telltale sign he was
holding onto his temper as hard as she was censoring hers.
"I also need you to trust me."

"Have you not been listening?"

He slammed his palms on the desk. "I have been listening, and I want to protect the life you've built for yourself.
But that can't happen until I find what I'm looking for. And
you're the only one who can help me."

"Why?" She threw her arms open wide, hoping to catch
a single shred of truth. "What are you looking for?"

"A vial once owned by Anne Capel."

"A vial from a seventeenth-century witch? Do you
know how crazy that sounds?"

"Yes, actually. I do."

She gritted her teeth and turned back to the window.
Garza and Philip were walking toward Mamie's Café across
the street from the church. A battered Texaco sign blew
in the breeze, and a row of motorcycles lined up along the
clapboard side of the station-turned-café.

"Juliet?" Rafe came up behind her. "Please. If you don't
help me, others will get hurt."

"Now you're blackmailing me?"

"No, I'm asking you." His breath against her neck sent
tingles up her arm, and she lowered her head. "If I succeed,
I promise I'll leave town and you can get on with your life."

She shifted to see his profile. "How do I know you're
not lying?"

He put his hands on her waist so gently she felt the heat
more than the pressure. "I swear on my mother's grave."

She turned, only to find him inches away. With her back

against the window, his enormous body in the way, and his hands still on her waist, she was trapped. His touch burned through her dress, his masculine heat filled her lungs, pushing up her breasts. Her breaths sounded shallow, and she fought the urge to press her hands against his chest. To see if his heart was beating as fast as hers. "If I help you, I need something in return—besides you leaving town."

His eyelids lowered, his focus entirely on her lips. "Anything."

"I need your signatures on the deeds to Capel land. My father added your name, and I can't sell my land without your signature."

He released her and crossed his arms. "Selling your land is a terrible idea."

She slipped by him and moved into the open space. Being so close to him left her hot and shaky. "I didn't ask for your opinion. Only your signature."

After a minute of intense silence, he nodded. "Once I get out of here, we can start—"

"I don't think so," Calum said from the doorway. "Juliet, I apologize for interrupting but I need to talk to my client. We have things to figure out."

"Like what?" Rafe asked.

Calum straightened his jacket, and then his tie. "*Things.*"

Grateful for the reprieve, she said, "I have to set up for a funeral this afternoon, and I'm working late tonight on a new project." No need to tell them what that project entailed. She headed for the door but paused to glance back at Rafe. "Meet me at the store tomorrow morning. We'll get started then."

Because the sooner they began, the sooner he'd leave.

Rafe's scowl deepened while Calum took her arm and led her outside to the porch. "You called earlier?"

"It's not important," she said. "I figured it out." There was no way she was asking him for money now that she knew he was involved with Rafe's mess.

Calum looked at her sideways. "You okay?"

She almost snorted. "You're asking me that question?"

"I'm just...worried about you. I can only imagine how hard this is."

"I'm fine, Calum. Really. Now I'm going to ask Philip if he can give me a ride back into town. And I'd appreciate it if you found Rafe some clothes. The clean kind that fit."

Juliet left the rectory and, once she hit Mamie's Café and convenience store, headed directly for the restroom. She gripped the sink and reviewed her reflection in the mirror. Her hair had come loose. Long, damp tendrils framed her pale face. Dark circles surrounded her eyes.

What was wrong with her? *Why did I agree to help him?*

Turning on the faucet, she splashed cold water on her face until her fingers tingled.

Everything will be okay. As long as she relied on herself, she'd survive. After fixing her hair, she left the restroom only to see Philip leaning against the beef jerky stand, hands in his pockets. "Do you want me to take you home?"

"Thank you. I need to get away from all of this."

He reached for her. But she moved away, and he dropped his hand. "Are you okay?"

"Yes." Except she wasn't the only one with Rafe issues. "Are you?"

"Sure."

That didn't sound promising. "Where's Pops?"

"With Grady. Jimmy asked the families to split their search of Capel land. Which means the Marigny boys, who are currently filling their pieholes with peach cobbler, will make up a bullshit story to cover the fact that they did nothing."

She attempted a smile until one of the Marignys wolf-whistled from the other side of the store. And this was why she never came to the Isle.

She followed Philip around the beer case to find Detective Garza at the counter, holding water bottles, surrounded by curious local men. She pushed through and moved next to Garza as he placed the water on the counter and adjusted his stance to show his holstered weapon. "How much?"

"Two forty-eight." CJ, the man behind the register with the Harley T-shirt and dish towel thrown over his shoulder, nodded to her. "Hey, Juliet. Who's your *friend*?"

"Detective Garza," she said. "You should be nice to him."

Garza flashed his badge, and the men dispersed, most of them going back to the sandwich counter.

"Oh." CJ straightened his shoulders. "Aren't you from Maryland?"

"Trenton," Garza said, pocketing his change. "It's in New Jersey."

"Huh." Then CJ fixed his gaze on Juliet. "Is it true you're selling your land?"

Before she could answer, Etienne, one of the Marigny boys seated at the lunch counter, asked, "How does your husband feel about that?"

She faced the line of men seated like frogs on logs eating hamburgers and fries. "Rafe and I are divorced."

"Rafe's a fucking traitor," another man said. "An animal. Should've been hanged."

"Not surprised a dead body shows up the day he returns," said a third. "No good ever came from a Montfort marrying a Capel. Gerald should've stopped that marriage."

"Only thing that land is good for," said another, "is killin' and buryin'."

CJ threw his towel at Etienne Marigny and headed for the grill. "Shut up, eat up, and help the sheriff. Or I'll throw you out."

The men went back to their food, CJ flipped burgers, and she glanced at Garza. "Philip offered to take me home."

Garza nodded, handed her a water bottle, and followed them into the sunlight. Once she retrieved her workbag and camera, Garza opened Philip's car door for her. She got in, collecting her dress before closing the door.

"Wait!" Jimmy jogged over and scrunched down to meet her gaze. "One of the Toban boys found an SUV he didn't recognize near the Capel land border, not far from Boudreaux's restaurant. I ran the plates. It's insured and registered to a law firm in New Orleans. Beaumont, Barclay, and Bray."

"So?"

Jimmy held up a set of keys. "ME found this in the victim's pocket. Same make and model of that SUV."

"Which makes them evidence." Garza took them and read the engraved key chain. "*Occidere, et non occidit*. Kill or be killed."

Jimmy frowned. "You know Latin?"

"A bit."

She opened her bottle and took a drink. "The victim was driving that rental?"

Jimmy nodded. "Juliet, remember what happened after the brush fire in your back meadow months ago? What we found after recovering Senator Wilkins's body?"

She pressed the cold bottle against her cheek. "There was a johnboat at the dock."

"So?" Garza asked.

"So," Jimmy added, "right before the fire, Juliet's daddy cut off the bush roads on the property. Everyone, including

Senator Wilkins, knew Gerald shot first, asked questions never. Yet, despite the danger, Wilkins used a boat to traverse the tidal estuaries across Juliet's land. And in that boat, we found Wilkins's jacket with a business card for Beaumont, Barclay, and Bray."

She'd forgotten that. "You think Senator Wilkins's death and today's murder are connected?"

Jimmy lifted an eyebrow. "Yes. I'm just not sure how."

"You should know," Garza said, "that Detective Legare never believed Wilkins got caught in a brush fire days after a tropical storm."

Jimmy hissed. "You opening the Wilkins and Legare investigations again?"

"Maybe," Garza said.

"Be careful," Jimmy said. "Legare was a great cop. Now he's dead."

So now maybe two deaths were related to today's victim? Was this the kind of *weird* Rafe had mentioned earlier? She hoped not.

"I will." Garza shut her door. "I'll keep in touch, Miss Capel."

Philip drove away but had to make a U-turn. As he shifted gears, Rafe and Calum came out of the rectory and met the group near the church.

Again, she noted Rafe's graceful movements.

"Look at the way Rafe walks," Philip said. "It's odd."

"Very."

"Is it true those are names on his arm?"

She finished the last of her water and screwed on the top of the bottle. She didn't care. So why had she been trying to read the ink? "I'm not sure of anything anymore."

Her phone buzzed with a text from Mr. Delacroix.

*Can't wait to see the designs you come up
with for the Prideaux House. Can you have
preliminary renditions by Friday?*

Full-color renditions were a lot of work. Still, she texted,
Yes.

As Philip drove, she glanced back one last time. Rafe
stood with his hands on his hips, staring at her.

She turned, hating the fact that her face felt hot. As Philip
hit the bridge leading to Skidaway Island, another text came
in. But this one wasn't from her lawyer or Mr. Delacroix.

*Love alters not with his brief hours and weeks
but bears it out even to the edge of doom.*

CHAPTER 9

RAFE TRACKED PHILIP DRIVING JULIET AWAY. SEEING HER again had been harder than he'd expected. Maybe it was the longing to hold her that left his chest caved in and his arm muscles contracting. Or maybe it was the fact that she was in danger, because of his own stupidity, that made his stomach hurt like he'd been gutted with a wire hanger.

After Philip's car disappeared toward the bridge off the Isle, Rafe studied the group only to realize there was one man he didn't know. The same man who'd interrupted his dealing with Tommy and had stood too close to Juliet.

Rafe held out his hand. "Rafe Montfort."

"Detective Garza." After the firm shake, they dropped their hands. "Do you think a sniper took out the man we found on your ex-wife's property?"

The cop was direct. Something Rafe respected. "That's the theory."

"It's almost two miles from the river to the manor."

"Not an impossible hit," Rafe said to the group. "With the right weapon."

Jimmy cleared his throat. "Is this connected to what Pops told us is happening at Juliet's Lily?"

"What are you talking about?"

Calum laid a hand on Rafe's arm, as if knowing he had little patience left for bullshit. "She's been dealing with vandalism. Detective Garza is on the case."

She'd mentioned that earlier but had downplayed the

severity. Rafe addressed Garza directly. "Have you caught the vandals yet?"

"Not yet."

"Not surprised," Pops said. "SPD can't find shit."

"Pops? Enough." Jimmy blew out an exasperated sigh and issued orders, sending different groups on their way. He ended with, "I want every inch of those twenty-three hundred acres scoured."

Rafe expected the men to argue. After all, they'd feared Gerald and had treated Juliet with disdain most of her life. Instead, they left with promises to check in.

Jimmy commanded respect and regard? Interesting.

"Remember." Jimmy held up a hand. "We have a rogue sniper on the loose."

Rafe clasped his fingers behind his neck. He didn't love sending these men out to chase a phantom. By now whoever killed Escalus would be long gone along with any trace that Rafe had ever been there. "How do you know the killer didn't hit his target and disappear?"

"What are you sayin', Son?" Pops said.

"Capel land is a jungle. There's no way twenty or so men—even experienced hunters and trackers—will clear that property. If it was a friendly kill—"

"What's that?" Jimmy's hands landed on his hips as if annoyed someone would question his knowledge or tactics.

"A shot for a specific person with the killer moving on without hurting innocents."

An assassination. Except no one said the word aloud.

Jimmy sighed. "Pops, Grady, do the best you can. Tommy can load the teams up with SAT phones. They don't work great out there, but it's all we have."

Garza added, "We have a heroin issue in town right now, Sheriff. But if you find evidence, I'll get you men."

Garza's phone buzzed, and he stepped away to check the message.

Jimmy nodded at Rafe. "You joining us?"

Before Rafe could answer, Calum said, "I need time with my client."

"Rafe knows that land as well as Grady and Pops."

"Rafe and I have lawyer/client things to discuss."

Since there was no chance of putting Calum off, Rafe said to Pops, "I'll return the truck, get my things, and use the Impala to follow Calum into town. I'll leave you Calum's cell phone number so you can reach me."

Pops nodded.

"Fine," Jimmy said, pointing at Rafe. "Don't you leave Savannah. You hear?"

Rafe shrugged. Who was he not to follow orders?

Nate hauled the rum cases to the edge of the truck and jumped down. His boots thudded in the alley behind Rage of Angels club. The odor of puke and piss churned his gut.

"I can't believe you took that call." Pete rolled a dolly around. "And you agreed to be Montfort's PO. When Colonel Torridan finds out—"

"*He* won't."

"*He* will." Pete swept a bandana over his face. "And *he'll* be pissed."

"*He* won't if you don't say anything." Calum believed Montfort held their only hope. Considering Nate was out of clues and almost out of time, he agreed.

"This sitch sucks," Pete said.

Nate handed Pete a case to load onto the dolly. Part of the bouncer/security deal. Toss out drunks at night, refill the bar the next day. At least Deke paid them extra for lifting and carrying. With what they earned from scraping assholes off the floor and protecting women performing down-and-dirty acts in the bathrooms, they could eat, sleep, and get to the gym. Because beating down random guys in the gym's ring was Nate's favorite part of the day.

"What about Juliet?" Pete loaded another case.

Now she was a problem. Which was why Pete had agreed, at the start of the mission, to "meet" Samantha. Since their only clue was Juliet's eight-petaled lily, Pete was using Samantha to gather intel. But all Pete had found was a girlfriend and shit for evidence.

Nate lowered his case onto the cart. "I'm counting on the fact that Juliet hates Rafe more than she hates me and won't tell him."

"Crash-and-burn factor is huge."

No kidding. Too bad he couldn't erase the memories he still carried. Especially that moment during the interrogation when tears stained Juliet's cheeks. He rubbed the sweat off his brow with his arm. Figures fate left him with the crippling memories and took those that could've saved his men.

Pete whistled low as Sally, the red-haired, green-eyed, double-D waitress, came out of the club's back door. She wore a short skirt and tiny T-shirt and carried two paper cups with steam rising from them.

"Hey, Pete. I got two coffees. You want one?"

"Thanks." Pete took his and gave her his trademark smile filled with sunshine and unicorns, while Nate, apparently, didn't warrant a casual *hey*. Then again, he wasn't doing the sideways tango with the club's waitresses. Until he freed his men, it was celibacy all the way. He'd taken a vow and everything.

Since Pete had stopped working to stare at Sally's breasts,

Nate said, "What are you doing here, Sally? Don't you come in at seven?"

"Deke might let me dance, but I have to audition." She twirled, holding her coffee high while her skirt flew out, revealing a purple thong. "Want to watch, Pete?"

Nate looked away while Pete said, "I'd love to, Sal, but I gotta get this stuff stocked."

"Since when can Deke hire?" Nate asked Pete.

"None of your biz," a husky male voice said from behind him.

And speak of the devil's younger, meaner minion.

Deke came around the truck with a big ole fake smile plastered across his ugly-ass face. The guy had to have broken his nose ten times to get that look between busted and pounded. His dark hair hung in oily strands. He'd topped his black tee, leather pants, and Doc Martens lace-ups with a crucifix. If that didn't qualify as heresy, Nate didn't know what would. Add in the overly developed biceps and Deke was half Orc, half Death Eater.

Unfortunately, Deke was also Nate's supplier of Z-pam, the anti-seizure drug, stronger than anything available in the U.S. and only sold in Canada, that semi-controlled his seizures without knocking him on his ass.

"Hey, Deke." Sally twirled again. "I was just saying—"

"Get ready." Deke licked his lips. "I want your ass tight and your tits high. And no platforms. This is a classy club."

Sally hurried inside, but Nate had seen a tear. Once this mission ended, and he reentered the real world with health insurance, doctors, and pharmacists, the Time of Deke would end. Hopefully with Deke screaming *please stop* and *don't hurt me*. He was the definition of *dick*.

Deke came closer, and Nate smelled his sour breath. "You got somethin' to say?"

Had Nate said *dick* aloud? "Since when do you hire and fire?"

Deke's sly smile reminded Nate of that story about the snake that'd had its head partially cut off and still ate its own body.

"Haven't you heard?" Deke's lips curled. "Earl resigned. I'm the manager."

Wasn't that a kick in the ass. Deke was now their boss. Let the fuck times roll.

"The girls are my responsibility." Since Deke was self-absorbed enough to believe they cared, he kept yapping. "And the security staff. Watch your p's and r's. Or you're out."

Nate kept the laugh in, but Pete's snort could've been heard in Charleston.

"You mean q's." Pete spoke low, but Nate heard the *asshole* at the end. "It's p's and *q's*."

With a resounding *fuck you* and a requisite middle finger, Deke headed into the club.

Nate sighed. "I can't wait for this day to end." Except fate decided to squeeze his balls once more and his cell phone rang. Blocked ID. Which meant it was their *real* boss, Colonel Kells Torridan, wanting an update.

After pointing to Pete to stand watch, Nate answered, "Walker."

"Nate," Kells said in his straight-shooting style. "Where are we?"

Fucksville. "We have a lead." *Don't ask what it is.*

"What is it?"

Pete held up one hand surrender-style because the other held a hot cup of coffee.

"A guy who might help," Nate said.

"I don't need to remind you how important this mission is."

Yet you do…

"And I don't want to add to your stress."

Yet you will…

"But we have a problem."

Like you not telling me Montfort had been released from prison? Or the fact that you've given me shit for intel? "Problem?"

Pete mouthed, *What now?*

"The Prince," Kells said. "One of his warriors is in Savannah, but I don't know why."

"We'll watch for him."

Pete tilted his head and mouthed, *Him who?*

Nate wrapped one arm around his waist and bowed. Pete's eyes went cartoon-wide.

"I could come down there," Kells said. "Help you out."

"No need, sir. We can do this alone."

Pete nodded so hard he spilled his coffee.

Nate was tempted to ask his boss about Montfort but didn't. Either Kells knew Montfort was out of prison and had a reason for keeping quiet or didn't know and would be pissed. Either way, keeping Kells away was a priority.

"Find out what that lily means," Kells said. "And stay away from men who bow. They're vicious killers. If they see you, they may decide you fit their elimination profile."

"Yes, sir." Nate slipped the phone into his pocket. While Pete paced the area between the club's moldy brick wall and the truck, Nate filled him in.

When he finished, Pete said, "There may or may not be a Fianna warrior in town."

"We can handle one."

Pete frowned. "We work with Montfort and keep it a secret from Colonel Torridan."

"Then we pray Rafe doesn't find out what I did to Juliet." The tic above Nate's eye started again. Which meant one thing. Incoming seizure. He pressed the palms of his hands against his eyes.

Pete came over and gripped Nate's shoulder. "You okay?"

"Yeah." Nate dropped his hands and dug his fists into his thighs. He had to be okay.

"If Montfort agrees to help us with this mission, our men in prison can never find out."

"If they're out of jail, they won't care." That was the only reason he was doing this.

"The Fianna may be here to retrieve him."

Nate hadn't thought about that. And he should have. "Or kill him."

"We might have one shot to convince Montfort to help us, without him finding out what you did to his wife, before the Fianna gets to him."

Nate held up his cell. "Calum texted. We're meeting Rafe here at the club. Nine p.m."

"Why don't I take the meeting? I didn't know him well. We'll leave you out, make sure he doesn't discover you're a first-class asshole who intimidates women."

Nate *was* an asshole. Except he'd already considered Pete's option and dismissed it. Nate might have screwed over his A-team in a way he couldn't remember, but he was no coward. "I'll meet him."

"You're the boss."

Nate ran his hands over his head. A pre-seizure headache brewed, and he needed more coffee and ibuprofen to ward it off. Unfortunately, he had to wait eight hours before taking another Z-pam. While he was in the prison hospital, they'd given him harsher meds that added hallucinations to his already screwed-up life. Since then he'd experimented with OTCs, coffee, and illegal Canadian epilepsy drugs until finding the right balance. Wasn't a great solution, but it kept the shakes and seizures under control. Kind of.

Pete locked up the truck. "We need to make Montfort want to help us. You could lie and tell him if he doesn't we'll send him back to prison."

"Wouldn't stop him from taking off. If I can't convince him, we grab Juliet."

"Whoa!" Pete held up his hands. "I'm not good to go with this."

"I won't hurt her."

"There have to be limits to what we're willing to do."

"None of what we do here in Savannah will matter if we succeed."

"Not true." Pete pushed the cart, spewing filthy water in its wake, and headed inside. "We might free our men, but no amount of penance will change the fact that we'll be the only Green Beret unit ever dishonorably discharged. Everything we do matters more now than ever."

Although Pete was right, it made no difference. If the mission failed, so did they.

Once alone, Nate threw up behind a Dumpster until his stomach emptied and curled in on itself. His own past was kicking his own ass in his own personal octagon. *Hooah*. He ended up on his knees, staring at the graffiti on the wall across from him: a skeleton fist gripping a pirate's sword. Blood dripped down the blade and formed words beneath. *Sans pitié*.

He reached for the medal around his neck that wasn't there, then felt for the handkerchief in his back pocket. Sometimes prison seemed like the easier choice. But he had to pull himself together for Pete's sake. Besides Nate's meds, there was only one other way to deal with these hole-in-the-head Hallmark moments. An hour in the ring with his sparring partner.

He found his phone and texted, Meet me in the ring?

The text came back instantly. **Yes.**

He prayed a beat down would help him deal with Pete's inevitable disappointment and Rafe's inevitable bullshit. One thing Nate knew for sure: whatever line had to be crossed, he'd be the one to jump. And like the pirate's slogan on the wall, he'd do it without mercy.

Balthasar held the phone against his ear and slammed his fist into the plaster wall of his safe house. Sand and concrete landed around his feet. Dust motes attacked while sunlight cut through transom windows. Escalus dead. Romeo free. The rumors true.

How had Romeo been released? Not even the Prince had that power. Despite the whos and whys demanding a reaction, preferably with knives, Balthasar stayed inside. The slats crisscrossing broken windows allowed him to study the world undetected. Thunder rolled, and dark clouds marched toward the city.

Escalus was a trained warrior. A master soldier. An assassin of repute and renown. But so was Romeo. And Balthasar should know because he'd trained them both.

"How now, Balthasar," the Prince answered.

"Pray tell, my lord. How did Escalus meet his demise?"

"Romeo slayed Escalus. A fatal blow until Arragon offered the final strike."

Arragon had executed Escalus? "I understand not."

"Were you aware Escalus made a deal to sell the vial you seek?"

A docent stopped across the street, telling tourists about the ghost in the house where Balthasar squatted. "No, my lord. Is there proof?"

"Yes."

The Prince didn't offer anything else, and Balthasar didn't understand. He and Escalus had been in the city for months, building their presence for a long-term operation. If Escalus had planned on betraying Balthasar, he would've suspected. "Our mission is in play."

"You've not found the vial."

"No." He paced off his restlessness. Inaction made him feel like a socket spewing sparks, waiting for someone to turn off the damn fuse.

"Escalus made a deal with another buyer to sell the vial and leave the Fianna."

Impossible. "I would have known."

"Yet you didn't."

Was that an accusation? "My heart lives with the Fianna."

"Then understand what I have to do. I've set up a contest between you and Romeo. Whoever finds the vial first and returns to me will receive a full pardon."

"I've not betrayed you."

"I don't know that."

"And the one who returns last?"

"Faces the Gauntlet."

Bullshit. "Romeo slayed Escalus, forfeiting his own life." Considering how many brutal punishments the Prince had handed out through the years for similar infractions, with Balthasar directing most of them, the rule was immutable. "'Tis our law." Their. Fucking. Law.

"Romeo is different."

Everything with Romeo was different. Which meant that Balthasar, the Prince's second-in-command, now had to prove his innocence? And risk the Gauntlet? *Fuck that.* "Romeo deserves a just punishment."

"Romeo must live for now. You've until Sunday to find the vial and return."

"And Torridan's soldiers?"

"They know not what they look for. As long as they don't threaten the mission, leave them. The vial is vital for the Fianna. Understand?"

"Aye." Because following the Prince's orders was what drove him. Unlike Romeo, Balthasar believed in the Fianna's calling. In their mission to force peace where there was only strife. To protect those who suffered under the control of evil men. "And Escalus?"

"He stays where he lay."

Balthasar's breath formed a knot in his chest, and he took out his gun. No Fianna warrior had ever been left behind, and Escalus couldn't have done what he'd been accused of. Escalus, unlike Romeo, had been a true believer. "Why?"

"Escalus was found on Capel land, and the SPD has his body. Retrieval would bring attention to his death."

Except Balthasar had ordered Escalus to go to Thunderbolt, not the Isle of Grace. Balthasar pressed the gun's butt against his forehead. *Had* Escalus betrayed him?

"Romeo's return and Escalus's death must be a shock, and your task isn't easy. Although Escalus went rogue, there's no shame in honoring those we've loved."

The phone went dead. Despite the Prince's assurance, there *was* shame in defeat.

Balthasar sat at the table loaded with knives and weapon-cleaning supplies. With ease, he popped out his clip, disassembled the nine-mil, and started oiling and polishing. The Prince had always preferred Romeo. His transgressions forgiven faster, his insubordination tolerated instead of reprimanded. He couldn't read Latin or speak in Shakespearean verse. He'd even forced the Prince to recruit him or kill him in the Gauntlet.

And what did Romeo do? He survived a corridor of forty

Fianna warriors on both sides, each holding two weapons. That night, Romeo became the Prince's favorite. Romeo, who spoke his mind despite consequences, who didn't care about the chain of command and contradicted orders in public, whose ruthlessness shocked the rest of the brotherhood.

The Prince protected Romeo because he was the only one with a reason to survive. They all lived without hope, in extreme circumstances with extreme penances, punishing themselves until their minds and bodies broke or they died. But not Romeo. He treated the Fianna as a game, as if one day the warriors would put away their weapons and go home to the women they loved. That's why Balthasar didn't just dislike Romeo, he despised him.

But something else bothered Balthasar. This morning, he'd sent Escalus to search county property records in a warehouse near Bonaventure Cemetery. Not to the Isle of Grace.

Balthasar reassembled his gun while studying the street through the slats. Pete White Horse strode by with groceries. Balthasar's restlessness rushed back, and he reloaded the clip. He had seven days to find a vial they'd been searching for for months—he slammed the clip into place and stood. If Escalus had planned on selling the vial, he might've had more intel than he'd shared.

Ten minutes later, Balthasar had torn apart Escalus's room. The laptop was on, but he hadn't found Escalus's journal. When Balthasar entered the Fianna's secure server and scanned the files, he found a link to cameras on Juliet's Lily, the Liberty Square construction site, and the Savannah Preservation Office. Escalus had even set up the feed to go to his cell phone.

They'd been authorized to follow Juliet but not record her.

The next file was named *BBB*. Balthasar clicked it and was prompted to enter a password. After three failed attempts, the file automatically locked. *Fuck.* He shut the laptop. The only thing preventing him from firing rounds into the wall was the fact that Romeo was even further away from finding the vial than Balthasar was. And that gave him an idea.

He grabbed a notebook and pen from a makeshift desk and made some notes. A few minutes later, he heard a buzzing sound from the pillow. When he stripped off the case, a burner phone fell out. He answered on the fourth ring.

A male voice said, "Deke and I got the stuff. It's taking down the city, man. Hope you're right about this vial. Meet us at Rage of Angels. Midnight."

"Aye."

"Straight savage, my man. *Straight. Fucking. Savage.*"

CHAPTER 10

RAFE WAS GOING TO KILL CALUM.

Rafe left Pops's trailer bathroom, showered and dressed in his last pair of clean jeans and T-shirt. His duffel and Escalus's backpack lay in Pops's family room while Calum talked on the phone in the kitchen.

When Calum ended his call, Rafe hit Calum in the chest with his fist. "You got me out of prison to help you find Eugene Wilkins's murderer?"

Calum rubbed his sternum. "That's part of the deal."

Typical Prioleau bullshit. "And the rest of your plan?"

"Need-to-know basis."

"Fuck you." Rafe paced, everything familiar yet not. The shabby couch sat next to a new leather chair. The record player console held a flat-screen TV. His mother's photographs stood in frames and were pinned to walls.

"Are we done?" Calum asked. "You can pace in town. And I'd appreciate less cussing."

"*Why?*" The word came out with so many sharp edges he should've tasted blood.

Calum crossed his arms. "Eugene Wilkins started your release process ten months ago. I finished it when he died."

"I don't care about *whos* and *hows*. I want the damn *why*."

"You spent two years in a Russian prison and nine months in Leavenworth's isolation. I thought you'd be happy to be out."

"My release means I have to deal with my past shit and

fix yours while protecting you all." Rafe threw a remote against the wall. It left a mark and fell to the floor. The lives of everyone who might be involved with Calum's *plans* were now Rafe's responsibility.

Calum took out his phone and started texting. "I thought you'd be happy. You were in *isolation*. In *prison*. You were alone."

Rafe fixed a glare on Calum. "*I wasn't alone.*" Not with his monstrous past drilling into his conscience on a daily basis. In some ways, prison had offered the only relief he'd had since leaving Nate and his A-team. Since leaving Juliet.

Now Rafe was free to eat, shower, and put on new bandages. Free to clean and retie his blue ribbon. But none of it mattered if his liberty meant more innocent people got hurt. And there was no going back. He had to find the Prince's vial and finish what Calum started. Rafe's army duffel, with the few things he still owned, was ready to go to one of Calum's apartments stocked with clothes and food. Like it had all been planned.

Because it fucking had been. "I deserved to be in prison. I didn't need you to save me."

"This isn't about you, Rafe," Calum said, still on his phone. "It's about Juliet. If you'd trust me, you'd realize that my mess, Walker's mess, and yours are connected to your wife."

"How does Walker factor into this? He should be in Afghanistan with Kells Torridan."

Nate was the perfect soldier, and Colonel Torridan had made his favor for Nate clear. Which had been fine with Rafe. The last thing he'd ever wanted was attention from one of the two toughest colonels the Army's Special Forces Command ever trained. Nate had been a good guy and an even better commander. Until their last night together when Rafe ignored Nate's order. But bullshit orders deserved to be ignored.

Finally, Calum put the phone away. "Nate needs your help as much as I do."

"I doubt that." Rafe threw his duffel over his shoulder, grabbed Escalus's backpack, and found the Impala keys. His muscles ached. Even his toes hurt. And he was so damn tired. Still, he trudged through the wall of heat and humidity to the car.

"Things have changed since you left," Calum said, hurrying to catch up. "For Juliet. Walker. Myself."

Rafe opened the trunk and dumped in the bags. "Now you manipulate and bribe people to get your own way? I thought you didn't want to become your father?"

"You've no idea what the past eight years have been like. For any of us."

"You're right." He shut the trunk and headed back to the house. He needed his weapon, ammo, and one more thing. "I don't. But I also don't twist events for my own benefit."

"That's an activity you save for the Prince."

Rafe spun around, teeth clenched. "What do you know about the Prince?"

Calum wiped his brow with a handkerchief. "The Prince is an arms dealer with a private army. Except no one knows what his army does, and no one who joins ever leaves."

Rafe pressed his fists into his thighs. No one outside the brotherhood knew the truth. At least not anyone alive. "You freed me knowing I had a death sentence on my head?"

"The people you love are safer with you here in Savannah."

"You're wrong." He went back to the house, Calum trailing. "You have no idea what followed me home."

"It didn't follow you. It was already here. It killed two men and drove a third to suicide."

Rafe paused on the back steps leading to the kitchen. "What are you talking about?"

Calum stood three steps below, his hand on the rail. "Nine months ago, Eugene Wilkins died in a brush fire in Juliet's back meadow. After Eugene's death, Gerald went into a paranoid rant. Juliet tried to talk to him, but he fired a shotgun at her."

"Gerald fired a gun at his *own daughter*?"

"Gerald wasn't right in the head." Calum pushed past him and went inside. He found two Cokes in the fridge and tossed one to Rafe. "Gerald was terrified of something. Shut off access to the property. Felled trees over roads. Wouldn't work with Detective Legare on Eugene's case."

Rafe pressed the cold can against his hot forehead. "How am I involved?"

"Your Interpol file. The file Eugene helped Legare find."

Bullshit. There were no public records on the Fianna. The Prince had minions everywhere, desperate for cash, willing to do his bidding in every level of every government.

After securing his weapon, Rafe drank his soda and ID'd the photos on a bookshelf.

Calum opened his can and followed. "Something Legare read in your file prompted Eugene to start your release paperwork. But first he had to get you out of that Russian prison."

Rafe had wondered who'd gotten the extradition. He finished the Coke in one gulp, and the fizz settled in his empty stomach like a grenade filled with Pop Rocks. "What did they read?"

"Two things. The first was a name. Romeo."

He scanned the photos around the trailer and acted dumb. "What does it mean?"

"No idea. Even though Detective Legare deemed Eugene's death an accident, something was found nearby that made Legare question whether Eugene had been murdered. Words cut into the dirt near the dock where he'd tied up his boat."

Behind a beat-up copy of *The Shining*, Rafe saw a gold frame holding the photo taken years ago. His momma helping Juliet with her veil on their wedding day. A study in smiles, tears, and sheer happiness. He took the photo from the frame and shoved it into his back pocket. "What words?"

Calum pulled out his phone and handed it over. "These."

It was a photo of a verse cut into the sandy dirt, the indentations lined with pebbles to keep their form. OH ROMEO, ROMEO, THE HEAVENS DO LOUR UPON YOU FOR SOME ILL, MOVE THEM NO MORE BY CROSSING THEIR HIGH WILL.

Every vertebrae clicked into place. "It's from *Romeo and Juliet*."

"Yes. Sheriff Boudreaux thought kids might have written the words. But I don't agree. Neither did Detective Legare. The words are cut too perfectly. The verse too sophisticated."

A Fianna warrior driven by control and precision had carved this warning for Rafe. Except he'd been in prison at the time, and the Prince had known that.

"And Gerald's delusions?" Rafe handed the phone back. "How do I connect to those?"

"After Eugene's death, Gerald screamed about being hunted by men who bow. The Interpol file said the men who work for the Prince sometimes bow before killing."

F. U. C. K. "That's odd."

Calum stared at him. "That's all you have to say? Your Interpol files says you worked for the Prince as one of his bowing men—"

Rafe snorted and found the ammo bag.

"And you went by the name *Romeo*. At the same time,

a verse from *Romeo and Juliet* is found near Eugene's body and your father-in-law starts raving about men who bow."

Rafe moved into Calum's personal space until he could see the silver specks around the edges of his blue eyes. "This is *me* telling *you* to let it *go.*"

"Eugene and Legare are dead. Murdered by these *bowing men.*"

"You got me out of prison to ask questions I can't answer?"

"I got you out to fix this. Find out who killed them and why, and you keep your freedom."

And there it was. The Prioleau ultimatum. "Send me back."

Calum's eyes narrowed. "I've been able to keep this quiet, but Eugene and Legare were killed by the same person. Eugene died in the back meadow of smoke inhalation, but the ME found a small wound, like a pencil had been driven through his neck. Two weeks later, Detective Legare was found in the cemetery, with another verse near his body as well."

Rafe released a breath. "Did Legare have a puncture in his neck?"

"Yes. Then, weeks ago, Walker shows up making inquiries about eight-petaled lilies. And the last place I saw those flowers was in the back meadow almost twenty years ago. I believe that's what Eugene was looking for when someone killed him."

"You mentioned a suicide?"

"Gerald Capel hanged himself in the manor after Legare's death."

Rafe sank onto the couch and ran a hand back and forth over his shorn head. This he'd not seen coming. "The chandelier?"

Calum squinted. "How'd you know?"

"It doesn't matter." Rafe's heart ached for his wife. "I don't believe it. Gerald might've been a mean old SOB, but he was no coward."

"Agreed," Calum said. "Two deaths, one *possible* suicide, and Walker's search have Juliet's land in common."

And two had been killed with a misericord. A Fianna weapon of choice. But how did the vial tie in? If a Fianna warrior killed Eugene and Detective Legare, maybe even Gerald, Nate could be next. "Is Nate the second part of your plan?"

Calum tapped his Rolex. "In exchange for being your PO, I told him you'll help him. You'll meet him at Rage of Angels Club. Nine p.m."

"That PO story is bullshit, and Garza will figure it out." Rafe got up and Calum followed him out of the trailer. "You could hire every PI in the country. Why me?"

Calum paused near a red Ferrari parked next to the black Impala. "Because this is personal. To you as well as me and Juliet. This mission of yours is worth the risks."

Rafe tossed the ammo into the front seat. "Because you're not the hired gun."

"I'm not hiring you."

"Right. The blackmailed gun." He looked toward the glory cross against the tree line. "This isn't about Juliet. Or even Detective Legare and a dead senator. It's about protecting the Prioleau family name."

"Self-pity isn't an attractive quality." Calum opened his car door. "Besides, if you don't agree, I'll send you back to prison before you turn on that car."

"What do you really want?"

Calum got in and adjusted his rearview mirror. "Once, a long time ago, you and Juliet were my best friends. Maybe I want us to be happy again."

Rafe leaned his forearm on Calum's car roof and bent

down. "You can't live in the past. None of us can. And no amount of money can change that."

"Maybe not. But I'd give anything to make things the way they once were."

"Considering your *anything* includes enough money to move governments, tides, and the weather, what would you be willing to do?"

"Manipulate." Calum put on his sunglasses. "Lie. Maybe more."

Rafe stared at his oldest friend. "Kill?"

"I haven't thought about it."

"You should decide what your limits are before events roll out of control and you become a man you don't recognize, a man who makes the angels cry. If you don't set lines you won't cross, nothing can stop you. Not even yourself."

"Is that why you sent Juliet that letter?" Calum's voice cracked like a hammer hitting ice. "Because you couldn't stop yourself?"

"I miscalculated." Rafe wanted to say *fucked up*, but that implied he'd made a mistake. His decision to leave his men, destroy his marriage, and abandon Juliet had been a choice.

Calum nodded. "Did she—"

"Drop it." Rafe stepped away and crossed his arms over his chest.

Calum nodded. "We have an appointment, and I want to get you settled in your apartment. Then we'll talk about Juliet."

Calum revved the engine with the confidence that came from a boatload of money and a shitload of power. For a moment, Calum reminded Rafe of the Prince.

"Fuck. You."

"While we need to address your use of foul language in public, we have an appointment before you see Walker."

"Who the *fuck* with?"

Calum smiled and shifted the car into gear. "My tailor."

Nate dropped the weights on the metal stand in Iron Rack's gym. The *click-bang* reverberated around men lifting and fighting in the ring. Pete had offered to finish the bar restock and grab groceries so Nate could work off his testosterone high. For the first time in days, he felt focused. Muscle-fatigued, but with a Z-pam-inspired alertness that kept him ready. Ready for anything. Ready for anyone. Ready to fight in the ring.

He'd taken another pill, eight hours early. But he was meeting Montfort later and needed the boost. He'd get more pills from Deke after getting paid tonight. Fuck the seizures.

Nate hopped on a treadmill, set it to *shred*, and thanked the gym's management for the hard-core music selection. He settled into a punishing rhythm and studied the room: the perimeter, entrance, and emergency exit. As far as pay-by-day gyms went, Iron Rack's was perfect. No female distractions, basic amenities, and enough weights to make the Hulk happy. There were even two skull-and-crossbones pirate flags covering the picture windows facing the street. It made him feel like he was working out "under the black."

And that stale odor of male sweat and hormone-fueled hostility? Hell, he was a soldier. That scent had melted into his skin years ago. But it was the ring that drew him. The beatings he'd taken and given burned the edge off his emotions. He now craved the daily physical stress that controlled his aggression. As he hit his stride, the front door opened and his sparring partner strode in. Average height, he wore track pants and a long-sleeved T-shirt.

Nate hopped off the treadmill. "Ready to hurt?"

"It won't be me in the infirmary today." The guy smiled without showing his teeth. "And I'm not giving up my winning streak."

Nate pointed to the ring. "Fists or Kenpo sticks?"

"Fists."

"Perfect." Except for the fact that Pete hated Nate's pastime and was probably rehearsing his nightly lecture about spiritual balance and karma.

Nate picked up his bag, when his sparring partner gripped his shoulder.

"I need to know…you okay? No headaches? No high?"

"My migraine meds are working, so I'm cool."

"Just making sure. I'd hate to take advantage of an addict."

"Good. Because I don't want any pity fights."

"No pity. No mercy. Got it."

They hit the ring. After having their hands taped, Nate pounded his fists. Although he was a failure who controlled his seizures by double-dosing illegal prescription drugs, with Rafe's help Nate would be redeemed. Because he sure as hell wasn't an addict.

His sparring partner stretched, his arms flexing. "Ready?"

Nate smiled wide. "Make me bleed."

CHAPTER 11

At nine p.m., Rafe parked the Impala and headed into the club.

After leaving the tailor where Calum had ordered him clothes, including a tuxedo, they'd eaten dinner and dropped his stuff off at one of the many apartments Calum owned. It was down a tiny alley across the courtyard from Juliet's Lily, above Dessie's Couture dress shop. Rafe had wanted to storm Juliet's building, but her store was closed and her apartment above the store empty. When he tried to break in, Calum waved his I-can-send-you-back-to-prison card.

Unfortunately, for now, Rafe had to play by Calum's rules. Rafe had seventeen dollars left from what his lawyer had given him three days earlier. And the account he'd had while working for the Prince was gone. So Rafe had to take Calum's food and clothes until he earned some cash. Hopefully before he ran out of gas.

Once Calum left to bother someone else, Rafe had returned to Juliet's store, but everything was still dark. Since he couldn't find her, he figured he'd stick with Calum's plan for now. Maybe Nate would have answers.

Rage of Angels sat at the end of the River Walk. Demon chanting oozed out of speakers. The eighteenth-century building had white pentagrams on the windows, and the heavy beat of death metal pulsed. Rafe passed a line of goth adults and addressed the man in leathers. "I'm here to see Walker."

The bouncer nodded.

Once inside, Rafe waited for his eyes to adjust. It could've been one of many disgusting clubs in the many European cities he'd worked in. His gut heaved at the combo of overheated bodies, loud music, and incense as he pushed his way toward the bar. Stripper poles flanked the bandstand. High-end cameras watched the front door, bar, and main room. Iron cages hung from the ceiling.

"Walker?" he yelled over the crowd to the bartender.

The bartender made a call.

"What do you want?" The pissed-off male voice came from behind him.

When Rafe turned, he almost laughed. The guy had overly developed biceps and wore leather pants with a lace-up crotch. "I'm here to see Walker."

The guy pressed his ear radio and turned. His pants laced up front and ass. "Fine. But keep it short."

Rafe followed, pushing through the crowd, into an empty room with velvet wallpaper, couches interspaced with booths, a bar, and a mirrored wall. An exit put them in a service hallway. The right door opened into a dressing room with high heels and colored feathers tossed about. A glass bowl of condoms sat on the dressing table. One locker was decorated with glitter stickers spelling out the name *Jade*.

The guy pointed to a door on the left. "Ten minutes. Then I want you gone."

The guy left, and Rafe entered. Empty bookcases lined the office, with the mirror/window facing the velvet room. A desk stood in one corner, covered with tools and a microwave. Tables held laptops and screens, and a couch sat in the other corner.

"Ignore Deke. He's an asshole," a man said from the shadows. Tall with long blond hair pulled back into a ponytail and almost as wide as Rafe, Nate hadn't changed at all. Except for the wrinkles around the eyes and that scar on his cheek covered by fresh bruises.

Rafe would recognize those distinctive green eyes in any combat zone. "Nate."

"Rafe." Nate's jaw tightened, but he held out his hand.

Their shake was hard and fast, and they both went back to their scowls, arms crossed.

Nate spoke first. "I know this is awkward and you came because Calum made you."

"No one makes me do anything. You know that better than anyone."

Nate cleared his throat. "Let's state our goals and how we're going to help each other."

"I want to stay out of prison and protect my wife." Pretty basic as goals went, even if not the entire truth.

Nate looked down. "I need your help looking for something. I find it, we leave town."

"We?"

Nate pressed a button on the wall and leaned against the table holding laptops tied into security cameras. "I'm here with Pete White Horse."

Rafe remembered him. Good soldier. Intense. Quiet. The best kind to have on a team.

Pete came in wearing black cargos, a black tee showing off *real* tribal tats, and a black braid. Pete took his place next to Nate, arms crossed, like mirror-image twins. Great. Now the three of them looked tough and tight. No one spoke. Nate closed his eyes.

"Nate?" Pete touched Nate's shoulder. "You okay, bro?"

Time hiccupped in beats of three.

"Nate?" Pete used both hands to hold Nate's face. "Nate!"

Nate's eyes opened, he drew in breaths like he'd been diving, and his pupils enlarged. Pete let go and lowered the room lights.

Rafe pushed Nate into a chair. "What's going on?"

"How much have you told him?" Pete asked Nate.

Nate didn't respond, he just touched his neck, like he was looking for something, and then dropped his hand.

A heavy sensation invaded Rafe's stomach. "Told me what?"

Pete went to the water cooler and filled a plastic cup. "Ibuprofen?"

"Desk." Nate leaned over, his forearms on his thighs, his upper body shaking.

Rafe found the bottle in the first drawer and tossed it to Pete. Nate downed four pills.

Sweat glazed Nate's pale face, and his gaze danced around the room like on a sniper search. After two inhales, he sat back, spreading his legs to keep his large body balanced on the small chair. He closed his eyes again and ran his hands over his head. "I'm okay."

Liar. Now Rafe needed answers to a new set of questions. "What just happened?"

"Seizure," Nate said. "Followed by a headache. In a few minutes, I'll throw up."

"This was minor," Pete said. "Petit mal."

Something else Calum had left out. "Why are you getting seizures? PTSD?"

"Warlord POW camp." Pete moved a laptop and sat on the table. It sagged under his weight. "In Afghanistan."

Now Rafe felt like he was in that dream with the rabbit, a maze, and circling riddles. "How'd *that* happen?"

"Wakhan Corridor Massacre," Pete said. "Ever heard of it?"

"A native Wakhi tribe was murdered. Hundreds slaughtered, women and kids raped and burned. No one took responsibility." Even the Prince had been horrified by the brutality.

Nate shaded his eyes. "Pete and I need to find out who was responsible."

"Why? That happened years ago."

"Two A-teams, including mine, were accused of the massacre, tried, and sentenced."

In spite of the humming electronics, the room felt silent. Nate's story wasn't possible. He was the most rule-following soldier the army ever trained. "Bullshit."

"It's true," Pete said. "Nate was in command. After the massacre, two of our teams were ambushed near the site of the massacre and imprisoned as POWs. It took weeks to learn what they were accused of."

"Your A-teams were accused of this massacre, taken prisoner, and then released?"

"Rescued," Nate said. "After two years, Colonel Torridan rescued us. Except once home, we were secretly tried and sentenced for mass murder and treason. The rescue, trials, and sentencing are classified. No one knows the truth. Not even our families."

Rafe rubbed his eyes with two fingers. "Your two teams were found *guilty* of the Wakhan Corridor Massacre?"

"Yeah." Nate's voice barely qualified as a whisper. "Then dishonorably discharged and sent to Leedsville Prison in Minnesota."

It took power and money to ghost two A-teams. Even Calum couldn't swing that deal. Hell, even the Prince couldn't do it. "How many men are still in prison?"

"Ten. My A-team and Colonel Keeley's."

"Why was Colonel Keeley there?"

"Jack Keeley led the second team. His men, along with mine, got caught up in the ambush and ensuing nightmare."

Rafe paced, aware of the other men's breathing patterns, where their hands were, whether they were ready to fight. Except their lowered shoulders and hunched backs screamed *tired, defeated, discouraged*. "So why are you and Pete in Savannah?"

"Colonel Torridan has been searching for answers since the night of the ambush. Six weeks ago, he found two clues."

Pete snorted.

"Not great clues," Nate added. "Torridan got me released so we can investigate. If we find out who did this to us and why, then we can free the rest of our men. Prove our innocence. Reclaim our names. Win back our honor."

Hell of a mission. "If you fail?"

"Prison," Nate said. "For a long time."

Not only were Nate and Pete in danger because of Rafe's ongoing war games with the Fianna, their own stakes couldn't get any higher. And Calum had known this and not told him.

Big fucking surprise.

Pete eyeballed the bandages on Rafe's arm. Then his tats. "You here to help us?"

"Depends on your clues." *Please don't say a vial.* He couldn't execute these men.

"A flower," Nate said. "The night of the ambush, every wife in the unit received one. No note. No info on who delivered it. Just a bloom."

Rafe scoffed to hide his relief. "It took Colonel Torridan five years to find this out?"

"At the time, only four men were married. After the imprisonment, our families were thrown off post. And it wasn't just any flower. It was a lily with eight petals and no stamen."

Rafe's body locked down, from his jaw to his feet. Although Calum had warned Rafe, he hadn't been ready to hear it.

"A lily from your wife's property on the Isle of Grace." Pete glanced at Nate. "The second clue is a woman we can't locate. Anne Capel. Calum told us you knew her."

When this was over, Rafe was going to pummel Calum. Then shoot him. "The only Anne Capel with ties to that lily is dead. Has been for centuries."

Nate ran his hands over his head, and his shoulders shook. "That's not possible."

A knock pounded on the door as it opened. Deke's head appeared. "Time to work."

Nate stood, wobbled, and Rafe shoved Nate's ass into the chair. "I'm Walker's sub."

Rafe had just put his ass on the line for Nate? Calum would be proud. No, Calum had probably planned this.

"No deal," Deke said.

Rafe removed his leather jacket and threw it on the table between the tools and the microwave. "You want to be down one set of muscles tonight? Place looks packed."

"Fine." Deke scowled. "Do it now."

Juliet stared at herself in the full-length mirror of the club's locker room. She didn't want to be here. She didn't want to worry about creepy texts, Carina's bitchiness, or seeing Rafe tomorrow. Since she had no idea where Calum had taken Rafe, and she'd been so busy setting up for a funeral and inspecting the Liberty Square site, she'd put Rafe out of her mind. There was no room left in her heart for sadness and stress.

She wanted to be back in her apartment, working on

Mr. Delacroix's proposal, finishing the details for Liberty Square, booking new clients. But right now she needed to focus on her immediate problems.

In gold stilettos, she spun around to check the gold lamé micro-mini barely covering her bottom. She turned back to adjust the way-too-small gold halter top. Unfortunately, she'd lost ten pounds since she'd last danced, most of it in her breasts and her stomach. She added more bra padding because ridiculously inflated breasts might increase her tips.

"Hey, Jade." A woman in sweats came up beside her. "Haven't seen you in a bunch."

"Hi." Marylou, with blond hair and green eyes, had joined the club before Juliet left. "How's school?"

"Good." Marylou tied her hair up. "There's a new bouncer. He said hello to me."

A bouncer who recognized the need for the women who worked here to be seen as people of worth? Juliet applied her scarlet lipstick. "A miracle."

"His biceps are bigger than my waist." Marylou positioned her wig and started pinning. "He's a super hottie. And that's in jeans and a T-shirt. All muscle, tall, short hair."

"Don't you have a boyfriend?" Juliet didn't want to hear about Mr. Super Stud.

Marylou dropped her gaze. "He opened the door for me. A real gentleman."

Juliet brushed her own hair. Hers was much longer, almost to her waist, and dark brown, reminding her of mud. Except Rafe loved— She slammed her brush on the table.

"You alright?" Marylou had gone from blond to black in under a minute.

Juliet transformed herself from a brunette into a white blond with a terse, "Yes." Since Marylou still watched her, Juliet changed the subject. "How've the tips been?"

Marylou turned her lips pink. "I make a grand a night. Some girls make two. Except I can only get one night a week. Everyone wants to dance here because the money is so good."

"And Saturday?"

"Guaranteed six grand. But I haven't been able to get a Saturday in six months."

Not enough. "Is that from the cage?"

"Yes." Marylou mushed her lips together. "You can earn more on the floor. Lap dances are four hundred each. A thousand in a private booth."

Private laps could make up the difference. Juliet had done them in the beginning, hating every demeaning moment.

More women came in. Hair dryers flicked on, and the lights dimmed.

"Deke has been pressuring me to do more," Marylou said. "To—you know."

Yeah. Juliet knew. Besides the dancers, Deke had prostitutes who worked the rooms, using the coed bathrooms to complete their transactions. "Don't let Deke intimidate you. Don't let anyone tell you you're not strong on your own."

She dropped her arms and stared at herself in the mirror again. Long white-blond hair instead of her normal brown, a heart-shaped face, and red lips.

Samantha slid in next to her and adjusted her corset. Since she was a waitress, she could get away with a black mini, a corset, and high-heeled boots. "I hear there's a new bouncer."

Marylou giggled. "He's a stud muffin. You should see his tattoos. I almost fainted to see if he would catch me in those fabulous arms of his."

Juliet wished her only problem was drooling over the newest bouncer.

Deke stuck his head in the room. The music bounced off the hallway walls. "It's time."

She pulled him aside. "We need to talk."

He stared at her breasts and licked his lips. "On your next break."

With her head held high, she went for her cage.

CHAPTER 12

AT ELEVEN P.M., RAFE HEADED FOR THE CONTROL ROOM. He and Pete had already broken up fights in the bathroom and thrown out a drunk bachelorette party. He'd also met some of the strippers, most with eyes shadowed by self-loathing. He'd been extra polite to those he'd met.

He found Pete staring at the laptops. "How's Nate?"

"Out." Pete nodded to the couch where Nate lay beneath a plaid blanket either asleep or unconscious. From his shallow breaths, could be either.

Not feeling the love from Pete, Rafe studied the screens. A man with a heavily tattooed bare chest guarded the door to the velvet room. "Who's that?"

"Bruce." Pete adjusted one of the cameras. "The VIP room just opened. If he has a question about a patron, he'll radio. One of us should stay here for the rest of the night."

"We get to approve who gets in?"

"Yeah." Pete took a mug out of the microwave, and the scent of stale, reheated coffee filled the room. "After spending years in an A-team, it's a power rush."

Rafe heard the sadness in Pete's voice, but since he couldn't help, he watched the monitors. The main room had filled. Women stripped on the poles near the stage; others worked the cages above the dance floor. Too high to touch but close enough for men to throw in money. A leggy blond in a gold mini was the only dancer who deliberately kept her face hidden from the cameras. "Who's that?"

"Deke handles the women," Pete said.

"You don't care what goes on in the club?" Considering what Rafe had seen in the bathrooms, the women not only danced, they were for sale.

"I care about our mission. This job keeps us fed and pays for our shitty motel."

"Is that where Nate got beat up?"

"No." Lines curved around Pete's dark eyes. "When Nate gets stressed, he spars with the regulars at Iron Rack's gym. The more upset he is, the more bruises he gets."

"Nate went today after finding out I'd come home?"

"Yep."

Rafe wasn't the only screwed-up man in the room? That didn't bode well for the mission.

"What about yours?" Pete pointed to the bandages on Rafe's shoulder and arm.

They ached, but he'd had worse. Much worse. "A welcome-home gift."

"From that guy killed by a sniper on the Isle?"

"You heard?"

"Nate is your PO." Pete raised an eyebrow. "Did you know the victim?"

"The less I tell you, the better."

"Uh-huh." Pete went back to zooming cameras in and out.

The room filled with the hum of computers pumping out heat and the clacking of Pete's molars digging for diamonds. "What the *fuck* is wrong?"

"Colonel Torridan told Nate there's a Fianna warrior in town."

"The Fianna is my problem. I don't want you and Nate caught in the cross fire."

"Fine by me." Pete glanced at him, and then back at the laptops. "Is the Gauntlet real?"

The question Rafe had been waiting for all night. And he gave the three answers every soldier around the world wanted to know. "The Gauntlet's real. Most men die. I survived."

Pete stared at Rafe's arm. "And the tattoos?"

Now that Q was unexpected. "They mean what you think they mean."

"Oh," Pete said quietly. "Does Juliet—"

"She knows." And that's all he was going to say about it. He refocused on the security screens as the blond took off her bra, keeping her back to the camera. Despite the men throwing money at her, she danced as if alone.

"I want the truth, Montfort. You disobeyed Nate's orders once. Will you help us now?"

"Yes." If Juliet was involved with what happened to Nate and his men and that vial, Rafe was in. "What else did Torridan say about the lily?"

"Only that he traced it to Savannah. Why? Do you know anything else about it?"

Rafe tightened the camera view on Deke, near the blond, adjusting his pants.

"That lily grew on the Isle when I was a boy. We called it the Capel Lily because it appeared on Capel land. I haven't seen one since I was a kid."

"Damn it."

Rafe heard a groan from Nate and checked his breathing. Steady but shallow. "Does Nate remember anything else about the ambush?"

Pete took a bandana from his pocket, soaked it with water from the cooler, and put it on Nate's forehead. "Nate suffered a head injury during the ambush, and someone in the POW camp pumped him up with drugs. He lost his memories of that night. Whatever info he might have to help us is buried so deep, no one can access it."

Rafe felt Nate's wrist. Pulse was slow and erratic. How ironic that the man who needed to remember couldn't and the man who wanted to forget wasn't allowed to.

"Since we're in truth-telling mode," Pete said, "I'll share something Nate made me swear never to tell anyone. Not even Colonel Torridan. During the ambush, Nate saw a man on the other side of the ridge from where his team had dug in."

Rafe waited while Pete planted his hands on his thighs, his enormous upper body heaving. Whatever the secret was, it was a hell of a burden. "And?"

"Right before the first rocket-propelled grenade hit the unit's location, the man bowed."

That was seriously bad news. "Did anyone else see this… *bowing man*?" Rafe hated Calum's nickname, but it seemed less harsh than *soul-sucking assassin*.

"No. Two years later, after the rescue from the POW camp, Nate's memory was potholed. He didn't mention it because he didn't want Torridan to get wound up over something that might not have happened."

"That's the first good news I've heard all day."

"If Nate saw a bowing man on that ridge—and no one else did—what does it mean?"

Rafe shook his arms to stretch the twitchy muscles. His pain meds must've faded because the thudding ache felt like Escalus's knife was still stabbing. He found the ibuprofen bottle and downed four pills with a cup of water. "When a warrior makes himself known to another man, it's for one of two reasons. He's being recruited for the brotherhood or marked for future assassination. The fact that Nate is alive means it could've been a hallucination."

"Unless either one of those scenarios hasn't happened yet."

Rafe nodded. Truth was nothing if not honest.

"Do you trust Calum Prioleau?" Pete asked.

"Everything Calum does is for the purpose of destroying his enemies and protecting those he loves."

"And his city. He wants us to finish our mission and get out."

"That sounds like Calum. He adores Juliet like a sister and would do anything to protect her. With your intel on her lily, he thinks you're a threat to her as well."

"What about you? Calum got you out of prison, right?"

Rafe tilted his head.

Pete held up both hands. "I guessed. And I'd love to know how he did it."

"Piles of money and a sister who's a U.S. senator." Rafe went back to the cameras, to the woman in gold. The way she moved seemed…familiar. "If we succeed, we'll all get what we want."

"Except for Nate."

Something in Pete's voice sounded off, like the low drone of a helo with one engine blown out. "What do you mean?"

"Nate's seizures?" Pete's black eyes shone. "They're not just stealing Nate's memories. They're killing him."

CHAPTER 13

AT ELEVEN THIRTY, JULIET WENT INTO THE EMPTY LOCKER room for her break and stashed her tips. Her feet felt numb in the heels, and her back ached. *Thank God this day is almost over.*

Deke entered and closed the door. "How does it feel to be back, baby?"

She headed for the mirror and shoved pins in her wig. She could do this. No. Was doing this. Except this time on her terms, not Deke's. "First"—she stabbed another pin— "I'm not your baby. Second, I'm setting the rules." Finished with her hair, she returned to her locker. It still displayed her stage name. *Jade.*

He came up close. "What rules?"

She turned away from his garlic-stained breath. "I go on four times every night for the next nine nights, including Saturday." She had no idea how she'd handle stripping with the Rafe situation, but hopefully he'd be gone in a few days. And it wasn't like they were spending their nights together.

"No." Deke's hot hands found her waist. "You get two acts a night twice a week."

"Next rule." She pried off his sweaty fingers and checked her cell. No crazy texts. She threw it into her purse. "I choose the private laps."

Please God, if you're listening, make the private laps not necessary.

"Jade." Deke leaned against the locker next to hers, arms crossed, his gaze fastened on her breasts. "You're not the only woman here."

She slammed her locker door. "In return for my silence about your *other* job, I work off the books and keep all tips. You get the fifteen percent house take."

"It's twenty-five percent." He licked his lips. "*Baby.*"

Why hadn't she put on a sweatshirt before having this conversation? Because, to succeed on her own, she had to use all of her weapons. "I'm not the girl I was. I've learned a few things."

Deke's leer settled into a frown, and he stalked her. She moved until her back hit a locker. His hands landed on either side of her head, but she kept her chin up and her gaze firm.

"I can't wait to see what you've learned since you left me." The bulge in his pants grew.

She caught their combined reflection in the mirrored wall behind him. His predatory stance hid her body from view, but she didn't need to see herself to know her own strength. "Fifteen percent belongs to the house. That extra ten percent ended up in your pocket. But I'm not giving it to you."

He tried to kiss her neck. "No?"

"No." She ducked under his arm and crossed the room. Deke laughed. "If you want to do your thing in that cage, you'll do as I say."

Tremors rumbled in her stomach. "You want me, Deke?"

"You know I do." He opened his arms as if waiting for her to get on her knees. "I know what you are, Jade. We're the same. Both willing to do anything to survive."

Although they were nothing alike, she'd never go back to those dark nights on the streets, alone, hungry, and terrified. That meant lies had to be part of the plan. "If I make what I need, you get what you want."

His eyes widened as if she were already naked. "Now?"

"After—"

Deke threw her against the wall. Her head hit the concrete, and the room shimmered. He held her wrists over her head and pressed his erection into her stomach. His lips moved to her breasts. "I've waited too long."

No. She kneed him, catching his thigh instead.

He slapped her. "Bitch!"

She crashed onto the linoleum. Her head bounced on the floor, and everything shifted from light to dark. The stench of lemon bleach and Deke's sweat burned her nose. "No!"

His weight on her forced the last air out of her lungs. He gripped her wrists with one hand as his other forced her legs apart.

She bucked and kicked. "Stop!"

A door banged open, and male shouts filled the room. At the sudden lift of weight, she scrambled back against the wall. Her wig shifted, blinding her.

Fists cracked, and glass shattered. The crunch of metal sounded like cars crashing. But she didn't care. She had to get her stilettos off to run.

She kicked off the heels and fumbled with her wig. Bone cracked bone. Someone smashed into something metal. Her fingers dug for bobby pins, but the wig wouldn't come off.

Heavy boots beat the floor. "Grab him!" Pete said.

"Thtupid bith! Netht time—"

The thud of a fist hitting flesh answered. Followed by scuffling that got louder and then receded. A door slammed shut, leaving her in silence. She curled up and wheezed out short breaths. She wanted to throw up and fade away. Minutes or hours later, soft hands touched her shoulders, and Juliet jumped.

"You're safe." Samantha pulled out bobby pins and freed Juliet from the fake hair. "They took Deke away. He won't hurt anyone again."

Juliet stood, and Samantha wrapped a plaid blanket around her shoulders. "Deke didn't... I mean, you're okay?"

"No...I'm okay."

Samantha pressed her forehead against Juliet's until their noses touched. "Thank God."

Juliet shook like she'd been shoved in a barrel and rolled down a hill.

"Watch your feet." Samantha led her to a bench. "There's broken glass everywhere."

Juliet sat and pulled her hair behind her neck to survey the damage from the mirror's reflection. A beast had torn through the room. Some lockers were dented; others lay on their sides. Glass bowls had shattered, condoms and bobby pins flung everywhere. And her face—she had a bruise on her cheek, and her lips were swollen. She dropped her head. What was she going to do now?

"Is she alright?" a man said from behind them. "Do we need an ambulance?"

"No," Samantha said. "Juliet isn't hurt. I'm so grateful you got here in time."

The air hummed like static before a storm, and Juliet faced Rafe. He wore clean jeans and a black T-shirt, and his chiseled face was taut, eyes questioning, hands fisted. As he came closer, massive biceps flexed. The blue ribbon had been cleaned and tied tight.

He blinked, and his forehead furrowed. "*Juliet?*"

A vein pounded in his neck. He raised his tattooed arm to run his hand over his head. She stood, tightening the blanket around her. For some reason, he seemed larger than earlier in the day. Maybe because she felt so damn small and vulnerable.

Moving slowly, he took her free hand. His touch sent a hot rush through her body. She turned, crushed under the loss of her dignity, unable to bear his pity.

"*Please.* Look at me."

She broke away and licked her dry lips. This couldn't have been more of a nightmare if she'd planned it.

He rubbed a fist across his chin and glanced between her and Samantha.

Samantha moved until her shoulder touched Juliet's. "Didn't I meet you earlier today in Juliet's shop?"

"This is Rafe." Juliet swallowed, tasting blood.

"Oh." Samantha's eyes went wide, and then she scowled. "Your husband."

"Ex-husband." Juliet took Samantha's hand. "I'd like to shower and change before the girls go on their breaks. Can you make sure no one comes in?"

"No way." Samantha squeezed Juliet's fingers and glared at Rafe. "I'm not leaving you alone."

"Neither am I." Rafe kept flexing his fingers. "Why were you…"

"Stripping?" Juliet met his gaze. "It's—"

The door opened, and another man entered. "Do we need an ambulance? Or the cops?"

Green eyes. Blond hair. Large hands. Goose bumps clawed their way up her arms. Her toes curled against the floor. *Nate?*

"No ambulance," Rafe said, still staring at her. "And no cops. We'll handle Deke."

Except Nate didn't respond. His gaze had clasped onto hers, eyes wide.

Another locker fell, and she jumped. The jarring noise clarified things. She was in a strip club with Rafe and Nate.

She went to her locker and retrieved her bag. "Are you two working together again?" She hated the tremble in her voice and slammed the locker door shut.

"Juliet," Rafe said, "we have to talk."

"I just want to shower, change, and go home." Then she'd spend the rest of the night figuring out how to make twenty grand in nine days. "If what you want to talk about has anything to do with Nate, I've nothing to say." She avoided Rafe's pleading gaze and entered the shower room.

Her bare feet hit the cold tile, but before she could bar the door, it flew open. She dropped her bag as Rafe stormed in, nostrils flared. He shut the door with his boot. Then he locked it and stopped inches away. He used a finger to tilt her chin up, but she turned. Just not fast enough to miss the shadows darkening his brown eyes. The brown eyes she'd once trusted. The brown eyes she'd once drowned in.

With his thumb, he traced her swollen cheek. He swallowed, and she couldn't help herself. She followed the action. Her gaze skimmed his chest that rose and fell in undulations. He took her elbows and moved in. He didn't hurt her, but she felt the strength in his grip through the blanket. His breath grazed her hair, and her heart tumbled over itself.

His lips hovered over hers. "*Juliet.*"

She inhaled sharply. Of all the daydreams she'd had of seeing him again, she'd always pictured herself strong and fierce, armed with insults and indifference. Not shamed, tongue-tied, and on the verge of tears.

She pulled away and sat on a bench. Although she was grateful he'd saved her, she'd just lost her last chance to save everything that mattered.

He sat next to her. His knees almost touched hers, and he pressed his elbows into his thighs. "Why are you here?"

She was glad he sat on her right side. She didn't want to see his other arm. And while talking about this was the last thing she wanted to do, it might end the night sooner. "I need fast money to save my business." Her feet burned, and she realized they had tiny cuts, probably from the glass. "And Nate? You're working with your old unit again?"

"Not exactly." Rafe focused on her bruised cheek. "Nate is helping me. I'm helping him."

She snorted. "Nate wouldn't help a pregnant woman in a wheelchair cross the street."

Rafe frowned. "That's harsh."

Nate deserved it. "Although I agreed to work with you, if your plan involves Nate, I'm not interested." She stood. "Now I'd appreciate it if you'd leave so I can change."

Rafe gripped his knees with his fingers. He'd heard a woman's scream on his way to the VIP room and rushed in, not realizing the woman in gold had been Juliet. *His wife.*

Knocks banged on the door behind him as a cell phone rang.

Juliet answered her phone, "Juliet Capel," and turned away.

He unlocked the door to find Pete on the other side. "Everyone okay in there?"

No. "Where's Deke?"

"In the control room."

"I'll be there soon."

Pete left as Samantha scooted around them, heading to Juliet, who was still on the phone.

"Yes, Father Quinn," Juliet said. "I'll come right away." She hung up and turned on one of the showers. "Rafe, please go so I can change."

"Who was on the phone?"

"A client." She glanced at his tattooed arm, and then at the floor. "I need to swing by a work site before I go home."

He scowled. "It's almost midnight."

Samantha moved closer to Juliet. "The girls are coming in, and someone needs to tell them what happened."

"Nate can handle it," Rafe said.

"Your shoulder," Juliet said. "Are you bleeding?"

A stain bled through his T-shirt. The knife wound had reopened, and he hadn't even noticed. Except now that the adrenaline was wearing off, his aches rushed back. "It's nothing."

"You should get it looked at," Samantha said.

"A good thing to do *now*," Juliet added.

A cloud of steam from the shower reached for his wife. With her hair down her back, pale face, and dark eyes, she belonged in one of his erotic dreams. Not in a sleazy strip club. "I don't want you going anywhere alone. Get dressed and meet me in the control room."

The women glanced at each other, and then laughed.

Realizing retreat was the better option, he left the shower room and strode through the dressing room. But when he passed her locker, he slammed his fist into the center of the name *Jade*. Pain shot through his swollen knuckles and up his arm. The metal caved in on itself until the lock and hinges broke. He glanced back to see the women standing next to each other in the shower room doorway. They'd stopped laughing.

Juliet would never have to demean herself again. He'd make damn sure of that.

Outside the control room door, Pete stopped him. "I swear we didn't know Juliet worked here. This is the first we've seen her."

Rafe's heart braced against the memory of that moment when he'd stared into his bride's eyes. He knew that look. Had seen it on the battlefield, in the faces of the men he'd executed. They'd been the eyes of a woman who'd seen too much, had been hurt too many times, and was determined to protect herself. "I know."

"Samantha just told me Juliet worked here for years but stopped a while ago. Apparently, she needed money. Fast. Something about refinancing a business loan."

She'd worked here for *years*? And returned the same day he'd come home? The same day Escalus had died? Not a coincidence. "I believe you."

Pete's shoulders dropped three inches. "Good."

Now that blame had been redirected, Rafe entered the control room. Pete closed the door. Deke lay on this back, his hands and feet and mouth duct-taped.

Nate pointed at Deke. "This POS begged us not to call the cops. Said that as long as we didn't turn him in, he'd leave town."

"He'd come back."

Deke shook his head, banging it against the floor.

"You did a hell of a job on him," Nate said.

A knock sounded. The security camera in the hallway ID'd Samantha.

Pete let her in, but when Samantha saw Deke, she halted. "I need help in the dressing room. The women are *freaking out*."

"I'll go." Pete left and Samantha followed until Rafe blocked the door, stopping her.

"How could you let her strip? You're her friend."

A snarl marred her pretty features. "You were her husband. Yet you destroyed her. You're a monster. A cheat. A traitor."

"Samantha," Nate warned. "*Drop it.*"

She snorted. "Will we ever know why Juliet had such a strong reaction to *you*?"

"That situation was volatile by the time I got there," Nate said.

Rafe stared at his ex-CO. Juliet had had an unusually strong reaction to Nate. But with all the shit going on, did it matter?

Deke moaned on the floor, and Rafe kicked him in the ribs.

No. It didn't matter. At least not right now.

"Samantha?" Pete poked his head back into the room. "Where's Juliet?"

Samantha smiled liked she'd sucked the cream out of a French pastry. "She went to the cathedral."

Rafe clenched his fists. He was at the very end of his patience stick. "Alone?"

"Yep."

Pete took her arm as if he knew he had to get her out of there before Rafe forgot he'd never hurt a woman. "Please go tell the women everything is fine."

Samantha tossed her hair, stomped on Deke's balls, and left.

Deke curled up like a crumpled black-leather napkin, hard angles both turned in and sticking out. His muffled cry competed with a high-pitched ring from the speaker above the computers. Bruce's signal meant trouble in the VIP room.

"Who's that?" Pete pointed to the VIP room monitor.

Nate stepped over Deke to see the screen. Then he whistled low.

Bruce flashed a frantic hand signal.

"Hell, Rafe," Pete said. "That man walks like you."

The man wore leather pants and a black leather coat with a hood covering his face. He worked his way through the crowd, avoiding the women who sidled up to him. He moved with no jerky movements. The kind of gait that took strength, flexibility, and self-control to appear as if one skimmed over water. He oozed confidence and power.

Rafe planted his fists on the table. His nightmare was complete. "He works for the Prince."

The leather-clad man went through the emergency exit leading into the alley. The alarm started.

"Turn off the alarm, Pete. Then kill the security camera in the alley."

Pete clicked away, turning off the noise. "Why?"

Rafe didn't answer. "Nate, go to the cathedral. Watch over Juliet until I can get there."

"But—"

"You want my help, this is the deal. Go out the front. Don't let *him* see you."

"Who is he?" asked Pete.

"Balthasar. The Prince's second-in-command. If he sees either of you, he'll kill you."

Nate and Pete stilled, as if standing at attention.

"And don't let any of the women leave until I take care of Balthasar."

"What about him?" Pete motioned to Deke. Although his wrists were bound and tears stained his cheeks, he was trying to pull the duct tape off his mouth.

Rafe rubbed the back of his neck. He was out of time and options. "Deke remains here until closing. Then you and Nate will take Deke to the bus station and stay with him until he's gone. If he comes back, he's dead."

Nate frowned. "You sure Deke won't get loose?"

"Yes." Rafe grabbed the duct tape and moved his jacket to find a hammer and a nail in the toolbox on the table. His jacket fell on the floor and Pete picked it up.

Rafe knelt next to Deke and whispered in his ear. "Do you know what *sans pitié* means?"

Deke's swollen eyes went as wide as they could.

Yeah. Everyone in Savannah knew what that meant.

"Good. Because if you return, that's what you'll get." Rafe forced Deke's head sideways and against the floor. "Help me, Nate."

Nate knelt to hold Deke's head until one side was on the floor. Rafe ripped off a piece of duct tape and, starting at one side of the floor next to Deke's head, wrapped it along his forehead to the other until he was taped to the floor and couldn't move. "Hold his shoulders."

Nate pressed down Deke's upper body.

"Pete?" Rafe ordered. "Hang on to Deke's legs while I explain what happens when any man hurts the woman I love."

Rafe picked up the nail, and Deke whimpered.

"Fuck this," Pete said. "That's not the way we do things."

"Not the way *you* do things." Rafe ignored Nate's shocked gaze and focused on Deke's fearful one. "Let's see your ear."

Deke bucked.

"Dammit, Pete. Hold his legs." Rafe placed the nail in Deke's ear, held it steady, and swung the hammer, driving the nail into the floor. Muffled screams filled the room, and Rafe hit again. His stomach rebelled, but he kept his breathing steady.

Deke's eyes rolled back into his head, and he passed out. He'd never hurt Juliet again.

"Fuck. This." Pete crawled away until his back hit the wall.

Rafe stood and held out a hand to help up Nate, who'd gone as pale as the moon.

Nate scrubbed his hands over his head. "What've you done?"

Oh brother, so much more than that. "Avenged my wife."

Nate leaned over, hands on his thighs. His body heaved. Sweat stained his T-shirt.

Pete muttered, "We're fucked."

Rafe settled his hands on his hips and stared up at the stained ceiling. If they didn't get their shit together, this mission was over before it started. "This isn't the U.S. Army. This isn't an A-team. We're not a unit. We're three men being bitch-slapped by fate, hunted by warriors we can't see, and screwed by a situation we don't understand. If we want to survive, we have to play the game to win. We have to play my way."

Rafe pointed to the black monitor that used to show the alley but now hid a waiting Balthasar. "We play the game like Fianna warriors. No prisoners. No rules. No mercy."

"What are you going to do to Balthasar?" Nate asked. "Kill him?"

"No." That would escalate the situation and endanger Juliet even more. "I'll assess things and meet you at the cathedral. Watch over Juliet until I get there."

"We're fucked," Pete said again.

Nate wobbled.

Rafe gripped Nate's shoulders. "We need to be strong. We need to work together. Despite our screwed-up past, trusting each other is the only way we succeed. Got it?"

Nate helped Pete up, and they both nodded.

"Good." Rafe sighed. "If either of you have any influence with the Almighty, pray."

"Are you joking?" Pete asked.

"No. We need any help we can get."

CHAPTER 14

RAFE EXITED THROUGH THE KITCHEN. THE SOONER NATE and Pete understood Geneva Convention rules had no place in this fight, the better chance they had of surviving.

Did Rafe enjoy torturing men like Deke? No.

Was Rafe sorry? Let's add a *hell* to that *no*.

And if that asshole touched Juliet again, Rafe *would* kill him.

He entered the alley. Drizzle soaked his T-shirt. The stench of river mud irritated his throat. Last week, when he'd been in his cell dealing with the blackness of his life, he never would've guessed that six days later he'd be meeting Balthasar. Fate liked to fuck him over and then stand back and laugh.

"Romeo." Balthasar emerged. "My brother lives."

Rafe hit his chest with a fist and bowed his head. "It grieves me to lay my gaze upon you, Balthasar. What do you require?" The words barely made it through his gritted teeth.

Balthasar hugged the shadows cast by the anemic street light. "The truth about a mis-justice done this day."

Talk of mis-justice from a man who dealt out death with the same precision with which he spoke? Super. "Do you speak of my freedom?"

"Your freedom is an abomination I care not about."

"It's Escalus's release from this world that troubles you?"

"My tears would wash our brother's wounds, except Escalus betrayed our brotherhood and his body remains in this world."

Rafe rubbed his forehead. While verse had come more easily for Escalus, neither of them had worked as hard at the Fianna's language requirement as Balthasar. He was a powerful, deadly perfectionist. So Rafe stopped trying to be something he'd already failed at. "Where's Escalus?"

"In the morgue."

Rafe raised his head, the drizzle rinsing his face. Fianna warriors, even errant ones, were always returned to the brotherhood. "The Prince has his reasons."

"'Tis our way to honor our dead brothers. Have you forgotten?"

As if that could happen. "No."

Balthasar moved until Rafe saw himself reflected in the other man's eyes. "Pray tell, Romeo. What was the cause of your fray with Escalus?"

"He threatened my wife."

"And you took his life?"

"I wounded him. Arragon slayed him."

"Which leaves us at odds."

"Did you know Escalus had been planning to sell that vial to a third party?"

"No. 'Tis a fiendish lie."

"The Prince's second-in-command didn't know Escalus had gone rogue?"

Balthasar's lips turned into thin lines. "In the two thousand years of our brotherhood, there's been only one record of cowardice, of a brother leaving those he loved behind, of turning traitor. And you've performed these wretched deeds *thrice*."

Rafe's hands formed fists. "How long did it take after my arrest in St. Petersburg for the Prince to make you his second-in-command?"

Balthasar growled.

"It must kill you that I'm grateful to be done with that life, grateful you took my job, grateful for the years in prison that gave me distance and perspective. You must hate that I see you for what you are. An insecure man desperate for approval."

"I may seek approval from those I respect, but neither the Prince nor I relish what we do. Our ends and our means are equal in weight and stature. Whereas you—" Balthasar glanced at Rafe's bleeding, swollen knuckles. "Your means far outweighed your ends. Never was a soldier more brutal than the one called Romeo."

"I fulfilled my orders with precision and skill."

"You relished each and every kill."

Rafe's throaty laugh echoed. "We are Fianna warriors. We seek vengeance on behalf of those who can't, those who are too weak or poor or incapable of violence. That was my purpose. Until it wasn't."

"No one leaves the brotherhood."

"I never cared about the rules. Just ask Walker."

"The rules care about you."

"Fuck the rules. Fuck the Prince. And fuck you. I've more important things to do tonight than deal with your bullshit."

"You need your wife's forgiveness if you wish to succeed."

გ

Balthasar adjusted his gloves while Romeo bared his teeth.

"My wife is none of your business."

"Your wife despises you. I watched while she read that letter, how it broke her." He paused. "Don't you wonder why she hates Walker?"

Romeo frowned. Balthasar could tell from the way Romeo's eyelids twitched that he wanted to ask about Walker, but that would be a sign of weakness.

"Next week," Romeo said, "after I win back my wife and find that vial, we're going to have an adult male *conversation*."

"Then you'll return with me to meet the Gauntlet. As is your fate."

Romeo scoffed. "While you're begging for your life, ask the Prince why he tried to recruit Nate Walker."

"You speak of nothing." Balthasar pointed to the club's back door. "You'll not win back your wife. I'll destroy her first."

Romeo's hit came hard and fast, throwing Balthasar against the wall. Romeo had gained in strength and speed, but Balthasar was willing to let Romeo play the wounded, righteous hero. Romeo never could control his emotions, and Balthasar had his knife ready.

Romeo pressed a forearm against Balthasar's windpipe and took a short metal rod from Balthasar's coat. Instantly, a thin, razor-sharp sword extended, and Romeo pressed the tip against Balthasar's neck. "Do you remember Athens?"

Balthasar ignored the sting. "Aye." Athens had been Romeo's first assignment with Escalus. A brutal display that left a message not to fuck with the Fianna. That city still belonged to the Prince.

"I've learned a lot since then," Romeo said. "How to drive a man so mad he prefers the cold ground to his lover's warmth. So insane he begs for the end, no matter how painful."

"Who taught you all you know?"

Romeo released Balthasar and threw down the misericord. Balthasar retrieved it, retracted it, and shoved it in his coat pocket. Then he grabbed Romeo's arm and whispered in his ear. Romeo struggled, but Balthasar tightened his hold and kept talking. Lady Juliet had always been Romeo's greatest weakness. That also made her the game's greatest pawn. When Balthasar was done, he let go.

Romeo stumbled back, shaking. He leaned against the wall and scraped his hands over his head. "It's not true."

"Ask Lady Juliet. Or Walker."

"I'll kill Walker." Romeo glared at Balthasar. "And Kells Torridan. Then you."

"A battle, then. You fight to win your lady's affections while I destroy them. Pray, have you explained the names on your arm yet?"

Romeo straightened his shoulders. His powerful chest undulated with rage, and his eyes glittered with the ruthlessness he was known for.

When Romeo refused to respond, Balthasar bowed at the waist. "Until next week."

"Fuck you." With that oh-so-eloquent farewell, Romeo left.

Once alone, Balthasar took out his cell phone and dialed. Lennox answered, "Need you help, Balthasar?"

"Did you recruit Torridan's man Walker?"

"Not I. Perchance another did. Why?"

"It matters not. My thanks." Balthasar hung up and rubbed his eyes. No one was recruited without his permission.

"Hey." The male voice came from the shadows. "It's me." Escalus's contact. "Show yourself."

A young man in a hoodie and ripped jeans emerged. His features were so sharp that if one were to run their hands over his face they'd receive a palmful of papercuts. "Where's E?"

"Dead."

"Oh." The man scratched his head. "And you are?"

"Escalus's partner." Balthasar bowed his head. "Balthasar."

"E didn't mention a partner."

"He didn't mention you either."

The man frowned "True. I'm Eddie. And Deke's inside. Without him we can't get any more zombie heroin."

Heroin? Balthasar had watched for weeks as that new drug decimated the addict class. "Escalus was involved with that?"

"*Dude*, E brought it—and Aemon—to the city. Except E killed Aemon a few days ago. Sliced him with that sword thing and dumped his body nearby. Aemon was a computer wiz but didn't have the proper respect. You feel?"

"Who's Aemon?"

"Where've you been?" Eddie ran his hands through his hair until it stuck up like brown toothpicks. "Aemon's the uber-top guy in the org. Except for my cousin. My coz wasn't happy about E killing Aemon, but E was like you. *A fucking tank.* And my cousin needs him." The kid's eyelids dropped. "My cousin isn't going to be happy about E's death. He had this *thing* for E. He counted on him."

These were the people Escalus betrayed him for? "I'm here now."

Eddie popped gum in his mouth. "You have E's laptop?"

"Yes, but not the passwords."

"Deke can fix that. I was inside watching. Deke's busted up and stuck in the club's security office. I also got a lead on the vial."

Balthasar nodded. "I'll retrieve Deke. Meet us at the safe house." After giving Eddie the address, Balthasar said, "Hurry. We've work to do."

Eddie disappeared, and Balthasar hid until someone came out to dump garbage. He caught the back door and, once inside, used a service hallway to bypass the kitchen. He stayed in the shadows, watching the locked security office, until a female voice asked, "Are you lost?"

Balthasar turned to find a stunning redheaded woman in a too-short skirt and too-small bikini top. She had the body of a teenager and the eyes of a combatant. He'd always been highly attracted to females, which was why his tithe had been celibacy.

A Fianna warrior was required to break every link tying him to the real world, and this woman, with the *come fuck me* lips and full breasts, would be another one of the Prince's trials.

He bowed his head. "I was waiting for someone but now can't remember why."

"I can help." She giggled and held out her hand. "I'm Sally."

He pulled her against his hard body. Heat built up in his veins, and his breath shortened. Sally gasped, her eyes closed. His cock pressed into her stomach, and from the way she chewed her bottom lip and moaned, she felt his length and width grow. Yes, he'd more than enough to satisfy any woman and had left many complete in both bliss and exhaustion.

He kissed her hard, both sucking and biting her lips. The ache in his lower stomach sought relief by pressing his hips against hers. When he raised his head, his hands gripped her ass. She rubbed against his body like she wanted to crawl inside him. From her nipple rings and the way she swirled her tongue, she obviously had other skills. His body responded with a flash of heat, and he grabbed his arousal. It'd been so long since he'd cared for this rebellious part of his body, he almost climaxed from his own touch. "Can we go someplace private? Someplace with a locked door?"

She glanced down to his hand holding his cock through the leather, and her eyelids went halfsies. She dragged him to the security office door and punched a code into the keypad. Before hitting the overheads, he forced her against the wall, her legs around his waist, his lips on hers. He ground his hips against her core through their clothes. His cock swelled even more at the scent of their arousal.

While he fondled a breast, he flicked his wrist, protracting the blade. The misericord slipped beneath her ear, into her neck. Her eyes widened before she slid down the wall and slumped on the floor.

Then he turned to find Deke struggling against ducttape ties. Keeping the deadly sword visible, Balthasar knelt and smiled.

CHAPTER 15

JULIET HIT THE CATHEDRAL WHEN THE DRIZZLE STOPPED. Dark clouds had snuffed out the stars.

Her cell phone buzzed, and she checked the message.

Lady Juliet, make haste. Time is short.

She glanced back. Other than cop cars lining the street, the area surrounding the cathedral was dark and empty. She hurried up the steps, and the gargoyles in the spires snarled at her.

This had to be one of the worst days she'd ever had—other than those weeks after Rafe had sent her that letter, those weeks spent with Nate Walker. How could her life have crashed so quickly? She stood on the edge of losing everything, with Rafe as a witness. But she wouldn't cry. She'd do what she always did. She'd rely on herself. She'd survive.

Once in the narthex, she sucked in the frigid, incense-filled air. Police checked the pews with flashlights, searching the transepts and sanctuary. Her sneakers scuffled on the marble floor. There were no overhead lights on, but every votive candle had been lit, illuminating the main church, keeping the corners in shadow.

"Miss Capel!" Detective Garza strode down the aisle toward her. "Are you alright?"

She met him halfway. "Why wouldn't I be?"

"Father Quinn called a while ago."

Not wanting to admit she'd walked fourteen blocks in

the dark, dodging heroin addicts in the alleys, she focused on the two dozen cops. "What's going on?"

Garza reached for her face but dropped his hand. "What happened?"

She turned and saw Father Quinn standing in the shadows next to the main altar. "I fell at the work site."

"Do you want to talk about it?"

"No." She hiked her bag on her shoulder and regretted her short tone. Then she noticed the dark circles under Garza's eyes and the hair that looked like he'd been running his hands through it all night. "Are you alright?"

"Besides finding a dead kid near the River Walk today, the murdered man out on your property, and the flood of heroin overdoses, I'm fine."

"That's awful." She needed to remember that other people had problems too.

"I'm sorry." He scrubbed his fingers through his hair. "I shouldn't unload on you or talk about other cases. It's unprofessional."

"It's alright." She offered a half smile. "I know all about bad days."

He took her elbow and led her to the main altar. "Have you been here since setting up for tomorrow's funeral?"

"Not since my foreman, Bob, and I finished around seven p.m." She peered over Garza's shoulder to check out the ficus trees in the sanctuary, ivy roping along the altar rails, and white lilies in the two side chapels. "Is something wrong?"

"Yes."

Father Quinn stood in the right transept, facing the altar that held the statue of Mary. He held a phone to his ear. Instead of his collar, he wore jeans and a blue golf shirt. The cold air was thick with the fragrance of vanilla-scented candles. "Good evening, Father."

Father Quinn pocketed his phone. "Juliet? Are you hurt?"

"I'm fine—" She stopped. Behind him the stone pots she'd just ordered, carved with her Juliet's Lily logo, had been pulverized. All of the white Madonna lilies had had their heads cut off. The blooms outlined a pile of potting soil spread beneath the statue. In this four-foot-by-two-foot dirt rectangle, someone had scrawled the words JULIET, HERE'S SUCH A COIL. TO REVERSE A PRINCE'S DOOM, STOP THY UNHALLOW'D TOIL. "Who did this?"

"We were hoping you'd know," Garza said.

"I've no idea."

"Did you show her the other one?" Father Quinn asked Garza.

"There's more?"

Garza led her past the main altar to the north transept. Father Quinn followed.

"I locked up at ten," Father Quinn said, "and went to eat. When I returned, I noticed lights flickering through the transept window. Every candle in the church had been lit, the fuse box had been destroyed, and incense had been burned. Then I saw this."

As in the other chapel, her pots had been destroyed, flower heads cut off to line another rectangle of dirt in front of the Altar of Reservation. This message said DRAW THE SHADY CURTAINS FROM AURORA'S BED. THY HUSBAND IN THY BOSOM THERE LIES DEAD.

"Miss Capel," Garza said. "Do you know what this means?"

"No." That was the truth. She had no idea what tonight's vandalism or the crazy texts meant. The only thing she was sure of was Rafe was involved. She just didn't want to discuss her relationship with her ex-husband.

Garza's cell rang, and he held up a hand. "Excuse me. I need to take this."

Since everyone was busy, she walked down a side aisle, staying out of the way. She sank into a pew and leaned forward, her head in her palms. What was going on? And more importantly, what was she going to do?

"Don't scream," a man said behind her.

She turned. Even in the shadows, she recognized Nate. She'd put up with a lot today. Two strikes of vandalism. A bank loan disaster matched by real estate issues. A narcissistic senator. A rogue ex-husband. A murder on her land. Crazy texts. Deke. And this cathedral disaster. But she wouldn't put up with Nate. "Go. Away."

"I'm here to help."

She snorted. "Did Rafe send you?"

"Yes."

"Then he doesn't know what you did to me eight years ago?"

Nate's green eyes begged her. That's when she noticed the scar on his cheek, the worry lines around his eyes, his shaky lips. "Not yet."

"You saw what Rafe did to Deke," she whispered. "I wonder what he'll do to *you*?"

"Kill me. But, for now, Rafe asked me to watch out for you until he can get here."

"What for?"

Nate waved his hand around the cathedral. "You're at the center of this mess."

"Ridiculous." Shivers ran up her back. But was it? Really? She left the pew.

He followed her to the confessionals. "If you can't trust me, trust Rafe."

Before she could respond, Garza maneuvered between her and Nate. "What's going on?"

Nate held out his hand. "Nathan Wall."

She snorted. Another lie? Why was she not surprised?

Nate sent her a warning glare. "I'm Montfort's parole officer."

Garza crossed his arms over his chest. "What are you doing here?"

Nate shoved his hands in his back pockets, his nonchalance loud and clear. "I heard about the incident from the police scanners. I knew Miss Capel had been setting up for a funeral. I decided to check it out."

She started to reply but stopped. She didn't want to give the detective any more reasons to ask questions about Rafe. She just wanted this night to end.

"You follow the ex-wives of all your parolees?" Garza asked Nate.

"Only the ones who need help."

"Uh-huh." Garza turned toward her. "May I speak with you alone?"

She nodded and followed him to the front of the church.

"Why is Wall here?"

"I don't know." Was that her sounding so exasperated? Probably. Except it didn't matter because it was the truth.

From his slight scoff, he didn't believe her. "Does Wall bother you?"

She pointed at the chapel. "All of this bothers me. The vandalism. The dead man on my land. My loan."

"What loan?"

She told him the story, finishing with "Someone's targeting me, and I don't know why."

Garza glanced back at Nate. "Do you know a man named Escalus?"

"No." She followed Garza's line of sight to see Nate texting. "Why?"

"According to the ME, that name was tattooed on the

arm of the victim we found on Capel land. Same name I read in a journal the sheriff found in that rental car."

"What journal?"

"This afternoon, Sheriff Boudreaux sent me a diary belonging to Escalus because it was written in Latin."

The detective was full of surprises. "You know Latin?"

"Yes." Garza showed her a photo on his phone. It was of the dead man's arm with a tattoo of a sword piercing a heart and the name *Escalus* scrawled below. "The journal has a leather cover embossed with this same image, and his name was inside." Garza swiped the screen, finding another photo. "This is the first page. Read the first line."

She took the phone as the cathedral doors shut with a bang, and she saw Rafe grab Nate's arm and drag him into the shadows.

"You should know," Garza said in a conspiratorial voice, "that I've called my military contact. I'm looking into your husband's release."

"Ex-husband," she said softly. Rafe had Nate cornered.

"Miss Capel, are you familiar with the graffiti around town with the words *sans pitié* beneath a skeleton hand holding a cutlass?"

The question startled her, and she gave the detective her full attention. "It's the Prioleau family sigil."

"It looks like a pirate flag."

"During the seventeenth and eighteenth centuries, the Prioleau family ran a pirate empire from the mid-Atlantic to the Caribbean. By the Revolutionary War, they were wealthier than King George. By the Civil War, they were the most powerful shadow family in the country. The Prioleaus are huge benefactors in this city now."

Garza nodded, his gaze going back to Rafe and Nate. "The Prioleau tag was painted near a murder victim we found today. The boy had a hole in his neck. I was hoping the tag would be a clue."

"Probably not."

"Thank you. I couldn't get anyone in the station to tell me what it meant."

She could only imagine how hard it was for a man from New Jersey to fit in. In Savannah, if people didn't know you, they knew your family. If they didn't know your family, you were nothing. "I'd like to talk to Father Quinn. I have to fix this by tomorrow."

"When you're ready, I'll have an officer take you home." He nodded to her hand, and she realized she still held his phone. "Did you read the first line?"

She blinked before giving his cell back. Then she focused on Rafe, who leaned against a column, a few pews away, staring at her. The first sentence on the first page of the diary had started with one word. *Romeo.*

CHAPTER 16

RAFE STAYED IN THE DARK. AWAY FROM CANDLES. AWAY from cops with flashlights. Away from Nate. Rafe had come in ready to throw Nate into one of the stained-glass windows and then rip him from balls to neck.

But Rafe had stopped himself. First, he wasn't sure if what Balthasar said was true. Balthasar was a master manipulator. Yet Kells Torridan was a cold-blooded Special Forces commander devoid of emotion who gave no quarter. It would be like Kells to mentally torture a defenseless woman in the name of protecting his men. While Nate would pay for what he'd done, the real blame lay at Torridan's boots.

Second, Nate's problems were connected to Juliet, so until that mess was figured out, Nate had to stay alive. At least Rafe now understood her reactions.

Juliet stood in the north transept with Father Quinn. She'd changed into yoga pants and a sweatshirt. Her braided hair was twisted into a knot that hung low against her neck. Rafe remembered the weight of her hair, the sensation of the strands dragging across his naked chest, the scorching heat left behind.

He ached to go to her. Instead, he focused on every sound: footsteps, male conversations, Juliet's softer voice.

Nate came up next to him, pocketing his phone. They'd had a brief conversation when he'd arrived, but Rafe had tabled the real issue of Nate's evisceration. The one good thing Rafe had learned from the Fianna? Extreme self-control.

"I don't get it," Nate said. "Why defile a church?"

"Balthasar didn't defile." Rafe caught the candlelight glinting off the silver combs in Juliet's hair. She rubbed her neck and passed the altar. Had she looked at him? "Balthasar desecrated."

"There's a difference?"

"A desecration ruins the sacred, like a consecrated cathedral. Or a marriage." She moved closer. His heartbeat kicked up, and he crossed his arms so he wouldn't reach for her.

"Hey." Nate nudged his shoulder. "You with me?"

"A defilement ruins the profane. The real world."

"*Our* world." Nate's voice scraped gravel. "You're sure—"

"Positive." Rafe would recognize Balthasar's work anywhere. Although Rafe wasn't sure which angered him more: the desecration, what Nate had done, or the fact that Juliet might have walked here alone in the dark.

A text hummed. Nate pulled out his burner phone and showed it to him. "What does this mean?"

For never was a story of more woe.

The caller ID was blocked, but Rafe knew who'd sent it. "Balthasar's idea of a joke."

"That freak has my cell phone number? *Fabuuuulouuuus.* We're supposed to be staying below the fucking radar."

"Balthasar knows I have to win her trust. So he's making her not trust me."

"Is this *The Dating Game*? We have work to do, except I have a Fianna warrior on my phone and a detective on my ass. We can't keep up this parole thing." Nate held out his cell. "Pete left a message. Garza requested info about you from every military organization around. It won't take long for him to put this together. Or Colonel Torridan. And when *Kells* finds out I'm working with you, I'm back in prison."

Rafe dragged his attention from his wife and planted it on Nate's scrunched-up face. Rafe was moments away from going primitive. "Cut the self-pity or I walk."

"What are you—"

"I don't give a shit about Torridan or what he wants. I don't care about you or Pete."

Nate blinked. "You agreed to help us."

"That was before I spoke to Balthasar."

Rafe's eyes must've shot fire because Nate sank into a pew and scrubbed his face with his palms. "I was under orders."

"I don't care."

"I wish…I'm sorry, alright? We got your letter, for fuck's sake. You'd gone AWOL. Betrayed us. Betrayed your country. What the hell were we supposed to do?"

Rafe gripped the pew and got in Nate's face. Rafe spoke slowly and carefully so Nate would realize how close he was to being annihilated. "Not emotionally torture a defenseless woman with enhanced interrogation."

Nate stood. "I didn't have a choice."

"You always have a choice, and the irony is that what you did eight years ago may have destroyed your chances of succeeding now."

"What do you mean?"

"You humiliated her and stripped her of power. A person doesn't just *get over* that kind of interrogation. Abuse like that forms scar tissue preventing them from trusting others. You and Torridan may have ruined the woman you need to save your men."

Nate ran his hands over his head. "I'm fucked."

"We're both fucked."

"Does that mean you're still helping us?"

"I'm helping myself. I have a week to do something for the Prince. In order to do that, I have to win back my wife's trust, which will be harder now that she knows I'm helping you."

"Where does that leave me and Pete?"

"Not sure. Don't care. The only reason you're not dead is because killing you would condemn your men to prison for something they didn't do. But when this is over, there *will* be a reckoning. In the meantime, stay away from Juliet."

"My operation is connected to your wife."

"Connected to her lily."

Nate sighed like a teenager. "I'd give anything to know what a stupid fucking flower has to do with a Special Forces operation on the other side of the stupid fucking world."

"Right. Divert blame to the fucking flower."

"What are you doing here?" Juliet's voice came from behind him.

Rafe turned slowly, taking half breaths along the way. Her face glowed without all the heavy makeup she'd worn earlier. But her eyes seemed heavier, the circles beneath darker. And the bruise on her cheek made him want to beat Deke again. "I heard about the break-in. I was worried."

She wrapped her arms around her waist and sent Nate a glare that could strip paint off a bumper.

Nate held up both hands. "I'll wait for you outside, bro."

Once Nate left, Rafe said, "Let me take you home. We can talk there."

Detective Garza appeared. "Why are you here, Mr. Montfort?"

To save my wife. "To protect Juliet."

Garza's eyes narrowed tighter than a gun spring. "Miss Capel is safe. I guarantee it."

"How can you when you've no idea what's right in front of you? This vandalism isn't random." Rafe pointed to the broken pottery. "Calum told me that over the past nine months, pots decorated with Juliet's lily were broken and her store windows were destroyed. Is that true?"

"Yes," she said.

"So?" Garza asked.

"One thing is being destroyed. Every image of Juliet's lily."

She covered her mouth with her hand.

Garza rubbed his chin with his fist and focused on Juliet. "The pots. The windows. They all had your logo?"

She nodded and sank into a pew.

Her shoulders shook, and Rafe wanted to sit down and wrap his arms around her. Instead, he said, "Tonight's different. Things have escalated. Not only was your logo destroyed, whoever did this sent you a message."

Garza's phone rang, and he answered. A moment later, he covered the speaker and said to Juliet, "I have to take this. Officer Holmes is waiting outside to take you home."

Since Rafe needed to see Nate first, he gently touched her shoulder. From his height, he could see the engravings in her silver hair combs. Eight-petaled lilies. "Can you go with Officer Holmes? I'll meet you back at your place soon."

"It's late—"

"I know. But we're running out of time."

After a moment, she nodded, and he led her outside. Across the street in a garden square, Nate stood with his arms crossed.

Rafe opened her car door.

As she got in, she said, "Nate is Colonel Torridan's lying puppet."

Rafe shut the door and double-tapped the roof, and the car sped away.

Then he made his way across the street. Nate had no idea how lucky he was to be alive.

Nate waited for Rafe with his arms crossed. He wasn't sure which worried him most: Rafe working for the Prince or the fact that Rafe knew about what Nate had done to Juliet.

Rafe's self-control would only last so long. A judgment was coming that would make Deke's beating look like a handshake. But the fact that Nate was still standing meant one thing: Rafe needed him.

Nate wasn't surprised Rafe had heard so quickly. The surprise had been that Nate hadn't figured out Rafe was still working for the Prince. Then again, considering the headspace Nate occupied right now, he wasn't up on his game. Hell, he wasn't even sure he knew what game they were playing.

He closed his eyes and clasped his hands behind his neck. Colors flew behind his eyelids, and his larger muscle groups felt like they'd been tased. He couldn't afford to faint, and he had another hour before he could take his next pill. His last pill. Because without Deke, no more Z-pam. *Shit.*

"As much as I want to kill you right now," Rafe said in a rough voice, "you've got to chill. You can't help your men if you lose it."

Nate opened his eyes. "You're still going to help us? Despite what I did?"

Rafe shoved his hands in his coat pockets. Probably where he kept his gun. "Yes."

"Why?"

"Because your men are innocent. When this ends—"

"I did the deed. I'll take the punishment."

Rafe nodded.

The tic above Nate's left eye kicked in. "This clusterfuck we're in? It's epic."

"It's always epic." Rafe glanced at the cathedral with its flickering lights through the stained-glass windows. "Does Torridan have any idea who set you up? Any idea who has money and motivation to take down two A-teams?"

"Besides the Prince?" Rafe shifted his attention back to Nate. "There's a list of arms dealers, drug kingpins, and tribal warlords. You probably know most of them personally."

Rafe frowned. "This attack on your team took cunning, a ton of money, and a load of logistics. But the fact that you weren't all killed sounds like it was personal."

"Again, the Prince comes to mind."

"The Prince doesn't act on emotions. Everything is logically thought out, every action considered. The Fianna is all about self-control and obeying orders."

Nate raised an eyebrow.

"I never said I was a great warrior, Nate. The Prince threw me in prison because I got tired of the bullshit and wanted out."

"I'm feeling sorry for the Prince and Colonel Torridan."

Rafe crossed his arms and stared at his boots. "The Fianna has this rule. Once you tithe, you belong to them forever. Three years into the gig, I walked away and went rogue. Except I got caught."

"That must've sucked."

Rafe shrugged. "Pete told me you don't remember much from the night you were ambushed or the POW camp. That you're not sure if you saw a man bow."

"Hell." Nate was going to murder Pete. "I don't know. Maybe. We were dug down in a trench, it was dusk, and when I did a perimeter check, I saw...something."

"Details count."

"A man in the distance, in a combo of tribal dress and desert fatigues, sword strapped to his back. He stood there, eerie as shit, backlit by the dropping sun. Then he bowed."

"Halfway? Or all the way to the ground?"

"To the ground."

Rafe's gaze narrowed. "You're marked for execution."

"Then why am I still here?"

"Because you were captured, and when you came home, you were convicted and sentenced. Fianna assassins only take care of things when traditional justice looks away."

Nate threw himself onto an iron bench in the shadows. "If I'd been freed after the rescue—"

Rafe sat next to him. "You'd be dead."

"And now that I'm out?"

"The Prince probably wants to know what you're looking for."

Nate squeezed the bridge of his nose. He had to remember to breathe. It helped keep the seizures at bay. "If I don't succeed, I go back to prison for a lifetime. If I do succeed and get our convictions overthrown, I'll spend the rest of my life running from a Fianna assassin."

"Yep."

"I'm screwed either way."

Rafe clapped Nate on the back. "Welcome to the Screwed Every Which Way Club."

Nate ran his hands over his head. "I have to try, Rafe. I'd rather be dead than responsible for my men spending their lives in prison. I'm working the mission."

"While I'm more selfish than you are, I get it."

"And your deal with the Prince?" Nate glanced at Rafe, who'd crossed his ankles and was staring at the candlelit cathedral. "What about that?"

"I have to find something from the seventeenth century. The only clue is Anne Capel."

"The same Anne Capel I'm looking for? The dead one?"

"Yes."

"And this Anne Capel is your wife's ancestor? Which is why you have to woo Juliet?"

Rafe nodded.

"Fan-fucking-tastic." No way was this going to end well.

Voices came from the cathedral and Garza ran down the steps, jumped into his car, and tires screeched on the pull-out.

"That can't be good," Nate said.

Rafe stood. "You okay dealing with Deke?"

"Pete and I can handle it." Nate got up too. As tired as he was, he still had work to do. "What about this nonexistent plan to save our asses? If it depends on you making nice with Juliet, we're doomed."

"After I talk to her, we'll figure it out. In the meantime, stay away from men who bow."

"You sound like Torridan."

"I hate to say this, but sometimes Torridan is right. Now get some sleep. You gotta keep those seizures under control."

Hooah.

Rafe walked away, and Nate unlocked his bike. Seizures were a bitch, but even more so when they meant you couldn't drive. His cell buzzed with a message from Pete, which left Nate wishing his heart would give up and stop beating. **Deke is gone.**

Nate dialed Pete. "What happened?"

"I was in the locker room with Samantha, and when I got back to the control room, Deke was gone. Except for the part of his ear he left behind. He must've pulled free."

"Any idea—"

"Fuck no. And I'm stuck here until closing."

"Deke's apartment is nearby. I'll check it out. I doubt he'd go to the cops or a hospital." Maybe Nate would find Deke's Z-pam.

"Deke had help. Someone knew the code and let him out."

"I'll be careful. And I'll be back as soon as I can."

Nate shoved his phone in his back pocket and hopped on his bike. His head started with the fuzzies that told him the drugs were wearing off. And now he was about to break and enter. Yeah. He was a hell of a hero.

A half hour later, Nate left Deke's apartment. Deke hadn't gone home, and there'd been no Z-pam.

On his way to his bike, Nate stopped. Someone was behind him. He'd left his weapons at the club, worried he'd be patted down in the church. He turned as a man drifted closer. Dark pants. Black hooded jacket covering his face and thighs. Steel-toed boots. The man stopped yards away.

The man hit his chest with his fist and bowed his head. "I am Balthasar."

Shit. Sweat dripped down Nate's neck.

Balthasar moved closer with the same weird Rafe-walk. "I'm here to make thee an offer. Join me, and all past sins will be forgiven. I can give you your heart's desire."

"You don't know shit about my heart."

"It weeps for your men, for what once was, for what you've become. If you join me, I'll give you the information to free your men."

"I thought I was marked for…you know, the other."

"If you join me, you'll be the one to mete out justice and punishment."

Nate scoffed. "What do you get out of this deal?"

Balthasar stopped inches away. "The vial."

Did Balthasar not understand the concept of personal space?

Nate took a step back. "No idea what you're talking about."

Balthasar advanced. "Your leader knows. As does our brother Romeo. Maybe you should ask them."

"If I had this information and joined you, what about my men?"

Balthasar clasped Nate's shoulder. "Their freedom depends on a fickle justice."

"No."

Balthasar's fist hit like a concrete block. Pain exploded in Nate's chest, forcing him to expel every last breath. He fell to the ground and rolled, blocking a punch with his arms. But he wasn't fast enough and the second hit slammed into his jaw, sending his head into cobblestones. Everything went starry, then black, and then the bright lights of a massive migraine sent him into a seizure. Balthasar kicked him in the ribs. Nate rolled into a ball, and the last thing he saw was a boot aiming for his face.

CHAPTER 17

JULIET GOT OUT OF THE POLICE CAR AND SHUT THE DOOR. SHE hurried down the dark alley leading to her apartment above her store. And the sky picked that exact moment to dump every raindrop God ever made. By the time she unlocked her door, she was soaked.

She turned on a light, passed the galley kitchen, the table holding her pot of gardenias, and headed for the bathroom. After taking a quick shower and changing into sweat pants, a cami, and a short robe, she went to the wardrobe in her bedroom. The eighteenth-century cupboard and dresser, two items she'd saved from her manor, barely fit with her double bed piled high with white pillows.

In the back of the cabinet, she found the digital lock box. After typing the code, she held the only present from Rafe she'd kept. Her Glock. She made sure it was loaded and laid it on her bedside table.

As much as she didn't want to deal with Rafe, she wished he'd get there soon. It was after one a.m., and she could barely keep her eyes open. To stay awake, she curled up in her bed with her sketchbook to work on her design ideas for Prideaux House. When her pencil skidded and her hand fell against her side, she slipped into longed-for sleep.

৶

Capel land, eighteen years earlier

"Run, Juliet!" the kids screamed at her. *"Run, little piggy!"*

Her feet slogged through the wet ground, marsh grass dragging her skirt. Her school bag bounced against her back, pulling her ponytail. *"Come on, Calum!"*

Calum tripped on a cyprus tree root. *"I can't!"*

She pulled him up.

"Run, Juliet Perdue!" the kids behind her chanted.

"Don't stop." She dragged Calum over a stream, her too-big shoes slipping in mud.

Her tormentors scrambled through the water. *"Juliet Porcelet. Who lives in a toilet."* They made snuffling pig sounds and laughed.

"Why are they so mean?" Tears streaked the dirt on Calum's face.

She headed toward her property line. They'd be safe there. *"Because they hate me."*

"Come here, piggy piggy. Juliet Porcelet. Who lives in a toilet."

Her heart burned in her chest, but she kept moving.

"Juliet Perdue! Who smells like a zoo!"

Jimmy Boudreaux grabbed her hair and then tripped. She tumbled down the ravine to another stream. Calum rolled next to her and helped her up. They crossed on river stones and used exposed roots to claw their way up the other side.

She was too afraid to look behind her. *"Get to the tree!"*

They climbed the oak tree that had guarded her family's property for hundreds of years. Mud caked the skirt of her plaid uniform, and runs laddered her tights. She'd lost her bow a mile back. She tucked her body into the branches, drew in painful breaths, and hung on. Calum clung to a lower branch. His blond bangs hung over his eyes. His uniform pants had a hole in the knee, and he'd lost his tie.

"Calum? Why did you follow me off the school bus? You were supposed to go to the Isle of Hope for the weekend."

"I don't like it there. I wanted to stay with you at the manor until your daddy comes home. I don't like that you're always alone."

"I can take care of myself."

Seven boys and two girls appeared on the other side of the water. One threw a rock, hitting the trunk.

"Jimmy Boudreaux throws like a girl!" Juliet yelled.

"What's wrong, Juliet Perdue?" Jimmy's face was as red as the rotten tomatoes he liked to chuck at her. "Are you lost, little piggy?"

"Go home," Angie Mercer shouted. "We don't want pig girls in our school."

Juliet took off a shoe and threw it at Angie. But Jimmy caught it and tossed it into the stream. It floated away. She had no other shoes. Which meant she wouldn't be able to go to school on Monday. She took off her other shoe and threw it. It slammed Jimmy in the forehead.

Calum laughed. "Get him, Juliet!"

"The Prioleaus can't protect you forever," Jimmy sneered. "My daddy says both your families can rot in hell."

Calum glanced up at her, his blue eyes now fiery instead of teary. "When we're bigger, we'll get them back. I promise."

Calum didn't understand. Even though she was only twelve, she understood that money could protect far better than size or strength.

A gunshot rang out, and her tormentors ran away. But not before Jimmy threw her second shoe in the water. By the time Jimmy disappeared, it'd washed away. Tears stung her eyes, and she bit her tongue. She wouldn't cry.

Calum climbed down first. When she dropped, her foot landed on a pinecone.

"Ouw!" She hopped around, the pain driving into her ankle. She still had a long walk, and it was getting dark.

Calum took her hand. "Can we go to the manor now?"

"We're going to St. Mary's. There's a phone in the rectory. We'll call your daddy."

"I'm not leaving you." Calum stared at her with an intensity that made him seem older. "But I don't know how to get to your manor by myself."

"There's a shortcut through the Cemetery of Lost Children. The scariest place on earth."

"I'm not afraid. My daddy says there are as many of my relatives as yours buried there. I'm sure they'll protect us."

She doubted it but took his hand anyway and led the way.

Thirty minutes later, barefoot, limping, and cold, she reached the cemetery's gates. Trees tightened around them. The pine straw offered a soft cushion for her sock-covered feet, but her ankle ached. She scanned the cemetery for anything that moved and adjusted her backpack. They headed toward the center where tall columns and crosses circled the one tomb she always avoided: St. Michael the Archangel.

Even though he'd lost his head, he towered over every other grave with a shield in one hand and a raised sword in the other. He was also naked with all of his parts showing.

Ewwwwww. "Don't look at the angel."

"I know what a boy looks like."

"You sound like Rafe."

"I wish he was here."

She did too. She held her breath; as they ran past Michael, she heard another shot. She stopped. Her heart banged so loudly she couldn't tell where the sound had come from.

"Could it be your daddy?" Calum asked.

"No. He's working the docks in Charleston."

Calum glanced behind them. "Maybe it's Rafe."

"Rafe isn't allowed to hunt alone." Although he did it whenever his father went to town. She quieted her breath so she could hear. An owl hooted in the distance, along with the rap-tap-tap of a woodpecker. A breeze chilled her, and the trees groaned.

She pushed her hair behind her ears, took Calum's hand, and

moved toward the darkest section of the cemetery. This area, behind pecan and mangrove trees that backed up to a river, scared her. It was unconsecrated land. If ghosts were real, this was where they'd live.

A twig snapped, and something pushed her to the ground. She tasted dirt and coughed until a person picked her up and tossed her over his shoulder. "Run, Calum!"

Calum screamed, and the man slapped him.

"Calum!" She hit the back of the bad man with her fist.

"Shut up, little girl," the bad man said in a harsh voice.

From her upside-down view, she saw his heavy boots, green jacket, and rifle. Calum's eyes went wide when he saw her being carried away.

Calum grabbed the bad man's leg. "Let her go!"

The bad man shifted her on his shoulder and reached down to take Calum's arm, dragging him along too. Calum fought until the bad man said, "Shut up, little boy. Or I'll pound you."

Calum hiccupped and dug his feet into the ground. But the bad man picked him up and carried him.

How could the man carry both of them at the same time?

"Juliet!" Calum sobbed. "My arm hurts."

She started to cry too, but when she realized where they were headed, she kicked and hit the man's back again. "Not here! Not here!"

The bad man dropped her, and his boot landed on her stomach. She tried to push it off, but he was too heavy. With Calum under one arm, he used a big key to open the iron door and tossed them in. She hit the hard floor as the door shut. The lock outside clanged into place.

"No!" She pounded the metal door until her fists hurt. "Don't leave us here!"

"Juliet!"

No one would ever find her.

"Wake up!"

Someone held her shoulders down, but she screamed again until her throat emptied of sound. "No!"

"Juliet." The firm voice pulled her forward. "Wake up."

She kicked, but there was a heavy weight on her.

"I'm here."

A breath coaxed her out from the darkness.

"Come. Back. To. Me." Now the voice held an edge.

She opened her eyes and gulped in deep breaths of cold air. A man sat next to her, warm hands on her shoulders. *Rafe?*

He covered her with a throw blanket, his hands sure yet gentle.

She sat up, trembling, keeping the blanket against her breasts. "*Sebastian was there.*"

Rafe took her shoulders, pulling her close until their foreheads touched. "Just breathe."

"We were in the cemetery."

He closed his eyes and tightened his grip.

Her hands pressed against his hard chest, for the first time feeing the hard muscles flexing beneath her fingers. It was like touching hot granite. "You're here?"

"I am." He opened his eyes. "Your door was unlocked. I've been sleeping on the floor."

That's when she noticed a blanket and a pillow on the floor next to her bed.

"Would you like some tea?" he asked softly.

How many times had he coaxed her out of her nightmares, settled her with tea, and then made love to her until she fell asleep? It'd been the only moments of her life when she'd felt safe and loved. "No."

"Do you want to talk about your dream?"

She scrambled out from beneath the blanket, stumbling over his lap, desperate for her feet to hit the wood floor.

"We know what happened. Someone threw me in Anne's crypt, and I stayed there until you found me."

"Have you had the dream a lot?"

"It's been nine months since the last one."

He swallowed. He'd taken off his leather jacket but still had on the black T-shirt that stretched across his chest, a bandage on his left arm, and jeans that rode his hips. He'd grown wider, stronger, so much more muscular. Surprising since she'd always thought he was in fabulous physical shape. But in the eight years he'd been gone, he'd turned from a young husband into a grown man. A grown man who made no move to hide the erection pressing against the denim or the blue ribbon he wore on his wrist. He'd always been confident about what he wanted, never shy about his needs.

She forced herself to look at his other arm. The moonlight exposed the words curved around the massive upper arm muscles, down his forearm, ending at his wrist. The light hair not only emphasized his strength; it couldn't hide what he'd done.

The names of every woman he'd slept with after leaving her.

He stood and flexed his hand, contracting the muscles along the length. The tattoos swept away any warmth she'd felt in his arms, and her shivering made it hard to swallow. Within the space of a breath, he pulled her close until their noses almost touched. One of her hands rested against his pounding heart. "What are you doing here?" she whispered.

"Waking you from a nightmare."

"Why are you *really* here?"

"Protecting you."

How was she supposed to bear this sadness all over again? "I don't understand."

"All I want is to save the life you've built."

She frowned. "You'll want something in return."

"There is one thing." When she arched her eyebrow, he shrugged. "To keep you safe, I need to find something. To do that, I need your help. There are bad people out there. Men who'll hurt you if I don't return with what I'm looking for."

"You know that sounds insane?"

"All of the vandalism, the loan being sold, the cathedral are related to one thing. *You.*"

"If I trust you, and we find this thing and fix my problems, you'll leave?"

"I'll do what's best for you."

So many emotions, so many thoughts driving garden stakes through her mind. But she wasn't stupid. Someone was tormenting her, and she had no idea how to stop it. Rafe might be the last person she'd ever turn to for help, but he might be the only one who could help her.

Her hands fisted against his chest. She'd always assumed this confrontation between them would be cold and bitter and ragged. She'd never expected to have this conversation in solemn, quiet darkness. "Rafe?" The word hurt coming out. Like knives carving each letter along the way.

"I'm here." He spoke with a soft drawl she used to love.

She rested her forehead against his shoulder. Now she knew the source of the heat. His body threw off enough warmth to reset the thermostat. *Why was she such a coward?* "That letter you sent me—"

"Things aren't what they seem. Just please trust that everything I've ever done has been for your safety." He paused. "We have one week to find what I'm looking for."

She raised her head to meet his gaze. Before he left, she'd been able to read his eyes. His secrets and dreams. His unspoken desires. Now there were shadows tinged with sadness and regret. The blazing fire she'd loved had turned to gray ash. And for some reason she didn't want to examine, it mattered. She blinked, determined to keep herself together and him separate. "Then we start tomorrow—I mean later today."

He held her head with one hand while his other arm wrapped around her waist. Her breasts flattened against hard chest muscles. His breath tickled her nose, warm and forceful. How could she consider being this close to him? Working with him? He brushed a kiss against her cheek. The sensation hit her system like the bottle rockets he used to shoot for her to see from her balcony, and she closed her eyes. His lips traced hers, and the tingle curled her toes.

How, after all these years, could she still be so susceptible to him? Because he'd once been her husband. The one man she'd loved beyond reason. Forever and always. She tilted her head, and the brush became a demand. The demand became an ache. And the ache became a need so great she threw her arms around his neck. Her world tilted, his arms tightened, and his lips explored hers as if he'd never kissed anyone else ever. The air around them vibrated, matching the motion of the kiss.

He broke away, leaving her a disoriented mess.

"Juliet." The word rolled like a wave break. Forward, then retreating. His body heaved, and he ran his hands over his prison-shorn hair. "I'm sorry."

Those words stung more than his rejection. He was sorry. Hadn't he said so in his letter eight years ago? "You should leave." She glanced at her clock. "It's almost three a.m. We both need to sleep."

And she needed to be alone. Because when he touched her, she melted. When he whispered, she caved. And when he kissed her, she begged for more. It'd always been like that. All he had to do was walk into a room, and she wanted him. When he looked at her, like she was the only woman he'd ever need, she dreamed of lying beneath him, his heavy body possessing hers. Her reaction to him was sad, pathetic, and wrong. She wasn't sure who she hated more: him or herself for her reaction to him.

Without warning, he swung her up and laid her on the bed. "I'm asking you to help me fix what I've ruined. Then your life can go on as it was."

Her eyes drifted closed. The nightmare's adrenaline rush left as swiftly as it came in, leaving her depleted. She heard the words, but his face blinked in and out of time and space. The bed sagged, and she scooted over so he could adjust his body. Then, just before sleep hit, she reached to feel his warmth.

No, she wasn't happy he'd been released from prison. She wasn't happy he'd come home. She wasn't happy he'd kissed her and she'd kissed him back. But she didn't want to be alone. And that was going to be a problem.

Rafe's heart ached for both of them. He'd arrived at her apartment to find her asleep and had grabbed a blanket to sleep on the floor—until her nightmare. Now she was curled up beneath the light quilt, trembling from the after-effects of the dream. He had no doubt the dreams were back because of him. They always appeared when she was stressed. Which proved, in spite of her cold-shouldering, that she was as affected by him as he was by her.

Still, despite their kiss having the power to blot out stars, he'd stopped it. Not because he wanted to. Not because he had that much self-control. He'd stopped it because he'd neither the right nor privilege to touch her. Instead, he placed his gun on the bedside, near her Glock, and lay next to her. When her hand found his chest, he covered her fingers, holding them against his heart.

His body burned for her. Sweat coated his forehead, and his arousal fought against the zipper. He needed her, wanted her, dreamed of driving into her with an intensity that almost made him reach for himself. Instead, he embraced the painful rubbing with the fervor of a penitent. Although he despaired of finding sleep, his mind closed the shutters. Days without proper rest, dozing on benches and bus seats, forced his body to shut down. Rolling to his side, he listened for her heartbeat, counting his, then hers, until they matched.

Nate opened his eyes, testing every muscle group, tasting blood. Despite his body screaming *Don't move,* he had no broken bones or fractured ribs. It took a minute to pull himself up and find his knife. Wobbly and achy, he checked his phone. Three a.m. Awesome.

Pete answered on the first ring. "Where are you?"

"Balthasar attacked me." *And for some reason left me alive.*

"Did he mention Deke?"

Nate hadn't expected sympathy, but an *Are you okay?* would've been nice. "No."

"What are we going to do?"

Nate didn't know. From his jittery hands and the flashing stars, he had to down as many ibuprofens as his stomach could handle ASAP. "Meet me at the motel."

"I'm here. I shut the club half an hour ago. You want me to come get you? Can you bike?"

"I'm fine." He took two steps and grunted.

"Samantha and I are coming. She's, uh, here with me."

"Stay put. I'll be there soon." He shoved the phone in

his pocket and felt something. A baggie with three pills. One day's worth of Z-pam. Balthasar obviously expected something in return.

Nate walked his bike toward the river. Where was Deke? How did Balthasar know about the Z-pam? And why had Balthasar been talking about a vial? That's when Nate remembered Balthasar mentioning two people who knew about the vial. Torridan, who'd obviously withheld intel. And a man named Romeo. A man Nate could only assume was Rafe.

CHAPTER 18

At seven a.m., Juliet stood in her workroom, staring at her floral refrigerators. She'd slept with Rafe. Not in the marital sense. They'd fallen asleep in her bed, when she'd been in that void between dreams and reality. But she remembered her hand on his chest. The warmth had burned through his T-shirt, to her heart, down to her toes.

They might be divorced, yet he still claimed her heart. And while she wasn't happy about that, she wasn't angry either. Maybe she was just tired.

Bob came in through the back door with a smile and a "Good morning, Miss Juliet," followed by Philip carrying a tray with two coffees and a bakery bag.

"Good morning." She opened her notebook on the worktable. "Bob, I spoke with Pearson's Nursery. They have enough lilies and can ship them this morning. Can you send someone to the cathedral to accept delivery?"

"I'll do it, Miss Juliet. I just left the planting crew at Liberty Square. As long as the city water workers get the fountain working and the electric system passes inspection, the square will be done by Sunday."

Thank God something was going right. Then she remembered that the workers had to be paid.

Philip handed her a coffee. "I heard about the church. Any idea who was responsible?"

Although he smiled, his voice sounded accusatory, like he was hurt she hadn't called.

She took a sip before answering. "No. I haven't spoken to Detective Garza yet."

Bob went through the new work orders, muttering, "I don't get what the world's coming to, Miss Juliet."

"I don't either, Bob."

"I'm glad no one was hurt." Philip squinted at her. "Is that a bruise on your face?"

"I didn't sleep well." She took money from her purse—her tips from last night. "Bob, here's three hundred dollars for the lilies. Please get a receipt."

"Will do, Miss Juliet." Bob pocketed the money and the work order.

She followed Bob to the lot behind her store where he'd parked the truck. "I have to take some personal time later. Samantha will be here, and I'll have my cell. If you need—"

Bob held up his hand, and a grin broke up his sun-darkened face. "All will be well, Miss Juliet."

She hoped so.

Inside the front room, she found Philip on his cell. She put down her coffee to eat her donut without dropping sugar on her dress.

Philip winked at her. "Thank you, Mr. Delacroix."

"What was that about?" she asked once he'd hung up.

"I'm working on a new architectural proposal worth a lot of money. Maybe enough so I can become a partner in the firm."

"That's wonderful." She popped the last bit of donut into her mouth. "What's the project?"

"Mr. Delacroix wants to restore Prideaux House. Once he buys it from the Habersham sisters. It looks like we'll be working together when you get the garden job."

"Great." She headed around her counter to find a tissue for her sticky hands. She was happy for him, but she didn't want the time they spent together to encourage his attentions. They were good friends, but *just* friends.

"Juliet? Have you told Calum about Carina not paying you?"

"No. Calum hates it when I bring up my problems with Carina." She wiped her hands and found her coffee again. "I need solutions."

"We'll do it together, if you let me." Philip took a gardenia out of the vase on the counter and tucked it behind her ear. She reached for it until he took her hand. "You love gardenias."

"That's why she wore them on her wedding day."

Rafe. Heat flashed up her arms to her face. She yanked her hand free and took out the flower, loosening strands along the way.

Rafe's gaze found hers, claiming something he didn't deserve, and she was grateful for the counter between them.

Philip crossed his arms.

Rafe picked up the flower she'd tossed on the counter. "You wore gardenias in your hair with your bridal veil."

"I remember." It'd been a simple event. Short dress for her. Dress blue uniform for him. Besides the priest, the only witnesses had been Pops; Rafe's mother, Tess; Philip; and Calum. The flowers had been a last-minute addition from Tess while they'd waited outside the church for Juliet's daddy to show up. Which never happened.

Rafe smiled. "Every time I smell gardenias, I think of our wedding night."

Philip snorted.

She forced herself to look at Rafe's tattoos. Except he'd traded his leather coat for a black field jacket over his black T-shirt. Instead of jeans, he wore black combat pants and boots. The blue ribbon around his wrist was visible when he moved his arms. Then she made the mistake of looking at his hands. Those hands that held her head at the perfect angle for his kisses.

Every breath stuttered. *Why do I feel this way?*

"What are you doing here?" Philip sounded like he was choking on his donut.

Rafe held out his hand. "Nice to see you too, Brother."

Philip took his hand but dropped it quickly.

Rafe shifted his attention to her. "Didn't Juliet tell you? We're working together."

"On what?" Philip spat out the question.

"For a way to sell her land," Rafe said before she could answer. "My name is on her deeds."

Calum entered in a gray linen suit, white starched shirt, and pink silk tie. "I didn't know we were having breakfast." He took a donut out of the bag on the counter and bit into it. Then he blew Juliet a kiss and licked sugar off his fingers.

She wanted to slap him but handed him a tissue instead. "What are you doing here?"

Calum smiled. "Reintroducing brothers to each other. And eating donuts."

Philip stared at Rafe. "Shouldn't you be standing trial for treason somewhere?"

Rafe smiled. Yet, despite the upward turn of his mouth, his lips were shut tight.

"Rafe is here at my request," Calum said. "He's also living in my apartment above Dessie's dress shop. Which, by the way, is closed for another week."

Juliet nodded. Lara, the owner, had called Juliet a few days ago to let her know. "Lara is staying in Paris for some more fashion shows."

"Rafe is living across the courtyard from Juliet?" Philip said. "Why?"

"Rafe needed a place. And you should know, Juliet, that I asked Rafe to convince you not to sell your land."

"We need to talk." She took Calum's arm and dragged him into the back room. Once near her floral refrigerators, she turned on him. "What games are you playing?"

He finished his donut and grinned. "No games. I think selling your land is a monumentally bad idea."

"You have no idea of the pressure I'm under—"

"Actually, I do." He found a towel near the flower sink and wiped his hands. "I know about your loan. I know Carina is a bitch. And I know what you were doing last night."

"Are you going to tell anyone?"

"Not if we strike a deal."

"What kind of deal?"

Calum took out his phone to start texting. "You work with Rafe to help him in his endeavor, and I won't say a word to anyone about your other job. Either last night or the past seven years."

"Six and a half years."

He glanced at her with a hooded gaze. "Six years, seven months, and three days."

She pressed the heels of her hands against her eyes. She couldn't have a headache yet. It wasn't even eight a.m. "If I asked you for money, would you lend it to me?"

"Nope."

She dropped her arms. "Would you ask Carina to pay her bill?"

"Wouldn't help." He stopped texting and held up his phone. "I've arranged dinner for you two to talk. Tonight. 700 Drayton. Eight o'clock. Bring your renditions and your best argument. Remember, Carina can smell insecurity and fear."

Juliet leaned against the table and sighed.

Calum squeezed her shoulder. "Don't worry. You have everything you need to succeed. If you help Rafe, he'll sign your deeds. Although I'll contest the sale any way I know how."

"I hate you," she said as her cell phone rang in her pocket.

Calum kissed her forehead. "You should get that. It's probably Detective Garza."

She pressed her ringing phone against her stomach and asked one more question. "Did you get Rafe out of prison?"

Calum shrugged and started texting again. Then he left the room, whistling the theme to *Star Wars*.

Once alone, she answered, "Juliet's Lily."

"Miss Capel. It's Detective Garza."

She sighed. "Good morning, Detective. Do you have any news?"

"Not yet. I've been researching Rafe's release. And I'd like to meet. In private. How about I swing by the store later. Around four?"

"Okay. Should I be worried?"

"Yes, Miss Capel. Very."

~

Rafe had had enough of his brother's glares. Considering Philip was, after all these years, still pining after Juliet, this second meeting of theirs could've been worse. There could've been blood. But right now Rafe's goal was to work with Juliet to find that vial. When Calum had shown up at the apartment where Rafe should've slept, half an hour after he'd left Juliet, he'd been glad. It meant it was time to get to work.

Ignoring Philip, Rafe checked out the security situation. Anything to keep his mind focused on things other than lying in bed next to his wife. High-end cameras. Double-bolt locks. Steel door leading to the back alley. Not great. But suitable.

He pulled in more scented air, her presence evident in every detail. The silver filigree floral bowls. The dainty halogen ceiling lights. The drawings of single blooms, outlined in gold, hanging on the wall. Tingles ran up his back, as if someone watched him.

When Calum came back into the room, typing on his phone, Rafe asked, "Why is Gabriel here?"

Calum talked and texted at the same time. "After Gerald's death, I hired men to bring back the only things of value left in the manor. Including Gabriel." When Calum put his phone away, he added, "I set up dinner tonight for Juliet and Carina to work out their financial differences. I expect both of you to be there."

After hearing the details, Philip smiled at Rafe through tight lips. "Do you have anything appropriate to wear?"

Calum answered first. "Rafe, the tailor will leave the clothes we ordered in the apartment. He has a key if you're not home."

Rafe nodded because there was nothing else to say. When Calum played chess, he moved all the pieces.

Philip's phone dinged. "I have to get to work."

Calum smiled. "I'll tell Juliet you said goodbye."

With a parting glare, Philip stormed out.

"Did you send Philip away?" Rafe asked.

Calum reached for the last donut. "I didn't think you'd mind."

Juliet appeared and snagged the donut out of Calum's hand. "Where's Philip?"

"Went to work." Calum took the donut back, broke it, and handed her half. "But cheer up, he thinks he's doing it all for you."

She punched him in the shoulder. "Don't be mean."

"I'm not the one who's leading him on."

"I'm not leading him on. I'm being gentle."

Calum smirked around a mouthful of donut. "How's that working?"

A blush rose from her neckline to her cheeks. In a blue strapless dress that skimmed her hips and hit her knees, and a white lace sweater barely covering her shoulders, she was a vision of everything beautiful in the world. Everything Rafe's world wasn't. Her hair, twisted up, showcased her graceful neck and shoulders. Even the long curls that had escaped only softened her businesslike demeanor. When he'd walked in and seen the flower in her hair, memories had hit like a bullet:

Juliet walking down the aisle to meet him.

Their first kiss as man and wife.

The way her body fit against his during their first wedding dance.

Juliet arching beneath him on their wedding night.

His jaw cranked, and his heart raced a beat he'd never felt before.

"Why are you still here, Calum?" She wiped donut sugar off her lips with a tissue. "Since you disapprove of my choices, maybe you should interfere in someone else's life."

Rafe chuckled.

As did Calum. "I wanted to make sure we're all getting along."

"I get along with everybody," Rafe said.

She coughed and took a sip of her coffee. "What are we looking for?"

Calum finished his pastry. "A seventeenth-century vial owned by Anne Capel."

She scrunched her nose. "Why would you think this vial is still around? Or that I'd be able to help you?"

"We believe"—Calum nodded at Rafe—"your lily is tied to the vial."

"How?" she asked Rafe.

Rafe shoved his hands in his jacket pockets. "I don't know."

"How does Nate fit into this?"

Rafe glanced at Calum. Then he decided he didn't give a shit what Calum thought. "If I tell you, you have to promise you won't tell anyone. It's the kind of classified that keeps A-teams from getting killed."

She nodded. "I promise."

He believed her. She'd been a wife in the unit and understood the risks. He told her about Nate's operation in Afghanistan and the massacre, POW camps, rescue, and imprisonment.

She paled and sat at a table beneath the picture window, cradling her coffee. "I knew something bad had happened…"

He sat across from her. "How?"

"Abigail, Liam Casey's wife. After I left Fort Bragg, Abigail and I kept in touch. A few years later, she called me from Rhode Island. She'd left Fort Bragg alone. Now she's a well-known botanical artist. Her original paintings hang in an exclusive art gallery in Newport, and I sell her prints on commission here in the shop."

"Liam is in prison with Colonel Keeley and two A-teams from my former unit."

"Are you sure you can trust Nate's story?" She tapped her fingers on the table until Rafe covered her hand with his. "If Nate was imprisoned, why is his hair long?"

An excellent question.

Calum sat in the third chair. "Nate and his men were sentenced immediately upon their return to the states. While his men went to prison, Nate was suffering seizures and taken to a medical facility in Maine. Maybe the hospital didn't bother cutting his hair."

"And Pete?" Rafe asked Calum.

"Pete and his A-team were in the Command Center with Kells Torridan outside the combat theater."

"Pete is still in the army?" she asked.

"Technically, yes. But Pete and Torridan's remaining men are facing trials of their own. They're accused of helping coordinate the massacre."

Calum added, "Because they're a flight risk, they've been suspended from duty without pay and have had their accounts frozen until the trials."

"Why is Nate here?" Juliet asked Rafe.

"Colonel Torridan found a clue about who set up the units in Afghanistan. He sent Nate and Pete to check it out."

"What kind of clue?"

"Five years ago, on the night of the ambush, four wives in the unit—including Abigail—received a flower. A rare white lily with eight petals."

Juliet sucked in her breath. "That lily hasn't grown on Capel land in decades."

"How would you know?" Calum said. "You own thousands of acres you never visit."

"Because my daddy hunted my lily with the same ferocity he hunted boars."

"Still," Rafe said, "it's possible the women were sent one of your lilies. It's also possible your lily grows elsewhere."

She shook her head. "I've never seen it in any textbook or grower's list. In grad school, I never mentioned it. Daddy was paranoid and delusional, and I was afraid of what he'd do to a grad student searching for a new species. I have no idea what my lily has to do with this vial or a Special Forces operation in Afghanistan."

"I don't either," Calum said. "But I know where to start. The Habersham sisters. They've been studying your lily for years." Calum kissed Juliet on the cheek and stood. "Don't forget dinner tonight. If you want your money, come armed with confidence."

A moment later, he was gone.

The silence between Rafe and Juliet stretched out. The space between them vibrated. His hand still held hers, but she seemed lost in thought. Although she'd covered the bruises on her face with makeup, it didn't hide the bluish stain. He wanted to ask her about the club and about what happened with Nate, but Rafe had no right to push.

He needed her to trust him enough to share her traumas without his prompting. If he forced her to talk before she was ready, she'd retreat and he might never be able to reach her.

The only problem with that plan was it meant lying to her. If she found out he knew about what happened with Nate and hadn't said anything, she might feel betrayed and powerless. Two things that would send her running out of his arms instead of into them. A calculated risk. The kind he was good at but also the kind he hated.

He squeezed her hand until she looked up. "Do you want to see the sisters?"

"It's early. We can't just drop in."

"You should go now." Samantha came in from the back wearing a long white skirt and black cami, her hair in a tangled braid. She scowled at Rafe. "I'll handle the store. The sooner you do whatever it is you're doing, the sooner *he* leaves. Right?"

Juliet glanced at him before standing. "I'll get my bag."

Once she left the room, Samantha turned on him. "You're a colossal asshole."

"What's wrong now?"

"Deke disappeared last night."

Rafe stood. "Excuse me?"

"Nate got beat up by some buddy of yours. And Detective Garza has some super-secret contact digging up info about you and Nate. Then Pete and I spent the night nursing Nate through the worst seizure ever." She rearranged flowers in a container on the counter, shoving yellow roses around. "Nate needs a hospital. I think his head might explode."

Rafe unlocked the phone Calum had given him earlier. "I'll wait for Juliet outside."

Samantha waved a hand in dismissal. "Pete and Nate are good guys, and they're trusting you are too. So even if you're not, pretend you are."

"Yes, ma'am." Rafe headed into the courtyard across from Dessie's dress shop. Garden statuary, including angels, almost-naked Roman women, and cherubs with flutes, lined the perimeter of the bricked-in area. Once in the shade, with the fountain as white noise, he took off his jacket. Despite the sweltering heat, keeping his arms covered while with Juliet was a priority.

Scrolling through his phone contacts, he silently thanked Calum for preprogramming numbers. Not sure which ones he'd use the least—Philip's or the tailor's—Rafe dialed Nate, who picked up on the second ring. "What happened last night?"

"Nate's asleep," Pete said. "Balthasar jumped Nate. Deke got away. Then Nate spazzed on a grand mal seizure."

"You're sure it was Balthasar?"

"He fucking bowed, bro. Then offered Nate a spot on Team Prince."

"Fuck."

"Yep. Then Balthasar asked about a vial. You wouldn't know about that, would you?"

Rafe sat on the edge of the raised fountain. While the cool mist coated the back of his neck and arms, he decided their only chance of survival was to go with the truth. "I'm looking for a seventeenth-century vial owned by Anne Capel."

"The Anne Capel Torridan wants us to find?"

"Yes. Did Balthasar say anything else about the vial?"

"Balthasar mentioned someone named Romeo, who I'm guessing is you, wants it. Balthasar also admitted that Colonel Torridan knows about the vial."

Whoa. "Wait. Torridan knows?"

"Apparently," Pete said. "But I'm not going to ask Torridan about it because we'll have to admit we're working with you. And that's not going to go over well."

True. "And Deke? How'd he escape a locked room when he was nailed to the floor?"

"Not sure. The security cameras don't record."

Why was Rafe not surprised? He rubbed his chin, feeling a light stubble. Juliet had always liked his stubble. "Deke has disappeared?"

"Yep." Pete sighed. "Calum called this morning and suggested Nate go to the Savannah Preservation Office to see if they have anything about Juliet's lily or Anne Capel."

"Good idea. Juliet and I are checking out a lead, and I'll be in touch."

"I'll be at the club earning cash to keep us fed and housed." Pete paused.

"What's wrong?"

"According to Luke, our unit's computer wizard, Garza's been poking around our shared history. The detective has access to serious black ops intel."

"One problem at a time, Pete. And don't forget—stay away from men who bow."

CHAPTER 19

THIRTY MINUTES LATER, JULIET AND RAFE FOLLOWED THE butler into the Habersham Mansion drawing room, which was furnished with Italian Renaissance antiques. The Habersham sisters, Miss Beatrice and Miss Nell, stood near French doors leading to the garden. Their heads were tilted, their whispers harsh. Once the butler left, the women greeted them.

"Welcome." Miss Nell waved to the love seat.

Miss Beatrice rang for the maid, who appeared quickly. "Four coffees, please."

The maid left, and Juliet and Rafe sat on the love seat. With his arm behind her, his heat scorched her right side and his scent tickled her nose. How was she supposed to concentrate?

"Thank you for seeing us," she said. "It's early."

Miss Beatrice shrugged. "Nonsense."

The two sisters—a widow and a spinster—sat on Louis XIV chairs opposite the love seat. They wore Dior silk suits, one in lavender, the other in rose. Each in matching Louboutin heels. Between them, the sisters' wealth almost rivaled Calum's.

"So," Miss Beatrice began, "you want to know the history of the Isle."

Miss Beatrice—the sister who'd snagged Calum's wealthy uncle and his estate known as Prideaux House—had always been the tough-talking businesswoman. Nell, more romantic, was the owner of Habersham Mansion. Since Miss Beatrice's widowhood twenty years earlier, the two sisters had lived at the mansion while Prideaux House had fallen into ruin.

The maid returned with four coffees and a plate of muffins. Once they were settled, Juliet said, "Rafe and I need information. Someone is targeting images of my lily."

Rafe added, "Juliet's store and her projects have been vandalized."

"Goodness," Miss Nell said. "Will ours be next?"

Rafe glanced at Juliet.

"The Habersham sisters were my first clients."

"You must see Juliet's garden," Miss Nell said. "We bought the houses around us and tore them down. It's now one of the largest gardens in the city."

"Except for Calum's garden," Miss Beatrice said.

Rafe nodded. "I'm looking forward to it."

Juliet finished her muffin and took a sip of coffee. It was so hard keeping the sisters focused. "You're not the target. My lily is. And Calum mentioned you were studying it."

"Not your lily," Miss Beatrice said. "We're studying the history of Anne Capel."

The murderess? "Why?"

Miss Beatrice drank her coffee and then dabbed her lips with a linen napkin. "Anne Capel was accused of killing forty-four children, and we're proving her innocence."

Rafe scoffed. "Anne was guilty, and the people of the Isle hanged her for witchcraft."

"Not exactly," Miss Beatrice said. "A mob led by Josiah Montfort attempted to hang Anne. Josiah was Anne's spurned suitor. His brother, Isaiah, was Anne's lover."

"The rope broke," Miss Nell added. "Anne survived the hanging, and everyone learned she was pregnant with Isaiah's baby."

Juliet placed her cup on the table between the love seat

and the sisters. "What does this seventeenth-century soap opera have to do with my lily?"

"Because," Miss Nell said, "Sarah Munro believes Anne *accidentally* killed those children *with* the lily."

"Sarah Munro?" Juliet asked, although the name sounded familiar.

"Sarah is a historian and an archivist with the Smithsonian," Miss Beatrice said.

"Is Sarah the woman who emailed me about visiting the Cemetery of Lost Children?" The request Juliet had declined.

"Yes," Miss Beatrice said. "Sarah is in town temporarily, working at the Savannah Preservation Office on another project for us, and offered to help sort through the documents."

Rafe glanced at Juliet. "What documents?"

She shrugged. She was as lost as he was.

Miss Beatrice turned to her sister. "Remember Rafe and Juliet's wedding day, Nell?"

Miss Nell waved her napkin as a fan. "Lovely."

"You weren't at our wedding," Juliet said.

"We saw the photos," Miss Beatrice said.

Rafe took Juliet's hand, and she let him. "What photos?"

"The ones Tess took," Miss Beatrice continued. "I think they're in Gerald's trunk."

"No," Miss Nell said. "We put them in the safe. To protect them."

Juliet took two deep breaths. "What trunk?"

"The trunk Gerald left you."

Juliet stood, with Rafe coming up behind her. "Excuse me?"

"Beatrice!" Miss Nell demanded. "Didn't you tell Juliet about the trunk?"

"That was your job, dear."

Juliet chewed her bottom lip until Rafe pulled her down to

the couch and put his arm around her shoulder. He was right. She had to hold her temper if she wanted more information.

"Why does Sarah think Anne killed those kids with Juliet's lily?" Rafe asked.

"*Accidentally* killed." Miss Beatrice sighed as if exasperated they couldn't keep up. "Sarah read about the poisoning in a book Gerald kept in the trunk."

"*Poison?*" Juliet shook her head. "My lily is poisonous?"

"*Of course.*" Miss Beatrice's politely worded *duh* made Juliet want to scream.

"I don't understand," Rafe said. "How could we not know this poison story?"

Miss Nell smiled over her cup. "Maybe you weren't paying attention."

Juliet wanted to laugh but was afraid she'd cry.

"Do you have the documents Sarah was working with?" Rafe asked.

"They might be in the trunk," Miss Beatrice said. "Unless Sarah still has them."

"My trunk," Juliet said. "Which my daddy left me. But no one told me about."

"Your lawyer, John Sinclair, was very specific," Miss Beatrice said. "We were told not to release the trunk until Rafe came home."

Juliet stood again. "You *knew* Rafe was coming home?"

Miss Beatrice stood as well. "John Sinclair told us Rafe would return, just not when."

"How did John know?"

"Gerald told him. Right after Gerald added Rafe's name to your deeds."

"Would you like to see your trunk?" Miss Nell rang the bell for the maid. "Now that Rafe is here, we can release it."

Juliet leaned against Rafe, and he tucked her beneath his

shoulder. She wasn't sure how much longer she could deal with the sisters. "I don't understand."

"I don't either," he said, his breath stirring her hair.

Miss Nell came over and touched Juliet's cheek. "Your daddy didn't want you opening the trunk alone. He wanted you to open it with your husband."

"*Ex*-husband. And how did you know my daddy put Rafe's name on my deeds?"

Miss Beatrice took a chain from around her neck and handed it to Juliet. It held a brass key. "We're the ones who recommended it."

Rafe tightened his hold. She wasn't sure what she would've done, but smashing the Limoges teacups seemed like a place to start. "I don't understand how my daddy knew Rafe would come home."

"Because he had faith," Miss Nell said. "Something you need a bit more of."

Rafe squeezed Juliet's shoulder as if knowing she was about to start throwing things. "Did you ever hear about a vial Anne supposedly owned?"

The sisters shared a look before Miss Beatrice said, "Call Sarah. I'll text you her number."

Juliet and Rafe shared an exasperated sigh.

When the maid appeared, Miss Nell said, "Escort Rafe and his bride to the guesthouse. Then bring in Mr. Delacroix when he arrives."

Miss Beatrice touched Juliet's arm. "You do know Mr. Delacroix is buying Prideaux House? Maybe you'd like to talk to him about the garden?"

"I'm already working on a bid for the redesign."

"Good. We'll add our recommendation."

Rafe's voice exploded. "What's up with the women of this city selling their property?"

"There's no need to raise your voice, Rafe Montfort," Miss Nell said as the maid led them away. "Juliet, show your husband our garden. It's so romantic."

Rafe had put up with many things while working for the Prince—lies, beatings, torture—suffering for the good of the brotherhood. But he resented being manipulated.

"Can you believe my lily is poisonous?" Juliet whispered as they left. "Or that the sisters never told me about my daddy's trunk?"

Rafe's hand rested on her lower back. "I don't know *what* to believe. And I think we need to be careful with *who* we trust. No matter how sweet *they* seem to be."

For all their gentility, the sisters hadn't become wealthy just through inheritance and marrying well. They were sharks. Prideaux House and the Habersham Mansion were the second- and third-largest homes in the historic district, after Calum's.

"I agree." Juliet glanced at him. "If the story of Anne's poison is true, do you think that's what's in the vial you're looking for?"

Sweat beaded his neck. "Anything's possible."

"Can you tell me why you have to find this vial? Or who wants it?"

"I don't know why. And I can't tell you who."

She sighed. "I just have to trust you?"

He studied her lowered head as they left the patio and entered a brick-walled garden that filled a city block. "Yes."

She nodded, and he ached to know her thoughts. He was asking a lot, and she had no reason to trust him. The fact that she was, even reluctantly, spoke to her strength and courage.

He followed her to a Pan fountain in the center of the garden with boxwood-lined paths running in spokes. Flowers and blooming trees stood in perfect symmetry. Scents of gardenia mingled with roses filled his lungs. He took her hand, and she didn't pull away.

Inside the guesthouse, they found the trunk beneath a window. She knelt and inserted the key. Musty air escaped, and they laid the contents on the floor. They organized stacks of oversized folders and a white dress wrapped in linen and, on the bottom, found a duffel bag loaded with enough guns and ammo to arm the Georgia militia.

Rafe lifted the heavy duffel and moved it out of the way. Although Juliet didn't seem interested in the arsenal Gerald had left her, they'd probably need it.

She sat on the floor, and he moved until their shoulders touched. The folders held architectural plans for Capel Manor. As Juliet studied the designs, he noticed an envelope marked with the name *Juliet*.

She opened it. "It's a copy of a detailed map of the Cemetery of Lost Children and the surrounding land."

Delicate leaves interspersed with swords, fish, and Juliet's lilies had been drawn within the margins, reminding him of a medieval text. He pointed to the photocopied image of a ragged edge and a cut-off compass rose. "The original must've been old. Maybe seventeenth-century. And it was torn."

"What are those numbers and letters written along the top?"

The ink was faint, but he could make out a partial alphanumeric sequence that had been cut off with the compass rose. "I have no idea."

She stood and smoothed out her skirt. "If there were documents about my lily and anything pertaining to Anne Capel, they're gone."

Rafe refolded the map, placed it in the envelope, and put it in his jacket pocket. "Maybe Sarah has them."

Juliet rubbed her fist along her forehead. "There's no information here. And there's still so much we don't know. Like why my daddy put your name on my deeds."

Rafe stood and took her hands. They were freezing. "Or how Gerald knew I was coming home."

"It was Gerald's idea to extradite Rafe, and Senator Eugene Wilkins agreed to do the work," Miss Nell said from the doorway.

Juliet drew away from him as Miss Nell entered, holding an accordion file. "Why would my daddy want Rafe free?"

Miss Nell cupped Juliet's face with one hand. "My dear, you've had so much sadness in your life. Your momma dying when you were a baby. Your daddy being a man who knew he couldn't be a good father. He was looking out for you."

"By finding my ex-husband? By killing himself?"

"Gerald knew Rafe would protect you with his life." Miss Nell looked at Rafe. "Isn't that so?"

"Yes, ma'am." Although Rafe and Gerald had had a difficult relationship, they'd always had concern for Juliet's safety in common. "That's what you and Miss Beatrice were talking about when we arrived. You were arguing about whether to tell Juliet the truth."

"The truth about what?" Juliet demanded.

Rafe touched her shoulder. "Gerald was murdered."

Miss Nell pressed a birdlike hand against her chest. "We believe so, yes."

Juliet sank onto the edge of the bed. "What?"

Miss Nell handed Rafe the file and sat next to her. "The last year of Gerald's life, something frightened him terribly. He was terrified on your behalf and begged Eugene to bring Rafe home. Then Gerald asked us to help sort out the history of the Isle and the story about Anne Capel. After Eugene's and Detective Legare's deaths, we recommended that Gerald put Rafe's names on the deeds to Capel land. Whatever was happening, it was happening on that land. And we thought adding Rafe's name would give you another layer of protection."

Juliet frowned, and Rafe took her hand.

"Gerald's actions," Rafe said, "no matter how old-fashioned, don't account for his suicide."

Miss Nell nodded. "Beatrice and I believe the same person killed Eugene, Detective Legare, and Gerald. We just don't know why. Or what Gerald was so frightened of that he'd seek Rafe's extradition and our help to study the history of Anne Capel."

Rafe swallowed before opening the accordion file on the bed.

"What are they?" Juliet asked Miss Nell.

"Tess's photographs. Since Pops and Gerald never got along, she gave them to us for safekeeping, not long before her death. Beatrice and I thought it was time to give them to you."

Rafe laid out his momma's photos, all of them exquisite, and chose one of Juliet in a white sundress sitting at the end of a dock in the back meadow. Through the hazy glaze of floating dandelion seeds and humidity, her bare feet splashed the water, her hair hung to her waist. He remembered this. It was her fifteenth birthday. Even though he'd always adored her, it was the moment he realized she was the only woman he'd ever love. He'd been nineteen, and it was the day he started keeping count. He married her four years later.

Juliet sifted through others while he found a wedding

photo. They were leaving the church, laughing. He clutched her free hand while her other held a bouquet of white gardenias, pink roses, and lavender.

"Miss Nell," Juliet said softly, "what was Eugene looking for the day he died?"

"Your lily. He thought if he could find one and have it analyzed, maybe he could prove Anne's innocence."

"Anne died over three hundred years ago," Rafe said. "Why does her story matter?"

"It mattered to Gerald, and he believed it would matter to Juliet. When he came to us for help—which was an extraordinary act in and of itself—we said yes."

"You all were working on this together?" Juliet asked. "You, Miss Beatrice, Eugene, and my daddy?"

Miss Nell nodded. "When Eugene died, Calum joined our little group. And Sarah has been doing some research for us."

Rafe stacked the photos. "Why do you think Gerald didn't kill himself?"

"Gerald wasn't a coward. Beatrice and I believe the three men were murdered looking for the secret behind Juliet's lily. Calum believes it too."

Rafe's phone rang. It was Pete. "I have to take this."

Juliet nodded. "I'll pack up the photos. Can I get the trunk later?"

"Yes," Miss Nell said. "Rafe, you can take the call in the garden. I want to show Juliet the dress Gerald saved for her. It was her momma's wedding gown."

Juliet wiped her cheeks with the heels of her hands. "I'd love to see it."

Once outside, Rafe answered, "What's up?"

"A new problem."

After Pete finished, Rafe sat on a bench. The scent of roses he'd savored earlier now burned his nose. "*Fuck.*"

"The word of the day," Pete said. "What do we do?"

"Let Calum know we'll be there soon."

"And Nate? He's at the gym."

"Tell Nate to stay put. I don't want him near Garza." Rafe shut his phone and went to get his father-in-law's arsenal. That *probably* had become a *definitely*.

CHAPTER 20

JULIET WENT UNDER THE YELLOW POLICE TAPE, WITH RAFE behind her, and entered Rage of Angels. Police cars, ambulances, and cops surrounded the club. A kid in a hoodie hovered.

She and Rafe stepped aside as men wearing coroner jumpsuits pushed a gurney.

It was true. Rafe's hand pressed her lower back, and they went into the locker room. The warmth from his touch eased the tightness in her body. She appreciated the support as she took in the destruction. Bent lockers lay on their sides. Upside-down chairs leaned against broken mirrors. Glass crunched beneath shoes. Blood stained the floor.

Last night she hadn't understood the force of Rafe's anger, but today she was grateful. As confident as she was in her own strength to survive, Deke was physically stronger. If Rafe hadn't appeared, Deke would've raped her.

She inhaled, exhaled, and met her next challenge of the day.

Detective Garza stood in a circle with Pete, Calum, and Samantha and said, "I'd like to speak to Jade. A witness said she'd been beaten last night by a suspect."

Juliet swallowed the bitter taste in her mouth and said, "I'm Jade."

Calum came over and kissed her cheek. "Hello, beautiful."

Samantha hugged Juliet. Garza's face shifted from assessment to astonishment to anger. Not that Juliet blamed him.

Last night she'd lied when he asked what'd happened. And now that he knew the truth, she could only wonder what he thought of her.

"Is it true?" Juliet asked Samantha. "Is Sally dead?"

Samantha pulled away, wiping her cheeks with her palms. "Yes."

Garza cleared his throat. His friendliness from yesterday was gone. "Sally's body was found behind the Dumpster in the alley. A stripper named Marylou ID'd the body." Garza motioned to Calum. "The body was left near a tag of the Prioleau sigil."

Calum took out his phone and started texting. "Could it have been a heroin death?"

"No," Garza said. "Sally was murdered. Near your family's crest."

"One has nothing to do with the other. My mark is near every building I own. Although it looks like graffiti, I assure you it's not."

"With respect, Mr. Prioleau, you don't seem surprised to find a body on your property."

Calum nodded as if expecting the question. "Like many women, Savannah is lovely and gracious during the day, but when the sun goes down, her demons appear."

"That's dark." Garza's voice reeked of sarcasm.

Rafe picked up two chairs so Juliet and Samantha could sit.

"Do you have any idea who did this?" Juliet asked.

"Possibly." Garza held up an evidence bag with a cell phone. "We found this. It belongs to Deke Hammond. Marylou said Deke is the manager."

They all nodded.

Garza put the cell into his coat pocket. "When was the last time any of you saw Sally?"

"Before I went on break at eleven," Juliet said.

"On a pole around ten forty-five," Rafe said.

"Samantha and I saw her at midnight," Pete said. "After her last shift ended."

Garza picked up his notebook and pen from the dressing table. "What do you know about Deke Hammond?"

Pete shoved his hands in the front pockets of his black combat pants. His lip piercings glinted. "Deke is the club's manager who also runs two side businesses. One with women. The other with drugs. But Sally wasn't a prostitute, and she didn't use."

Garza wrote while he talked. "You don't think this is Deke's work?"

"No," Pete said. "Deke is an asshole, but Sally was making him money. His money stream is something he didn't screw with."

"Yet last night," Garza shifted his focus to Juliet, "he attacked you."

Juliet raised her chin. "I refused Deke so he tried to rape me. Rafe stopped him."

Now Garza looked at Rafe. "How, exactly, did you stop him?"

"I hit him."

Juliet glanced at Rafe's hands, but they were in his jacket pockets.

"Did Deke need medical attention?" Garza asked Rafe.

"No."

"What time did Deke leave?"

"Between eleven forty-five p.m. and one a.m.," Pete said.

"You're not sure?"

"It was a crazy night," Pete said. "I left Deke in my office to keep him away from the women who wanted to pound him. When I returned, Deke had disappeared."

"You didn't call the police?"

"Didn't have time."

"Uh-huh." Garza kept writing. "Do each of you have people who can vouch for your whereabouts the entire night?"

"Sure," Pete said. "Bartenders. Dancers. Patrons. I closed the bar at two a.m. Samantha and I were the last ones to leave."

Samantha squeezed Juliet's hand and nodded.

"I need to speak to Deke," Garza said. "Any idea where he is?"

"No." Pete paused. "But I have his address."

Calum looked up from his phone. "The club is closed."

"Great," Pete muttered.

Samantha laid her head on Juliet's shoulder. Juliet could smell her friend's honey-infused shampoo and feel her erratic breathing. She knew how much Samantha needed this job, and Juliet prayed she could save her own business and give her friend a raise.

Garza pointed to the cameras in the hallway. "The security tapes?"

"There aren't any," Pete said. "The cameras inside the club are live-feed only. The dancers don't want their moves on the internet."

"External cameras?"

"Not working."

"Not surprised," Garza muttered.

Calum cleared his throat. "Do you have a time of death?"

"After midnight." Garza tapped his pen on his notebook. "No one saw Deke leave?"

The four shook their heads in unison.

"That's enough questions, Detective," Calum said.

Garza scoffed. "According to Marylou, Rafe beat up

Deke so badly his face looked like he'd been crushed by a dump truck."

Juliet bit her lip, hating the fact that she hoped the description was true.

"If you find him," Rafe said, "you can see for yourself."

"I will." Garza's gaze drifted to Juliet. "Could Deke be your store's vandal?"

"No," Juliet said. "I haven't worked here in nine months and only did so last night to help pay back my loan. The loan I told you about. Could Sally's death be connected to the death on the Isle?"

"Possibly," Garza said.

"Dammit," Rafe said harshly. "Stop throwing around veiled accusations and tell us your theory."

Garza moved into Rafe's personal space. "I believe someone killed Sally to send a message to *you*."

Rafe raised an eyebrow.

"And," Garza continued, "I want to know every move you made last night until now."

"Rafe was with me all night," Juliet said. "He slept… nearby. Just in case."

"The entire night?" Garza kept his voice level, but harsh undertones leaked out.

"Yep," Rafe said.

She wasn't sure if it was Rafe's careless attitude or the confidence rolling off his muscled frame like paint fumes, but Garza's face had turned red and sweat striped his neck.

"Detective?" Calum spoke casually, as if they were at tea instead of an interrogation. "Do you have evidence supporting your supposition?"

"I do. After studying Sally's body and the body of the man killed yesterday, as well as speaking with my military contact, I believe Sally was murdered by a man with a tattoo of a sword piercing a heart, the mark of the Fianna." Garza stared at Rafe. "And the only Fianna warrior I know of is *you*."

Rafe's jaw clamped, and he crossed his arms. "Ridiculous."

"What are you talking about?" Pete asked.

"I'm talking about things that've happened since Montfort arrived," Garza said. "The man shot yesterday had a tattoo of a sword piercing a heart, with *Escalus* inked below."

"Maybe it was his mother's name," Samantha offered. "Or his lover's."

"I considered that, until hunters found a rental car with a journal in the glove box. The name *Escalus* was imprinted on the leather cover."

Rafe wished he could kill Escalus again. That was a mistake that sent warriors to the Gauntlet.

"One of the interesting things in this journal," Garza continued, with his arms crossed and focus completely on Rafe, "besides the fact that it's written in Latin, is the page numbering. The left page number starts at 2018 and continues until the last entry, 4897. The right page number starts at 57 and ends with 512."

Although Rafe played the clueless card, he knew that journal. They'd each received one. He'd cheated by writing in French while Escalus, a stellar student, had learned Latin. Writing in the book had become a nightly ritual for both of them until Rafe had gone to prison. "Do you know what the numbers mean?"

"Not yet," Garza said. "According to what I've translated so far, Escalus worked for an arms dealer known as the Prince and the Prince's secret army called the Fianna, a secret unit of highly trained, dangerous men."

Rafe kept his piehole shut. Too bad Garza had read that

journal, because when this was over, there was nothing Rafe could do to save the detective.

Juliet glanced up at Rafe before asking, "What does the Fianna do?"

"Assassinations," Garza said. "Arms deals on the Prince's behalf. They even police armies and militias. They follow strict rules regarding the way they talk, walk, and kill. Most importantly, they're protected by lots of money."

"The Fianna is a myth they told us in basic training," Pete said. "If we didn't follow the rules of warfare, the Fianna would find us. Torture us. Speak in verse. Bow before killing. Standard stuff to scare recruits."

"Did it work?" Samantha asked.

"I never believed, but my buddies did."

"You're ex-military too?" Garza asked.

Pete shrugged. "Sure."

"They speak in verse?" Juliet now stared at Pete. "What does that mean?"

Garza answered instead. "According to Escalus, when Fianna warriors speak to each other or a potential victim, they use Shakespearean language. They memorize every one of the Bard's plays and poems and use the same types of words and speech patterns."

"Why?" Juliet asked.

"They're big on self-mortification and self-discipline. They train naked in the woods in winter and hunt each other, and if one makes a sound, he's tortured. They learn how to move their bodies with stealth and silence. Before a recruit becomes a warrior, he makes a tithe and faces the Gauntlet."

"Except," Pete said, "they're *not* real."

"But it's interesting," Samantha said. "Go on, Detective. What's the Gauntlet?"

"A lane formed by seasoned warriors. Up to forty on each

side, holding different weapons. Whips, chains, knives. If the recruit makes it to the end alive and pronounces his tithe, he's bound for life to the Fianna army. He can never leave."

Rafe snorted. Although he wanted to correct Garza and refute the Wikipedia propaganda the Prince updated himself, anything Rafe said would put Juliet and his family in more danger.

"The man who died near my manor was a Fianna warrior?" Juliet asked.

"Yes. Escalus had a hand-drawn sketch of your house in his pocket. There were also notes about windows. Does that mean anything to you?"

"No." Juliet kept her hands clasped in her lap. Rafe knew he'd be lucky if she ever looked at him again. "What's a tithe?"

"A guarantee of fealty," Garza said. "The recruit offers up the one thing that ties him to this world. After tithing, he's in, body, heart, and soul."

Rafe exhaled and kept his arms crossed and hands fisted. He needed to end this convo now. "Pete is right. The Fianna is a myth. Just ask Interpol. They've never found any evidence of the Fianna's existence."

"Because," Garza said sharply, "everyone who knows about the Fianna is dead."

Calum stopped texting long enough to say, "What does this have to do with Sally?"

"It's not a coincidence," Garza said, "that the death of a Fianna warrior on the Isle corresponds with Shakespearean verses left in the cathedral and two dead bodies—a young man we found near this club and Sally—both of whom I suspect were killed with misericords. A weapon Escalus describes in his journal."

"How is Rafe—*my client*—involved?" Calum said.

Garza held up his cell phone. "Escalus wrote about his days as a recruit and the men training with him. One, in particular, went by the name *Romeo*." Garza handed his cell to Juliet. "A man I believe is your ex-husband."

∽

Juliet took the phone, hoping no one noticed her hands shaking. Had Rafe left her to join the Fianna? To become an assassin named Romeo for an arms dealer and his secret army?

The screen photo showed three men near a European medieval church. Two men stood opposite, and another in the center held his hands out as if brokering a truce. "What's this?"

"The man in the overcoat, with his back to the camera, is believed to be the Prince. The man in the center with the jeans and scarf is Escalus."

She squinted. Escalus's profile was shadowed. "How do you know?"

"There's a wound on his thumb identical to one on the body yesterday."

The third man, taller than the other two in leather pants and a hooded leather jacket, stood with his arms crossed. Although she couldn't see his face, she'd recognize Rafe's exasperated stance anywhere. "Is this you?"

Rafe's jaw locked down, his dark eyes narrowed into knife edges directed at Garza.

Samantha leaned over to look at the photo. "Where'd you get this?"

"Interpol," Garza said. "My military contact believes the third man is Romeo. At the time this photo was taken, Romeo was not only the most brutal Fianna warrior, he was the Prince's second-in-command."

Rafe's pupils had darkened, and his nostrils flared. There wasn't an apologetic feature on his face. Her blood rushed so fast a roar filled her ears. "Is this true?" she asked him.

"No." Pete took the phone and tossed it back to Garza. "Rafe left his unit because he's a traitor. Nothing more."

"*Juliet.*" Rafe spoke her name on the exhale, breathy and deep with his drawl that softened the hard consonant. The same way he'd spoken when they'd been in bed together last night.

She faced Garza again. "That photo you showed me last night. The one with the tattoo of a heart and a sword and Escalus's name beneath. Which arm was it on?"

"His left arm."

If she took off Rafe's jacket, yanked off the bandages, would she find a similar tattoo?

"This misericord that killed Sally," Samantha said to Garza. "What's that?"

"A small, sharp sword that, when shoved underneath the arm, pierces the heart. Or, if thrust behind the ear, takes out the brain stem. It's a sudden, almost painless death that leaves little blood and a small entrance wound."

"That doesn't mean a Fianna warrior killed Sally," Samantha said.

"No," Garza said, "but after studying the ME reports on Eugene Wilkins and Detective Legare, I discovered they were all killed the same way."

Juliet stood. "That's not what we were told. Eugene died in a fire, and Legare hit his head."

"I know the stories," Garza said. "It's also possible your father didn't commit suicide."

She clasped her hands behind her neck. While knowing her daddy hadn't committed suicide would help her grieve, his murder made everything worse. It meant his paranoia about men who bowed had been true, and she'd ignored it. She'd left him in this nightmare alone. How could she not have believed her own father?

Calum snapped his fingers. "I figured it out. I worked against Garza getting this job. I wanted someone I could trust, except I was overruled. My sister hired you to find out who murdered her husband, didn't she?"

Garza scowled. "I don't know what you're talking about."

Calum's eyes shuttered. "Now who's telling lies?"

"This isn't about me," Garza said. "This is about the Fianna killing people in my city."

"No, Detective. This is about my family. My people. *My* city."

"Believe what you want." Garza stood tall, taking Calum's accusation on directly. "But two people, possibly three, were murdered within nine months. And yesterday I realized those deaths, Miss Capel's vandalism, and the cathedral mess are tied to Montfort's return." Garza shifted his attention back to Rafe. "Do you remember your mother's death?"

Rafe's eyes blackened into polished stones. "Yes."

That'd been an awful time. Juliet and Rafe had been married for two years, and his mother's sudden death had devastated them all.

"We went to her funeral," Juliet said. "After returning to Fort Bragg, Rafe's unit left on a mission." Then, months later, she'd received his letter, and her world had fallen apart. "Why does my mother-in-law's death matter now?"

"Because," Garza said, "when I pulled up her ME report, Detective Legare had added a handwritten note about a small hole beneath her armpit. I believe Tess Montfort may also have been killed with a misericord. Possibly by a Fianna warrior."

The air in the room felt hot and heavy. The AC compressor kicked on, and Pete's breathing echoed. But Rafe's heart, beating fast and furious, had to be obvious to all in the room. His neck muscles bulged, and his hands balled.

Juliet licked her dry lips and asked him, "Is this true?"

"I don't know." The harshness of his voice offset his whisper.

No one spoke. Even Calum—who'd stopped texting— kept his peace.

"There've been so many secrets and lies." Juliet's voice shook. "So many people hurt. Sally. That teenage boy. Eugene Wilkins. Detective Legare. My daddy. Maybe your momma. Is Garza right? Are all those deaths connected to you?"

"For the record," Garza said, "I believe they are."

Rafe's eyes turned into brown pools of melted glass. She could see her own reflection on their surface, feel the heat through her dress. All. True. "You worked as an assassin? And somehow our families got involved?"

No words, but he didn't need any. The intensity of his regard said it all. *Yes.* He'd left her to work for some mythical army that killed without remorse or shame. And everyone else had paid the price.

Rafe's voice shattered the fragile silence. "There is a Fianna warrior in town named Balthasar. He killed Sally. If you go after him, he'll kill you too."

"Detective." An officer popped his head into the room. "Chief needs to talk. Pronto."

Garza pointed at Rafe. "This isn't over."

"It is until I say so," Calum said.

Garza pulled an envelope out of his jacket. "This is for you, Miss Capel. It's what I was going to give you later this afternoon. Do with it what you want."

Once Garza left, Samantha asked Rafe, "Are we in danger because we know this?"

"Yes."

"If we're already screwed," said Pete, "we deserve the truth."

Rafe crossed his arms and spoke through gritted teeth. "The truth is I'm responsible for every life here. Including Garza's."

Samantha took Juliet's hand and squeezed. Juliet squeezed back. While she was furious about what she'd learned, there was nothing she could say or do to make this better. But maybe if she and Rafe could find that vial, this whole nightmare would end before anyone else got hurt.

"So…" Pete ran a hand over his head. "How do we work the mission?"

"We win." Rafe sighed. "Where's Nate?"

"Getting beat up at the gym," Pete said.

"Give Nate this map." Rafe took Juliet's envelope out of his jacket and handed it to Pete. "Tell him to haul ass to the Savannah Preservation Office and talk to Sarah Munro. We need any info we can get about that map and Anne Capel. I doubt there'll be anything online. Then take Samantha to Juliet's Lily. Stay with her and watch out for anything strange." Rafe turned to Juliet, his jawline sharp enough to cut steel. "Change and pack whatever you want to bring to the Isle. Bring your gun."

"Why?"

"We're going to your manor to see those windows. We're going to find that vial before Balthasar kills again."

CHAPTER 21

BALTHASAR PLACED HIS SNIPER RIFLE NEAR THE WINDOW OVER-looking the city. Attics weren't his thing—too many child-hood memories. But this one was secure and had electricity.

After retrieving Deke, dumping Sally, and meeting Walker, Balthasar had waited for Eddie to move his gear into the safe house. Eddie even brought a cot for Deke to recover on.

Deke lay on his side, ear bandaged, hopped up on pain meds. Unfortunately, because of Romeo's beating, Balthasar had to wait for Deke to wake before hitting the laptop. Deke had until noon to recover.

Heavy steps on the stairs meant Eddie's return.

The moment Eddie entered with an armload of groceries and ammo, Balthasar said, "What happened at the club?" Although he didn't trust the younger, skittish man, Eddie knew about the Fianna. Whether from Escalus or Eddie's still-unnamed cousin-slash-boss was TBD. Regardless of Balthasar's unresolved feelings about Escalus's betrayal, Balthasar had a job to do and few leads. Eddie held the only way forward.

At least, according to Eddie, Romeo had less intel than Balthasar.

"They found Sally," Eddie said. "Unfortunately, the cops discovered Deke's cell. Almost caught me, too. I hid in the ladies' shower room and overheard that detective talking. What a strange accent. From Pennsylvania or something."

"The point?"

"Garza found E's journal, translated it, and told them about the Fianna."

Garza had Escalus's journal? Balthasar ran his fist over his chin. "Did Montfort speak?"

"No." Eddie went to the coffee pot and started a fresh brew. "Except to say you'd take out everyone in the room including the cop because they now knew about the Fianna."

Romeo knew Balthasar well. "What are their plans?"

"Montfort gave that Indian a map and told him to find Walker."

Balthasar took his weapon from his waistband and laid it on the table. "What map?"

"Not sure. Montfort wants Walker to go to the Savannah Preservation Office and meet a Ms. Sarah Munro. She may be able to help him find out what the map means. Then Montfort told the Indian—"

"White Horse."

Eddie scratched his head. "Montfort told White Horse to protect Samantha at Juliet's Lily while Montfort and Juliet search Capel Manor to find the windows."

"What windows?"

"Right. You don't know about those." The coffee hissed as it filled the pot. "My cousin told me the manor has stained-glass windows with clues to where the vial is. Except the manor is in ruins and the windows are probably broken. That's what E was looking for yesterday when he got dead."

The aroma of fresh coffee filled Balthasar's head. "Follow the lovers. Find out about those windows. I'll handle Garza and Walker."

"And White Horse?"

"Deke will monitor White Horse. But you're my eyes and ears at that manor."

"What about my cousin? We're late checking in. If my

coz finds out Escalus died and I didn't tell him, I'm—" Eddie used a spoon to make a slashing motion across his neck.

Balthasar poured two cups of coffee. One for him, one to wake up Deke. "I can't contact your cousin until I get that computer working. Unless there's another way?"

"Only by secure laptop." Eddie pointed at Deke. "My boy can barely walk and talk."

"I'll care for him." Like Balthasar had cared for so many Fianna recruits, including Romeo. After a long sip of the hot coffee, Balthasar added, "If you fail—"

"I know." Eddie dumped sugar into his cup and shrugged. "*Death will follow.*"

Nate met Pete outside Iron Rack's gym. Nate's body hurt, his head pounded, but his vision worked. It'd been a good fight.

He adjusted his bag on his shoulder. "Hey."

Pete handed him a laundry duffel and an envelope with Juliet's name on it. Threw them was more accurate. "Here."

"Thanks." Nate hadn't thought about laundry in days. "What's this?"

"It's a map. Montfort wants you to go to the Savannah Preservation Office and talk to Sarah Munro. Figure out what the map means and see what you can learn about Anne Capel." Pete headed into the gym.

Nate carried the duffel on one shoulder, shoved the envelope in his back pocket, and grabbed Pete's arm. "What's up?"

Pete knocked him off. "Seriously? You have no idea of the danger we're in. We have no jobs. We're broke. And you're fighting random losers to make yourself feel better."

Only bad shit put Pete in this kind of mood. "What happened?"

"Sally was murdered behind the club last night by Balthasar." Pete pulled the HELP WANTED sign off the front door and went inside.

Nate followed Pete back into the gym. "What are you talking about?"

Pete stopped at the front desk painted to resemble a Jolly Roger flag and addressed the check-in guy wearing a black T-shirt with a skull and crossbones. "I'm applying for the self-defense instructor job."

"Yeah?" The guy took the flyer. "You trained?"

"Trained. Certified. Experienced. Krav Maga is my specialty. But I teach tae kwon do, karate, and basic street fighting. Considering the pirate theme going on here, I can also do fists, knives, chains. Whatever you need."

The guy nodded. "Leave your number, and the owner will call."

After Pete did, he turned and left. Again, Nate followed him. "What's that about?"

"We have no money, and because the club is closed, we have no jobs."

Nate grabbed Pete's shoulder. "Talk to me."

After Pete went through the morning's events, including Garza's Fianna rant, Nate said, "Shit."

"That sums it up." Pete went down the street and turned left.

Nate, still carrying the duffel and his gym bag, ran to catch up. "Where are you going?"

"Where the fuck do you think? To protect Samantha and stop whoever's killing people we know. You need to get to the SPO. Unless you don't want to win this fucking war?"

"Of course I do."

Pete stopped and pushed him. "Then act like it. Do

something. Anything. Hell, cry about Sally or go after Balthasar. The old Nate would've been on this with helos and guns."

"You don't think I can do that? Because I'm not crying over a dead stripper?"

"Jeez, Nate, when did you turn into a coldhearted bastard?"

"I'm…fuck." Nate dropped both bags onto the sidewalk. He was a bastard. Hadn't he been telling Pete that for weeks now?

Pete sighed. "If we don't find that vial before Balthasar does, if we don't figure out what Juliet's lily has to do with a Spec Forces op halfway around the world, we're screwed. Abso-fucking-lutely screwed. My team—including me—goes to prison for helping your team, and you end up back in the psych ward."

Pete was right. Nate picked up his bags. "I'll go to the SPO, and then meet you at Juliet's Lily."

"Good."

"Wait…will Juliet be there?"

Pete walked away. "She and Montfort went out to the Isle to see some windows. But don't worry. I'm an experienced Krav Maga teacher. When she returns, I'll protect you."

An hour later, Nate sat—showered, in clean clothes, with coffee—at a table beneath an oak tree in the Savannah Preservation Office gardens. The patio fountain provided white noise and, when the breeze blew, a cool mist. The SPO antebellum mansion housed the preservation society offices, library, and reading room.

He'd gone in, but the assistant with long brown hair and too many arm tattoos had taken the document and told him to wait for Miss Munro, the temporary archivist. Then the assistant gave him a book about the history of Savannah's isles. Since the AC was acting up and it was cooler outside, he'd chosen the garden.

He squinted at the fine print. He preferred math equations to reading. His struggle with mild dyslexia didn't help. Neither did Pete's anger still ringing in Nate's ears. He *hadn't* been holding up his end of the mission. But he'd rather have gone out to the Isle with Rafe than do library duty. As Nate reread the same sentence three times, his cell phone rang. "Walker."

"There's news," Kells said. "The trials for my team start Friday."

"I thought we had weeks!"

"Things have changed. If you don't find new intel to prove our innocence, the men who rescued you will be dishonorably discharged and imprisoned as well."

"Why? Your team wasn't there. You weren't the operational commander."

"You entered the country under another commander's control, but the mission was mine. That secret congressional committee says it has evidence proving my team was involved with the massacre at the planning stage."

Nate rubbed his forehead. He'd thought the charges against Kells's team would be dropped. "You were all at HQ that night."

"Doesn't matter, Nate. Someone wants to pin this on *all* of my men. And by tying the team that stayed behind to the planning of your and Jack's mission, we're culpable."

"How many men?"

"Ten including me. Between my team and the two in prison, that's three A-teams and two colonels."

All because of Nate's inability to command. "I'll have info by the end of the day."

"I hate that this falls on you and Pete, but it does."

So man up. "I'll call later."

Nate hung up and reached for the medal around his neck that wasn't there anymore. The colors behind his lids were bouncing. A roar in his head threatened to send him into unconscious land. He opened his eyes and found a pill. He'd taken two of the three to get through last night and had one left. He swallowed it with coffee, savoring the burn in his throat. He was pressed against the wall with a knife at his jugular. Yet, instead of diving into the books, he worried about where he'd get his next hit.

CHAPTER 22

JULIET SAT NEXT TO RAFE IN THE IMPALA, WITH HER BACK-pack on the floor and her daddy's duffel in the trunk. Besides her weapon, she'd brought flashlights, ponchos, water bottles, and granola bars. She'd also changed into jeans, a T-shirt, snake boots, and a field jacket. It'd been nine months since she'd been to the manor, and she had no idea how much more it had declined.

Was she surprised Rafe had left his unit to join a super-secret group of highly skilled soldiers? No. Despite enlisting in the army at nineteen, he'd always done his own thing.

He'd barely spoken since picking her up. But, as angry as she was, she had to take some responsibility. She could've worked harder to get him to answer her questions—before Sally's murder—yet Juliet had chosen the fearful path. The path of self-pity. And where had that led? Vandalism and death.

Her cell phone buzzed with a text from Samantha.

> *Sold all of Abigail Casey's botanical prints to a sexy stranger. $3000. Hope I get paid tomorrow.*
> Wonderful. Everyone gets paid tomorrow.

Even if Juliet had to steal the money to do it. Now that she knew Abigail's husband, Liam, was in prison with the rest of Nate's men, Juliet was sure Abigail would appreciate the sale. Maybe Abigail would have enough capital to design the line of stationery they'd discussed to sell in Juliet's Lily.

Yay! Painters are here to finish your logo on the new windows. Will send pics.

Before Juliet could respond, her phone rang. It was her lawyer. "Hello, John."

"I have two interested buyers for your land. One of them is a cash transaction and he's not as concerned about the King's Grants, although I warned him he could lose up to forty percent of the land to the federal government without them."

"The land isn't up for sale yet."

"I only talked to my well-connected clients. Most of them weren't interested without the King's Grants."

"I'm going to the manor now. I'll call when I find them." She hung up and held the phone in her lap.

"What was that about?"

"Besides finding your vial, I need to find the King's Grants proving King Charles gave my family the land on the Isle of Grace."

"Why?"

"If I can prove the land was granted by King Charles, the federal government can't claim protected wetlands. Without the grants, they could take forty percent of the property."

"You're still thinking of selling?"

"I have no other way of refinancing my loan and staying in business. Even if I could sell my land to cover the expenses of my refinanced loan, I still need Carina's money to finish the Liberty Square project. If Carina doesn't come through with what she owes me, I won't be able to pay the city's workers. If I don't pay, the city will sue me and I'll be bankrupt by the end of the summer."

His hands loosened on the wheel. "You'll persuade her tonight."

"She hates me."

For the first time since leaving the city, he glanced at her. "What happened to Calum when we were kids wasn't your fault."

"I let Calum lie for me. Because of that lie, his parents sent him away. Carina will never forgive me for that."

"You were twelve. You're not responsible for what happened."

"I guess." Juliet sent more texts to Bob, and he sent her a photo. The new fountain at Liberty Square would be hooked up tonight, weather permitting. The water guys and electrical workers had come to a truce. Probably due to the donuts she'd sent to the work site earlier.

Once finished with her texts, she stared at the blowing palmetto trees as they crossed the only bridge leading to the Isle of Grace.

"You should open Garza's envelope. That way we can get the fight over with."

She threw her phone into her backpack. "What fight?"

"I'm talking about the way you sink into yourself when you're annoyed or frightened. How you separate yourself from the real world when you don't want to feel pain or get hurt."

Wow. They were going to do this now? "Instead of throwing myself into a gauntlet of eighty men with weapons and chains? Would you rather I hold a knife at your throat and tell you what I really think of you?"

"At least that would be the truth." Once exiting the bridge, he pulled the car over and hit the brakes.

She braced herself against the dashboard. "Because you're the beacon of honesty?"

He faced her, his gaze fierce and determined. "You lie by omission. You're so afraid of feeling pain that you can't rely on others. It's so self-destructive, you won't argue or confront them when they've done wrong."

She got out of the car and slammed the door. He followed, and she stared at him over the roof. "I don't know what you're talking about."

"You should be pissed at me. I hurt you. I've done terrible things I'll never be able to redeem myself for or be forgiven for. Yet you won't talk about it."

"Because you won't answer my questions."

"Maybe you're asking the wrong ones."

"Maybe I don't know what to ask."

He took off his jacket and threw it into the back seat. "I'm not wearing it anymore."

"I don't care about your arm. Or that tattoo under the bandage. Maybe I'm not asking the right questions because your answers don't matter."

"You're lying. You're not asking because you care too much. Because if you know the truth, there's a chance you're going to get hurt again."

She closed her eyes and turned her back to him. "I agreed to help you. And you promised you'd leave. Why can't we do this without any talk of the past?"

"That's not possible." His voice sounded closer, and she opened her eyes. He stood inches away, his chest moving with every breath. "Every time we look at each other, we remember."

Despite what she'd said about not caring, she avoided looking at his fully tattooed arm. And the blue ribbon around his other wrist. Focusing on the muscles contracting beneath his T-shirt wasn't helping either. "No, we don't."

Now who was lying?

He pinned her against the car, his larger body covering hers. "I remember what it was like between us once. The last time we were together."

She licked her lips and kept her gaze on the pulse at his neck. She remembered too. "It doesn't mean—"

His lips found hers. His arms held her tight, one around her waist, the other behind her neck tilting her head at the perfect angle. He refused to hide his strength or his erection. As the kiss increased, her resolve weakened from those memories of the last time they'd made love. That last day of August when they'd gone hiking and found themselves at a secluded waterfall. They'd eaten a picnic and made love in the water, beneath the pine trees, under the stars.

Just as she kissed him back, he lifted his head. The yearning in his eyes threatened to leave third-degree burns on her heart. "You remember."

She pressed her fists against his chest—that solid wall of uncompromising muscle. "It doesn't matter."

He gripped her shoulders. "I need to know that when you read that letter you were in the same amount of pain I was in."

She pushed harder, but he only came in closer. "You're the one who caused the pain."

"Didn't you hear anything Garza said?"

"You left your unit—you left me—to work for an arms dealer with a god complex."

"Think harder, Juliet." Now Rafe's hands held her waist, their hips still meeting, his erection cutting into her stomach. "You're a smart woman. I can't tell you what happened, so you'll have to be the one to figure it out."

Why was he doing this to her? She punched his chest but he didn't even blink. "I don't understand."

"I know." He rested his forehead against hers. "I swore an oath I can't break."

"You swore to love me above all others until death do us part."

"That's all I've done."

She scoffed. "How?"

"If I speak, we both die."

She shook her head. Her lips were tender, as if she hadn't been kissed in years. Which was the truth. "We know about Escalus's journal, so we're all in danger."

"Pete, Samantha, Calum, and Garza. They're expendable to the Fianna. You're not. You're the only leverage the Prince has over me. If I don't fulfill my duties, they'll kill both of us." Without warning, he let her go and headed to his side of the car.

He'd kissed her like she'd brought down the stars from the sky, and now he was walking away as if it didn't matter?

She ran over and grabbed his arm. "I don't know why you came back. I don't know what you want or why you kissed me, but I'm counting the minutes until you leave." He stared at her hand on his bicep covered with names. She wiped her hand on her jeans.

How could she have let him kiss her?

"Now that I'm seeing vestiges of the girl I fell in love with, I might stay."

She went for her side of the car. "That girl disappeared years ago."

"She's just lost. And I'm going to bring her back."

She got in and waited until he turned the car on and began driving. "Nothing can bring her back. She died from a broken heart. And I swore I'd never let that happen again."

"Whatever you say."

Ignoring him, she found Garza's envelope and opened it, determined to prove him wrong. She found four pages. One was a photocopy of the picture on Garza's phone. The second was a copy of a journal page. The print was perfect, tiny, and impossible to read. A sketch took up half the space: a drawing of Rafe with eyes filled with so much pain she wondered how he could bear to stay alive. It was dated February fourteenth of the year she'd received his letter. The day he'd abandoned her.

The third sheet was a State Department transcript requesting Rafe's extradition from a Russian prison to the United States. Garza had highlighted the application date and Eugene Wilkins's signature. The fourth paper was a DoD form detailing the terms of Rafe's incarceration at Leavenworth. Again, Garza had highlighted the date.

The road shifted from paved to gravel, and Rafe tightened his grip on the wheel. "What are they?"

"A photocopied page from Escalus's journal. Your extradition paperwork signed by Eugene Wilkins with the transfer date—the same day Eugene died. The last one is your Leavenworth paperwork." She dropped the papers into her lap. "You arrived in Leavenworth the day my daddy died."

Rafe turned onto a dirt road that led to the river and public dock. Once he'd parked next to a blue IoG bus, he took the pages and checked the dates.

"It can't be a coincidence," she said.

"It's not."

Her breath caught in her throat as she realized something. She had her own anger, regret, and sadness to carry, but she'd been able to emerge from the nightmare of their past to make a life for herself. While Rafe—she glanced at his hard jawline and powerful body—was still in the nightmare.

"Rafe?" She touched her bruised lips. She tasted his peppermint mouthwash and would have to wash his scent out of her hair. But those concerns were secondary to her fears. "Is Garza right? Did the people we love die because of you?"

"Yes." Rafe tossed the papers into the back seat and got out. "Now you're asking the right questions."

CHAPTER 23

RAFE GRABBED HIS FIELD JACKET FROM THE BACK SEAT. THE Prince had been playing these life-and-death mind games since Rafe had shown up in their camp eight years ago. Regardless of how cold this sounded, none of those deaths mattered now. What mattered was finding the vial and keeping his wife alive. And while those things were vital, he'd added another item to his to-do list: bringing his wife back from the reserved woman she'd become.

Last night he'd thought it'd be better if she kept up the independence routine. Except after watching her this morning with her daddy's things, he realized she hadn't grown stronger.

Although she could start a business and fend for herself, she'd become more vulnerable. The tensile strength of the steel cage surrounding her only proved how emotionally fragile she'd become. If he was going to leave her again to rejoin the Fianna, he needed to know she could take care of herself. Not just financially but in the way that let her live a full, happy life. A life with a husband and kids. A life without him.

She appeared with their backpacks. Her lips were swollen, and he hoped he hadn't hurt her. Once Rafe loaded the rifle on his shoulder and the machete on his hip, both courtesy of his father-in-law's duffel stashed in the Impala's trunk, he followed her to the water. There were a few canoes and johnboats with outboard motors on cement blocks.

The dock was a forty-square-foot block of treated pine that floated during high tide and sat on pluff mud during low tide. He took one of Grady's weekly tidal charts from a plastic holder on the light pole. "What's the bus for?"

"The Isle bought it for hurricane evacuations and Tourist Wednesday. Which is today."

"What's Tourist Wednesday?"

"To raise money for the general fund, the Isle offers tours of the marshes and swamps. The tour starts at Calum's plantation on the Isle of Hope, Tommy Boudreaux brings them by boat up the Black River through my land, Grady leads them through the swamps near the back meadow, and the day ends at Boudreaux's restaurant."

"Why?" Gerald never would've allowed such a thing.

She hopped over a pile of coiled ropes. "Since the Isle has no development and the land is pristine, eco-types and bird watchers love it. They pay for the experience."

On the far edge, she reached for a tarp covering two boats. He helped her unfold the canvas to reveal a new canoe and an old johnboat with a new motor. Paddles lay in the bottom of the canoe. A red jerry can sat in the boat. "Which one?"

"The canoe. The johnboat won't make it through the marsh grass."

"You two heading to Capel Manor?" Jimmy Boudreaux came down the path, his badge glinting in the sun, his hat pulled low.

Rafe nodded. "Your hunters still out there?"

"No. When Grady lost the trail, the search was over."

Juliet shaded her eyes with her hand. "Is Tommy on the river today with a tour group?"

Jimmy pointed to a dot on the horizon. "He's taking them to the back meadow to fish."

Rafe glanced at her. "You let them fish?"

"For an extra fee," Jimmy said.

She eyed Jimmy. "It doesn't hurt that they end up at your family's restaurant."

Jimmy shrugged. "When Boudreaux's Cajun Shack showed up in that *Off the Beaten Path* tourist guide, we spent too much time rescuing people searching for it. This is simpler."

Deep in the woods along a narrow river, Boudreaux's was an outdoor Cajun joint with plywood floors beneath the trees, coolers of beer along the edges, and a cooking shack that made the best gumbo Rafe had ever had. "I thought Gerald shut Boudreaux's down."

Juliet found her straw hat in her backpack and put it on. "Before he died, Daddy and Old Man Boudreaux came to an agreement. Jimmy's daddy admitted the restaurant was on Capel land, but as long as he gave the Capels a monthly stipend, it could remain open. Although there's no way my daddy would've gone for tourists. The Boudreauxes didn't have the guts to mention this plan at the town hall meetings until my daddy was dead."

Jimmy smirked. "You shouldn't complain. The money you make between the land access and Boudreaux's rent pays your taxes."

"Is this true?" Rafe asked her.

For the first time, her smile didn't seem forced. "Yes."

It was a brilliant business plan. "Will the tourists be near the manor?"

"No." Jimmy unclipped a transmitter from his belt. "Take the SAT phone. Tommy has one on the boat. And Grady always carries his. When you return, leave it in the rectory. If you're not back by seven, I'll come out after you."

"Thanks," Rafe said, surprised by the offer.

Jimmy clapped him on the shoulder. "Be careful. The only thing that place is good for now is kindling."

A few minutes later, they had the canoe in the water, backpacks and weapons loaded, with Juliet sitting forward while he sat aft. He'd found an Atlanta Braves hat in Calum's apartment, and she wore a straw hat that was sexy as hell. It took heavy paddle work to move into the deeper part of Black River. When the canoe stabilized, he let the current take them. Thirty minutes later, they made it to the opening of Snake Creek.

He steered through marsh grass and muddy waters. Birds flew overhead, and the heat shimmered on the water. As they paddled around a bend, a swath of Capel land opened up. Thousands of untouched acres of marsh and woods and streams. Egrets skimmed, looking for food. A porpoise appeared in the distance. "You can't sell this property."

"I have to save my business," she said softly. "It's all I have."

"This land is a part of you. A part of your family's history."

"A history of murder and curses?"

"No family is perfect."

Her laugh sounded weak, like she wasn't convinced.

The grass closed in on them, and the paddling became harder. If they missed the tides, they'd be stuck out here. She pointed right. "Head through those reeds."

He steered the boat into the nonexistent path until they were surrounded by mangrove trees and swamp.

She pointed left. "You'll have to push us in."

The curve led into a tidal creek, and he saw a dock ten feet ahead. It took all his strength to guide the canoe to the platform, using the paddles to control the balance. Once they hit, Juliet tied the canoe to a post. After unloading the backpacks and machete and tossing his hat into the boat, he held out his hand.

She hesitated, and then accepted it. Heat, not from the weather, shot through his body. The brim of her hat hid her eyes. He took it off.

"What are you doing?"

"Looking at you."

"Why?"

"Because you're beautiful." He pressed her palm to his chest. He wanted her to feel what she did to him. His heart bounced around like it was spring-loaded, and he kissed her.

This kiss wasn't one of desperation, like on the road. This one was sweet like a first time, soft like froth on the water. When her lips moved beneath his, his arm snaked around her waist and brought her in close. His body shook with the force of what he wanted. So many years of dreaming of this, his mind couldn't keep up.

A squawking bird broke the spell. She pulled away and took her hat. "We need to go."

Right. The mission. He helped her with her backpack. Then he slipped his on and adjusted his rifle over a shoulder. His free hand held the machete. "Which way?"

She pointed into the thickest part of the marsh. "There's a path."

He doubted it but didn't want to argue. He wanted to focus on the kiss. And what it meant. "You know we need to talk about it eventually?"

"What?"

"The three times I've kissed you."

She grabbed the machete and led the way. "There's nothing to talk about."

〜

Nate raised his arms, stretching the tight muscles. The reading hadn't been that bad. Anne Capel had been a kick-ass seventeenth-century woman.

"Hello?"

The female voice shook him out of his stupor, and he squinted from the glare. The woman stood nearby, carrying an armload of books. He took them from her. Born and bred in North Carolina, he always rose for a woman when she addressed him. And he always carried her books.

"Hey." That's the best he could do?

She waved to the second seat at his table. "May I?"

"Sure." He placed the texts between them and kept the moan in. He'd been hoping for a SparkNotes version. "Are you the archivist?"

"Yes." She held out her hand. "I'm Sarah Munro."

He took her smaller hand in his. In that moment, his heart exploded, the force causing everything around him to become silent. Like the sound wave after a rocket-propelled grenade hit. Her long brown hair was tied up into a messy bun, and curling tendrils framed her face. The pink sundress and sweater made her seem ethereal. Her glasses emphasized brown eyes.

"I'm Nate." He took out the white handkerchief he kept in his back pocket and wiped down the other seat for her. He made sure to keep the embroidered strawberries hidden.

Once they sat, she said, "You're interested in Anne Capel and this map you dropped off." She pulled it out from one of the books. "Early colonial history is my specialty."

"I didn't know one could get a job doing…that." *Way to go, Prince Charming.*

She scrunched her nose. "I'm a historian on loan to the preservation office from the Smithsonian. My specialty is 1650 to 1713."

He shoved the handkerchief in his back pocket. "The golden age of piracy to the end of the Revolution?"

"Among other things, yes." She smiled for the first time. "I'm interested in this map. Where'd you get it?"

The lower half of his body woke up, and he shifted to make sure his hips were under the table. "A buddy had this trunk—"

"I understand." She gave him another one of her asteroid-blasting smiles. "That happens a lot around here." She laid the map on the table. "Although a copy, it appears to be a map of an old cemetery on the Isle of Grace."

"Is there anything special about this map?"

"Possibly. While the leaves decorating the edges are lovely, they're not the most interesting thing." She took a magnifier out of her dress pocket and held it over a corner. "The top of the original is torn, but you can see there was once a compass rose."

He looked closer. Only the *W* and *E* could be seen, but from the scroll work, they had been compass directions. "Most maps have a compass rose."

"Except the way this map is oriented, true north is off by thirty degrees."

"Does it matter? It's old. And what about those scribbled numbers and letters along the top. What do those mean?"

"Interesting." She put down her magnifier. "I'm not sure. The map may be related to the history of Anne Capel, who lived on the Isle of Grace."

"Yeah." Now this he could talk about. "I've read about her. She was quite a woman—for the seventeenth century."

"I agree." Sarah adjusted her glasses and opened the top book. "Anne had a love affair with Isaiah Montfort, got pregnant, was accused of murdering forty-four kids with an herbal potion she'd made, was hanged for murder and witchcraft, and, when the rope broke, was pardoned. Then her lover's brother burned down her house and killed Isaiah. She went on to live in isolation and died in 1703, leaving a son named Lawrence."

"Was that the child she had with Isaiah Montfort?"

"Yes. Anne never married after Isaiah's death. And that supposedly started a long-running feud between the Capel and Montfort families."

"Did she murder those kids?"

"I don't believe so. Anne was a renowned herbalist. I believe she was helping them and it went horribly wrong."

"Have you ever read about a vial she may have hidden?"

Sarah shook her head. "I'm sorry."

"That's alright." Nate smiled at her when he really wanted to do more. Like kiss her senseless until all her clothes fell off.

"Are you a history buff?"

Only if it saves my men. "Sure."

She touched the map again. "I'd love to see this cemetery. But it's on private land. I've emailed the owner but I've yet to get permission to go out there."

"There've been a lot of deaths on that Isle."

Sarah smiled wryly. "Now you sound like my boss." She stood and brushed a stray curl off her shoulder. "I have to get back to work, but I've brought more books worth reading. When you're done, drop them off inside. If you need them tomorrow, my assistant will reserve them for you."

He stood and shoved his hands in his front pockets. "Thanks."

She walked away. And, for a brief moment, she glanced back.

"She's beautiful."

Nate turned to find a shadow behind the oak tree. The man wore a hoodie that hid his face. "Did you kill Sally?"

"Yes. Have you thought about my offer?"

"To join the Fianna? No, thanks." Nate sat and opened books, hoping the monster would go away. It was daylight, and Nate was in public. The chances of being beaten again were slim, and now he was armed.

"What if I offered you information that could save your men?"

"I wouldn't believe it even if you had it. Which you don't. Now go away."

"How are your headaches?"

Truthfully, now that Sarah was gone, his head hurt like he'd shoved it in a blender with stereo speakers. "Fine."

"Have you ever wondered about where the headaches come from?"

"I know how they started." In a warlord's POW camp.

"Yet, despite the pills, you still have them."

"What do you care?"

"I have what you need. You have what I need. One day's worth of pills for one map."

"The map is meaningless."

Balthasar laughed. "Then you wouldn't mind giving it up for three pills."

Too bad Nate's burner phone couldn't take photos. Conflicted, he sat back. It wasn't as if the map was *of* anything. And without a compass rose, it *was* broken.

"I know those pills are the only things that help your pain," Balthasar said. "Too bad they're addictive."

The pills weren't the problem. The headaches and seizures—caused by his time in the POW camp—were the issue. After another long minute, Nate handed Balthasar the map. In return, the warrior gave him three pills.

"Now leave," Nate said.

"If you want more pills tomorrow, the price is the journal Detective Garza is reading."

"How do you know about that?"

"Deke is quite the informant. He also discovered Garza has his cell phone. The one he used to make his drug deals. I hope your name isn't in there."

Nate rose, but Balthasar had disappeared.

Dammit. Nate packed up the books. Once he handed his stack to the assistant and put them on reserve, she gave him a note from Sarah. "Miss Munro had to leave for a family emergency, but she wanted me to give you this."

> *Nate, I just heard from a colleague that there are no satellite photos of the Isle of Grace because none have ever been taken. There are only two reasons for this. One, the Isle is mostly uninhabited, so it doesn't matter. Two, someone paid someone off to make sure no aerial photos would ever be taken. My bet is on the latter.*
>
> Sarah

Why was he not surprised?

As he shoved the note into his pocket, his phone buzzed.

You will join us or suffer the consequences.

Nate left the SPO, texting Pete. CC

"Fuck you, Balthasar." Those three pills had bought him one more day, and he had to make the most of it before Montfort found out. Nate removed the SIM card and smashed the phone against a rock. On his way out of the garden, he threw the SIM card into the fountain and the phone in the garbage. He didn't have a plan, but he

had a goal. He just hoped Pete remembered that *CC* meant
cells compromised.

Then Nate prayed that Pete still cared.

༄

Rafe went up the porch stairs first, testing each one for rot.
By the time he dropped his pack and turned to help Juliet,
she stood next to him.

She started taking things out of the bags. "Should I bring
my gun?"

"Yes. I'm worried about snakes." He shifted his rifle to
his back and left the machete on the ground. He had his
nine-mil in his back waistband and two knives.

She took off her hat and placed it on a poncho. "I
haven't been inside since my daddy died. Jimmy hired men
with an electric scissor lift and it took them hours to get
here. Even longer to maneuver over the mud flats. Inside,
the floor was so rotted, they built cross supports to keep it
from falling through to the subbasement. So"—she pointed
to the tattered police tape—"don't expect much."

He took her hand and led her in. "What happened to
the chandelier?"

"The men with the lift had to take it down to get my
daddy."

Rafe studied the two-story ceiling. "How'd Gerald get
up there?"

"He stood on a ladder, tied a rope around the chandelier, and jumped." She wrapped her arms around her waist.
"The ladder was nearby when I found him."

"Bullshit." Rafe put a hand on her shoulder and squeezed.
"I've known a lot of tough men and your daddy wasn't only
the toughest, he was the most stubborn. Gerald would never
commit suicide. And he sure as hell wouldn't hang himself."

She nodded. "Where do we start?"

"Upstairs and work our way down."

Besides the staircase with newel posts elaborately carved with leaves, the first floor had four rooms off the foyer, two on each side. The kitchen and glass conservatory ran along the back of the house. A study hid beneath the stairs. Gabriel once stood near the front door, protecting everything and everyone. The upstairs had six bedrooms, and the landing overlooking the first floor had been a ballroom. Now the space was a field of animal droppings and mold.

"Let's check my room first."

Once upstairs, they found her bedroom empty, the French doors leading onto her balcony open. After testing the wood, he went outside.

"Be careful," she said.

"I will." He took the scope off his rifle and scanned the river. He followed the path they'd walked to the house. When he shifted the scope upward, past the tree he used to climb to her balcony, he found what he was looking for. "Look."

She stepped onto the balcony, and it groaned. "Will it hold?"

"For now." He handed her the scope and pointed to the river. "Can you see the canoe?" She nodded, and he moved the scope up and to the right. "See the fire lookout tower? I think that's where the sniper stood when he killed Escalus."

"It's almost two miles away."

"It's where I'd take the shot from."

She handed him the scope and followed him inside.

The rest of the bedrooms were empty, with holes pitting the floors. "I've always loved this house," he said, leading them into Gerald's bedroom.

She went to her father's closet where he'd kept one of his safes. "Why?"

Rafe stood next to her, contemplating what it'd be like to restore and live in the manor. Raise a family here. "Imagine what it looked like with the carved molding and decorative ceiling plaster. Fireplaces in every room. I bet it was beautiful."

"I'm sure it was," she said from the closet. "There's nothing here. The safe's gone—Rafe!" She screamed as the closet floor gave way.

He grabbed her hand before she dropped. He ended up on his stomach while her legs kicked back and forth below her. He saw the kitchen sixteen feet down.

"Stop moving and look at me," he ordered.

She tried to grab his wrist with her other hand, but she didn't have the strength. His grip on her wrist slipped, and his arms burned. "Juliet!"

She raised her head, eyes wide.

"I'm going to pull you up. Stop swinging your legs."

She slowed and closed her eyes.

"Throw up your other hand."

She reached, and he grabbed her other wrist. His muscles strained until he thought his shoulders would dislocate. Slowly, he moved backward using his elbows and knees. When she was at the edge, he maneuvered until he had dragged her through.

They both collapsed on the floor. And when that groaned, he rolled them toward the wall and threw off his rifle. She shook and he held her in his arms, both of them curled into one another. Her heart beat as fast as his, and he pressed his lips against her hair. They were both covered in dirt and grime, but he didn't care. They were safe.

CHAPTER 24

JULIET CLUNG TO RAFE. THE FLOOR HAD DISAPPEARED SO quickly, and she'd been suspended solely by Rafe's strength. She had no idea how he'd pulled her up. Her arms ached, and the adrenaline rush left her nauseated and shaky.

He kissed her head, and she wanted to snuggle in closer. Instead, she backed away.

"Let's finish so we can leave." She hated this place. Being in her old room had filled her with painful memories. Like the summer night Rafe strapped a telescope on his back and climbed her tree so they could seek out the Pegasus constellation. She also hadn't wanted to talk about his work as a sniper. Assassin. Whatever.

Yes, she was a coward.

He helped her up and found his rifle. It didn't take long to check out the first floor sitting room and conservatory. Most of the windows had been broken, and closets were bare. The kitchen was a giant crater, so they stayed out. Her father's study had a space in the wall where the second safe had been. On the other side of the house, the living room was a bird habitat. That left the boarded-up dining room.

"Looks like the dining room is our last chance to find the vial, grants, or windows."

"Give me your coat," he said as he took off his own. "It's too hot."

She tossed it to him, grateful for the cooler air against her skin. They'd left them on to protect them from debris and mosquitos, but he was right. They were overheating.

He disappeared for a moment and came back with a crowbar from his backpack. Without his jacket, his muscled chest and arms seemed so much more powerful. The hair on his arms barely covered the contracting muscles in his forearms and biceps. The way his wide chest rose with each breath left her light-headed.

Every time she saw him in a T-shirt, she was reminded of how much he'd changed. She'd thought the man she married was hot. What was she supposed to do with the supersized version? *Look at the names and ignore the blue ribbon.*

Still, another voice in her head said, *His strength just saved you.*

She bit her bottom lip and led the way. "I've no idea why my daddy closed up the dining room. I don't ever remember eating in there. He must've been crazy."

"I used to think that, but now I'm not sure." Rafe used the crowbar to pry off the two-by-sixes crossing the double doors. Once they were down, he pushed the doors open, and she flicked on the flashlight. All of the windows were covered by plywood. She held the light while he worked on freeing them, inside and out. An hour later, mottled sunlight filtered in. Except for the interior wall with the fireplace, the octagonal room was made up of twelve ten-foot-tall, stained-glass windows with marble pillars between them.

"Wow," she whispered. "They're beautiful. In a horrible kind of way."

"I can't believe we didn't know these were here."

She went to the farthest window, with the Roman numeral *I,* and pulled out her phone to take photos. A woman on the balcony of an Italian villa was dropping a lily—*her* lily—to a man. They were both dressed in late Renaissance costumes, and behind him stood an oak tree and a yew tree. "She's Italian, but he's English. From the clothes, I'm guessing late fifteen hundreds to early sixteen."

"He looks like he should be in an old pirate movie."

Juliet snapped a picture of a square in the corner with the initials *JL*. "I wonder if JL is the artist."

"Maybe."

She moved to the next one. The second showed a king signing a stack of papers, with the Charleston coastline in the background. "I bet that's King Charles signing the King's Grants."

In the third, a man planted crops in her back meadow. Behind him, a ship was coming in from the ocean.

"That ship's flying a black pirate flag," Rafe said.

Number four had the same pirate ship, but this time the farmer was lying on the ship's deck, his neck slit. She took a photo of the pirate standing over the dead man. "He's holding a vial."

"And look at that second pirate flag flying beneath the skull and crossbones. It's black with a white Capel lily."

She'd never seen that before.

The fifth window was a scene of brightly dressed people in the back meadow dancing around a maypole surrounded by lilies. Dead men lay on the side.

Window number six? A pregnant Puritan woman holding a mortar and pestle with children in the field behind her.

The seventh window showed dead children stacked up around the pregnant Puritan woman, with a broken rope around her neck. "That must be Anne Capel," Juliet said.

"Probably."

In number eight, a pregnant woman held a dead Puritan man while a house burned behind her.

"These are dark." Rafe took her hand, and they stopped

in front of the ninth window. Anne was handing a velvet-lined box with two vials to two men in tricorn hats and capes who were bowing to her. One of the men was giving her a scroll in return.

"At least we know your vial is real," she said.

They went to the tenth window, where a Puritan girl was burning at a stake. Two women stood behind, crying. "One of the crying women is an older Anne."

"Look at eleven," Juliet said. A young man was being dragged away by the same two bowing men, the burnt girl lying in a grave in front of him. "What are they doing?"

"No idea."

The twelfth window showed two pirates on the deck of a pirate ship. The first was an older version of the young man from the previous window. His face was carved out by years in the sun and punctuated by brilliant black eyes. The other man, with a scowl etched in hatred, held two bloody swords. The two bowing men lay at his feet, throats slit. This pirate flag had a red heart with a sword going through it and *sans pitié* on the bottom.

"It's the Prideaux pirate flag, similar to Calum's sigil," she said.

Flying beneath it was a flag with nine vertical stripes: five red, four white.

Rafe pointed to it. "That's the rebellious stripes flag. A sign of the Sons of Liberty."

"This last scene takes place during the Revolution."

"And our pirates were revolutionaries."

"Who are those dead bowing men?"

Rafe's face hardened. "They're Fianna warriors. And I'm guessing they burned the pirate captain's wife, and he got his revenge."

"That's gruesome." Juliet peered closer to take another

photo. "There were Fianna warriors in the seventeenth century?"

"The original Fianna warriors were Irish, pre-Christian Druid soldiers who fought off the Romans during the invasion of Britain."

He'd given her information? A miracle. "Pete said that was nonsense."

"Some of what Garza said was true, some wasn't."

She'd love to know which parts were true, but Rafe would only share when he was ready. Or when she had the right questions. "Why are they in my windows?"

"One of the jobs of the Fianna is to protect secrets. It looks like they're putting Anne and her vial under their protection."

She scrunched down to take more photos with better light. "Is that a normal Fianna thing?"

"The vial must be dangerous for the Fianna to be involved. Maybe the same reason the Prince wants it now."

The room temp had risen, and she wiped her arm across her forehead. "At least we know there were King's Grants and a vial. What I don't get is what my family's history has to do with Nate's operation in Afghanistan."

Rafe met her near the fireplace. "I have no idea."

"Why would anyone give each woman of the unit one of my lilies?"

"My guess is to send a message. The setup of Nate's men was well planned and well funded. It was also personal."

"What do you mean?"

"Nate and his men could've been executed. Instead they were held prisoner for two years. It's expensive to run a POW camp."

"You'd know this from experience?"

He shrugged and ran his hand over the fireplace mantel

that was almost as high as his shoulders. "This isn't just about Nate and his men. Someone wanted to send a message to Kells Torridan."

"You said Kells told Nate about Anne Capel. Does Nate know how Kells found that name?"

"Great question." Rafe blew the dust off his fingers. "And I doubt it. Kells has a reputation for keeping his intel close and his officers in the dark."

She rubbed a damp strand out of her eyes. "Kells always was a controlling bastard."

Rafe wiped his fingers on his pants before tracing her cheek with his thumb. "Kells does what's best for his men. Regardless of whom he hurts."

Rafe dropped his hand, and she exhaled, unaware she'd been holding her breath.

"Are you okay?" he asked softly.

No. "Yes." She held onto the woodwork he'd dusted with his fingers. Then she ran her hands over it, feeling the intricate pattern. "This feels hand-carved."

His flashlight moved across the length. "The design matches the carvings on the staircase's newel posts."

Thunder rocked outside, reminding her their time was short. Wanting a few more moments without the world pressing in, she blew away dust to expose the intricate pattern. "Oak leaves intertwined with yew leaves."

A branch cracked outside, and a man screamed.

Rafe took her hand, and they ran into the foyer.

The man screamed again, and Rafe said, "Stay here." With his rifle ready, he took off.

A chill went down her spine, and she followed him around the side of the house. If there was something to face, they'd do it together. A gunshot splintered the air, and the sound wave silenced the chatter of insects. When she caught up, Rafe stood over a teenage boy with a dead copperhead snake near his leg.

Rafe aimed his rifle at the boy, who scrambled back. "What are you doing here?"

"I was just checkin' out where they found the dead body."

She touched Rafe's shoulder. "He's one of the Marigny boys. Eddie, right?"

"Yeah." The kid, no more than seventeen, raised both hands. "Like I said—"

"I heard what you said," Rafe said. "Leave now. And next time you show up on my wife's land, I won't ask before shooting."

The kid scrambled to his feet, his shirt dirty, his boots worn. "I wasn't doin' nothin'."

"You're trespassing," she said. "And I'll make sure Sheriff Boudreaux knows about it."

"Like Jimmy'll care what you say? Juliet Perdue who lives in a zoo? The little lost girl who married the fucking traitor?"

Rafe shot into the ground near the kid's feet. Eddie turned and ran.

When he disappeared into the woods, she said, "Let him go. He's not worth it."

"Nothing good ever came from the Marigny family."

"People used to say that about the Capel family."

Rafe hooked the rifle on his shoulder, and she walked into his arms. There were still so many things between them, so many unanswered questions, and being with him required a trust she wasn't sure she was capable of. But in this moment, she pretended the past eight years hadn't happened. That they'd lived a happy, married life. That they still loved each other.

～

Rafe held his breath. Her head rested against his chest, and her hands were on his waist. Slowly, he enclosed her in his arms and listened to her breathing. This was the first time she'd initiated physical contact with him that wasn't due to stress or surprise. His body heated up and hardened. While he didn't hide his arousal—he'd never lied to her about how she affected him—he didn't move either. Whatever happened in this next breath had to be up to her.

If given a choice, though, he'd loosen her hair. Since returning, he'd only seen it up, braided, or beneath a wig. He'd yet to see it flowing over her shoulders and caressing her breasts. Bare breasts, preferably. His hard-on pressed against his zipper, ready to get on with that plan. He groaned against her head. She smelled of lavender and sunshine, and he wasn't sure he'd ever let her go.

Thunder rumbled again, and she whispered, "We should leave."

He released her, and his heart wept for the loss while his body ached with unreleased tension. Sighing heavily, he adjusted his rifle and took her hand. The agonizing truth speared him in the gut. No matter what he did with the rest of his life, which probably included dying violently in service to the Fianna, he'd never love another woman.

Like he'd told Escalus, Rafe could leave her if he had to. It wouldn't kill him, but it would destroy him. If all the stars in all the skies fell to earth sending the world into darkness, it wouldn't compare to the desolation of losing Juliet.

CHAPTER 25

NATE LOCKED HIS BIKE, SHRUGGED ON HIS JACKET, AND went inside the police station. When Nate arrived at Juliet's shop with new burner phones, he'd told Pete that Deke was working for Balthasar and got confirmation that Garza had Deke's cell phone. It'd been bad news all around, and now someone needed to get that diary from Garza.

Nate didn't know that much about the Fianna, but he was sure of one thing: when the Fianna realized Garza had the diary, they'd come and Garza would die.

Although Garza wasn't Nate's responsibility, he couldn't face any more casualties.

Nate stopped at the main desk. The din didn't help his headache. "Detective Garza?"

The officer didn't even look up. "Second floor. Third desk on the right."

"Thanks." On the second-floor landing, Nate hit the vending machine for two sodas. He found Garza hovering over a desk, writing, and handed him one. "Detective?"

Garza wore a blue blazer over a white shirt and jeans. He shut the journal and notebook. He was translating the diary. "Wall."

Nate smiled. "Call me Nate."

Garza pointed to a wooden chair. "I was going to ring you."

Nate sat, stretched his legs, and opened his soda. "It's my day off"—which explained his lack of uniform—"and I wanted to check in after this morning's incident at the club. Bad news about that murdered girl."

"Yes, it is." Garza moved the journal into a drawer and locked it. "I dug into Montfort and got an interesting report from a contact."

Thank God Pete had filled Nate in on this part. "I know Montfort was extradited from St. Petersburg and sent to Leavenworth."

Garza sat, opening his can with a *pop-fizz*. "Did you know there was no trial?"

Nate nodded, pretending to look clued in. But he'd noticed something on the far corner of Garza's messy desk and was having a hard time concentrating. An evidence bag with Deke's cell phone. "There's a lot of secrecy surrounding Montfort. I've learned when the Army hides the facts, there's a good reason. You should let it go."

"Montfort isn't an ordinary ex-con. He worked for the Fianna—"

Nate held up a hand. "We don't talk about that group in public."

"If they're assassinating people in my city, I need to know about them. Fuck their secrecy. Fuck their rules. And fuck their warriors. I've been up against worse. I'm not afraid."

Nate leaned forward and lowered his voice. "The Fianna doesn't care. If you get in the Fianna's way, its warriors will eliminate you."

"I'm supposed to let dead bodies pile up?"

"I didn't say that." Nate heard voices and pointed to a group of cops facing a wall covered in notes. "What's going on?"

"My chief's put every extra detective onto this zombie heroin task force. Thirty-four people have died, hundreds are in the hospital, and our cages are full of silent dealers."

"You're not working the heroin epidemic?"

"No." Garza tapped his fingers on his desk. "I don't know how yet, but I'll prove Montfort is responsible for Escalus's death."

"No way Montfort could've pulled the trigger and made it to where he was found."

"Sounds like you're on Montfort's side."

"I'm on the side that keeps us both alive." At least that was the truth. "I'd help if you had evidence connecting Montfort to both murders. But you don't."

"Two people—Sally and a John Doe we found near the club—were killed with a misericord within thirty-six hours. I know the misericord is a close-quarters combat weapon favored by Fianna warriors, and I believe Montfort is one of them."

"Do you have proof?"

Garza rummaged through his papers and found an eight-by-ten photo.

Nate's heart rate kicked up. "Who are they?"

"The one in the middle brokering the peace is Escalus, the man killed yesterday on Capel land. The one in the wool coat is the Fianna's leader."

Garza handed Nate a magnifier to hold over the Prince's photo. Holy. Shit. "The third man with his face hidden?"

"Montfort."

Obviously. Nate would know that pissed-off attitude anywhere. "It's not a clear photo. It wouldn't hold up in court." He stood and accidentally dropped the photo on the floor.

Garza retrieved it and threw it on the desk. "Too bad."

Nate clapped him on the shoulder. "I'll keep an eye on Montfort. If anything strange happens, I'll let you know. In the meantime—" Nate pointed to the journal hidden within the desk. If he couldn't take the journal, the least he could do was offer a warning. "Leave the Fianna alone. Before they figure out who you are."

Garza stood, arms crossed. "Is it true they bow before killing?"

"I hope not." With a nod, Nate turned and bumped into a detective standing behind him. Shorter than Nate, the detective wore khakis, a white shirt, and a red tie, which seemed out of place with his chest holster. The gun accessorized his frown. "Excuse me."

"This is my partner, Detective Elliot," Garza said.

Nate held out his hand. "Nice to meet you."

Instead of shaking, Elliot glanced at his phone.

Okay. Feeling the animosity, Nate double-timed it downstairs. Outside, he called Pete.

"Hey," Pete said. "Get the diary?"

"No. But I think I just ID'd the Prince."

"Seriously?" Pete spoke in hushed tones, as if in awe.

"Yes," Nate said, unlocking his bike. "This might be the leverage Kells needs to keep you out of jail. I also took something else. Deke's cell phone."

Balthasar studied the map on the table in the safe house and, thanks to Deke, had Escalus's laptop turned on and files open. The Prince had been right. Escalus had not only promised to give the vial to Eddie's cousin, Escalus had coordinated the influx of heroin into Savannah.

Unfortunately, the laptop held no clues about the vial, the windows Eddie had sent photos of, or the map obtained from Walker. From Escalus's notes, the cousin was a low-level player who'd made inquiries about the vial and had told Escalus about the manor's windows. Unfortunately, now the cousin was Balthasar's only source of intel about the vial. That meant Balthasar had to play whatever game the cousin wanted in exchange for info.

Working with Eddie's cousin wasn't a Fianna-approved plan, but considering Balthasar was proving his own innocence, he'd risk the Prince's anger.

Deke moaned from his cot. "I need another pill."

"No." Balthasar positioned his compass. From what he'd overheard at the preservation office, the pretty historian didn't know much about the map. Although she was correct about the compass rose being off by thirty degrees. "You're in pain from the withdrawal. Not the beating."

"Fuck you." Deke curled up on his side, protecting the bandage over his ear. "I did what you asked. I followed Pete and his girlfriend."

Balthasar despised weak men. After barely surviving the Gauntlet, Romeo had stumbled, on his own, to the first aid tent. "If you'd like, Montfort can finish what he started."

"No!" Deke's lips pulled away from his teeth. "That bastard has serious anger issues."

"Don't we all." Balthasar clicked open a file named *SEBASTIAN* and found pages from a warrior's journal. According to Escalus's notes, Sebastian had once been a Prince who'd searched for Anne Capel's vial. Because of his failure, Sebastian lost his title and disappeared.

How was it Balthasar had never heard of Sebastian?

Eddie arrived with brown bags smelling like hickory smoke. "I got Angel's BBQ."

"I'll take two sandwiches," Deke said from the bed.

"Dude, I only had money for four. B gets first dibs."

"Deke may have mine," Balthasar said, still reading about Sebastian.

Eddie dumped the bags on the weapons table. "Did you contact my cousin?"

"Yes." Balthasar shut his laptop and stood to stretch his tight biceps. He wished he'd taken time to go for a run this morning. He needed to work off this restlessness before tonight's event. "Your cousin wasn't happy with Escalus's death or my taking Escalus's place. Still, despite your cousin's suspicions about my ability to retrieve the vial, he's giving me a chance to prove my loyalty." The words burned. Fianna warriors were only loyal to each other and their Prince. They proved themselves to no one.

Eddie shrugged. "My cousin tests everyone who works for him." He opened the food bag and popped fries in his mouth. "He called me to check up on you and give me the scoop about tonight. But I vouched. Told him you were more badass than Escalus."

Balthasar bit his tongue until he tasted blood. The idea that a Fianna warrior needed anyone's recommendation was ridiculous. But since now was not the time for pride, he said, "Thank you."

"No prob." Eddie handed a sandwich wrapped in foil to Deke, then pulled a box of blond hair dye out of another bag.

"What's that for?" Deke asked, already two bites into his food.

"Your disguise. B's orders." Eddie sat on the shabby couch to eat from the bag. "Do we have what we need for tonight? My cousin's plan was very specific."

Although Balthasar resented being forced to do anything, especially work with amateurs, his cathedral stunt had only brought Juliet and Romeo closer together. That left Balthasar with few options. Hence Eddie's cousin's plan.

Moving into the corner, Balthasar stopped near a table covered with a sheet. He whipped it off, exposing two stacks of C-4. "We're ready."

CHAPTER 26

JULIET CLUTCHED HER PORTFOLIO, AND PHILIP HELD OPEN the door of 700 Drayton, the restaurant in the Mansion on Forsyth Park hotel. Rafe had stayed outside to call Pete.

Both Philip and Rafe had arrived at her apartment to pick her up and, after recovering from her shock at seeing Rafe in dark wool dress pants, black button-down shirt, and navy silk tie, she'd convinced them they could take one car.

As they went upstairs, the scent of roast chicken made her stomach gurgle.

Philip glanced back. "You look beautiful."

"Thanks." The silver lace shift was the only fancy thing she owned. Months ago, when Dessie's Couture opened across the courtyard from Juliet's Lily, she'd been tempted to go in. But there was no way she could've afforded couture prices. Even worse, if Calum had heard she'd gone in there—not an impossibility since he owned the building—he would've insisted on buying her something. While she wasn't too proud to ask him for business help, she'd never accept his charity.

They entered the cocktail lounge, a dimly lit, elegant space with a granite bar and leather couches. Beyond the bar was the restaurant with tables set up in a hexagonal room. Picture windows overlooked Forsyth Park and its fountain across the street. She and Philip had to wait for their drinks. The bar was unusually crowded for a weeknight.

Carina, in a red silk wrap dress, stood nearby with her champagne, surrounded by men. A diamond necklace sparkled, and crystals lined her stilettos heels. Even though

Juliet loved her own dress, she felt like a country girl when compared to Carina's sophistication.

"Hello, beautiful." Calum appeared in a perfectly tailored tuxedo and dropped a kiss on her cheek.

No doubt Calum and Carina were the two most elegant people in town. "What are you doing here? I thought you weren't helping me with your sister."

"I'm not." Calum nodded to a corner where Mr. Delacroix and Detective Garza talked. "Tonight's the Savannah Friends of the Police dinner downstairs."

Philip arrived carrying two glasses of wine, and she took one. It was cold and delicious.

"I'm off." Calum nodded toward the dining room. "I want to speak to the Habersham sisters before dinner."

Juliet watched while Calum went to the table near the biggest window. He bowed over both of the sisters' hands.

"I wonder what it's like," Philip said, "to be one of the richest people in the city."

"Those things don't matter." She sipped her wine, wishing Philip would stop comparing himself to others. "Look at Eugene Wilkins. He had everything and died a horrible death."

"Agreed," Mr. Delacroix said, coming up behind her. "I hope you don't mind my joining you. I couldn't help but overhear."

Tonight, Mr. Delacroix wore black dress pants with a white dinner jacket and bow tie.

"Not at all." She smiled. "Philip and I were discussing life goals."

"One of mine," Delacroix held up his whiskey, "was always to be independent. Never to rely on others financially or emotionally. I've always taken risks others were afraid to face."

Philip nodded. "You wanted more than you've had?"

"Yes. More money. More experiences." Mr. Delacroix smiled at her. "More women. For some, it's the adrenaline rush that makes them feel alive. Feel more like a man."

She studied her wine glass. So much of what he said reminded her of Rafe's letter.

"I want to build a life with a fulfilling career and a family," Philip said.

Delacroix clapped Philip's shoulder. "I've seen your designs for my new mansion. It's why I chose your architecture firm and why I'm asking you to lead the design group. You were the only one with the guts to suggest we rebuild while at the same time recovering the windows and moldings and other elements. It's brilliant."

Philip smiled wide.

"That's wonderful," Juliet said to Philip. "Your first big project from the ground up."

"I haven't forgotten you, Juliet," Mr. Delacroix said. "I like the idea of you two working together to rebuild that property."

If she had to stay up for the next two days, she'd have those renditions done by Friday. "Thank you, Mr. Delacroix."

"Here's to the new Delacroix Mansion on Pulaski Square." Mr. Delacroix held up his glass, and they toasted.

A huge clap of thunder rolled, and the lights flickered.

"Looks like that storm has arrived," Delacroix said. "I'm off to dinner. I hope you celebrate this evening."

"We will," Philip said. "Thank you."

Once they were alone, Juliet clinked glasses with him again. "I'm so happy for you."

"What are we celebrating?" Rafe's voice cut through her like a razor over glass. She knew the cut was there but didn't want to move or else she'd break in two.

Philip's smile evaporated. "I got the job to rebuild Prideaux House."

"Congratulations." Rafe picked up the portfolio she'd rested against the wall. "Let's talk at our table. Carina is with the Habersham sisters, and it looks like Calum is annoying her."

Juliet agreed. The last thing she needed was a sibling argument to ruin her chances of getting paid.

Rafe took her hand and led her to the Habersham sisters' table. "I hate to interrupt," he said, "but I wanted to tell the sisters how lovely they look tonight."

Juliet didn't roll her eyes. But she wanted to.

Miss Nell turned a few shades pinker than her silk dress. Miss Beatrice held out her hand for Rafe to kiss.

Carina, standing nearby, tilted her head. "You haven't changed at all, Rafe Montfort."

"Carina, darling," Calum said in his deepest Southern drawl, "it's not nice to tease a man recently released from prison."

"Rafe has always taken care of himself," Carina said. "I'm sure he's not afraid of things that go bump in the night. Unless he's the one doing the bumping?"

"I only bump things in the night that deserve it," Rafe said.

Carina narrowed her gaze.

"I believe our table is ready." Philip waved to the four-top with the hovering waiter.

"Please, Rafe," Miss Nell said. "Would you, Juliet, and Philip join us for dinner?"

"Remember, Nell?" Miss Beatrice said. "We're going to that dinner downstairs. We got the table to stay away from the crowds in the bar."

"That's right," Miss Nell said. "We're not comfortable in bars."

"*You're* not comfortable in bars," Beatrice corrected.

Calum offered the ladies a short bow. "I'd be honored to escort you both."

Miss Beatrice nodded. "We'd be delighted."

"You're going to that police dinner?" Carina said to Calum. "Whatever for?"

Calum grinned. "To make new acquaintances and strengthen old friendships. Something you might want to do before Election Day."

Carina opened her mouth, and then closed it.

"Will we see you later?" Juliet asked Calum. "Philip has good news."

Calum nodded. "I heard. I think you'll do a wonderful job rebuilding the mansion."

"Rebuilding the mansion?" Miss Beatrice said, taking his arm. "Surely not mine."

Calum led the sisters away. "Did you hear Vivienne Beaumont is coming to town? She's hosting a salon at the Ravenels'. It will be *un grand scandal.*"

"*Noooo,*" Miss Nell said. "I want to hear *everything.*"

Once they left, the waiter led them to their corner table. Juliet leaned her portfolio against the window overlooking the square. Rafe and Carina sat on either side, and Philip was across, frowning.

Carina ordered champagne and appetizers. "I haven't eaten all day. It's hard being on the campaign trail and talking to random people about their pathetic lives."

Rafe winked at Juliet. Carina had always been like this.

The ensuing silence fueled the awkwardness between the brothers. Between Carina and everyone else. Juliet decided to get things started. "Carina—"

"Juliet," Carina said sharply, hiding behind the menu. "I don't want to talk about money. *C'est très impoli.*"

"It's even ruder not to pay your bills. Especially ones you're contracted for."

Carina snapped the menu shut, and the lights dimmed. "I hope there's a generator."

"There is." The waiter appeared with four glasses of champagne and left the bottle. "I'll be back with your appetizers."

"Good." Carina played with her flute.

Juliet wanted to get to work, but Rafe reached beneath the table and squeezed her hand.

"Since you don't want to talk money," Philip said, "what do you want to talk about?"

"How about the fact that Juliet is the reason my brother was sent to boarding school when he was eleven? And when he came back at sixteen he was so traumatized he barely spoke?" Carina's smile was so tight Juliet thought her lips would snap back.

"Instead," Philip said, "let's talk about your party."

Juliet appreciated Philip's attempt to divert Carina, but Juliet knew it wouldn't work. "Calum being sent away wasn't my fault."

"You weren't living in secret in his room at our Isle of Hope plantation for two weeks? You weren't stealing our food? Sleeping in his closet?"

"It wasn't like that."

"Things are never your fault. I told Eugene I didn't want him to give you the square project. You're the sleeping princess who refuses to wake. By day, you're the gardener—"

"Landscape architect."

"By night, you're nothing but a strip—"

"What was Eugene doing in the back meadow when he died?" Rafe's voice cut through the tension.

Carina's shoulders popped up so fast the diamonds

around her neck threw prisms. Then she glared at Juliet. "He was helping *you*."

"How?"

"Don't play the naive heroine. He was looking for your lily while Calum searched for your King's Grants."

Juliet put her glass down so she wouldn't snap the stem. "Excuse me?"

"Calum didn't tell you?" Carina snorted elegantly. "Eugene was part of some group, along with Grady Mercer, who devoted their lives to eradicating your lily."

"Why?" Philip asked.

"Because it's poisonous." Contempt laced Carina's voice. "It's the lily Anne Capel used to poison all those kids."

"That's crazy," Philip said.

"What do the King's Grants have to do with anything?" Rafe asked.

"King's Grants were pieces of land granted by King Charles to the Lords Proprietors who ruled the Carolina Colonies, including parts of Georgia and the Savannah area."

"We already know that," Juliet said.

"Well." Carina spoke as if they were all in kindergarten. "Since nothing is free, those grants were issued with stipulations. If the owners haven't broken the stipulations, the grants supersede federal authority."

Philip frowned. "What stipulations?"

"Like the land owner could never build a barn. Or maybe they couldn't own horses or raise sheep. Some could own land to the low-tide mark, others to the high-tide mark. My guess is they were rules set up by the Lords Proprietors to keep certain people from doing certain things." Carina paused to dab a napkin against her red lips. "As long as the owners haven't broken the stipulations, the government can't take their land. Since Juliet's family has held the land for over three hundred years, if she sold it now, the federal government would take up to forty percent due to wetlands regulations."

Philip leaned his elbows on the table. "But if she has the King's Grants—"

"And can prove she's never broken the stipulations, not only would she own all of the granted land, but she'd probably own it out to the low-tide mark. Since King's Grants supersede state and federal rules, the government can't appropriate her land or regulate her usage of it. Ever."

Juliet hated asking Carina for anything but did anyway. "If I sell?"

Carina shrugged. "If the grants allow a sale, then you sign them to the new owner."

"Do you know what the stipulations on my land are?"

"No. That's why Eugene and Calum wanted to find them. Gerald believed one stipulation was that the lily never grow on the Isle, so he asked Grady, Eugene, and Calum to help. All to protect your inheritance." That last bit was laced with a sneer.

Juliet sat back and sighed. "Why didn't Calum tell me any of this?"

Carina took another sip of champagne and pursed her lips. "Ask Calum."

Rafe, who was still holding Juliet's hand, shifted it to his thigh. Heat burned through his pants, his muscles beneath her fingers bunched, and his foot tapped.

He vibrated and held on firmly, as if forcing her body to resonate at his hotter, higher frequency. She drank her champagne and forced herself to remember why they were there.

"I understand Calum's interest, but why was Eugene involved?" Philip asked Carina.

It was a good thing Philip could speak because Juliet had lost the ability to make simple sounds.

The waiter dropped off plates of appetizers, and Carina ate a mushroom cap. "Eugene loved the stories of the Prideaux/Prioleau pirates and the legends of Anne Capel and the Prioleau sigil."

Juliet took another sip, and the bubbles tickled the back of her throat. "I saw your sigil today." She coughed, trying to gain some traction in her voice. But it was difficult with Rafe moving her hand…higher. "In a window in Prideaux House."

Carina waved a hand, her diamond rings glittering. "Not unlike the Prioleau mark Calum pays people to paint all over this city." She handed her glass to Philip to refill. "During the golden age of piracy, the Prideaux pirates dominated the coastline. Many citizens were hostile, but those who raised the Prideaux flag or a black flag with a white Capel lily were allies. Eugene's fascination with our history got him killed."

Juliet switched to water, except she spilled it because her free hand shook. The other was still held captive against Rafe's thigh.

"You're worried about Calum." Rafe spoke casually, as if he wasn't at all affected by her touch. "That's why you hired Detective Garza to look into Eugene's death."

Carina took her refilled glass from Philip. "Yes."

Lightning flashed, and Juliet looked out the window. The park's lights were on, and the street was empty except for a man in a hooded coat standing near the fountain. He stared in her direction, but when she blinked, he was gone. Yet, in that moment before he disappeared, the man bowed.

CHAPTER 27

RAFE SAT BACK, ENJOYING THE FEEL OF JULIET'S HAND AGAINST his thigh. While he dreamed of more contact, he cherished this moment because it might be all he'd get.

Juliet's face paled. "Rafe—"

"Excuse me." Nate appeared and gripped Rafe's shoulder. "Can we talk?"

Rafe raised Juliet's hand that'd been on his leg and kissed the palm. "I'll be back."

Once in the bar, Nate ordered a ginger ale while Rafe ordered scotch. "What's up?" He wanted to return to Juliet.

"Did Pete tell you I ran into Balthasar?"

"Yes. Pete filled me in on what happened to you at the Savannah Preservation Office and police station. He also gave me your new phone numbers and told me he's taking Samantha to her third job." Rafe swallowed his drink and let the burn trail down his throat. "When Samantha is done, they're going to the motel. Pete doesn't want either of you to be alone. He's a good guy."

Nate nodded and leaned against the bar. "The SPO had some info about the Isle but nothing new."

"Not surprised." Rafe ordered another drink. It'd been a long time since he'd tasted Calum's forty-year-old favorite. "Pete told me about the trials on Friday."

"How can the government bring charges against Torridan's team? They weren't in the country and had nothing to do with what happened."

"Torridan's team handled the planning, and Kells is

your CO, regardless of whether he was the theater commander. Even though Kells's team wasn't there, they were
involved." The bartender placed Rafe's new drink on a
napkin, along with a bowl of pretzels. "I still think this
clusterfuck is personal. This was planned with the goal of
bringing down Kells Torridan."

"That's what Jack Keeley told me before they threw him
in jail with the other men."

"Jack's a smart and experienced soldier. I've never
trusted Kells, but I trust Jack."

Nate ran a hand over his head. His long hair was still tied
behind his neck with a rubber band. His green eyes were hazy,
as if he'd gone without shut-eye for a few days. "I tried to get
that journal from Garza, but no luck. Although I warned him."

"If Balthasar knows Garza's read the journal, it's too
late." Rafe savored his sip. "We have our own problems."

"Except I don't know what to do next."

Rafe gripped Nate's shoulder. "Get some sleep.
Tomorrow meet me at the apartment across from Juliet's
Lily. You know it?"

Nate nodded.

"Oh-nine-hundred hours. Bring Pete. We'll figure out
a plan."

When Nate didn't respond, Rafe exhaled loudly. "What?"

"Garza called an hour ago. He knows I'm not your PO.
He also knows my real name, rank, and serial number. As
well as Kells Torridan and the 7th Special Forces Group."

Rafe finished half his drink. Screw savoring. "How'd
that happen?"

"Garza's partner saw an employment photo with my
name at the club. Since every cop is busy tonight, Garza
wants me downtown tomorrow morning. Seven a.m.
Otherwise he'll issue a warrant."

"Well," Rafe said on a sigh. "*Shit.*"

Nate popped a pretzel into his mouth and mentally walked through the mess he'd made of the day. He couldn't even decrypt Deke's phone. "There's something else. I saw a photo of you, Escalus, and the Prince. Escalus was pleading with the Prince on your behalf. Not unlike how I'd get between you and Torridan."

Rafe raised an eyebrow.

Nate raised one back. "I realized something. I think I know who the Prince is."

"Those who talk—and hear—die."

"I'm already marked. I've seen a man bow."

"We don't know that." Rafe grabbed a few pretzels. "If you tell Kells, he'll be marked too."

"I have another option." Nate watched the ice in his glass melt. "Balthasar made me an offer. Join him and he'll give me the intel I need to free my team."

"Balthasar doesn't know shit. Don't let him screw with your mind." Rafe finished his scotch. "I'm headed for the restroom. We'll meet tomorrow. Now go sleep. You look like hell."

Rafe left, and Nate finished his soda, the ice hitting his lips. Maybe Rafe was right. Nate could take another pill and sleep. That would leave one more pill for tomorrow. Time enough to fess up to having given away the map.

"Nate?" The female voice sounded hesitant.

Juliet appeared with her hair pulled back in long curls. Her silver dress showed off her slim figure. She'd changed since he'd interrogated her. Her eyes seemed darker and older, almost like Rafe's, as if the world was too heavy a burden. "Rafe is in the restroom."

"I'm here for another drink while Philip tries to get Carina to understand the importance of paying her bills."

Pete—having heard from Samantha—had filled Nate in about Juliet's money problems and Carina's bitchiness. "Is it working?"

Juliet shrugged. "Philip has always been good with Carina."

The bartender handed her a glass of wine. Her fingers played with the stem, and she looked everywhere except at Nate. "Rafe told me what happened in Afghanistan. I'm sorry."

"Rafe shouldn't have told you. It's classified."

"I know how to keep a secret," she said sharply. "I never told anyone about what you and Colonel Torridan did to me."

Nate watched her fingers trace the delicate glass stem. "Calum knows."

She met Nate's gaze, her eyes wary. "How?"

"I assumed you told him."

"No." She looked away again. "I haven't told anyone. Rafe doesn't know."

Nate swallowed the ice, and the cold hit his molar with the metal filling. Pain fired up the nerves. He gritted his teeth and closed his eyes. "Juliet?"

"Yes?"

He opened his eyes and met her stare. "I'm sorry." There was so much more he wanted to say, but he'd never been great with words. "Really sorry."

She wiped her lips with a napkin. "Was the interrogation your idea?"

"No. It was Torridan's. For the record, Jack Keeley was against it."

She half smiled. "I always liked Jack."

"Everyone likes Jack." Too bad he was in jail. "He thought interrogating you was barbaric."

"Then why didn't he stop it?"

"He wasn't in charge."

"And you were following orders?"

Nate crossed his arms over his chest and leaned his back against the bar. "This isn't an excuse, but it was a god-awful time. First Colin disappeared. Then we discovered Rafe left to join the Fianna, and the unit was devastated. We were paranoid and scared and watching each other, trying to guess who'd be the next to leave."

"I didn't know Colin disappeared. What happened to him?"

"No idea. Went out on a mission and never came back. Then Rafe went to look for him, and the next thing we knew he'd sent us some bullshit letter about needing more from life, more adventure, because apparently being an elite soldier in the U.S. Army had too many rules. He was suffocating." Nate made air quotes around the last word.

She swirled her wine. "I received a letter saying the same things. How he was tired of his life, of all the rules, and wanted out." She shook her head. "I remember how he fought with everyone. His arguments with Torridan."

"You want to know why the whole story is bullshit?" At her nod, Nate leaned in to whisper, "Because I've never seen a man more in love with a woman than Rafe is with you. Even if he hated us—the A-team he'd spent years training with—he never hated you. You were—and always will be—his reason for breathing."

"I've seen his tattoos."

"Everybody knows about those. Hell, what with the Gauntlet, tattoos, and prison time, Rafe is an urban legend in Special Forces. But the more I learn, the more I question what's true."

She wiped her cheek with two fingers. "All those names—"

Nate took her hand and squeezed. "Pay attention to the facts we know: He made it through the brutal, medieval Fianna training. He survived the Gauntlet and became a full-fledged warrior, a damned hard thing to do considering the ninety percent death rate. He went to a Russian prison and survived. Then he emerged from Leavenworth as if it were a summer vacation. Because he certainly doesn't act like a man who's been imprisoned for years."

She reclaimed her hand but shifted closer. "Pete said the legend of the Fianna was a story told around army campfires."

"There's always an element of truth in fairy tales." A thunderclap shook the building. The lights flickered off and came back on.

"That doesn't mean—"

"Rafe and I have a lot of shit between us." Nate flexed his hands against his thighs. The returning restlessness meant incoming seizures. "We haven't spoken in eight years. Last night we had things to settle, but the first thing Rafe asked about was you. That means one thing. You're the reason he's back. You're the reason he's playing these games with the Prince. For Rafe, everything is—and always has been—about you."

Juliet took another drink. Could what Nate said be true? "You don't know that."

"Rafe is in love with you," Nate said. "Whether you believe it or not."

"I'm glad someone's talking sense to our girl." Miss Beatrice came up next to Nate and patted his arm. "Although I'm sure there's a lucky woman waiting for *you* to notice her."

"Not at the moment, ma'am," Nate said, smiling.

"Miss Beatrice," Juliet said, "this is Nate Walker. Nate, Miss Beatrice Habersham."

Nate took Miss Beatrice's hand and kissed the back of it. She blushed but didn't pout or flutter like Miss Nell. Miss Beatrice was too confident for such flirtations.

"It's a pleasure to make your acquaintance, ma'am."

"And yours, Mr. Walker. Are you a friend of Juliet's?"

He glanced at her, his green eyes filled with apology and shame. "I am."

The deep scar on his cheek made her realize that none of them were getting out of this unscathed.

Miss Beatrice took her wine from the bartender. "Then convince Juliet that true love only comes around once in a woman's life."

Juliet frowned. "That didn't end so well for me."

Miss Beatrice patted Juliet's hand. "Your story barely had a chance to start."

"Quite true," Nate said to Miss Beatrice. "May I buy your drink?"

"No, thank you. I forgot something in the dining room. I was also hoping to have a word in private with Juliet, if you don't mind?"

"Not at all," he said. "I was just leaving. And Juliet, I'll see you and Rafe tomorrow morning to, uh, finish our project."

"Okay." Juliet bit her lip, debating whether to say more. Maybe instead of worrying about how not to get hurt, they should focus on minimizing the scar tissue. "Thank you for your apology. Maybe things aren't the way they seem."

Nate nodded and headed for the stairs until being cornered by Detective Garza.

Meanwhile, Miss Beatrice took something out of her purse and dropped it in Juliet's hand. A man's gold ring. "Do you recognize it?"

Juliet held it up. Worn engravings decorated the ring. "Was this my daddy's?"

"Yes. Although your mother didn't live long after your birth, your father never got over losing her. She was everything to him."

"More so than me." She hated the whiny-sounding words, but they were the truth.

"Your father was never good at expressing emotion, yet toward the end of his life, his every thought was about your safety. He asked me to give this to you when the time was right."

"Why tonight?"

"Because tonight I realized you love Rafe."

The room suddenly felt too hot and too small. A tingly feeling started in her arms, ending at her fingertips. "I don't."

"Rafe broke your heart, but he's back now. Don't throw away this chance because you're afraid to love again. Or afraid to rely on another. Be brave, my dear. Be strong. Be dauntless."

Juliet slipped the ring on her thumb. She'd had a forever-and-always kind of love, and it died a brutal, bloody death.

Miss Beatrice kissed her on the cheek and left for the dining room.

Juliet pushed away her glass. It'd been a long day, and she had a buzz from the alcohol. She didn't normally drink, yet she'd had two glasses of wine and a flute of champagne without eating dinner.

"Are you alright?" Rafe put a hand on her lower back and slipped in next to her.

Warmth traveled up her spine, and she nodded. Would she ever not respond when he touched her? "I needed a break while Philip sweet-talks Carina."

"Philip was always good with her." Rafe kissed her cheek, and his breath brushed her ear. "You look beautiful—"

A loud boom ripped through the room, and the force threw her to the floor. Rafe landed on top, his body protecting her from the exploding mirror behind the bar. The lights went out, and another blast knocked over tables, chairs, and drinks. The shock wave threw glass and splintered wood from the dining room into the lounge. Screams echoed, and she covered her ears. Debris fell from the ceiling, and a moment later everything sounded heavy and hushed. Emergency lights in the corners kicked on, adding an orange sheen to the room now covered in dust and debris.

Rafe helped her to her feet. Everyone around them was shouting, running toward the exit. Some were covered in blood. Others were disguised by drywall dust and dirt.

He dragged her to the other side of the bar. "Stay here. I'm going into the dining room."

"I'm going with you." She followed him and could barely make out the situation. The safety lights helped but also cast shadows. Four windows were gone, and across the street the park lights were out. The buildings around the square had gone black.

Driving rain made the dirty floor slippery. She tasted ash and ran over to their now upside-down table and found Philip on top of Carina beneath the table, pinned down by a ceiling beam. They were both covered with dirt and blood.

She reached Philip, and he lifted his head. "Carina's hurt."

Nate and Detective Garza rushed in while Rafe went around to the other side and tried to pry off the beam.

"Here," Nate said, "I can help."

"You two get the beam, I'll take Philip," Garza said. "Juliet, hold Carina's head steady."

When Rafe said, "One, two, three," they lifted the beam high enough for Garza to pick up Philip.

Juliet coughed into her shoulder. Her eyes burned. "Shouldn't you wait for the paramedics?"

"We have to evacuate," Rafe said, still holding the beam. "We can't rule out another explosion."

"Hurry," Nate grunted. "This thing is heavy."

After moving Philip to safety, Garza came back for Carina. Juliet took Carina's shoulders while he dragged out her legs. She was covered with cuts, but there didn't appear to be any broken bones. Garza lifted her into his arms, and Rafe and Nate lowered the beam. The floor shuddered, and more of the ceiling tiles fell.

She crawled to Philip, her hands scraping on glass and splintered wood. "You're bleeding." She opened his jacket and saw a gash on his abdomen.

"Shit," Philip muttered before his eyes fluttered.

"It's okay, Little Brother," Rafe said. "Can you stand?"

Nate and Rafe helped get Philip upright.

"Juliet?" Rafe adjusted Philip's weight against his shoulder. "Use the flashlight on your phone to lead us out of here."

Using her light, Juliet illuminated the path into the bar. People were crying and stumbling around. She turned to check on Philip when her light landed on a nearby table covered with a piece of steel. Miss Beatrice was buried.

Juliet rushed over. Miss Beatrice couldn't be dead. Except when Juliet shifted the debris, she saw a piece of pipe had impaled Miss Beatrice's chest. She stared up, her eyes blank.

Juliet covered her mouth, holding in a scream.

"Rafe?" Nate asked. "Can you carry your brother alone?"

"Yes." Rafe shifted his body under Philip's shoulder.

Nate came over to pick Miss Beatrice up. He was as gentle as he could be. "Let's go."

With Juliet's light, they tumbled out of the ruined dining room into the bar's chaos. People were rushing to the stairs as sirens blared.

"Juliet," Garza said. "To the right, on the other side of the bar. There's another stairway."

She found the stairwell and finally got them to the back door.

Outside, the rain slashed her arms and soaked her dress. She breathed in fresh air and coughed. Ambulances had set up in a semicircle, and fire trucks pulled in. First responders were installing a triage tent with tables and beds. People huddled in groups, all with wide-eyed stares.

Two EMTs brought a gurney, and Garza laid Carina on it. A third EMT held an umbrella over her as they rolled away. A firefighter helped Rafe carry Philip and get him under the tent to lay him on a table.

Nate carried Miss Beatrice to a bed beneath the tent and laid her down. Then he covered her with a sheet.

"Juliet!" Samantha and Pete were on the other side of the barricade. Samantha, ignoring the rain, ran to Juliet. She threw herself into Juliet's arms, and they both sank to the ground. Juliet was vaguely aware of Pete holding the umbrella over them.

"What happened?" Pete asked.

"An explosion," Juliet said. "Nate is with Miss Beatrice. Carina is unconscious. Philip is hurt."

"Where's my sister?" Calum appeared holding an umbrella, except it was still closed. His tux was covered with dirt and soaked through, his tie gone.

Rafe took his arm. "Carina is on her way to the hospital.

She's unconscious but no apparent broken bones. They're checking her for internal bleeding."

Juliet left Samantha to hug Calum. "Are you alright?"

"I was lucky," Calum said against her wet hair. "Delacroix and I were outside having a cigar when the explosion happened. We evacuated the private dining room and gathered everyone in the park. That's where the cops are setting up their control center. But the power is out in most of the historic district."

"Are there a lot of wounded?" Samantha asked.

"More scared than wounded," Calum said.

Juliet laid a hand on his arm. "Miss Beatrice. She was in the dining room when it happened. She didn't make it."

Calum swallowed, and his eyes went shiny. "Miss Nell—"

"I don't know how to tell her."

Calum let her go but still held her hand. "Dammit, Rafe. What happened?"

"That's what I want to know." Garza joined their circle, his mouth tight and grim.

Rafe opened Calum's umbrella to hold it over Juliet, and then placed a hand on her shoulder. She was grateful for his warmth and the respite from the rain. "An explosion."

"Don't be a dick," Garza said. "You know as well as I do this comes back to you."

"Bullshit," Nate said. "It could've been a ruptured gas main."

"Know what's bullshit?" Garza's face turned into a snarl. "And a crime? Pretending to be a parole officer. How about we talk about that downtown."

"You've no evidence," Calum said. "Rafe's release was legal. I have the paperwork. He wasn't issued a PO. He was a free man when he left Leavenworth."

"So why lie?"

"It seemed like a good idea at the time," Calum said. "And Nate isn't meeting you tomorrow morning at the station. At least not without his lawyer."

"This is what you Prioleaus do? Manipulate situations to work in your favor?"

"Why not?"

Garza put his hands on his hips, but Juliet interrupted the argument. "Please. Can we not fight about this now?"

"There are still people inside who need help," Nate said. "Pete and I are trained—"

"No," Garza said. "Check on Philip and Carina at the hospital, and then go to bed. Because, trust me, tomorrow you'll have a lot of explaining to do."

"You're right." Rafe spoke so harshly they all stared at him. "Everyone, including Garza, meets us at Calum's apartment tomorrow. Oh-nine-hundred. Don't be late."

CHAPTER 28

Two hours later in Calum's apartment, after showering and changing into yoga pants, a cami, and a zippered sweatshirt, Juliet said, "Thank you, Calum," and hung up.

She leaned back in the window seat and watched Rafe make dinner in the galley kitchen. He cooked on a camping stove because the power was still out. Clouds hid the cathedral's steeple while candles cast an intimate glow.

She opened the window even more, hoping for a breeze. Without AC, the humid air settled on everything, and the night-blooming jasmine plant on the kitchen table filled the room with a sensual fragrance. At least the thunderstorm had moved on. In the distance, police and fire truck lights flashed.

According to the news on Calum's shortwave radio, some citizens had taken advantage of the outage. That's why Rafe had insisted they go back to the apartment instead of staying at the hospital. Here he had weapons.

Her father's duffel bag was near the couch between Antoine's Tailoring shopping bags. When they'd returned from the hospital, they'd grabbed her gun from her apartment, adding it to her father's armory. She hoped they wouldn't need it.

Rafe put bowls of soup on the table bordering the kitchen and family room. He'd showered and changed into black sweatpants and a long-sleeved T-shirt. He added spoons and napkins. "What did Calum say?"

She stretched her aching muscles. "Philip is sleeping.

After stitching him up, they gave him pain meds. He'll stay in the hospital until tomorrow and should be fine as long as there's no infection. Did you talk to Pops?"

"Yes. I told him not to drive tonight. He'll come tomorrow to take Philip back to the Isle to recuperate."

"Calum offered his house. He said both Pops and Philip can stay as long as they want."

Rafe brought over a plate of buttered bread. "I'll let him know. And Carina?"

"No internal bleeding, but she has a mild concussion."

"And Miss Nell?"

Juliet rubbed her forehead. She wanted to forget seeing Miss Beatrice's broken body, but the image of Nate carrying her downstairs would remain. "Calum was with Miss Nell when she ID'd the body. She had to be sedated, and he made sure they admitted her to the hospital. He didn't want her to be alone."

Rafe took Juliet in his arms. She fit so easily, tucked beneath his chin with his arms around her. She rested her head against his chest. He'd insisted she pack a few things and stay with him. He didn't want her to be alone in the dark, and she didn't want that either. Since the apartment was bigger, with two bedrooms, it made sense.

"You hungry?"

"Yes." She hadn't eaten dinner, and the dull feeling from the wine had left, but now she was shaky and nauseated. "I'm jittery. Like I want to run a mile, then throw up and fall asleep."

He led her to the table. "Adrenaline. You're withdrawing from it."

She sat and unfolded a napkin. "Do you have a reaction to adrenaline?"

"Everyone does." He brought over two glasses of water.

"I've been trained to control my reaction so I can redirect the physical response."

"Did you learn that while working for the Prince?"

He glanced at her before taking his own seat. "Basic training."

"Oh." She took a sip of soup and closed her eyes. Canned tomato soup. The best thing she'd had in a long time. "Thank you."

"You're welcome."

She played with her soup, taking a few sips, gathering her courage. "Was working for the Prince like being on an A-team?"

He took a drink of water, as if biding time. "No. The army has one goal: to defend the U.S. Constitution. Everything I did with my A-team supported that goal. It was different with the Prince. Every rule, every decision had another purpose. Our missions were more intense, all our senses always heightened. We memorized poetry, spoke in rhyme, and, yes, trained naked in the woods in the middle of winter. There was no rest, no peace. That was the point."

"What do you mean?"

He took her left hand and rubbed her bare finger where a gold ring once marked her as his. "The men who work for the Prince are lost to this world. Their hearts broken by loss and despair, their souls damaged by years of combat and violence. With the sheer amount of physical and mental work required, there was no time to wallow in grief or self-pity. We were the perfect soldiers."

"Were you lost when you chose the Prince over me and your men?"

"I didn't choose the Prince. He chose me."

"You went AWOL to join his army."

Rafe's spoon hovered. He didn't seem that hungry either. "I left the unit against orders to look for a missing man. That's not the same as going AWOL."

"Not according to the U.S. Army."

He shrugged. "I never found the man and ended up in the Fianna."

"Did you know they might've killed your momma?"

He clutched the spoon with a white-knuckled hold, and the veins in his forearm bulged. "I knew it was a possibility. It was one of the reasons I joined. To find out the truth." He went back to eating soup and drinking water. He'd shut down and closed her out.

She still had so many questions. "Was working for the Prince worse than prison?"

Rafe took two more slices of bread, and said, "Prison, while horrible, was a penance of the mind. I was alone with myself, but I also knew I was doing no harm." He dipped his spoon in his soup again and stirred. "In some ways, it was a relief."

"Oh." They ate in silence until her throat closed. As hungry as she was, she had trouble eating. She tore a piece of bread, but it tasted dry. She drank water until her hands shook and the water spilled. She closed her eyes and rubbed her forehead. *What is wrong with me?*

She felt his heat first, and then his hands on her shoulder. He was behind her, his fingers rubbing her shoulders and her neck. His hands worked the knots until her toes curled and she sighed. She'd forgotten how strong his hands were. How safe he made her feel.

She opened her eyes, and everything tightened again. "Please stop."

He did. Except, instead of moving away, he took her hand and led her to the window seat overlooking the city. After covering her with a throw blanket, he left.

Her eyelids carried weights, but she couldn't sleep. She heard him in the kitchen, cleaning up, banging cabinets. He returned with a cup of chamomile tea.

"What are the chances of Calum stocking your favorite tea in one of many apartments he doesn't use?"

She sipped and settled against a pillow. The hot water eased the pain in her joints, and the chamomile calmed her restless mind. "When Calum has had enough of managing this city to his satisfaction, he invites me over for tea and jam tarts."

"You always were his best friend."

"So were you. Calum looked up to you, and you protected him."

Rafe sat across from her, one leg propped up on the seat. He exuded a fierce masculinity with no effort. He was, and always had been, confident in himself and his abilities. Even in bed.

Heat rose from her neck to her cheeks. She studied her teacup. "I'm not a good enough friend for him to lend me the money to solve this financial mess."

"You asked him?"

"Yes." She shifted when Rafe took part of her blanket and covered his legs up to his waist. His knee was pressed against her thigh. "Calum said I had everything I needed to fix it myself."

Rafe studied her with half-closed eyes. "He wants us back together."

"Calum wouldn't force that on us. Not after all the pain."

Rafe laughed. "Calum is all about the pain. Look at his relationship with Carina."

"What Calum wants doesn't matter. All I want is to find your vial and my grants."

Rafe's eyebrows took a downward turn. "Are you really selling your land?"

She took another sip. "John Sinclair has a buyer willing to pay cash."

"Why would you give up your inheritance? Your family's legacy?"

"You've seen the manor. You know about the murders. Anne's curse. Those windows."

Rafe took her free hand and put it on his knee so his thumb could rub her palm. "You belong there. In a home where you can raise your children, build a garden worthy of your talent. You deserve to break the cycle of poverty and sadness that's held your land captive for centuries."

"It would take a fortune to rebuild the manor, put in roads and the other things that would make it suitable for a family."

"If it could be done, would you do it?" He squeezed her fingers, and she noticed his bare ring finger on his left hand and the blue ribbon around his wrist.

Her wedding band was hidden in her jewelry box. Did he still have his?

She yanked her hand away, put her teacup on the floor, and buried herself in the blanket. "I've never thought about it."

"Not true. I remember sitting on your balcony while you told me what you'd do to the manor if you could. Modern bathrooms, a kitchen with marble countertops, a glass-walled conservatory. You had sketchbooks filled with garden ideas."

She pulled her knees up, dragging the blanket and exposing Rafe's legs again. Along with the erection tenting his sweatpants. She buried her face in the fleece. How could it already smell like him? "I wanted a parterre garden in the back with that thousand-year-old yew tree in the center, a vegetable-and-herb garden near the kitchen. I'd turn the back meadow into a wildflower garden and build a greenhouse."

"Don't forget the formal rose garden."

She raised her head and met his gaze. He hadn't moved, hadn't tried to hide his reaction to her. Even when his arousal jumped, he didn't break eye contact. He was as confident about how much he wanted her as he'd always been. "The property is wild. The manor isn't restorable. It would take Calum's fortune to make it a home."

Rafe crossed his arms over his chest, and even though he had on a long-sleeved shirt, she noticed the muscles shifting beneath. He was more comfortable with his own strength than any man she'd ever known. The epitome of a man physically at peace with himself. "I've never known you to give up on anything."

"I'm being realistic. The only thing I can save now is my business. It feeds me. It keeps a roof over my head and allows me to hire people who also need jobs. I never again want to rely on others for my own safety and survival. I also love it. It's the only thing I've ever wanted to do. The only thing I've ever dreamed of."

His gaze dipped. "What about children?"

She pressed a hand against her stomach. She'd wanted babies. As well as a loving husband who'd never abandon her. "I gave up on that eight years ago."

"You could've remarried."

The clouds parted, and she searched for the hidden moon; instead she saw the rising Pegasus constellation. "I still can."

The silence between them felt strained, maybe because he was sitting still. Her whole life, he'd been a mover. A man of action who could never just *be*.

"It's almost midnight," he said, "and I can't hear the birds."

"It's nighttime."

His gaze shifted to the cathedral's steeple. "It's just a saying."

"A Fianna thing?"

He chuckled. "A Gerald thing. When I was ten, he caught me hunting near the cemetery. He came up behind me and lectured me about protecting my perimeter. Then he talked about listening for the birds."

"I didn't know that." Rafe rarely spoke about her daddy. "What does it mean?"

"When you're in a new situation, listen for the local sounds. City noises could be car horns, vendors, airplanes. In the woods, it's the wind in the trees and the animals. Specifically, the birds. That way, when those sounds change, you'll know something's wrong. Like now. It's midnight, and I don't hear the church bells."

She followed his gaze. He was right.

They sat next to each other for a few minutes until he asked, "What happened to you after I left? After you got my letter?"

CHAPTER 29

JULIET FROZE. "YOU WANT TO KNOW WHY I WAS STRIPPING."

He lowered his arms and adjusted his hips, grimacing. "Among other things."

For a moment, she wondered how it would feel to reach out to him, hold his arousal between her hands, feel his hardness inside her, taste him… A blush worked its way up her neck, and she was grateful for the candlelight. "After…I got your letter, I had three days to move out. The army froze our bank account. All I had was the cash in my purse and the gas in our truck. Abigail and Charlotte, two of the other wives, helped me pack. When I got home, I found my daddy living in the trailer near Pops's property line."

Rafe's lips thinned, his nostrils flared. Almost like he was annoyed or frustrated. Like he wanted her to say something else. "Did you live with Gerald?"

"For a few weeks." She took the pillow from behind her back and held it against her breasts. "But he drank and was so paranoid, always worrying about men finding him. I got my waitressing job back at Boudreaux's, and one night Daddy set the trailer on fire. It burned down, and he returned to the manor. I think he did it on purpose. He hated living so close to Pops. I tried to stop him, but he couldn't be reasoned with. Then Old Man Boudreaux fired me."

"*Why?*"

"By then the Isle found out you'd gone AWOL and were accused of treason. Between my father's craziness and the Isle's anger, I went to town. I moved a lot, taking waitressing jobs. I wanted to go to school but needed a safe place to live. Then, one night, I waitressed at Rage of Angels. I saw the money the dancers made and realized if I did it a few nights a week, I could go to school. I ended up living with other dancers, worked at the club, and enrolled. After finishing my master's degree, I opened my shop and quit the club."

"Until last night."

"Because I need money for my loan."

"When you came home, did you ask Calum for help?"

"Calum was at Tulane, then Oxford. When he returned to Savannah, he bought the club." Her shoulders sank. "He never asked me to quit. He just took me to lunch a lot. When I graduated, he came to the ceremony."

Rafe was grinding his molars, and he only did that when he was mulling.

"If you have something to say, please do it."

"I'm proud of you."

"You're horrified."

"I'm sad that's what you had to do, but I'm proud of you for surviving. For how you fought for what you wanted. You haven't let anyone else define your success."

She frowned. "That silent *but* is a killer."

"When you're scared or threatened, you retreat into yourself. You don't seek help or ask for favors. Hell, when we were married, there was a part of you I couldn't reach, a part you held separate from me. No matter how hard I tried, I couldn't breach that wall around your heart. Sometimes being married to you was lonelier than being without you."

She blinked as a rushing filled her head. All she could see was the last line of his letter: *I need to be with a woman who's with me when I hold her in my arms. I need more life, more passion, more everything. More than you can give.*

She threw off the blanket and stood. "What you wrote in your letter was true? *Your* leaving was *my* fault."

"No." He stood with his hands out. "Leaving was all on me."

"You wrote that you were tired of me. You wanted a life of adventure, to travel the world, you wanted to experience other women."

He came toward her. She retreated until hitting a wall.

He cupped her face with his hands. His shadowed face was all hard angles and firm resignation. "I left you because I had to. Leaving you was the price of saving you." His voice shattered on the last word, mirroring the pain buried in his gaze.

She didn't understand why he had left, what he wanted, and how she still desired him. "I don't understand." She'd wanted the words to come out strong; instead they sounded like a plea.

He leaned his forehead against hers, their eyelashes clashing. "Please just trust me."

Pain bubbled up, spearing her heart. The room blurred. "I don't know how."

"Then let me remind you." His lips traced hers, gently at first, increasing pressure, until he was kissing her with a passion she remembered. His hard body against hers, an arm around her waist, a hand gripping her hair.

His breath warmed her, and his mouth made demands until she opened hers to him. His tongue slipped in, seeking anything she'd give him. Her lower stomach contracted, and her breasts pressed against his ridged chest muscles. She didn't want to ache for him. She wanted to be in control, to decide when and how to do the kissing.

As if sensing her conflict, his lips gentled. Caressed instead of ordered. Sought instead of took. He loved her in a way she hadn't felt in eight long years.

"Please remember," he begged, "what Garza said about the tithe."

It was hard to think with Rafe's mouth on her breast, sucking through the soft cotton, while her hand in his hair held him in place. *The recruit offers up the one thing that ties him to this world.*

His hands cupped her breasts as his lips moved up her neck. His arousal dug into her stomach, pinning her to the wall. She'd forgotten how large he was. Or had *that* grown along with the rest him? Her voice caught in the tangled web that had been their life together. "Was I what held you to the real world?"

His breath hitched, and the moment before his lips slammed onto hers, he said, "Yes."

With a soft moan, she kissed him back. The second she submitted, he lifted her so she could hook her legs around his waist. His erection ground against her center, and everything inside melted. He'd taken her against the wall many times, front and back, but she needed his hands on her breasts, his weight on her body. "Bed. Please."

He carried her, and she was suddenly on her back on the bed. After undressing himself, he pulled off her sweatshirt, cami, and pants. The only thing left were her black lace panties.

She lay before him, exposed, while he stood over her, holding his arousal. "You're so beautiful."

No, he was. He was so much larger and more muscular than a man had a right to be. Wide shoulders with enormous biceps and strong forearms. A stomach that had more muscles than she could count. His chest narrowed into slim but powerful hips. And she couldn't help but remember those thighs between hers, demanding erotic things she wasn't sure she was capable of, but as it turned out, she had been.

The humming in her body ratcheted up, and she felt like liquid mercury. Rolling around without direction, lost without boundaries. She held out her hand, and he took it. The sound of his heavy breathing kept her focused. His eyes darkened, and he licked his lips. Despite the lack of AC, she shivered. Her nipples hardened, and her breasts swelled. "*Please.*"

He dropped her hand to move to the end of the bed. With the male gracefulness she was getting used to, he slipped off her panties. Then, using his elbows, he balanced his larger body over hers. Their noses touched, his sex pushed against hers. "Are you sure?"

"Yes." She traced his chest muscles, feeling the indentations that hadn't been there the last time she'd seen him like this. His heart pounded beneath her fingers, the light hair rough against her smooth skin. When she brushed his nipples, he threw his head back and bared his teeth. His erection pressed in—then stopped.

Everything about him screamed primal male, and everything in her wanted him. She raised her hips and opened her thighs. He held himself with one hand, moving the head to tease her entrance, sending her into spirals of pleasure.

"I need you so damn much." His hands landed on either side of her head, making her his prisoner, his breath ragged and raw. "I've dreamed about this for eight years. I can't wait."

She held his face with both hands, kissing his nose, his cheeks, his lips. "Then don't."

"I know the first time I take you, it'll be over quickly. I want to enjoy you."

The first...of many? Her lips skimmed his neck, and she gripped his shoulders. She deliberately avoided the ink on one arm, the bandages on the other. "I don't want to hurt you."

"You could never hurt me," he said as he found a nipple. His mouth closed over the sensitive nub, and her body arched. A fire raged through her, and only he could put it out. Except he'd been propping himself up, not letting her feel the hardest part of him against the softest part of her. His mouth moved to her other breast while his free hand fondled the abandoned one. She gasped, desperate for *more*.

Beyond frustrated, she reached down and took his erection in her hands. It jerked in agreement. He lifted his head, his neck arched, the tendons straining as he hissed. She pulled and kneaded, his arousal hardening even more with her touch.

Finally, he gripped her hips, met her gaze as if daring her to stop him, and drove into her. Her head hit the headboard, but she didn't care. His eyes were closed, his fingers dug into her hips hard enough there'd be bruises. He filled her completely, and she felt a twinge of tightness.

As if knowing she wouldn't be used to his size, he held himself there. "*Juliet.*"

She bucked, desperate for movement. But he was stranded in a moment where each gasp became a groan. Deep inside her, his strength holding her still, his body became a single contracting muscle. A masculine machine with one purpose—to make love to her. His skin was drawn over his cheeks so tightly she saw his bone structure. Sweat coated his chest. He looked fierce and feral, and she wanted him more than she'd ever wanted anything else.

She tried to move her body, forcing the issue, except he was much stronger. Making him do anything was impossible. "Rafe. *Please.*"

He exhaled and began a slow back-and-forth movement. That escalated into a driving force that increased the firestorm. The sheer momentum of his thighs pressing hers farther apart so he could reach deeper inside threw her into an orgasm that lifted her off the bed. But that wasn't enough for him.

He pulled out and tossed her onto her stomach. Then he drew her hips up and slammed into her from behind. Her body shook with the after-effects of her climax, at the same time building to another. As he took her with a punishing rhythm, his breath came out in short, stuttered breaths. She exploded into a black void filled with shining stars.

She wasn't doing this alone. She reached behind to hold the back of his neck. He kissed her shoulder until her body clenched his sex, forcing his finish. He convulsed before his last two thrusts ended with a growl. Then he collapsed on top of her.

Her skin was so hypersensitive, his breath and his days' worth of stubble tickled her back. He rolled over, bringing her on top of him. Her breasts flattened against his chest. One of his hands pressed against her lower back while the other held her head so he could kiss her. But this time the kisses were softer than petals, more gentle than wings.

When he released her, his eyes glittered in the candle-light leaking in from the other room. "Are you alright?"

She kissed the center of his chest. "Better than alright." She laid her head against his heart and listened to its frantic rhythm. "I never want to move."

He threw a blanket over them. She was cocooned in his arms, held against his body, wrapped up in his scent, completely drained. He'd taken everything from her and, from his still-erratic breathing, had given it back. It had been so wonderful she knew, in that single space of time, she'd never love another man the way she loved Rafe Montfort.

～

Rafe sucked in a breath and closed his eyes. "Juliet." *I love you.*

For eight years, he'd never allowed himself to dream of her, to think about her, to imagine her in this way. To do so would've meant he couldn't live in his other world. It would've driven him mad.

"Rafe." She lifted her body slightly, and he saw her breasts pancaked against his pecs. Her hair hung around her shoulders, forming a veil that kept him in and the world out. What had he learned from the nuns in elementary school? *You veil what is sacred.*

"Yes?" He tucked a chunk of hair behind her ear, but it was so thick, it refused to stay.

"Kiss me."

His mouth captured hers again. He could smell her arousal, a tantalizing scent of lavender and sex. All female. All his. His hips arched, his balls tightened, and his cock hardened. *God, will I ever get enough of her?*

She shifted until she straddled him, flinging her hair back. The blanket fell off behind her. The moon had broken free from the clouds, offering its light at the perfect moment. She held her pale breasts out to him, and he took one nipple in his mouth, and then the other. He licked and nibbled, and she yelped when he gently bit.

When he lowered his head, she was smiling. Then, with one hand, she guided him in. His lungs exploded—or maybe it was his heart—and he closed his eyes. She was so tight, so perfect, he could barely process the fact that he was holding her hips and driving into her like a madman. All thoughts of gentleness and taking things slowly were replaced with a harsh hunger demanding satisfaction.

He'd wanted the second time to be about her. Instead, it was harder and faster than the first. He was ruthless, demanding things he'd no right to. When she grabbed his shoulders and met each thrust, he was sure he wouldn't survive. But this was a death worth enduring.

Moving his hands to her waist, he used his strength to sit halfway up while keeping the explosive rhythm. He dragged her head down for a kiss while his thighs forced hers apart even farther. She was slick and tight, a combo that allowed him to go farther, deeper, and faster. He heard her intake of breath and a small moan, and slammed her down with as much force as he could without hurting her.

Once she climaxed, he let go of what little self-control he had and detonated. He gripped her waist and in that moment of perfect pleasure and pain, threw back his head and let out a guttural cry. She drained him of everything he had to give her.

Exhausted, he brought her down. With one hand on her head and the other on her lower back, he kept her on top, her head tucked beneath his chin. Their hearts beat in sync, racing as if to catch up with the emotions spiraling out of control. After a few minutes of running his hands up and down her spine, a calm settled over him. Then he covered her with the blanket and used both arms to hold her close.

Soon he'd return to the Fianna. But after making love to her, after *loving* her, he'd no idea how he was going to leave her again. It would destroy them both.

CHAPTER 30

JULIET PUSHED THE HAIR OUT OF HER EYES AND CHECKED THE clock. The power was still out. She had no idea what time it was, and she didn't care. Curled up against Rafe's warmth, her head on his chest, a leg over his thighs, she hadn't felt such peace in eight years.

"Are you alright?" he asked gruffly.

She raised her head. His eyes were closed, his chest moving up and down as if he were running away. "I am."

"God, I've missed you. I just hope"—he swallowed—"I can make this better."

She kissed his chest. "I thought it was great."

He laughed. "I meant everything else. The past. The present. The future you want."

"You shouldn't have to carry that responsibility."

"I do." He opened his eyes and dragged her hair from her face. "I don't want to fail."

She yawned and laid her head on his shoulder again. "You always get what you want."

"Not everything."

"Then you'll have to try harder." She drifted away. Before her eyes closed, she noticed two things: his handgun on the nightstand and, leaning against the wall, her daddy's rifle.

∽

Capel land, eighteen years earlier

Juliet pulled up her knees and leaned against the door. Darkness swallowed them. "Calum?"

"I'm scared," he said between sobs.

She blew on her scraped knees. "Follow my voice." When she felt his hand, she pulled him close.

"We're going to die."

"Not if we're smart." But she knew the truth. They were alone, and no one was coming. "We have to break down the door." She stood and pulled him up. "Help me."

He sniffled. "We'll die here, and our daddies will be so angry."

"We're going to save ourselves."

She took his hand and led him to a corner where she knew an urn sat on a pedestal. She didn't want to think about what was inside it. "We need to lift it and throw it at the door."

"My arm hurts."

"I'll take most of the weight." They carried it toward a strip of light from beneath the door. "We'll throw and then back away so we don't get hit with shards. One. Two. Three."

The urn hit with a thud. It crashed to the floor, and the door remained locked.

"My daddy is going to be soooo mad," Calum cried.

She sighed. Hers would be too, if he were home. "We have to scream."

"The bad man might be out there."

"Pretend you're fighting with Carina."

Calum sniffled again. "I can do that."

"Help!" Juliet yelled as loud as she could with Calum screaming next to her. When she hit the doors, so did he. Ten minutes later, she slumped. Her throat hurt, and she was thirsty.

"Juliet, I have to go to the bathroom."

"I do too."

Calum sat next to her, his knees pressing against hers. "What now?"

She wouldn't cry. "I don't know."

"Juliet?" Rafe's voice came from outside the crypt. "Where are you?"

They hit the door with their fists. "We're in here!"

"Hide behind the tomb. I'll shoot off the lock."

She pulled Calum around Anne's tomb in the center. They knelt and covered their ears. "We're set!"

A moment later, an explosion blew open the metal doors. Light filtered in, dust floated, and her ears rang. Everything else went silent, as if the world was holding its breath.

She helped Calum up as Rafe ran in with Pops's shotgun. "What're you doing here?"

She grabbed both boys' hands and dragged them out. "We have to leave before he comes back."

Once they were outside, Rafe made them stop. "What's going on? What happened to Juliet's shoes?"

"We have to run," Calum said. "He has a gun!"

"I do too."

"Rafe Montfort." She stomped her shoeless foot, her school bag hitting her back. "You're sixteen. This man is, like, thirty. He's big and old and scary. We have to go now."

Rafe swung the shotgun onto his back. "Follow me. I've got the truck."

They ran until the scary man came out from behind a tree and grabbed her arm. "Isn't this a surprise?"

She kicked him until he backhanded her. Her head spun, and she saw flashes of light. "Now, young man," the man said to Rafe, "put down that gun."

Rafe pointed it at the man. "No."

The man swung her around. Her back was against his front, and he pressed a knife to her throat. "Are you willing to lose her?"

Rafe threw his gun, and the man tossed Juliet into Rafe's arms.

"It's never a good idea to choose a woman over your ideals," the man said, picking up the shotgun.

Rafe held her close, and Calum grabbed Rafe's arm. Rafe, being sixteen to her twelve and Calum's eleven, was taller than they were. But he wasn't as big as the bad man.

"What do you want?" she demanded. "This is my land."

"Aren't you the brave one?"

"You won't hurt them," Rafe said. "I won't let you."

The man tilted his head. "I've no reason to hurt them unless they get in my way."

"You locked us in Anne's crypt," she said.

"I didn't need children seeing what I was doing. Unless you can help me find Anne's Lament, I'll have to do something else with you three."

"You can let us go," Rafe said. "We won't tell."

"We don't even know what that is," Calum said between hiccups.

"No?" The man frowned. "I don't believe you."

"I swear it," Rafe said. "On my honor."

"Do you know what that means? What kind of vow you'd be taking?"

Rafe's arm tightened around her shoulder. "What do I have to do?"

"Come here." The man swung the rifle strap over his shoulder so it slung low on his back. "I won't hurt you."

"Don't go," Juliet pleaded. "He's bad."

"It's okay." Rafe kissed her head and stepped forward.

"Kneel and speak your name."

Rafe kneeled. "My name is Rafe Montfort."

"I'm Sebastian. Do you swear loyalty to me?"

Rafe nodded.

"No, young man. You must speak the words."

Calum clung to her hand. "This is weird."

"Shush."

"I, Rafe Montfort, swear loyalty to Sebastian."

The man tapped Rafe's shoulder with his knife. "Arise, Rafe Montfort, brother of Sebastian. From now until death you owe your loyalty to me. You'll never speak of this or of seeing me. If you do, I'll find the lovely Juliet and kill her."

Rafe came back to them. His walk was wobbly, and when she reached for him, he shook so hard she thought he might fall.

"How do you know my name?" she asked Sebastian.

"I know many things, Juliet of the lily. Now. Rafe Montfort, sworn brother of Sebastian, you'll not say a word of what you saw today. And if either of your companions speak—"

"We won't!" Calum's hand covered his heart. "We swear."

When Sebastian's gaze landed on her, she said, "I swear."

Sebastian put his hand against his heart and bowed his head. "Then it's time to run."

Juliet flung off the blankets. She was shaking and covered with sweat. She'd had the dream many times, but tonight's appeared in 3-D. Maybe it was the stress of the explosion or the emotions tied up with what she and Rafe had done. Either way, she needed fresh air.

Rafe slept on his stomach, so she covered him with a sheet and took a throw blanket to wrap herself in. She padded into the family room, sat on the window seat, and pushed the window open. The entire city was dark, and the candles had burned down.

Searching the sky, she found the almost-full moon and made out the constellations. How many times had she and Rafe laid blankets in her back meadow and mapped out Pegasus? Hundreds? Maybe more? Although it'd been eight years since he'd left, it'd taken less than two days for her to fall into his bed. And she hadn't been coerced. She'd craved his touch, needed his body moving over hers more than she'd needed anything else in her life.

"I was worried." Rafe wrapped his arms around her. His erection pressed through the blanket. Kisses landed on her shoulder where he pulled away the fleece.

He was naked.

She shivered. "I had a nightmare and didn't want to wake you."

"Anne's crypt?"

"And Sebastian." Juliet melted against his hard body. "I was so scared."

"We were kids." His whispers in her ear sent chills down her back. "He was a poacher."

"Who knew my name?" She shook her head. "Our fathers didn't think so. They also knew we were lying about you losing the shotgun."

"Sebastian disappeared before we told anyone. There was no point in worrying them."

She shifted to look at Rafe. "We lied and Pops beat you."

Rafe held her against his bare chest and rested his chin on her head. She sighed and snuggled closer. Had he always been this warm?

"Lying was our only choice."

"I didn't have to camp out in Calum's plantation on the Isle of Hope."

"Pops had called CPS. Telling him you were staying with Calum stopped the county from putting you in foster care. I couldn't bear to lose you."

"Carina caught me. Calum was sent to boarding school. You couldn't sit for a week."

He sat on the window seat and arranged her on his lap, her back to his front. He kept the blanket around her shoulders but left her breasts bare so he could hold them. "Meeting Sebastian is why I joined the army. I never wanted to feel that helpless again."

"That's how I felt the night I got your letter. Helpless."

"And powerless?"

She twisted to see him. Despite his warm hands fondling her breasts, his eyes had turned into black opals, his gazed fixed firmly on hers. There, in the dark depths, she saw sadness...and pity. *Oh God.* "You *know.*"

He brushed her hair off her face. "Yes."

Her heart hammered, and that jittery sensation came back. The one that followed every memory of those days with Nate. She struggled to get out of the blanket, off his lap. "*How?*"

Rafe spun her around and covered her with the throw. He held her so tightly between his legs, she couldn't move. "Balthasar told me. Nate confirmed."

"Yet Nate is still alive."

"For now." Rafe's sigh sounded like he'd been bench-pressing a semi. "I was on my way to give him the Deke treatment when I realized he's the only chance my former teammates have. Without Nate, they'll rot in jail for something they didn't do, and the person who set up my A-team will go unpunished."

Since her arms were held prisoner, she wiped her damp cheeks on the blanket. "I don't want to talk about this."

"I swear I *will* avenge you. Walker and Torridan will answer for what they did."

She nodded despite the fact that it felt like she was breathing air laced with crushed diamonds.

"And then you'll tell me what happened."

"No." She struggled until his hand brushed her nipples. Desire contracted her lower stomach.

"Yes." His hand slipped lower, until he found the part of her that was still swollen and tender from their lovemaking. "I don't want what happened in the past to hold back your future. Interrogating you like an enemy combatant was wrong. But you can't allow the past to have power over you. We'll discuss it, I'll destroy Torridan, and you can move on."

She bit her lip so she wouldn't moan. His fingers caressed, and she flung her head back. She wasn't sure about his plan, but she trusted the conviction in his voice. Although she wasn't ready to talk about what had happened, a spiral of relief wound through her heart. She no longer had to carry this burden alone.

The blanket slipped off her shoulders. "It was the worst February fourteenth I hope I'll ever have."

His fingers stopped moving, and her hips bucked involuntarily. "You received the letter on Valentine's Day?"

"Yes." She stretched her neck to see his face. His voice seemed…off. "Was that the day you joined the Fianna?"

"No." He removed his hand, tucked the blanket around her, and surrounded her with his arms. Then he stared out the window. "I tithed on St. Brigid's Day. February second." His voice had changed, sounding more business-like. More efficient.

She shifted to sit on her hip, half-facing him, still within his embrace. "You left in September, less than a week after your momma's funeral. I last spoke to you on Halloween. According to Nate, you disappeared November first."

"All Saints Day."

She tried to remember the details of that fall and winter. "Your letter said you weren't unfaithful until you left me."

The hitch in his breath could've been heard on the Isle.

"Rafe." She fought to keep the bitchiness out of her

voice. "What happened between November first and February fourteenth?"

His eyelids shuttered. "It doesn't matter."

"Considering we just made love, twice, it damn well does matter."

He lifted a shoulder nonchalantly. "I left my unit to look for Colin and met a Fianna warrior named Arragon. He took me back to the camp, where I started training."

She moved off his lap to stand, adjusting the blanket so it was more strapless dress than shawl. She remembered what Garza had said about the training. The brutality was almost pagan. She couldn't imagine there'd be a lot of time for dating—or random hookups. For the first time in eight years, something else occurred to her. When she was twelve, Rafe had lied and taken a beating to protect her.

Was it possible he'd done the same thing when he'd joined the Fianna?

He watched her like a hunter follows his prey. And for the first time since his return, she studied his tattooed arm. Visible by moonlight, she saw names inked in elegant cursive, from wrist to shoulder. At least sixty. Maybe more. All female. Yet, from their symmetry, it looked like they'd been tattooed at the same time. They were even alphabetical.

They weren't notches on a bedpost. They were a pre-ordered list.

"Oh God." She met his tortured gaze. "Your tithe was to break both of our hearts."

He moved quickly and tore off her blanket. One hand grabbed her bottom, pressing her against his erection. The other held her neck so his lips could take hers. She wasn't sure how, but they ended up in bed, with her on her back, his kisses working their way down her stomach. Heat rushed through her. *Will I ever get enough of him?*

When he pushed apart her thighs and buried his head between her legs, she held him in place. His tongue swirled and sucked while his hands kept her hips still. He knew what he wanted, and he was taking it. When he demanded a climax, she obliged. And when he slammed into her for the third time that night, driving into her core until she screamed his name, he made sure she knew the answer to her unasked question.

No. She'd never get enough of him. Without him, she'd never again feel whole.

At four a.m., Rafe checked the power and apartment's security. Naked and holding a gun, he checked every window and door. The candles had gone out, and adrenaline made his hands tingly. Something was wrong.

He went to the window seat and opened the pane. The moon was almost full, and the garden seemed quiet. No sound from the parking lot behind her store or the fountain. The only thing he couldn't confirm was the alley leading from her store to the courtyard and Dessie's dress shop below the apartment.

Had something moved?

A whippoorwill sang. Not the bird of the swamps. The call a warrior made when he sounded a threat. *Balthasar.*

Rafe shut the window and went back to bed. He wouldn't fight Balthasar now. When they met again, it'd be at a time and on a field of Rafe's choosing. Anything else would put Juliet's life in danger. And that's something he'd never allow.

Balthasar waited for Romeo.

"Pray tell, Balthasar." Arragon's voice sounded soft, absorbed by the moss-covered bricks. "What are you doing?"

Balthasar wasn't surprised to see Arragon. As the

Ghost, Arragon was the most experienced warrior in their brotherhood. He worked alone and performed the most covert of the Prince's orders. "What I've always done. The Prince's bidding."

"The Prince ordered you to return with the vial, not kill innocents."

"You understand not." Balthasar stood with his legs apart, ready to grab a weapon. "I sought knowledge from the fiend Escalus worked for. But to do so required a test."

Arragon gripped Balthasar's shoulder. "You've broken the Prince's trust and must return."

Balthasar shrugged him off. "I seek to prove my innocence."

"Yet a fair lady has met with death. Surely you didn't want to hurt those who've no say in this fray?"

"Her death was a message of strength."

"To whom? Escalus's fiend?" Arragon tilted his head. "Or Romeo?"

"This test was forced upon me."

"Thou are not a victim this night." Arragon's bald head shone in the moonlight. The fine, swirling tattoos looked like they'd been drawn on instead of inked. "The Prince gave Romeo a chance to redeem himself, as he gave you a chance to prove your innocence in Escalus's treachery."

"Which. I'm. Doing."

"Not when you cause such suffering." Arragon touched Balthasar's shoulder again. "Art thou so full of wretchedness that thou would desecrate a church?"

Balthasar flinched. "How could the Prince not want to know why Escalus betrayed us? Or with whom?"

"Because the Prince already knows."

Balthasar paced the small alley. "Then why does the fiend still live? You accuse me of hurting innocents, yet the Prince knew Escalus was poisoning this city for a villain?"

"The Prince has his reasons."

"The Prince has his favorites."

Arragon nodded toward Romeo's window. "Jealousy will destroy you, Brother."

"Why do you protect Romeo? He's fought every rule, every judgment, every commander he's ever had. Including you." The hypocrisy left Balthasar breathless. "There were two explosions tonight." Balthasar pointed at Arragon, in his combat pants, hoodie, and biker jacket. His arms were crossed, his attitude nonchalant, as if he'd not been handling plastic explosives earlier as well. "Pray, my brother. Who set off the second?"

"I had my orders."

Arragon had taken down the power grid moments after Balthasar's explosion. That meant Arragon had been following him. "How many were hurt?"

"I fulfilled my orders without pain. You disobeyed yours, and a woman died." Arragon held out both hands. "You were to seek the vial. Nothing more."

"If I return, will I be forgiven?"

"Once thou art shrived, after a time of penance and punishment."

The Gauntlet.

A text buzzed, and Balthasar checked his phone. It was from Eddie's cousin.

> I have much to offer. You can become a prince of your own making. I just need things in return, including Juliet Montfort. If interested, meet me in an hour at the train station. RLM

Balthasar gripped the phone. RLM was supposed *dead*. Yet RLM was offering opportunities that didn't include being bound to the Fianna. Opportunities of freedom and unlimited power.

Then the shock wave hit. The Prince knew RLM was alive and that Escalus had been working for him and hadn't said a word. The Prince had *lied*.

"My brother?" Arragon touched him for a third time, but Balthasar threw him off. "Will you return before this madness spreads and we lose you forever?"

Balthasar bared his teeth. "I'll *never* bow to Romeo."

Arragon sighed. "What shall I tell the Prince?"

Balthasar wanted to tell the Prince to go fuck himself, but that would only land Balthasar on a slab next to Escalus. "I'll consider his offer."

"The Prince will demand an answer before the next moon rises. In the meantime, no more brawls in these fair streets."

After Arragon slipped away, Balthasar studied Romeo's window and hoped, for the errant warrior's sake, that he was making good use of his last night alive.

CHAPTER 31

JULIET ROLLED OVER INTO A SOFTNESS THAT NESTLED HER aching body. Fleece blankets cradled her, and she smiled at Rafe's scent. She felt safe and loved. Then the noises hit her. Coffee pot gurgling. Grunting. *When had the power come back on?*

The clock on the nightstand blinked in frustration. The pillow next to hers had an indentation. Sitting up, she remembered where she was and what'd happened.

Explosion at the restaurant.

Coming to Calum's apartment.

Making love to Rafe.

Learning the truth about his tattoos.

She wrapped a blanket around herself and went into the kitchen. Once she poured a cup, adding too much cream and sugar, she saw the donuts. She bit into a jelly one when she heard grunting again. Carrying her coffee mug, she followed the sounds to the guest bedroom. Calum had filled the room with exercise equipment and a twin bed.

An army duffel, with its contents spilled out, blocked the door. In the corner, with his side to her, Rafe was doing pull-ups using a ceiling bar. She blinked against the sun glaring through the window. He wore his sweat pants, the rest of his body on display.

His eyes were closed, his breathing heavy, as he kept a steady pace. He bent his legs slightly so they wouldn't hit the floor. They'd made love in the dark, and she hadn't seen him this bare in eight years. While her hands and mouth had explored his body, touching him wasn't the same as looking at him in full daylight.

His massive arms, wide chest, and muscled thighs mesmerized her. All she could think about was the last time they'd been together—as in man-and-wife together.

They'd spent the day at a hidden waterfall. They'd made love in the water and fallen asleep in the sun, drunk on lemonade, humidity, and raspberry bars. When they'd stirred, he'd taken her on the blanket with such gentleness she could still feel his kisses against her tears. After the sun went down, they'd gone home with every intention of going to dinner and a movie. But when he joined her in the shower, their plans changed. Whispers turned to sighs, and they'd spent hours curled around each other's naked bodies until the phone rang at four a.m.

It was Pops telling them that Tess had died in the Cemetery of Lost Children. Almost a week after the funeral, Colonel Torridan told the unit to get ready for a mission. She and Rafe had spent the next few days arguing over things she couldn't remember now, all caused by her fear of losing him.

Months later, during her interrogation, she'd questioned what had happened to change everything. One thing she knew for sure—something every wife knew—was that up until he left, her husband had been hers. He'd loved her in all the ways a man loved a woman. The man she'd made love to that afternoon was not the man who'd abandoned his men, betrayed her, and disappeared.

She picked up a towel and noticed his back. Her cup smashed on the floor, porcelain and coffee flying everywhere. Deep scars covered him from his neck down to the low waistline. Lashes, knife cuts, burns, stitches. The scar tissue had to be half an inch thick in places. Other areas looked like the flesh had been gouged.

He dropped and spun around. He moved swiftly, swinging her up in his arms and taking her back into the family room. "Are you hurt?"

"No. But you were." How could she not have noticed last night? Then she remembered. He'd never allowed her to feel his back.

He dropped her on the couch, on top of suit bags, and then disappeared. He came back wearing the long-sleeved tee. After finding a garbage can and a roll of paper towels, he went to clean up her mess. She followed.

"What happened to you?"

"Nothing." He gathered the mug pieces and wiped up the coffee. "Be careful. You have bare feet, and there are shards everywhere."

She didn't care. Besides, he had bare feet too. "Why are you lying?"

"Because it doesn't matter." He carried the garbage can back to the kitchen.

She followed, and when he'd dumped everything, she grabbed his arm. "It was the Gauntlet, wasn't it?"

Rafe's gaze dropped to her fingers on his arm. "Do you know how much I want to kiss you right now?"

"You're trying to distract me."

"Is it working?"

"No." She let go. "Take a shower and get dressed."

"Yeah," he said heavily. "Okay."

But neither one moved. His lips lowered enough so his breath caressed her mouth. He pressed his lips against hers for the barest moment, the briefest rest. "Do you want to shower with me?"

"No." She pushed his chest. "Everyone will be here soon. I also have to check in with Bob, and I definitely need more coffee."

Rafe kissed her again before heading into the bathroom. When the water turned on, she sat on the couch. Someone had tortured the man she loved. And he discounted it as nothing. What kind of world had he been living in?

When he was done, he came out in jeans, boots, and a long-sleeved black T-shirt. "I'm making breakfast."

She avoided his outstretched arm and ran into the bathroom. It's not that she didn't want his touch; she just needed to process everything. After showering, she found her overnight bag and dressed in yoga pants and a cami. She heard him in the kitchen, the smell of bacon sizzling, the sounds of plopping and frying. Then she smelled peaches. He was making peach French toast. The same thing he'd ordered for them the morning after their wedding night.

She twisted her wet hair into a loose bun and straightened her shoulders. The shower helped with her confidence, but her emotions were as hot and raw as an exposed nerve. She passed the dresser and noticed a Dopp kit on top. She ran her fingers over the worn leather. The last time she'd seen this she'd packed it up for his final mission. Although it wasn't hers and she had no business opening it, she did.

Inside she found an open box of condoms. Her face warmed up. They hadn't used any protection last night. Who had these been for?

Juliet appeared as Rafe placed the plates of French toast and bacon on the table. She wore stretch pants that hugged her ass and a camisole barely covering her breasts. Her wet hair was twisted up, and her eyes shot bottle rockets.

He sighed. The post-sex rapport was gone. "You look beautiful."

She threw a box at him, and he caught it against his chest. "We didn't use protection."

He raised one eyebrow.

"Yes. I found them in your Dopp kit. Which I peeked into. But only because I was surprised you still had it."

He put the box on the table and went back to turning French toast. He loved it when she showed her jealous side. It made him feel like he could run the Army Ten-Miler and bench press an Abrams tank. "You gave it to me as a wedding present."

"And?"

He glanced at her. Now her hands were on her hips. "And what?"

"We didn't use protection. So why are you carrying around an open box of condoms?"

He faced her. After returning from the Isle yesterday, he'd found the box while going through Escalus's backpack. Since Calum had been in the kitchen directing the delivery of clothes, most of which Rafe would never wear, he'd shoved the box in his Dopp kit. Rafe hadn't wanted to deal with Calum's questions.

Why Escalus kept condoms in his backpack was a mystery. Most Fianna warriors, including Escalus, were celibate. "If I told you that box wasn't mine, would you believe me?"

She looked everywhere but at him. "I don't know."

"What if I told you the directions are in German and they're recently expired?"

She picked up the box to read it, and her eyes widened. "Oh. German."

"I'm pretty sure American drugstores don't carry expired German condoms. And they're not available in Leavenworth's commissary."

She chucked them in the trash and sat. The sizzling

French toast filled the room with a sweet cinnamon and peach fragrance.

He knelt in front of her, took her hands, and addressed her other worry. "While we were married, did we ever use protection?"

"No." She scrunched her nose. "We wanted a family. Except I couldn't get pregnant."

"That's not the only reason." His squeezed her fingers, wishing they'd stayed in bed. "I couldn't bear the thought of putting something between us when we made love."

She pushed him away and stood. "If the condoms aren't yours, whose are they?"

He rose and poured her more coffee with too much sugar and cream. "Escalus's."

"The guy killed on the Isle yesterday."

"I…inherited his backpack."

"Oh." She straightened her shoulders. "You were there. When he died."

"Yes."

She waved her arms. "You couldn't have killed him. He was shot from far away."

"I know." Still, Rafe appreciated her belief in him. He went back to the griddle and flipped the egg-soaked bread.

"But you were *with* him." She lowered her voice. "If anyone finds out—"

"They won't. You and the man who killed Escalus are the only ones who know."

"Who—"

"A warrior named Arragon." And that's all Rafe was going to say about that. He changed the subject and turned off the griddle. "While you were showering, I texted Sarah Munro, the historian Miss Beatrice mentioned yesterday.

She's doing research later today on the Isle, and I suggested we meet her at Boudreaux's. Two thirty p.m."

Juliet found her phone on the counter. "Bob texted too. The site sustained flooding last night, and the city's electrical crew can't work until it dries out."

Rafe indicated the plates on the table, hoping she'd remember their wedding morning breakfast in bed. "Why don't you eat before it gets cold?"

She got another message and texted back.

"Who's that?" He was annoyed she wasn't paying attention to him. Or the breakfast he'd made her. That she'd put up walls again. Damn Escalus and his stupid condoms.

"It's Philip. He wants us to visit."

Rafe took a drag of coffee. "*You*. Not *me*."

She dropped her phone. "Sorry about that." She picked up her cup. "I wish you two didn't hate each other."

"I don't hate him. Philip hates me because the woman he's adored forever wants me."

Rafe loved the flush that rose from her neck to her face. He was tired of hiding how he felt. And it was way past time she admitted her own feelings as well. He knew she was scared of her feelings for him. Hell, he was terrified.

"Just because we…" She lowered herself into the chair and bit her lower lip.

"Made love?" He sat and watched her carefully. "Three times?"

She ate some bacon. "That doesn't mean we're in a relationship." She spoke so softly, her voice reminded him of pencil-written words that'd been erased but still left a gray impression behind.

He got up to get more caffeine. "There's a hair dryer in the bathroom attached to the small bedroom."

"You're not eating?"

"I'm not hungry anymore." He kept his features as unconcerned and cool as she seemed to be. "You can wear the sweatshirt in my bag."

"Why?"

"Because if we're not in a relationship, you don't have enough damn clothes on."

She got up and headed for the guest room. Then she slammed the door so hard his mug fell off the table and shattered on the floor.

Juliet slammed the door of the spare bedroom. *Damn that man.*

Why was she so mixed up around him? Part of her wanted him to agree that they had no chance of having a long-term relationship; the other part wanted him to carry her back to bed.

She kicked his duffel, and more stuff fell out. After finding the hair dryer in the bathroom, she kicked his bag again. Except this time her big toe hit something hard.

"Ow, ow, ow." She hopped until the throbbing stopped. Although she didn't care what her lack of clothing did to Rafe, she didn't want to sit in front of the other men in her cami. It didn't take long to find a gray sweatshirt with a faded *ARMY* on the front. She unfolded it, and something fell out—a leather journal with an embossed heart with a sword through it.

Escalus had kept a journal, but had Rafe done so as well? She'd be surprised, since she'd had a hard enough time getting him to write a grocery list.

Once back in the master bedroom, she propped the book open on the dresser and dried her hair while she read. Diaries were private things, but he owed her so many explanations she didn't care. She started on the first entry written on paper thinner than onion skin:

> *November 2. All Souls Day.*
> *Northumberland, UK*

> *I am in.*

Unfortunately, the rest of the journal was written in French. As pages progressed, the French morphed into Latin. Two languages she couldn't read. She could only make out the names of cities and people, dates, and numbers at the top of each page.

The first six months he wrote a daily entry. Beneath each date on the left page, he'd written sequential numbers: 2190, 2191, etc. Another set of sequential numbers on the right-page corner started with 1.

Many pages had multiple dates and numbers, and some days and months were skipped. She flipped to the last page. The last entry was written in English:

> *September 29. Feast of St. Michael. St.*
> *Petersburg.*

> *4015 days. I have failed.*

The number in the right corner was 301. She flipped through, looking for names, but found no Juliet. He'd never written about her.

Rafe knocked. "Nate and Pete are here. I made more coffee."

"I'll be right out."

She also didn't see any other female names. She wrapped

up the journal in a towel and unplugged the dryer. After putting on the sweatshirt, she ignored the voices in the kitchen and went back to the spare bedroom. She returned the journal to Rafe's bag and the appliance to the bathroom. Back in the hallway, Samantha rushed into Juliet's arms. Today she wore black leggings, a lavender-and-black lace cami, and combat boots. Her reddish-blond curls danced around her shoulders.

Samantha squeezed. "I was worried about you."

Juliet hugged back. "I'm alright. How are you?"

Samantha let go but held Juliet's hand. "The explosion happened during my ghost tour of the tunnels. Once I got everyone out safely, I had to promise a refund. My boss is going to be furious."

"You stayed with Pete last night?"

"Yes." Samantha's nose scrunched. "I wish I didn't have to have a roommate. But now that the club is closed I may need a third."

Juliet led Samantha to the master bedroom. "I wish I could pay you enough so you didn't have to have roommates or give ghost tours."

"I don't mind giving tours. The people are nice, and it's fun to walk around the city at night. It reminds me of New Orleans. The irony is that yesterday I wanted to ditch my job at the club, but now that it's closed, I'm not sure what to do."

"Move in with me."

"In that tiny thing?" Samantha waved her hand around the bedroom. "Maybe Calum would give me a break on this one. It's his fault the club is closed in the first place."

Juliet slipped on her black flats while Samantha frowned.

"This bed looks like two people were in it, and they weren't sleeping."

A hot flush rose up Juliet's neck, and her cheeks itched.

"*No.*" Samantha covered her mouth with her hands.

Juliet went to the mirror to begin a dutch braid. Her cheeks were red, but the rest of her face was pale. She took a deep breath, and then exhaled. "Yes."

Samantha took over the braiding. "Do you know what you're doing?"

"No."

"Are you still in love with him?"

"I don't know." Juliet found the ring Miss Beatrice had given her the previous night and slipped it on her thumb. "There're so many secrets between us."

Samantha tightened her hold on the braid until Juliet yelped. "You're screwing a man who's completely into you, but he's also violent and untrustworthy, and you're not sure you're in love with him."

Could her life be any more messed up? "Yes." She handed Samantha a hair tie and met her gaze in the mirror. "I can handle this."

Samantha raised an eyebrow. "When *this* ends?"

Juliet spun around with a straight back, a silent resolution. "I'll deal."

Samantha hugged her again. "I'm not happy, but yesterday you wouldn't consider asking anyone for help. Today"—she tilted her head toward the male voices in the kitchen—"you're working with people who care about you. That's huge."

"I hadn't thought about it that way."

"I have. And if sex with the hottest man in town—besides Pete—is the reason, that's a good thing." Samantha took Juliet's arm and led her toward the kitchen. "I just hope you don't end up with another broken heart. You barely recovered from the last one."

Juliet blinked, hating the moisture behind her lashes. She hoped so too.

CHAPTER 32

RAFE POURED JULIET ANOTHER CUP OF COFFEE, HIS JAW cranking. Her comment about their not being in a relationship had hurt, and he regretted how he'd handled it. He knew her closed-off attitude hid fear—fear *he* was responsible for. But what more could he have done last night to show her how much he loved her?

Nate finished off Juliet's plate of French toast and poured his own coffee. His long hair was tied behind his neck. Despite the jacket he wore over his jeans and blue T-shirt, Rafe was sure Nate carried one if not two guns. He didn't even try to hide the knife sheath on his belt.

Nate placed his dish in the sink. "You okay, bro?"

"Great." Rafe turned too fast, and hot coffee burned his wrist. "Shit."

Juliet and Samantha came in, and he inhaled sharply. In his oversized sweatshirt and her hair in a complicated braid, Juliet was so lovely his chest ached.

Calum tossed a bag onto the couch. "Morning, beautiful."

Juliet went into his arms. "How's your sister?"

Calum wrapped her up, and Rafe hated him. Then he noticed Calum's puffy eyes and wrinkled tux. Calum had never gone home. As much as the twins fought, they were bound by a force field of love and loyalty. The kind of link Rafe had always wanted with Juliet.

Calum let go and pulled chairs out for both women. "Carina is awake and giving orders."

"I hate to ask." Juliet's forehead wrinkled. "What about my bill?"

Calum sat and cradled his coffee. "No idea."

"We have until three p.m." Juliet took the cup Rafe offered. "That's when the payroll company needs the deposit in order to cut the checks by six."

"One problem at a time," Calum said.

"Which is why I asked you all here this morning." Rafe stood against the counter, arms crossed. "We're tied together, fighting an enemy we can't see, for a reason we don't know."

Pete grabbed a donut and sat on Samantha's other side. "We need to catch Balthasar before he hurts anyone else."

"Amen, Brother." Nate leaned against the fridge as the front door opened.

Garza swooped by without a smile, dropped his jacket on a club chair, and went for the coffee. He wore his holster over a dress shirt, his weapon secured against the side of his chest.

Rafe locked the door and noticed Garza carried a knife in his back waistband and a leg holster beneath his jeans. The cop had loaded up too. Interesting.

Holding his mug, Garza sat on a stool, the heels of his boots hooked on the lowest rung. "I've had a hell of a night. So start talking." He stared at Nate. "Or I start arresting for impersonating a PO and stealing evidence."

The skin over Nate's cheekbones seemed tighter and more translucent than yesterday.

"What evidence is he talking about?" Calum asked Nate.

Nate tapped his foot. "I took Deke's cell phone because he was my only source of anti-seizure meds."

"You wanted his phone to contact his source?" Garza's voice reeked of incredulity.

"Pretty much. But the phone was encrypted." Nate drank his coffee and added, "I overnighted it to Luke. I'm hoping he can open it and give me a contact name."

Garza threw up a hand. "Who's Luke?"

"Our unit's comm expert," Pete said. "Think computer guru/wizard/god wrapped up in the body of a twenty-five-year-old Green Beret."

"That phone was evidence from *my* murder scene," Garza said. "I'm responsible."

"You'll get it back," Nate said.

"Then what?" Garza put down his mug and pressed the heels of his hands against his eyes. "You'll buy illegal drugs again?"

"It's not heroin or meth. They're anti-seizure meds." Nate paused. "They're legal in Canada."

Garza moved, and Rafe put a hand out to stop him. "It doesn't matter." Then he looked at Nate. "How're you doing without the drugs?"

"I have one left. I'm managing."

"Good." Rafe faced Garza. "Luke isn't going to tell anyone anything."

"How do you know that?"

"Because Nate's unit has their own shit to deal with." Rafe studied the room, his attention always drawn back to Juliet, who refused to look at him. "This is what we know. Someone's been terrorizing Juliet—vandalizing her store, destroying every image of her lily."

"He even stole her lily door knocker." Samantha held a black mug with *Got Ghosts?* stamped in white letters. "*Sooooo* creepy."

"Agreed," Rafe said. "The same lily was given to four women associated with Nate's unit the night they were attacked and imprisoned in Afghanistan."

"Where are your men now?" Samantha asked Pete.

"They're in Leedsville, a secret military prison."

"Never heard of it," Garza said.

Pete shrugged. "It's in Minnesota. The rest of us who were at the command center that night have been suspended and go on trial on Friday. Nate and I are here collecting evidence to save our unit."

"If you go on trial"—Samantha reached for Pete's hand—"will you go to Leedsville?"

"Yes." Pete kissed her palm. "And Nate returns to a military psych hospital in Maine. Our only clue is that lily, which Luke traced to Anne Capel in Savannah."

Rafe handed Juliet's phone to Nate. "At Juliet's manor, we found stained-glass windows that told a story about the lily."

"I see pirates," Nate said, flipping through the photos on the phone. "The archivist at the SPO told me the Capel family worked with the Prioleau pirates—"

"Prideaux pirates," Calum corrected.

"—in the seventeenth and eighteenth centuries." Nate handed the phone to Pete, and Samantha and Calum leaned over to see.

"I've never seen these at Capel Manor," Calum said.

Juliet sipped her coffee. "My daddy boarded them up."

"They're dark," Pete said.

Samantha snorted. "I'm not sure which is scarier— the window with the dead men on the pirate ship or the woman being hanged."

"That's Anne Capel," Juliet said. "Even though she was pregnant, they were executing her for killing forty-four kids with a poison she supposedly made from the lily. Except the rope broke and they let her go. A few days later, her lover was murdered by his own brother."

"Sarah, the archivist at the SPO, believes Anne was trying to help those kids," Nate said. "They'd gotten sick, and Anne was healing them."

Rafe pointed to another photo. "In another window, there's a woman, probably Anne, handing two vials to men offering a scroll in return."

Pete whistled and gave the phone to Garza.

"The man is bowing," Garza said.

"He's a Fianna warrior," Rafe said. "I believe Anne Capel made a deal with the Fianna to protect these vials. Which is why the current-day Prince knows about them."

Juliet fiddled with a ring on her thumb. "One of the vials may contain poison from my lily."

"And the Fianna wants the poison for its own purposes?" Garza said.

Samantha grimaced. "Even if a vial contains poison, it's three hundred years old."

"That might be the most important question of all." Garza started making another pot of coffee. He paused to glance at Rafe. "May I?"

"Go ahead." Rafe studied his squad while the water hissed. Samantha and Juliet both had dark circles under their eyes. Pete had traded his badass gunmetal lip piercings for a sleeveless black tank over black combat pants. Nate's pale face and darting eyes made him look strung out. Calum looked…unkempt.

Calum cleared his throat. "When did this happen between Anne and the Fianna?"

Juliet wrapped her hands around her mug. "Anne escaped hanging in 1677. In the window where she's giving away the vials, she has an infant. So it must be 1678?"

Calum crossed his arms. "King Charles signed the Carolina King's Grants in 1663. The Savannah grants were later, so the timing's right."

"What's a King's Grant?" Pete asked.

After Calum gave them a rundown, Garza's sigh screamed boredom. "So?"

Calum raised an eyebrow. "Maybe this Fianna warrior is offering Anne a King's Grant in exchange for the vials."

"Which would mean King Charles was in on the gig?" Garza said.

"It's possible," Rafe said. "A lot of monarchs worked with the Fianna until the American Revolution."

"Enough history." Garza poured himself a fresh cup of coffee. "Two explosions were set off last night: one at the restaurant and the second less than a minute later at the transformer in a tunnel outside the hotel. That's what took out the power grid. I had no idea there were tunnels in Savannah."

"Most are closed," Samantha said. "I give ghost tours of the safer tunnels and cisterns."

"How many dead?" Nate asked.

"Only Miss Habersham. Over thirty wounded. The restaurant blast was an expertly controlled explosion designed to blow out, not in."

Rafe wasn't surprised by the news. Just surprised the explosion wasn't larger. "We're lucky. Balthasar could've hurt more people. Last night made a statement without going for maximum damage."

"A statement to who?" Garza asked.

"Balthasar was telling me he could get to those I care about and telling you he could control this city by cutting the power."

"Why?"

"Is Escalus where you last left him?"

Garza dialed his cell. After talking to someone in the morgue, Garza threw his phone down. "Escalus's body is gone."

～

The fresh brew should've cleared Nate's head. Except everything was foggier than ever. And now Escalus's body was gone? "How'd you know, Rafe?"

Rafe shrugged and stared at Juliet, arms crossed. His silent stance was at odds with his jaw's crank-fest.

Garza rubbed his eyes with his thumb and forefinger. "Did Balthasar take Escalus?"

Juliet sighed. She seemed smaller tucked into a huge sweatshirt. The shadows under her eyes had darkened, and she stared at the photos while Rafe watched her.

"I think so." Rafe caught Nate studying him. Even though Rafe was visually stalking his wife, there was no apology or shame. "The Fianna brings soldiers back for burial."

"Back where?" Pete asked.

"Iona," Rafe said. "An island in the Scottish Hebrides."

"Oh." Pete clasped his hands behind his neck. "Okay."

"What will Balthasar do with Escalus?" Samantha asked. "Keep him iced?"

"Balthasar would've had a plan in place." Rafe paused to grind his chompers. "We should check out dry ice sales or temperature-controlled shipping."

"The chief has a detective on it." Garza started texting. "Looking for a safe house in the historic district might be a better bet."

"Good idea," Rafe said. "Balthasar must have a command center somewhere close to the explosion. He's too arrogant to leave. He'd never believe he'd get caught."

"I can help," Calum said. "I have listings of available properties in the city."

"There's something else," Nate said. "Yesterday Sarah

discovered that there are no satellite photographs of the Isle of Grace."

Rafe tilted his head. "None?"

"There's been a blackout over the Isle since aerial reconnaissance began."

"*Sheeeet*," Pete said. "That's too weird."

"That takes power," Garza said. "And money."

"Fianna money?" Juliet asked.

Rafe lifted a shoulder. "Don't know. What about the map?"

"Nothing." Nate studied his boots. "Compass rose was off thirty degrees. It's useless."

"Then why did my daddy hide it in my trunk?" Juliet asked softly.

Nate focused on the gold ring she wore on her thumb. "No idea."

Garza drummed his fingers on the table. "A law firm in New Orleans—Beaumont, Barclay, and Bray—paid for Escalus's rental car. Does that mean anything?"

Calum nodded. "It's one of the oldest firms in the country."

"They're corrupt as hell," Samantha added. "After my mom died, they sold her estate and accused me of stealing." Juliet took her hand, and Samantha half smiled. "I'm over it."

"I didn't know that," Calum said in a flat, hard tone.

"What does a corrupt law firm have to do with a Fianna warrior?" Pete asked.

Rafe held out both hands. "No idea."

At this rate, Nate's men were going to spend a combined four hundred years in prison.

Garza's phone buzzed. He read the text, and his shoulders slumped. "Escalus's journal is gone also. Taken from my locked desk. During the outage."

Nate washed out his mug and laid it on the counter to dry. "I have three questions." He faced Garza directly. "Why are we sharing with you? Why are you helping us? And how do we know you're not gathering intel to use against us?"

Garza crossed his arms. "Last night, after the debriefing, I walked home. On the way, I met a Fianna warrior named Arragon. He knows I'm translating Escalus's journal and investigating Rafe's release and Nate's background with the 7th Special Forces group. Arragon disapproved of all three activities and, after threatening my family in New Jersey, he bowed."

"Who's seen a man bow?" Rafe asked in a dark voice.

"Last night," Calum said, "before the explosion, I was outside with Mr. Delacroix smoking a cigar. A man across the street bowed to us."

"How low?" Rafe asked.

"Halfway. I guess."

"Could you tell what race he was?"

"It was too dark, and he was too far away."

Rafe turned to Garza who said, "Halfway. Dark-skinned. Bald, tattooed head. Not as tall as you but built like a gladiator."

All heads turned toward Nate. "In tribal dress and fatigues, all the way to the ground."

"Does it matter?" Pete asked him.

"Yes." Rafe collected mugs and spoons and stacked them in the sink. "Garza met Arragon. I have no idea who was in Afghanistan with Nate, and I'm not sure if Calum saw Balthasar or Arragon."

Juliet ran her top teeth over her bottom lip. Although

Rafe was in mission mode, he felt a sudden need to clear the room and kiss her senseless. "Juliet?"

"I saw someone bow in Forsyth Square last night. It was dark, and I thought I'd imagined it."

"What kind of bow?"

"He hit his chest with his fist and bowed his head."

Rafe exhaled. *Thank God.* "Samantha?"

"Yesterday, a man bought all of Abigail Casey's hand-painted prints. He was tall and muscular, dark-skinned, with a French accent. He had tattoos on his bald head. It was a huge sale—three thousand dollars. After I wrapped everything up…" She glanced at Juliet. "He hit his chest with his fist and bowed his head."

Pete frowned. "He didn't hurt you?"

"No!" She touched Pete's arm. "He was courteous and kind."

Calum looked at Juliet. "Were the prints Arragon bought the ones on the wall that looked like your lily in medieval prints?"

"Yes." Juliet tucked a hair behind her ear. "Abigail is a renowned botanical artist. I sell them for her on commission."

Nate and Pete glanced at each other before Nate said, "Did you ask Abigail to paint that lily? Or did she do it on her own?"

"I never asked her," Juliet said. "Abigail's specialty is roses. One day she sent me the lily prints, and they were perfect for the shop. I assumed she used my business logo as her inspiration."

"Who's Abigail Casey?" Garza asked.

"The wife of a man in Nate's unit," Juliet said. "We knew each other when Rafe was in the unit, and we've remained friends."

Nate clasped his hands behind his neck. "Abigail's husband is in prison with my men."

"So," Pete added to the convo, "Abigail, who received a lily herself the night of the operation, is incorporating them into her artwork, and the Fianna is buying it up."

"Seems like," was all Rafe could say.

Pete raised an eyebrow. "What's the difference between Arragon and Balthasar?"

Rafe poured the last of the coffee and drank it hot and black. "Arragon is a French Algerian with dark skin and eyes almost as green as Nate's. Balthasar has brown eyes and brown hair. It's possible Arragon is in town moderating this game between me and Balthasar."

"Is Arragon dangerous?" Pete asked.

"Lethal." Rafe put the pot in the sink. "But he's not here for you and Nate."

"That's a relief." Pete leaned back, balancing the chair on its back legs. "Although I'm feeling left out. I've seen shit."

"And the level of bows?" Garza asked.

"A head bow is a greeting or farewell. A half-bow is a watch-and-wait threat. But"—Rafe pointed at Garza—"that can easily turn into a full bow. Especially if you tell your superiors anything you've heard today or anything you read in Escalus's journal."

"Figured," was all Garza said.

"And a full bow"—Rafe sighed—"means you're marked for execution."

All eyes turned to Nate, who held up both hands. "Yes, I'm freaked out about what I may or may not have seen. But there's nothing I can do about it."

"Man," Pete said on an exhale. "It sucks to be you."

Nate gave him the finger. "Thanks, bro." Then he apologized to the laughing women.

Rafe squeezed the bridge of his nose, thinking out their next move. "We need to find the vial and the grants. Juliet and I are meeting Sarah the archivist on the Isle later. She may have some documents belonging to Juliet's father."

"I'll go back to the SPO," Nate said. "I'll see if I can learn anything else about Anne Capel and her lily."

"Good." Rafe gave another order. "Calum and Garza, find Balthasar's safe house. He's got to be in the historic district."

They both nodded.

"I'll handle the store," Samantha said. "Bob is at the work site, and the only thing scheduled is a wedding consultation."

"I have a job interview at two," Pete said. "I'll take Samantha with me."

"Interview for what?" Nate asked.

"Self-defense teacher at your home away from home. Iron Rack's Gym."

"Why? The trials start Friday."

Pete stood and held Samantha's chair. "Still need food and ammo, bro. And I want to start before the new owner takes charge."

"Excuse me?" Calum stood. "New owner?"

"Yeah," Pete said. "Place is for sale."

"Interesting." Calum grabbed the bag he'd dropped earlier. A minute later, they all held new burner phones. "Our numbers are programmed with our aliases."

Pete laughed. "I can guess who *GhostGirl* is."

Samantha smirked. "No laughing, *RezBoy*."

"I don't know whether I'm offended or just annoyed."

Calum clapped Pete on the back. "I'm sure you'll learn to love it."

"I'm *Copper*?" Garza said.

"It's pronounced *Coppa*," Calum said. "Very New York."

"I'm from New Jersey."

"Oh." Calum scratched his chin. "Right." He looked at Juliet. "You okay with yours?"

"*Petals*? Really?"

"Better than *KiteMan*," Nate said, scowling. "What does that mean?"

"You'll figure it out," Calum said. "I'm *SmartFox*."

"Good grief." Juliet and Samantha shared a smile. "I think we know who *LetsFight* is."

"I hit things too," Nate said.

Rafe laughed. "Maybe Calum will let you change your name to *FightsBack*."

"No." Calum started texting. "I'm going to see Carina. Pops will move Philip into my mansion until he recovers." Calum kissed Juliet on the cheek and opened the door to find Bob on the other side, his fist in the air, in the middle of a knock.

"Miss Juliet?" Bob took off his hat. "The windows."

Rafe took Juliet's hand and rushed out. The others followed until they stood in front of her store windows. Red paint covered her logo. But more worrying were the words scrawled below: A PLAGUE O' BOTH YOUR HOUSES.

CHAPTER 33

JULIET SAT IN THE HOSPITAL CHAIR WHILE THE NURSE CHECKED Philip's vitals and Pops and Rafe talked outside. She'd changed into a white eyelet sundress and sandals but now wished she'd brought her sweater. The AC was on full blast. As she waited, she checked her notes on her phone, trying to ignore the fact that she was freezing. She'd left Garza to handle the crime scene and Samantha to close the shop. Bob was overseeing the square, and Juliet had rescheduled the wedding consult.

She had almost everything under control. But she kept replaying her earlier argument with Rafe—the one about their non-relationship. She'd spoken out of fear and confusion, and he probably had too. She reminded herself that her feelings didn't matter. The only important thing was Balthasar's message.

Balthasar had bitten his thumb at Rafe, and Rafe had taken the bait. He'd reacted swiftly, giving orders and expecting everyone to meet back at Calum's for dinner.

When the nurse left, she stood near Philip's bed. "How're you feeling?"

Philip grimaced. "Who knew twenty-two stitches in the abdomen would hurt so much?"

"I'm so relieved." She smiled at the half-eaten applesauce cups on his bedside table. "Don't get used to living in Calum's mansion."

Philip started to smile, and then stopped. "Are you and Rafe still working together?"

"Yes."

Philip smoothed his blanket. "Were you afraid last night? You hate the dark."

"Actually..." She poured water from his pitcher and handed him the cup. "I spent the night in the apartment where Rafe is staying. He was worried about looting."

"I see." Philip took a sip before saying, "I'll be released soon. Pops is itching to get back to the Isle. He doesn't like being in town."

She nodded. Her daddy had hated coming to town as well.

"What about Carina?" Philip put the cup down, pressed his hand against his bandaged side, and winced. "Has she paid yet?"

"Nope."

"Juliet." He shifted his pillow and lowered his voice from a request to a plea. "Stay in town today. Irritate Carina's campaign manager until he pays you. Work on your renditions—"

"I can't." She moved to the window. The view overlooked a busy street.

"I've seen the way Rafe stares at you. And I'm wondering if you're not looking back at him the same way. Don't let him pull you into his world."

A nurse came in. "Bandage check."

Grateful for the interruption, Juliet found her purse and said, "I'll call you later." After shutting the door, she leaned against it. *What am I going to do about Rafe?*

"I don't care." Carina's voice across the hall sounded shrill. If she was awake and giving orders, she could handle a conversation about her unpaid bill.

Juliet drew up her shoulders and knocked on the open door.

"What is it?" Carina sat in her bed. The room's blinds

were closed, and the only light filtered in from the hallway. She wore a blue silk Chinese robe with gold embroidery. Her long blond hair was braided and thrown over one shoulder. Her campaign manager Henry sat nearby on a hospital chair with a laptop on his thighs.

Henry stood when he saw Juliet, placing the laptop on the rolling table. "I'm going for coffee. Would you like some, Miss Capel?"

"No, thank you."

Once he left, Carina frowned. "What do you want?"

My money. Instead, she started with, "I checked on Philip. He's being released this afternoon."

"He's lucky. Because of this stupid concussion, I can't leave for another day. I can't read, work on the computer, or be around light. How am I supposed to do my job?"

Seriously? Carina had a staff most CEOs would envy. "How are you feeling?"

"Horrible."

"Sorry to hear it."

"No, you're not." Carina waved her hand. "You just want my money."

"I want you to pay your bill. That's the expectation when someone's signed a contract."

"I didn't sign it. Eugene did."

"You approved the continuation of the project after his death. And when this is done, I'm never again entering into a working agreement with you."

Carina sat up and adjusted her robe. "Aren't you salty today."

"Just tired."

"You do look like hell." Carina's eyes narrowed, her eyelashes fluttering. "Tell me. Did the reunion with your ex go well last night?"

Juliet should've known better than to engage. "Have Henry text me."

"Were you and Rafe screwing last night?" Carina tilted her head. "You have that certain glow."

Juliet fisted her hands at her side. "None of your business."

Carina crossed her arms. "Lies never protect people. They only cause more pain."

"A politician lecturing about the truth. Is this a full moon thing?"

Carina shrugged. "Honesty is easier for everyone involved."

Juliet was halfway through the doorway when Carina said, "I loved my husband."

Juliet glanced back.

"With all my heart. But since I took over his Senate seat after his death, people assume I married him for political gain."

"I thought you married him for money."

Carina quirked an eyebrow. "He was a Wilkins. His fortune was half of mine."

"Is there a point?"

"A night of hard-core banging, and you're running for Miss Sarcastic." Carina straightened her blankets. "Eugene wasn't the only man I've loved. He wasn't the *first*."

Good grief. "TMI, Carina."

"Sometimes a first love is so powerful it eclipses all thought and reason. It draws you in even though you know it's dangerous. I also know second loves can be just as powerful. That's when you realize the light from the first wasn't fireworks, it was immolation."

"It's not like that with Rafe." Juliet hadn't gotten burned. She'd just died inside.

"Then run to your lover. Let him leave your heart in bits by the side of the road for the rest of us to pick up. Just like last time."

Juliet gripped the door handle. "I never asked for your help."

"No. You never do. But you expected Calum's. And Philip's."

"That's not true. Neither Calum nor Philip were around when I returned."

Carina stared at the window with the closed blinds. "Do you know what happened when I lobbied for Rafe's release?"

"That's obvious."

"They said no." Carina smiled as if waiting for that info to sink in. "I went to the DoD, the Justice Department, and anybody else I thought could help me. And they laughed in my face. As a widow in her deceased husband's Senate seat, I didn't have enough clout to get a parking space for my secretary, much less release an infamous traitor."

Juliet came back into the room and held onto the end of the bed. "If you and Calum didn't get Rafe released, who did?"

"No idea."

"Does Calum know?"

"No. He believes I saved his best friend, and I want it to stay that way." Carina blew a stray hair out of her eyes. "I don't want him to worry."

Was Carina daring her to keep the secret? It was obviously a setup for some payoff only Carina knew about. If Juliet played along, she'd solve one of her biggest problems. But how many others would she cause?

How could she demand honesty from Rafe if she was about to lie to him?

"It's not like you can trust Rafe anyway." Carina waved a hand. "I heard he has more than a hundred names on his arm. Do you think that's true?"

Bitch be damned. "I want the money in the payroll account by three p.m."

Carina's almond-shaped eyes flattened. The only thing she didn't do was lick cream off her lips. "I pay my bill, and you lie to Calum and Rafe."

Juliet would save her business. Then find the vial. And when this was all over, she'd deal with the fallout. "Whoever signed Rafe's release doesn't matter."

Carina laughed. "When Rafe leaves again, you're going to have bigger problems."

"Goodbye, Carina." Juliet shut the door and headed toward the raised male voices that could only belong to Pops and Rafe. Her phone rang, and she stopped. "Hello, John."

"Juliet, your deeds are ready for your ex-husband to sign. I'll text you my secretary's number. Remember, he'll need a witness that's not you."

"He'll bring Calum."

"Any luck finding the grants?"

"No." Juliet moved as a man pushed a gurney by. "I'm still looking. And the police investigations?"

"Sheriff Boudreaux said Tuesday's tragedy shouldn't hold up the sale. And the FBI dropped the investigation into Senator Wilkins's death. If you can find those grants with the stipulations in order and get Rafe to sign the deeds, the sale should go quickly."

"Thank you." Juliet hung up. Two problems almost solved. *But at what cost?*

She found Pops and Rafe in a waiting room.

"I'm tellin' you." Pops stood with his hands on his hips. "Stay away from the Marigny boys. There's bad blood there. Always has been. Always will be."

"Eddie was trespassing. I—"

Pops held up one hand in front of Rafe's face. "Your rights end here, boy."

She tried not to smile. Although Pops had to look up at his son, Rafe yielded by running a hand over his head. "Yes, sir."

"Good." Pops shoved his hands in the front pocket of his clean overalls. "I'm taking your brother to Calum's. Once he's settled, I'm going home."

Juliet took the soda out of Rafe's hand. The ginger ale tasted sweet and cold. "Pops, Calum said you're welcome to stay."

Rafe kissed her on the cheek, and his hand found her lower back.

"Too many people there up in my business." Pops's nostrils flared, and he headed for the door.

Rafe finished the soda and tossed the can into the trash. "Ready to meet Sarah?"

Juliet placed her hands on his chest. He'd changed into a short-sleeved black T-shirt with his jacket. She had not asked him to hide his arms, but he'd insisted. "Earlier, when we were talking about relationships—"

"It's okay, sweetheart." One hand cupped her cheek, and the other rested on her waist. He pulled her in until their hips met. She gasped from his heat, and he smiled. "I'm confused and overwhelmed too."

She traced the ribbon on his wrist near her face. The intensity in his gaze made her world unsteady, like any minute they'd fall down a rabbit hole. "You're never afraid."

His chest rumbled. "Not true. I'm afraid every hour of every day."

She closed her hand around his wrist, covering the blue satin. "You're the strongest man I know. What could you be afraid of?"

"Losing you." His lips traced hers. "I want to say good-bye to Philip."

After telling him about John's call, she stood on her toes, needing to be closer to him. "I got a text from Bob. When you're done, I need to check the Liberty Square work site before heading to the Isle."

Rafe kissed her hard then disappeared, leaving her trembling and alone.

CHAPTER 34

NATE ENTERED THE SPO'S GARDEN. BECAUSE OF THE POWER outage, the gym had closed for the day. But after meeting with Rafe, Nate needed to burn off this raging restlessness.

He bent over, hands on his thighs, and closed his eyes. He focused on the trickling of the fountain and the *clip-clops* of a horse-drawn carriage. What wouldn't he give for a place to rest his mind and his body? He craved deep sleep in fresh air where he wasn't woken by nightmares, that stabbing pain behind his eyes, or the remembered screams of his men as they'd been tortured in the POW camp.

Breathe in. Breathe out.

"Are you alright?" The feminine voice floated over him, cooling his heated body.

He opened his eyes and stood. He blinked until she came into focus. Sarah. "Hey."

She wrapped her white lace sweater around herself, her arms inadvertently pushing up her breasts. "You look… tired."

She wore a flowy blue skirt and white camisole, had pulled her brown hair into a high ponytail, and stared at him like she was about to call 911.

He forced himself to breathe. "Not enough sleep last night."

"I hope they catch whoever set off that explosion." She walked toward the SPO, and he followed. "I was thinking about you this morning." She wrinkled her nose. "I mean your map."

The map was better than nothing. "I'm here to do more research."

"Your books are in my office. I'll bring them to you in one of the reading rooms." She smiled again. "The AC is working today."

He followed her inside, and cold air swept over him. He hadn't realized how hot his skin had gotten, and he'd been unsuccessfully ignoring the aching hard-on. "Thanks."

She disappeared behind the staircase while he went right. The North Reading Room welcomed him with a large fireplace, library tables, and chairs. Dust motes floated as if knowing they weren't allowed to land on the highly polished wood. It smelled like every other building in this city: wood oil laced with mildew.

Wooden crates lined the back wall, beneath a picture window overlooking the garden. File folders lay on top in perfect piles.

Sarah carried in a stack of books. "Those crates are filled with seventeenth-century pirate weapons I'm auctioning off in a few weeks on behalf of Calum Prioleau and the Habersham sisters. I just finished authenticating them."

"Sounds interesting." Not really, but he didn't want to be rude. He took her books and placed them on the table. "May I stay for a while?"

"Yes." She pressed a finger against her lower lip, and he wanted to kiss them both. "Did you bring your map?"

He sat and adjusted his jeans. While the pressure of his arousal against the zipper diverted him from the pain in his head, he needed to pull himself together. "No. Why?"

"I had an idea, but I can't be sure without seeing it again." Sarah sat and opened *The Chronicle or Discourse of Virginia*. "There's a compilation that had similar maps in it."

"I was wondering why that book was in the pile." He

hadn't been, but wanted to appear interested in something other than her neckline.

She opened it to a section titled "White/Hariot Maps." "This chapter is worth reading."

"Are there SparkNotes?"

"Nope." She tapped the page with her finger. "In 1582, Sir Walter Raleigh decided to map out the New World and hired Thomas Hariot and John White. Hariot was a famed mathematician and navigator, John White a renowned artist. Together, they compiled a book of navigational maps of the New World titled *Arcticon*."

"You think my map is from that book?"

"I'm not sure your map is old enough."

Okay. Now he was confused. "It's not from the book."

"No." She found her glasses in her skirt pocket and put them on. "After White and Hariot died, their apprentices did the newer work. These new maps were added to the *Arcticon* as a supplement."

Nate wanted to care but wasn't sure why he needed to. "So?"

"That compass rose on your map reminded me of the White/Hariot supplemental maps I've seen." She adjusted her sweater. "*The Arcticon* disappeared in the seventeenth century. I've only seen copies of the supplemental maps in the British Library in London."

"We can't check this famous book because it's been missing for four centuries."

She smiled again, and sweat dripped down his neck. "Three and a half. But if your friend's find is a copy of an original White/Hariot supplemental map and he could find the original and prove provenance, it could be worth millions." She stood and straightened her skirt. "If your friend wants me to look at the original, I can give him my opinion. I'm here for a few more weeks before I go back to the Smithsonian."

Nate stood and shoved his hands in his back pockets. It was either that or kiss her until she begged him to strip her naked. *Jeez Louise.* How had he ever considered himself an officer and a gentleman? "I'll tell him. Thanks."

"One more thing." She brushed back a stray hair. "Because of Elizabeth I's use of privateers and appeasement of pirates, many map makers added hidden messages, like those Easter eggs programmers hide in computer games. Call it seventeenth-century leverage."

With his men facing trials, Nate knew all about leverage. Or lack thereof. "Like treasure?"

"Some things, like diseases and remedies, were more valuable than treasure."

"You mean crude biological agents and cures?"

"Yes."

He ran his hands over his head to stop the flashing lights. "How effective were these weapons?"

"Very. The goal was to kill in small bursts, making it seem like a controlled epidemic but not create panic."

"Is it possible those forty-four children supposedly killed by Anne Capel were murdered with one of these weapons?" He picked up *Discourse* and flipped through pages. "What if those kids were infected and Anne was helping them and they died anyway?"

"It's possible but still speculation."

His phone hummed. Someone, probably Pete, had given his new number to Kells. *Fantastic.* "Can I come back? There's something I have to do."

"Yes. We close at five." For some reason her voice sounded more…*efficient*…than before, and she glanced at her watch.

"Will you be here?" he asked, hiding the disappointment in his voice.

"No." She went over to the crates near the window and started stacking files that already looked organized.

Was he making her nervous?

"I'm leaving soon," she said, glancing at him. "My truck is being repaired, and I'm picking up a rental car to do some research on the Isle of Grace."

The tic above his eye started up again. The air around him hummed. Something didn't feel right. "What kind of research?"

"The Isle's sheriff has asked me to archive the Isle's historical records, and I'm picking up some boxes. But first"—she paused to lay out the files and restack them *again*—"I thought I'd check out the Isle itself. It's supposed to be beautiful."

"Most of the Isle is privately owned land."

She frowned, and now she squinted at him. It was adorable. "You sound like my boss."

Nate crossed his arms. He understood what she wasn't saying. She was interested in that cemetery on Juliet's land. Although he'd no reason to care, he didn't want Sarah going out there alone. Not until this mess with the Fianna and the vial was squared away. "Aren't you meeting friends of mine later at Boudreaux's restaurant? Juliet Capel and Rafe Montfort."

"I am." Sarah tilted her head. "But how—"

"Rafe and I go way back. Army buddies. Do you know how to get to Boudreaux's? It's buried deep in the woods." That's what Rafe had told him, anyway.

"No," she said. "I was hoping my GPS could help me."

Nate chuckled. "There's no service out there." He paused and then asked quickly before he lost his nerve, "Would you like me to take you?"

Her eyes widened, and she backed up a step.

His cell hummed again, but he ignored Kells's call and texted Rafe and Calum instead. "I'm just offering. I have to go out there anyway"—which wasn't true—"and I know how to get to Boudreaux's." Also not true. When he was done with his text, he shoved his phone in his pocket and held out both hands, palms up. "I can also help you with the boxes."

"Do you think Miss Capel will give me permission to explore the Cemetery of Lost Children? I believe it's on her land."

"You can ask, and I'll vouch for you."

Sarah chewed her bottom lip, clearly still unsure, when her phone buzzed. She pulled it from her skirt pocket, read the text, and gave him a beautifully raised eyebrow. "Did you just text Mr. Montfort and Calum Prioleau? Because they say you're a stand-up guy and that I have nothing to worry about."

Nate smiled wide. "What time should I pick you up?"

"I'm meeting Sheriff Boudreaux at St. Mary's Church on the Isle at two p.m. to get the boxes. Then I'm going to Boudreaux's."

"I'll be here at one fifteen." He desperately wanted to kiss her cheek. Instead, he gave her a lame wave and left the building. While he hated leaving the beautiful woman who smelled like gardenias, he had to call Kells back. For the first time in Nate's career, he'd let Kells's call go to voicemail. When Kells didn't pick up, Nate left a message. Then he dialed Calum. "Where are you?"

Calum put him on speaker. "At the station with Detective Garza."

"I'm on my way. I fucked up. We need to find that safe house today."

Nate hung up and unlocked his bike. His phone rang

again, and this time the caller ID said Sergeant Turner. "Luke, tell me you have what I need."

"I texted you the number I believe is for the Z-pam contact. You sure you want to keep taking those things? They're far stronger than what's available in the U.S. And the FDA had serious reservations about their addictive side effects."

"Fuck the FDA."

"*Okaaay.* Just don't let Kells find out you're taking illegal meds. Or tell him I helped you. He's in a vicious mood."

"Agreed. I also need a favor. Check on Abigail Casey. She's in Newport."

"Liam's wife? Why?"

"She's drawing that lily. It may cause unwanted attention. Make sure she's safe."

"Got it." Luke paused. Despite awesome computer skills, Luke was still an old-fashioned note-taker. "I also discovered Deke is moving high-powered heroin. One hit and people are sent into seizures, comatose states, even death."

Nate remembered hearing about it at the club. They'd had overdoses, but Deke had taken care of them. *Shit.* Deke had been dealing heroin and cleaning up the mess while Nate and Pete had been working there. "What does that have to do with us?"

"Since our public defenders suck, I've been compiling the evidence against us. I built a database of numbers your in-theater commander called and received the night of the operation. A number on Deke's cell matched an outgoing call on your commander's SAT phone."

Nate closed his eyes. "Have you told Kells?"

"I can't without admitting I have Deke's phone, which will lead to questions neither one of us can answer."

Because lies and secrets beget more lies and secrets. "Can you trace it? And find out why a scumbag like Deke would be receiving phone calls from the same number my commander called the night our lives were fucked?"

"The number doesn't work, but it was for a law firm in New Orleans. Beaumont, Barclay, and Bray. I'll let you decide how to tell Kells."

Wow. Hell of a not-coincidence. "And the other thing I asked you to check?" Nate didn't want to say *Prince's identity* on an unsecured phone.

"Can't confirm. I'll keep checking."

"Thanks, Luke." Nate hung up and texted the dealer's number Luke had sent him.

Need Z-pam. Interested in making a deal?

The text came back. *$20/pill. Cash. ROA alley. 5 p.m.*

For the first time in forever, Nate climbed on his bike without feeling like a loser. Soon he'd have enough pills to get him through the next few days. As much as he dreaded admitting he'd lost the map, he had his first clue.

Then he remembered. He didn't have a car because he wasn't supposed to drive. So how was he going to pick up Sarah?

Nate felt like a non-driving loser as he headed into the SPD's conference room and locked the door. Calum and Detective Garza were huddled over maps and photos. Calum had showered and changed into pressed jeans, a white dress shirt buttoned to the neck, and a gray vest. Garza wore his holster and the scowl he'd had on earlier.

One of the maps on the table was an enlargement of the

historic district. Red circles dotted the paper, and a few had black lines through them. "What's this?"

Garza snapped the cap of a red Sharpie. "Calum's listing of properties for sale in the historic district. The black lines are ones that've burned down."

"Unfortunately," Calum said while texting, "arson's a problem."

Nate had noticed. "How many do we have to check out?"

"Thirty-two," Garza said. "What's this about you fucking up?"

Nate paused to take a deep breath. "I don't have the map anymore, and we need it."

"Where is it?" Calum asked.

"Balthasar has it."

Calum and Garza stared at him.

"Why?" Garza used his inside voice, which Nate hadn't been expecting.

Kells didn't have an inside voice.

"I traded it for something."

"Wait." Calum laid his phone on the table. "You saw Balthasar?"

"Yesterday," Nate said. "At the preservation office. I'd just learned that the map meant nothing."

"Then you handed it to Balthasar?" Garza said.

"Tell me you didn't trade our only clue for drugs," Calum said carefully.

"Anti-seizure meds." Nate paused. "They're legal in Canada."

"Shit." Garza hit the table with his fist. "What the *fuck* were you thinking?"

"I was on the verge of a migraine, waiting for a seizure."

Calum's lip curled. "You didn't tell us this morning?"

"I didn't think it mattered. Yesterday, the map meant nothing."

"You coward." Garza pointed at Nate's chest. "You didn't want Montfort to know."

"Or Juliet," Calum added.

Nate sank into a chair and ran his hands over his head. "If we can find Balthasar's safe house, maybe we can get that map back."

Garza hooked and unhooked his holster safety strap. "Why does the map matter now?"

"It may lead us to the vial."

"*Dammit.*" Garza kicked a chair across the room. "If you're high—"

"I'm not." After telling them Sarah's stories, Nate stood to take the coming punishment. He'd screwed up and deserved their anger.

Garza fisted his hands until Calum held up one hand. "We've had setbacks, but we're not done. Like Nate said, if we can find the safe house, maybe we can stop Balthasar before he hurts anyone else or finds the vial."

Garza picked up the chair he'd kicked.

"The goal is," Calum said in his teacher-speaking-to-child voice, "to recover the map before Rafe finds out. Because I, for one, have no interest in having that conversation."

"Agreed," Nate said. "Where do we start?"

"What makes you think we're going to let you help us?" Garza asked. "You might run to Balthasar and tell him our every move."

"I won't."

"Huh." Garza raised an eyebrow. "Why did Balthasar visit you yesterday?"

Calum, who was texting again, said, "Good question."

Nate sighed. "Balthasar has been recruiting me for the Fianna since Montfort's return."

Calum sat. "That's unexpected."

"*Shiiiiiiit*." Garza rubbed his chin that hadn't seen a razor in a week. "We have thirty-two properties to check, and I can't tell my chief what's going on because he won't believe me. Even if he did, we'd all be assassinated by bowing men. We need a plan that works."

"Balthasar's safe house will be two stories, if not more." Nate studied the map's red circles. "He's an experienced sniper. He'll use his scope to check his routes. He'll also need exits and entrances that seem unused but can be secured from inside."

Calum took the marker. A minute later, he'd eliminated eleven properties.

"Water's not that important," Nate said. "But power is. Especially if he has to hook up to the internet. We should look for properties near power and open Wi-Fi sources."

Calum crossed out ten more circles.

"Samantha mentioned tunnels." Garza pointed to a café on East Bay Street. "Do any of these properties have access to tunnels? That might be how Balthasar was able to set off the explosions and get away."

Calum chewed the inside of his cheek before crossing off seven more circles.

"How'd you know that?" Nate asked.

"I know my city."

Garza cleared his throat. "That leaves five properties."

"Another thing," Nate said. "This morning you mentioned a law firm in New Orleans."

Garza put on his jacket, adjusting the holster beneath. "What about it?"

"I talked to Luke. He told me Deke received phone calls from the same firm. And my CO—"

"Colonel Kells Torridan?" Calum asked. "The one Rafe told me about?"

"No. The night of our ambush, while waiting for a rescue or backup or a missile strike, my in-theater commander was making calls. To Beaumont, Barclay, and Bray."

Garza said, "Fuck."

Calum straightened his vest. "What does this mean?"

"No idea," Nate admitted.

Garza took out his weapon and checked the clip. Then he slammed it back in and chambered a round. "If whoever's behind this was willing to sacrifice two A-teams, they won't stop for us."

Calum pointed to one of the circles. "Start here. It's an abandoned house with a trap door in the kitchen leading into a subbasement." After Calum gave them the lowdown on the other four properties—all of them uninhabitable— Garza and Nate agreed to split up. "And watch out for rats."

"Fuuuuuck." Garza headed for the door. "I'll be back."

While Calum studied the map again, Nate glanced at his watch. It was almost noon, and he had to check his assigned locations and get to Sarah's by one fifteen. "Calum? Can I borrow your car?"

"You're not allowed to drive." Calum tapped Nate's head. "Seizures. Remember?"

"Can I also borrow your driver?"

"Does this have anything to with Sarah Munro and the text I sent for you?"

After laying out the situation with wanting to keep Sarah out of that cemetery, Calum sighed heavily. "I'll have Ivers waiting for you at the club. That's near the last location on your list."

Nate clapped Calum's shoulder. "Thanks."

Garza returned with two string backpacks filled with flashlights and water bottles and tossed one to Nate. "Let's do this thing."

To which Nate responded, "Hooah."

CHAPTER 35

Two hours later, Rafe stepped on the gas, and the Impala pulled out of the mud. He'd forgotten how deep in the woods Boudreaux's was. "I thought Old Man Boudreaux kept these roads cleared."

Juliet sat with her hands tucked between her knees. In her white dress, she reminded him of the young bride he'd married. Yet only more beautiful and confident. Two traits that were definite turn-ons. Then again, everything about Juliet turned him on.

"He died months ago. Jimmy and Tommy own the restaurant now."

Daaaaamn. "The Isle is losing its patriarchs."

"Grady and Pops are the last ones. The Marignys don't count." Juliet's voice trailed off until she said, "What's wrong? You've barely spoken since we left Philip."

The trees pressed in when the road went from gravel to dirt. "Philip told me I should do what I need to and disappear so you can live your life."

Although there was no chance he'd be able to stay with her, he'd been praying for a miracle. Like, once he returned the vial, the Prince would free Rafe despite the fact that no Fianna warrior had ever left the brotherhood alive.

By making love to her, he'd promised a future that wasn't real. Yet, if the opportunity came again, he'd love her again. He had no choice in the matter. He was a selfish bastard.

"Philip's opinion doesn't matter." She pointed left. "You missed the turn between those two palmettos."

Rafe did a ten-point turn, avoiding a mudpit and a ravine. "Philip wants what's best for you."

"I can make my own decisions. And although I'm scared to death, I'm choosing to be here with you." She rubbed the back of his neck. "What about you, Rafe? What do you want?"

He glanced at her wide eyes and soft lips and wanted to slam on the brakes and make love to her in the back seat. Her honesty speared him in the gut, leaving him shaky. He couldn't stay with her, and he couldn't leave her. What the hell was he going to do? "Since I can't guess the future, I want to rewind time to our second anniversary."

Her face flushed. "I remember."

Talk about a memory burned into his cerebral cortex. He'd taken leave from training at Fort Bragg, and they'd met their families at Boudreaux's. They'd eaten Cajun food on picnic tables. Danced barefoot in the early September summer heat on wooden boards beneath oak trees. Moved to a band playing Zydeco waltzes and Cajun two-steps until the sun rose.

That was the last night he'd spent with both of his parents.

She traced his ear with her finger. "Do you hear that?"

It came in slowly. A Zydeco waltz wafted through the woods. The vegetation thickened until Rafe turned onto a bush road and, fifty yards down, parked near the river. "Everything changes. Except for Boudreaux's."

She reached for her door handle.

"Wait." He came around to open her door. The heat slammed into him, and the spicy scent of Cajun food made his stomach growl.

"You can take off your coat," she said softly. "It's too hot."

"Are you sure?"

At her nod, he chucked it in the back seat, took her hand, and led her to the cooking shack with shutters painted blue to keep away the local *haints*, a.k.a. the Isle's restless spirits. He gently pushed her against the siding, his hands landing on either side of her bare shoulders. He needed to breathe in her scent. "It's my turn to apologize."

She held his face in her hands. "What for?"

He pressed his forehead against hers. "For everything."

"Rafe?" She swallowed. "Are you asking for forgiveness?"

"Forgiveness is a gift I don't deserve." Their eyelashes caught. "I need you to know…" He tickled her jawline with his lips. "There are so many things I can't tell, so many things I regret, but there's never been a moment when I haven't loved you."

"Rafe." Her voice came out scattered, like it had been drawn through a sieve. "*Please.*"

Her rapid breath pushed her breasts up and down, each time rising higher. His hands moved to her rib cage, his thumbs cupping her breasts. "I love you. If we lived a thousand years in a thousand lives, I would find you and love you and make you mine."

She stared up at him, and for the first time there was no anger, bitterness, or wariness in her eyes. Just raw, anguished pain. But beneath the pain, there was something else—a smoldering he remembered. An awakened desire.

His thumbs made small circles along the fuller curves. She leaned into him. His lips slanted over hers. His world exploded with images of her straddling him, beneath him, in the shower. Every memory he had of her left him blind, deaf, and breathless. Her lips softened, and he held her head at the perfect angle. He pressed his hard body against her smaller curves, making sure she knew how she affected him.

But since he was trying to change from the monster he'd once been back into the honorable man he'd always wanted to be, he broke the kiss. "Let's find Sarah and Nate."

Rafe had been surprised to learn Nate was coming with Sarah but relieved when Nate explained he was keeping the curious historian off Capel land.

Juliet touched her swollen lips and took Rafe's outstretched hand. His body ached, and sweat beaded his brow. He focused on his environment.

People sat at picnic tables lined with brown paper, and a band played near the wooden dance floor beneath overhanging oak trees. Lights were draped from tree to tree. He was drowning in memories. Holding her against his chest. His hand on her lower back. His breath in her ear, whispering things husbands asked of wives.

Before Rafe lost his mind, Tommy came out of the shack. Juliet stiffened, and Rafe's hand settled on her shoulder. Tommy wore a white apron over jeans and a white T. Only on the Isle would the head cook of an outdoor gumbo hut also work as the deputy sheriff.

"What are you two doing here?" Tommy met them, wiping his hands on the apron. The bruises on his jaw and around his eye were purple and swollen. They were lucky Tommy didn't throw Rafe out on his ass.

"Meeting friends," Rafe said, "not from the Isle."

"Hopefully they won't get lost." Tommy scanned the surrounding tables, and Rafe noticed what Tommy noticed. Three Toban brothers and their sons were at a table near the largest oak tree. All ex-Navy. Next table over sat six distant cousins on his mother's side—the Marigny men his father despised—all ex-Army. The table on the left side of the dance floor held Grady Mercer and four of his nephews. All ex-Marines.

An AWOL ex-Green Beret imprisoned for desertion and treason might not be welcome. "How about that table near the tree line?" It was away from the men and heavily shaded.

"Great," Tommy said. "There's soda and beer in the coolers and sweet tea in the dispensers." Coolers lined the dance floor, and a nearby table held a sports dispenser and red Solo cups. "Grab some drinks, and I'll send over a bucket of boiled shrimp."

The band was on break, and murmurs swept through the area.

Juliet poured two teas. "Are they talking about me or you?"

"Probably me." Rafe took a sip, and the sweetness hurt his teeth. He'd forgotten how sweet *sweet* could be. "Although I hear whispers about dead bodies and ghosts."

She sat at their table, and he followed. "I can't wait to sell my land."

Tommy appeared with a stack of napkins, and the Cajun band geared up with "Iko Iko."

Rafe pointed to the security cameras in the trees. "Having trouble?"

"Teenage stuff." Tommy wiped his hands again. "It's been dicey since my daddy died."

"Juliet told me. I'm sorry."

"Times are changin'. The younger ones don't want to come to the woods to drink and dance where there's no Wi-Fi." Tommy nodded to a couple near the cooking shack clutching a copy of *Off the Beaten Path*. "Whatta ya know. Tourists. Excuse me."

The band started a creole waltz, and Rafe dragged her up. "Let's give the locals a reason to chatter."

༄

Rafe swung Juliet around before bringing her close. And she let him. Although he didn't flaunt his arousal, he didn't hide it either. After each swing, her dress flowed, and her hips brushed his.

It'd been so long since they'd danced. She'd forgotten how he'd take the lead so she could close her eyes and float through the muggy air tinged with Cajun spices. The waltz felt weightless and sensual, every third beat her rubbing against his body. Since his return, her emotions had been blowing around like dandelion seeds. Fears about trusting him, loving him, losing him fought intense desire and yearning. She was sixteen again with no idea what to do with it all.

He whispered against her hair, "This was our wedding waltz."

She remembered. They'd come here after the church ceremony and danced until they left for their one-night honeymoon in Charleston. He spun her again, but on this return, he wrapped an arm around her waist and kept her close. The dance became a sway, and a flush rose up until her cheeks felt hot.

"The day you graduated high school I told your daddy I was going to marry you."

She checked out his wide, laughter-free eyes. "You did not." *Did he?*

He nodded. "I decided the night of your senior prom."

"I didn't go to my prom." She couldn't afford a dress and didn't have a date.

He frowned, as if hurt. "We danced to the whippoor-wills under the full moon."

She rested her head against his shoulder. "You climbed my balcony and convinced me to come with you."

"You wore a white dress."

A worn sundress, threadbare and thin. "You stole a canoe."

He'd paddled her to the back meadow. With a blanket and a basket of food, they sat on the dock eating PB&J sandwiches, lemonade, and his momma's brownies.

He kissed her head. "We danced in the grass until the full moon turned in."

She moaned. "That was the night I fell in love with you."

His body stiffened, and then shifted back into the weightless movement she was still getting used to. "Nate and Sarah are here."

Juliet pulled away and wiped her damp hands on her skirt. Sarah and Nate poured themselves iced teas before they headed over, every man in the place watching.

Juliet went to the table, and Rafe's hand rested on her lower back. Like he'd always done. Like he couldn't help himself.

Sarah held out her hand and introduced herself. "I'm Dr. Sarah Munro."

Juliet shook Sarah's hand and smiled back. The pretty historian had long brown hair in a high ponytail and wore a long blue chiffon skirt, white camisole, and white Keds sneakers. She placed her straw bag on the table and blew a stray hair out of her face. Sarah wasn't at all how Juliet had pictured her. Sarah seemed more like a kindergarten school teacher than a PhD historian with the Smithsonian.

But the most interesting thing about Sarah? Nate hadn't taken his gaze off her since arriving.

"I'm glad you two found the place," Juliet said.

Sarah grinned. "I've always wanted to come to Boudreaux's. And I'm glad Nate offered to bring me. I never would've found it on my own."

Nate glanced at Juliet. "Thanks for sending me detailed directions. This place defines *the middle of nowhere*."

Juliet smiled. "Yes, it does."

Rafe laughed. "And the people of the Isle like it that way."

Once they sat, Sarah started. "I spoke with the Habersham sisters yesterday. They mentioned you wanted to talk about your lily?"

Juliet sipped her tea. "You heard about Miss Beatrice?"

"I did." Sarah clasped her iced tea. "I'm so sorry. I hope they find who did it."

"I hope so too." After filling Sarah in on some of the details of their search, Juliet ended with, "Rafe and I need to know more about the lily and Anne Capel."

A waitress dropped off two baskets each of fried shrimp and fried oysters.

"First of all," Sarah said, and peeked at Nate, "my specialty is early colonial American history. What I know about the lily and Anne Capel I've learned from diaries and journals from that time period. Primary sources, but without public records it's still hearsay."

"It's more than we have now." Rafe handed Sarah the phone photos. "We saw these windows at Capel Manor."

Sarah wiped her hands on a napkin and scrolled. "Wow. These are...disturbing."

"Very," Juliet said. "Any idea what they mean?"

"This first one?" Sarah pointed to the image of the woman handing a lily to a man. "The man is Alexander Capel. The woman is his wife, Countess Violetta Priuli. It's 1583 in Verona, Italy, and the flower she's holding isn't a real lily. It's a hybrid Glorious Lily and White Hellebore."

Juliet coughed on her tea. "It would be extremely poisonous."

"It was." Sarah ate a shrimp and wiped her hands on a napkin. "Sixteenth-century Italy was known for STDs and poisons. The Priuli family created your 'lily' to treat syphilis, but it quickly became known as a tasteless and odorless poison that could be mixed with water or food.

"Unfortunately, the poison was easier to make than the cure, and the Doge stepped in. Anyone caught growing the flower, making the poison, or using it was executed. When the Priuli family was charged with cultivating the lily, the family fled Italy."

Rafe squinted at the photo. "How did this lily end up on the Isle of Grace?"

"Alexander Capel was an Englishman who owned property in Charleston. By 1633, he and his wife's family were ensconced there. Since Alexander was a noble, the Capels were included in the highest social circles. The Priuli family, still carrying the stigma from the Veronese scandal, changed their name to Prideaux. But it wasn't enough to hide what the family had done in Verona. While the Capels rose, the Prideauxs, unable to overcome their family's past, became pirates.

"By 1637, both the Capel and Prideaux families were settled on the Isle of Grace and the Isle of Hope. Then Countess Violetta made a trip home to Verona and, unbeknownst to her husband, returned with lily bulbs."

"Why?" Juliet asked.

"This story comes from second- and thirdhand sources, but from what I can piece together, Violetta was upset over her birth family's inability to rise up Charleston's social ladder. Her family was descended from Italian royalty, yet in the New World, the Prideauxs were reduced to common thieves. She wanted her Prideaux family to succeed in their new career as pirates and take down the very society who'd refused them." Sarah paused to sip her iced tea and steal another look at Nate.

And Nate looked back. "Violetta wanted revenge?"

"Yes." Sarah wiped her lips with a napkin. "Alexander owned land from Charleston down to Savannah. After a few false tries, Violetta—a renowned herbalist—discovered that the poisonous lily loved the high level of phosphates in the soil on the Isle of Grace. She encouraged Alexander to settle down here and, being a man who'd always preferred adventure to civilized life, he agreed to move to the wilderness."

"Why bring the lily back to life?" Rafe downed his tea and started popping shrimp. "Weren't there easier ways to seek revenge?"

Juliet took a few shrimp, but her stomach revolted.

Sarah glanced at Nate for the millionth time, and Juliet hid her smile behind her cup. "Because," Sarah said softly, "Juliet's lily could be weaponized."

When Rafe and Nate exchanged a *holy shit* look, Juliet took Rafe's hand. He returned her squeeze.

"It's a matter of leverage," Sarah said. "The Prideaux pirates would poison someone and demand ransom. If the family paid, they were given the antidote. If not, the victim died."

"That's awful." Juliet flinched. "No wonder the Prideaux pirates became so rich and powerful."

"Exactly." Sarah took some oysters and ate them one by one. "After Alexander and Violetta died, their son, Theodore Capel, married Eliza Prideaux. Eliza died giving birth to Anne Capel. Theodore raised Anne, and together they grew the lily and supplied the Prideaux pirates with the poison and antidote.

"It wasn't uncommon for the people of the Isles to put a black flag with a white lily in their window to tell the raiding pirates they were loyal to the Prideaux family. But after Anne and other families on the Isle became Puritans, things changed. She convinced her father that what they were doing was evil. Before Theodore died, he applied for King's Grants for his land on the Isle of Grace and requested a stipulation that a woman could own the land. He wanted the land grants to protect his daughter. King Charles agreed but added another stipulation that the lily never be cultivated on the Isle."

Rafe handed Juliet a napkin filled with oysters. "So that's one of the Grants stipulations?"

"I haven't seen them," Sarah said, "but I believe so."

Nate took more napkins from the passing waitress and handed them out. "I bet the Prideaux family wasn't happy about it."

"They weren't. But by then they were so feared that the threat of the poison was enough. The real problem was Anne. In the seventeenth century, scattered Puritans, Native Americans of the Guale tribe, and wild animals occupied the Isles of Grace and Hope. There was little community, and settlers made their own peace with the natives.

"After Theodore's death, Anne—now a devout Puritan ashamed of her part in providing poison to the pirates— retreated from society and learned natural healing arts from the Guale women. She never married, but in 1677 she had an affair with Isaiah Montfort and got pregnant. It was a huge scandal, and Isaiah's brother, Josiah, was jealous.

"Then an epidemic arrived. Anne searched for a cure, but when children died, she suspected her lily was the cause and parsed the stipulation of the King's Grants. Since cultivation means to 'grow or raise under controlled circumstances,' she decided that didn't include wild lilies. And the lily reappeared on Capel land."

"Why?" Nate touched Sarah's hand. "Anne knew it was poisonous."

Sarah withdrew her hand to take another sip of tea. Juliet couldn't help but notice Sarah's hand shook and that she watched Nate from beneath her long lashes.

"The lily was both the poison *and* the antidote," Sarah said. "Anne believed someone was using the lily to cause the malady afflicting the children. Therefore, she could cure it with the antidote derived from the same flower. But the children died and were buried in the Cemetery of Lost Children. Then the settlers turned against Anne.

"After Josiah burned her house and killed Isaiah, Anne disappeared into Capel land, only seeing those brave enough to find her. Capel land has always been the backdrop for violence."

Juliet smiled at Rafe. "Another reason to sell."

Rafe ignored her and swiped the manor's photos again. "What about these other windows?"

"I'm not sure. Although…" Sarah scrolled to the last one. "See this inscription? I've seen that before, in a diary I was translating."

Worked into the bottom of the stained glass were the words: *Sinn ag loighe ar in lucht romhainn, lucht oile orainn san úaigh.*

"It's Old Irish," Sarah said.

"*We rest on those who came before us and others will rest on us in the grave,*" Rafe said in a hushed voice with a hint of reverence.

Nate stared hard at Rafe while Sarah said, "You're right. It's an obscure text used by a cult of ancient Celtic warriors known as the Fianna."

Nate stood. "I'll be right back."

Once Nate left for the restroom, Rafe snagged Juliet's hand and put it on his upper thigh. She felt the vibrations of his foot tapping beneath the table.

"Sarah, in your research," Rafe asked, "did you find references to a vial Anne owned?"

"Not directly." Sarah held up the photo of Anne with the two men. "After those children died, Anne never allowed the lily to be grown on her property. She went to great lengths to eradicate any wild plants. And there's one story I can't corroborate, but it's about a deal Anne made with someone to help prevent the lily from ever being used again for nefarious purposes."

"She's handing them *two* vials," Juliet said.

"Before Anne eradicated the lily, she made one last dose of the poison and the antidote and hid them for safe-keeping. Since you never know if or when a disease will pop up again, you keep the chemical compounds to make more antidotes."

"Rafe?" Nate strode over, his face one hard glare. "We have a problem."

"Shit." Rafe took Juliet's elbow, and she stood. "Time to go."

That's when she noticed men around them. All staring at Rafe.

CHAPTER 36

RAFE KNEW EVERY MAN STANDING. THREE TOBAN BROTHERS and their four sons. Six Marigny brothers. Four Mercer cousins. Six Boudreaux men. Two Legares. And two Prioleaus—the poorer Prioleaus. "Nate?"

"Yeah?" Nate came up next to Rafe so they stood shoulder to shoulder.

"Let me handle this. And watch out for the women."

"You sure, bro?"

"Yes." Rafe didn't want anyone involved in any more of his life's shit than necessary. Once Nate backed up two steps, Rafe met the gaze of the biggest badass of the group, Francois Marigny. One of Rafe's many second cousins. "Frankie. You look…concerned."

"Concerned?" Francois spat. "What the hell you doin' here, Rafe? You're supposed to be in prison. You know, with the other fucking traitors."

The other men murmured, some inched closer. Frankie's youngest brother, Etienne, in a black hoodie, protected Frankie's left side. Etienne's long, narrow nose, flanked by beady black eyes, looked like a steak knife sticking out of his thin, angular face.

Rafe moved in front of Juliet, while Nate covered Sarah. "I'm here to see my wife."

Francois's gaze slid to Juliet. His brown eyes brightened. "She doesn't belong to you anymore. We heard you ditched her."

Rafe fisted his hands. "Since when do you listen to gossip?"

Etienne spoke up. "We don't want trouble. We just don't want you here."

"And I don't want you here," Juliet said from behind him.

The men laughed.

Juliet pushed Rafe aside. "Boudreaux's is on *my* land. I can invite or disinvite anyone I want. *Permanently*."

"You gonna let your woman fight for you?" Francois taunted. "We heard how you beat up my nephew Eddie yesterday. Kid was so terrified he pissed his pants."

"I did not," Eddie said from the back.

Rafe crossed his arms over his chest. "Eddie was trespassing, about to be snake food. And my woman can fend for herself. Gerald made sure of that."

Francois reached out to touch her hair. "Is that a threat?"

Rafe pulled up Francois by his T-shirt until his feet dangled. "You touch my wife again, you'll regret it."

"I ain't afraid of you," Francois sneered. "And the next time you touch my kin—"

Rafe tossed Francois onto the table. His back smashed the shrimp baskets, and the sweet tea splashed in three different directions. "If any of the assholes from your family trespasses on Capel land again or looks at my wife, he'll answer to me. And it *will* hurt."

"Hey." Tommy ran over. "Rafe, let him go."

Grady took Juliet's arm. "I think you and your man should leave."

Juliet shrugged him off. "They started it."

"Probably," Tommy said, "but it'd be better if you left. You know, until people forget?"

Rafe let go and glared at Tommy. "That I betrayed everyone I love?"

"Yeah."

"Except we won't ever forget what you did, Rafe." Francois, now splattered with tea, scrambled to stand again. "You disrespected the uniform. Abandoned your men. Betrayed your wife."

Etienne added, "Prison was too good for you."

Juliet moved into the center of the scene. Despite her shorter stature, her glare reminded Rafe of her daddy at his angriest. From the way the others backed away, they remembered too.

"If you can't be civil, I'll shut down Boudreaux's like my daddy always wanted." With a toss of her braid, she walked away as if she were queen of the Isle. Which, considering she owned more than half of it, was kind of true.

Rafe's heart swelled with pride. Juliet, in her white dress and with blazing brown eyes, had taken on almost every man on the Isle.

Sarah followed Juliet while Nate protected Rafe's back. Everyone else returned to their tables.

"Come on, Rafe." Tommy grabbed his shoulder. "We need to talk."

Although Rafe never walked away from fights, he and Nate followed Tommy. Whatever the deputy had to say, he'd better use few words. Juliet was waiting.

Juliet fell against the truck. The metal's heat burned through her dress. The Isle's summer sounds, which used to comfort her, now made her irritable.

"Juliet?" She opened her eyes to find Sarah nearby, her arms wrapped around herself. "Are you selling your land?"

"Yes." Juliet waved toward the men staring at her. "There's no reason not to."

"I may be an outsider, but even I know that if a developer

turns your land into a resort with golf courses and condos, it'll change the Isle."

Juliet crossed her arms over her chest. "It's Wednesday afternoon, and half of the Isle's inhabitants are *here*."

"Hunting, fishing, and construction work happen in the early hours. That's how these men make their living. I also know from the Habersham sisters how these men treated your father." Sarah pointed at Tommy, who had Rafe up against the cooking shack while Nate appeared to be reasoning with them. "How unkind they were to you. But that doesn't mean you're not a part of this place. Considering you own more than fifty percent of the Isle, what you do will change the lives of everyone living here."

"That's quite a guilt trip." Juliet rubbed her forehead with the back of her hand. "Since I can't find the King's Grants, it probably won't matter."

Sarah glanced at Rafe and Nate again before going to a black car, with its engine running, parked a few feet away.

Was that Calum's Bentley? With Ivers asleep in the front seat?

When Sarah returned, she handed Juliet a canvas messenger bag. "This is for you."

Juliet took it, surprised at the weight. "What is it?"

"It's a book I borrowed from your father's trunk. It belongs to you."

Juliet pulled it out. The leather was so old and worn it left her hand covered in orange dust. "*Hume's History of England*? It looks old."

"It is."

Juliet flipped through the pages until finding the chapter marked with a velvet ribbon. "Ancient Order of Druid Priests and Warriors." It was written in Old English. She also found a loose paper with scrawled writing on it. Her daddy's handwriting.

> *All warriors tithe until death. No way out.*
>
> *Extreme self-discipline: daily training, fasting, penance, celibacy, speak in well-mannered verse; courteous; memorize twelve books of Gaelic poetry; fluent in Latin; keep a journal; must learn how to walk.*
>
> *Vows: to protect women, children, noncombatants; cut all ties to previous life; give up own life for a fellow warrior; hunt down/kill rogue mercenaries; serve one master.*
>
> *Twelve floggings: one every month*
>
> *If vows are broken, lives of recruit and all of his loved ones are forfeit.*
>
> *Must survive the Hunt while naked. Must submit to the Gauntlet.*

"After reading this book," Sarah said softly, almost conspiratorially, "I started researching the Fianna. They existed during Anne's time, a fact confirmed by that window inscription. It sounds crazy, but it's possible they still exist. It's also possible they want to either use your lily as a weapon or prevent it from being used as such."

"It's not crazy." Juliet shoved the book into the bag and put it in the car beneath her seat. "The sisters mentioned other documents in my daddy's trunk. Do you know anything about those?"

"Gerald brought some documents for me to look at. The maps were incredibly fragile. He refused to leave them with me to study, and I have no idea what he did with them. If you find the maps, though, I'd love to get another look at them."

"I'll let you know," Juliet said. "Hopefully I'll find the grants as well."

Sarah brushed a stray hair off her cheek and stared down at the ground. "I know your father and you forbade anyone going out to the cemetery on your property—"

Juliet touched Sarah's arm. "I can't allow anyone out there right now. A man was murdered yesterday, and they haven't caught the killer. But if things change"—like if Juliet built a real road and people stopped dying on her property—"I'll take you there myself."

Sarah nodded. "I'd appreciate that." She glanced at the men again before asking softly, "What do you know about Nate? He seems nice but…troubled."

Considering Nate's uncertain future and complicated past, Juliet didn't know what to say. Mostly, she wanted to spare Sarah the kind of heartache that came with loving men like Rafe or Nate. Men torn between the families they loved and their need to prove themselves. Their desire for love and their instinct to protect. Then Juliet remembered how Nate had helped beat up Deke, how carefully Nate carried Miss Beatrice out of the restaurant, and his plan to protect Sarah from the cemetery. "Nate has a good heart. He's honorable and protective." As Juliet said the words, she realized they weren't just true, she actually believed them. "He's a man worth loving."

Sarah gave her a half smile. "Thanks."

Juliet nodded and noticed Rafe and Nate striding toward them. Despite Rafe's size, he moved in that weightless, graceful way she'd become accustomed to.

"The book mentions that Fianna warriors fall to the ground," Sarah said, "repeatedly, until their movements lose stiffness. As if bones, muscles, and tendons are stretched and realigned."

Floggings. Gauntlet. Hunt. What else had Rafe suffered while he'd been gone?

He stopped close enough for his breath to tickle her ear. "Let's go."

"You didn't hit Tommy." Juliet stood on her toes to kiss his cheek. "I'm proud of you."

Rafe grinned. "You're a good influence."

Nate came up next to Sarah, holding a red Solo cup. "I think it's time to wake Ivers. I promised him some lemonade for the drive home."

Sarah nodded at Juliet. "It was a pleasure meeting you. I wish you luck with your search for Anne's Lament."

Juliet and Rafe shared a confused glance. "Anne's Lament?" Juliet asked.

"Yes." Sarah hiked her straw bag higher on her shoulder until Nate took it from her. "That's what historians call the legend of Anne Capel and the forty-four children. They even say she's protected by three archangels."

Juliet squeezed Rafe's hand. "That's what Sebastian said. Do you remember?"

Rafe nodded.

"Who the hell is Sebastian?" Nate asked.

"Cemetery trespasser from years ago," Rafe said, "looking for Anne's Lament."

"*Greeeaaaat,*" Nate said. "More competition."

"Excuse me?" Sarah looked at all three of them.

Nate shook his head. "Never mind. We should leave."

After they said their goodbyes, Nate took Sarah's arm and led her to the car.

Once Ivers drove away, Juliet said, "Sebastian was looking for the vial."

"Yes."

"Do you think he was a Fianna warrior?"

Rafe stayed silent a long time, his breathing strong and steady.

"Rafe?" She tugged his arm. "When you were sixteen, did you make a vow to a Fianna warrior to save me and Calum?"

Rafe's exhale was explosive. "Apparently so."

"What do we do now?"

"We need to go to where we last saw Sebastian. We need to visit Anne Capel's tomb."

CHAPTER 37

RAFE PARKED THE TRUCK AS CLOSE AS HE COULD TO THE CEM-
etery and opened Juliet's door. They'd stopped by Pops's
trailer to get the cemetery keys and switch cars. While
there, she'd changed into the jeans, T-shirt, and field jacket
she'd thrown into the car before coming out to the Isle.
Rafe had also found snake boots in the barn.

He got out and opened her door.

"I wish I hadn't forgotten my own boots," Juliet said.
"These are too big."

He scrounged through the back of the pickup and found
Gerald's duffel while Juliet adjusted the boots with ladybug
faces painted on the toes.

He concentrated on the weapons. "My momma loved
ladybugs."

"I miss her," Juliet said softly.

"I miss her, too." He'd take the shotgun, his handgun,
the machete, and two knives. "Do you have your gun?"

"In the pocket of my field coat."

"Good." Although it was beastly hot, they understood
the risks of traveling on foot without jackets and boots.
He slipped on his field jacket and loaded up with ammo
and flashlights. He gave her a backpack he'd filled with
water and more ammo. Once he slung the shotgun onto
his back and held the machete ready, he took her hand
and led the way.

A minute later, she said, "Is it true you were flogged
once a month?"

He stopped and stared at her. "What are you talking about?"

"Sarah gave me a book. It had a chapter on ancient Druid warriors."

Rafe's snort startled nearby birds. "*Hume's History of England*?"

"How'd you know?"

He shook his head and kept walking. "I've read it. And no, I wasn't flogged every month for a year. I can't imagine how that'd go over with the brotherhood."

"What about the Hunt? What's that about?"

"Juliet—"

"This situation can't get much worse, and I've a right to know."

She had a point, and he was tired of being evasive. "The Hunt is the last training period before a recruit is accepted into the brotherhood. He's chased through the woods in the middle of winter, naked, with a staff as a weapon. And his hair, which he was forced to grow during the training period, is plaited."

"Why?"

"Because that's how they did things during Roman times. He has to hide, evade, and take out as many hunters as possible. Every branch he breaks and noise he makes, even each hair that's out of place, is counted against him. But, eventually, he's captured. Then he's buried up to his chest in a pit with his nondominant arm free and uses the staff to fight off twelve men. If he wins, he's dug up and allowed to enter the Gauntlet."

"You're buried naked?"

He glanced at her concerned frown. "That's what you're thinking about? Not the fact that he's being attacked by twelve highly trained men at the same time and only has one arm and it's freezing cold?"

"That's bad too. But weren't you worried about bugs?"

He laughed out loud. "I thought you'd be impressed. Instead you're worried about spiders crawling up my a—"

She covered his mouth with her hand. "Don't be crude. And I am impressed. Just wondering why that kind of training is necessary." Her head tipped to the side. "Since you're a warrior, I suppose you passed this training?"

He smiled wide. "Yep. Wish you'd been there. I was totally buff and hot."

She passed him. "You're impossible."

"And still hot."

She laughed, and the tightness in his chest dissipated. He'd never talked about these things. Not even with Escalus, and they'd trained together. Yet bringing them out into the open made the horror seem less…horrible. Maybe that'd been the point of the secrecy. Once you release the memories, they lost their power.

When they reached the headless archangel in the center of the cemetery, Rafe turned left. It was a twenty-yard direct line from St. Michael to the iron doors of Anne's crypt. Rafe gave her the keys, and she flipped through the ring until finding the right one.

The doors opened easily, and he slipped the padlock into his coat pocket, trading it for a flashlight. "Ready?"

"Yes." She threw the keys into her backpack, found her light, and used her bag to prop open the door. "Let's do this quickly."

He switched on the light and went in. Dust motes scattered through the beam, and his boots left impressions in the dirty floor. Juliet coughed next to him. A marble tomb lay in the center. Four pillars stood in the corners, three holding urns. "I don't see anything unusual."

"The urn I broke is gone."

He swung the flashlight around. "There's no place to hide anything in here."

She tilted one of the urns to look inside. Then the other two. "They're empty."

They met over Anne's tomb, and she wiped off the dust on Anne's crypt, exposing a carving of her lily. "Do you think there's anything in here?"

He laid down the machete, knelt, and ran a hand around the marble edges. "It's sealed." He used the light to trace around the bottom. It was a solid piece with no joints or obvious openings. "I can't imagine anything was buried with Anne. That'd mean someone else would've been in on her secret."

"You're afraid to open it."

He glanced at her and caught her smile. "I'm not big on desecrating burial sites."

She moved to kneel next to him. "I can't wait to tell Samantha you believe in ghosts."

"I don't believe in ghosts. I just don't want to see another dead body."

Her smile fell away, and she touched his cheek. He closed his eyes and pressed his face against her hand. "Have there been many?" Her voice sounded soft and far away.

He opened his eyes and met the brown gaze he'd dreamed about for the past eight years. "Too many."

She kissed him gently on the lips. "I'm sorry."

When she withdrew, he said, "Don't be. The choices I made, along with the consequences, are mine to live with."

She stood and ran her hand along the tomb one last time. The edges had been etched with a design. "The carvings on this tomb are intertwining yew and oak leaves. Like the carvings on the mantel."

"And on your map." He stood behind her and looked

over her shoulders. "Except those sketches also had swords, lilies, and fish worked into the design. I get the lilies, but I wonder what the swords and fish are all about."

"No idea." She glanced back and held up her hand. "May I see your phone?"

He frowned. "What for?"

"Didn't you take a picture of the map before you gave it to Nate?"

"My burner phone doesn't take photos." He kissed her neck, loving it when she shivered. "I assumed you took a photo."

She pressed back against him, and he wrapped his arms around her waist. Her lavender scent, her softer body against the hard length of his, made him want to leave this place forever and go back to the apartment. He was tired of mysteries and secrets and dead things.

"Why would I do that?"

"When we were married, you were always the one snapping pictures."

Now her eyes were closed, and she leaned most of her weight against him. "That's ridiculous."

"And you did take all the photos of your windows yesterday."

"This was my responsibility?" She snorted. Delicately, of course. "You're the one who came home with crazy stories of lilies and bowing men."

He shrugged. "And you let me kiss you anyway."

"We handed over our only clue without taking a picture." She turned so he could see her narrowed eyes. And was that a slight smile? "What is wrong with us?"

He kissed her cheek. "I know I was distracted."

She pushed him away. "Then let's go home."

He couldn't agree more.

They gathered their things, and he locked up. After adjusting the shotgun, he saw Juliet standing a few feet away, her hands on her hips, staring at St. Michael. "What's wrong?"

She pointed to the naked angel. "Sarah mentioned that Anne's secret was protected by three archangels." Juliet turned in a full circle. "Michael ahead of me, Anne behind me," she stretched out her arms in opposite directions, "the other two would be on either side."

"I'll go right, you go left." He kissed her quickly. "Be careful."

It didn't take long to lose sight of her behind two large mausoleums and a grove of pecan trees. "Can you hear me?"

"Yes. Do you see anything?"

"Not yet." He was in the center of four limestone headstones. The only unusual thing was an empty plinth block with ELIZA PRIDEAUX 1600–1652 carved on the front. The yew-and-oak-leaf motif had been cut along the edges, interspersed with Juliet's lilies. He walked around, seeing smaller tombs and mausoleums but no angels.

He went back to Anne's tomb. "Where are you?"

"Over here!" He followed her voice until he found her between a crypt and an angel. Her backpack lay on top of a flat tomb nearby.

The archangel, while not as imposing as Michael, was eight feet tall on a four-foot plinth with THEODORE CAPEL 1590–1670 carved on the front. Again, yew and oak leaves had been etched, but this time with fish.

"It's Raphael," she said. "He's standing on a fish and holding a staff, his angelic symbols."

He pointed to the inscription *Efficia fret quietum* on the scroll in Raphael's other hand. "This same scroll is on a relief of St. Raphael in the Doge's Palace in Venice."

"I'd love to go to Venice." She touched the angel's face. "Is it as romantic as it seems?"

"I didn't go for the romance." He took her hand and held it against his heart. "We'll go there for our second honeymoon. After lots of wine and a dinner of *bigoli in salsa*, we'll walk the streets and eat meringues. You'll love them. They're bigger than Calum's head."

She hit him in the chest with her free fist. "We never went on a first honeymoon."

He caught that hand and kissed it too. "We honeymooned in Charleston."

"One night at the Mills House Hotel. And we didn't leave the room."

He raised an eyebrow. "We were busy. Like last night."

She yanked her hands out of his and cupped his face. "We need to focus."

He covered her fingers with his. "I found a plinth block on the other side that probably held another angel. It has Eliza Prideaux's name carved into it along with lilies."

"Eliza was Theodore Capel's wife and Anne's mother. And the map's decorations were yew and oak leaves combined with swords, fish, and lilies."

Rafe glanced back toward the statue of St. Michael hidden behind many crypts and trees. "Swords are the angelic symbol of Michael, fish are the angelic symbol of Raphael, while lilies are the angelic symbol of..."

Juliet grabbed his arm, her eyes widening into brown pools. "Gabriel."

Rafe ran a hand over his head, trying to work this out. "Gabriel lived in the manor."

"My daddy moved him in when I was six." She squinted at Raphael. "But why?"

Rafe knelt and ran his fingers along the bottom carvings

until he felt a metal pin. When he pulled, a spring-action hinge popped and a door opened. He dragged out a steel box, and she lifted the top. Inside, wrapped in canvas, was a stack of yellowed, folded documents, and a manila envelope with Juliet's name on it.

He handed her the envelope while he looked at the documents. They were very fragile and crumbling maps. He rewrapped them so they wouldn't disintegrate.

"Rafe, look." She'd opened the envelope and laid the contents on the ground to show him the scrawled signature of King Charles I of England. "My King's Grants."

Juliet gripped Rafe's hand. "This means the vial could be in Gabriel or Michael."

He stood and adjusted the weapon on his back. "Stay here while I check Michael."

Before she could protest, he disappeared. She wasn't sure she'd ever get used to the graceful way he moved. Next to him, she felt like a clunky cow. She sighed and put the decrepit documents in the box. Luckily the grants weren't as fragile.

How could she be holding documents signed by King Charles I that'd been touched by Anne? And her father? Each grant was folded in thirds and still held the remains of the royal wax seal. Although Juliet could make out the names on the grants, including the King's and Theodore Capel's, the rest of the writing was in a beautiful yet hard-to-read script.

"Don't move." Rafe's harsh command made her freeze.

A second later, something whizzed by her head and cut her ear.

Rafe yanked her up and wrapped his arms around her. "Are you alright?"

"I think so." She pressed her face against his chest. His heart beat faster than hers, and she held on, hoping to ease his fear as well. Although she'd no idea what he was afraid of. "What happened?"

He sprinkled kisses on her head, her nose, her cheeks until he found her lips. When he released her, he said, "Storm's coming."

A clap rumbled, and she looked up. The tree canopy hid the sky, but she could feel the rising static. Something dripped down her face, and she touched her ear. Her fingers came away red. "Why am I bleeding?"

He pointed to the tree behind her. She turned, still within his arms. There, held against the trunk with its head almost severed by Rafe's knife, was a diamondback rattlesnake.

Her legs wobbled, and he tightened his hold. "I never heard him."

"He wasn't moving. But his head was raised. He must've been sleeping in the tree."

The diamondback rattler was the most venomous snake in Georgia. "Thank you."

He rested his cheek against her head and rubbed her lower back. "I'm sorry I cut your ear. He was about to strike."

"I don't care. It doesn't hurt."

He kissed her again, this time with lingering pauses and rising pressure that mirrored the growing storm around them. "Please, Rafe. Let's go home."

CHAPTER 38

BALTHASAR STOOD NEAR THE WINDOW OF HIS SAFE HOUSE. Coffee brewed while he scrolled through the photos Eddie had sent. Romeo holding Juliet in his arms, dancing, whispering in her ear. When he found one with Rafe's hand dangerously close to her breast, Balthasar hit send.

Balthasar took no pleasure in destroying Philip's dreams. Balthasar's priority was finding the vial. But to do that he had to separate Juliet from *all* those she loved.

Snores came from the corner where Deke was sleeping off his meds. Steps sounded, and Eddie entered.

"It was so cool, man." Eddie threw a bag down and beelined for the coffee. "You got my pics, right? I mean, they're killer. *Straight savage,* my man. Straight. Fucking. Savage."

Balthasar shoved his phone in his back pocket. "What else did you learn?"

"So." Eddie took a long sip. "They talked to some girl from that Savannah history place."

"The historian at the Savannah Preservation Office?"

"Yep. Didn't hear what they said 'cause I couldn't get close enough. But then things went *bam!*" Eddie grinned. "The men of the Isle surrounded Rafe. Taunting him about going AWOL. Then I stepped in and came *this close* to taking him out." Eddie put down his mug and held his thumb and forefinger an inch apart. "Because Juliet was there, I backed off. But Rafe knew who was in charge."

"Indeed." As if Eddie could ever come close to touching a full-grown Fianna warrior.

"I get why Rafe came home. Juliet is smokin' hot. Can't imagine doing *that*."

Balthasar grabbed Eddie by the neck, lifting him off the ground. The boy sputtered, his face turning red. "Although Romeo is my enemy, Juliet is the great love of a brother. She won't be defiled in words or deed."

The boy's head bobbed as he gripped the fingers around his throat. Finally, the moment before Eddie passed out, Balthasar released him.

Eddie fell to the ground, clutching his throat.

Balthasar went back to his coffee. "Anything else?"

Eddie threw himself on the ratty couch. "Yeah." He coughed, and Balthasar handed him a water bottle. "Rafe and Juliet were going to the cemetery to see Anne Capel's tomb. But Escalus already did that, so they won't find shit."

Balthasar went back to the window and drank his coffee. The river flowed in the distance. "Is that all?"

"I took notes on my phone so I wouldn't forget."

Balthasar waited while the boy scrolled.

"The historian gave Juliet a book. Humor in history."

"*Hume's History of England*?" If that was the best the historian could offer, there wasn't anything to worry about.

"That's it. She also called the story of the lily *Anne's Lament*."

That jived with something Balthasar had read in Escalus's notes. "Anything else?"

"The historian mentioned that Anne's Lament was protected by three archangels, *aaaaaand...*" Eddie snapped his fingers. "Something about Juliet's lily being a weapon."

A weapon?

Balthasar went back to his desk, to his only real clue,

to read the map for the millionth time. The broken compass rose and the leaves decorating the edges only added to his belief that it hadn't been worth the pills he'd given to Walker.

"Apparently Rafe met a Fianna warrior named Sebastian when he was a kid."

Balthasar raised his head. "Excuse me?"

"Crazy, right?" Eddie took another gulp of water. "Sebastian was looking for Juliet's lily. And Rafe saved Juliet by pledging his life or his honor or something."

"You learned this from eavesdropping?"

"No, man." Eddie burped. "My cousin told me."

Balthasar opened the laptop, his hands hovering over the keyboard. He'd read Escalus's file on Sebastian, and there'd been no mention of Romeo. As Balthasar stared at Escalus's notes, three things popped out: *Anne's Lament. Three archangels. The warrior Sebastian.*

And the lily was a weapon.

Balthasar's heart sped up with the sudden adrenaline burn. He stretched his arms over his head, enjoying the tight pain of his muscles stretching. His body hummed with growing aggression. He never felt more alive than when he was about to crush his enemies.

He pulled up RLM's secure email.

> **B:** *Will have vial tonight.*
> **RLM:** *Excellent. Bonus offered for JM and her grants.*
> **B:** *Not sure about grants. Can provide JM but require backup. Will need extraction when operation concludes.*
> **RLM:** *BBB mediator will fill you in on details and capabilities.*

Once he signed off, Balthasar handed Eddie two twenties. "Get dinner. We've much business and little time."

"What are we doing?"

Balthasar smiled. "Retrieving my vial and killing Romeo."

Eddie smiled, his crooked teeth skewing his lips. "You met my cousin last night?" His voice sounded breathy, edged with awe. "You're *all* in?"

Balthasar hit his chest and bowed his head. "I am."

Eddie whooped and jumped around the room. "And you'll tell my coz I did good?"

"Yes, Master Eddie." Balthasar clapped him on the shoulders, and Eddie tried to hide his wince. "I'll tell him you just won this war."

"Straight. *Fucking*. Savage."

Nate waited for Ivers to drive away before he slipped beneath the police tape, got into the club, and found the manager's safe. He only took the cash he and Pete were owed. It wasn't a lot, but Nate didn't need much. Just enough for pills and two days of food. The way things looked now, on Friday he and Pete would be going back to Kells and admitting defeat.

It wasn't just the day's failures that had put Nate into a funk. After searching for the safe house earlier, Nate had texted Garza and Calum to announce that—big fucking surprise—the two he'd checked out were a bust. Garza's three properties had been the same. Then Nate had met Ivers here at the club, and they'd picked up Sarah.

It'd been awkward in the back of Calum's car. Going and coming, she'd sat against one window while he sat against the other. They'd talked about simple things like the weather and the previous night's blackout. When they'd picked up the boxes for the SPO, she'd barely looked at him. If he asked her anything personal, she shut him down.

Even at Boudreaux's, in that sensual atmosphere of barefoot dancing and sultry music, she'd kept her attention on Rafe's phone and her history lesson. She hadn't glanced at the dance floor and had had little reaction to Rafe's confrontation with the men on the Isle. It was as if she watched everyone from behind a mask of textbooks and memorized facts. As if she studied the world but was afraid to be a part of it.

Yet when Nate touched her hand, a spark of desire shot through him, leaving scorch marks behind. He *still* burned from her touch, his body *still* rock-hard from the shock. And from her sudden inhale and instant withdrawal, he knew she'd felt it too. Why she pretended otherwise didn't make sense. *Nothing* about Sarah Munro, PhD in early colonial American history, made sense.

The church bells rang as he entered the club's alley, and he counted five chimes. Someone coughed; a young man stood in the shadows. Dirty jeans. Black Converse sneakers. A gray hoodie hid his face.

Nate moved slowly. His weapon was in his back waistband, and he pulled out a roll of four fifty-dollar bills. "Ten Z-pam."

"Put it behind the Dumpster's left back wheel."

He did.

The kid hovered. "You sure, man? My shit is pure. More so than that asshole Deke's."

"S'all good." As long as it kept the seizures at bay, Nate didn't care how high he flew.

The kid took the money and left an envelope. "Straight savage, my man." Then he ran.

Nate retrieved his pills and checked his phone. No news from Garza or Calum or Pete.

Once in the security office, Nate downed a pill. Then he went to set the alarm on his phone only to discover his phone was on low battery. Since he didn't have a charger, he turned it off and set the alarm on the microwave instead. Then he lay on the couch listening to the rain tapping the roof. A horse and carriage clip-clopped by.

It didn't take long for that weightless feeling to kick in. For him to fall into that space where regrets and recriminations floated away. For the silence to muffle the pain in his head so his body could rest. As the walls melted, his nightmares and fractured memories morphed into a woman with long brown hair and a name spoken on a single breath. *Sarah.*

Juliet kept the duffel with her daddy's armory and the King's Grants at her feet in the Impala.

Since they had left Pops's trailer and grabbed the car, Rafe had driven like demons chased them. His knuckles crowned white as he death-gripped the wheel. His left foot drummed a hole in the floor. She closed her eyes and leaned back. She needed a hot shower and a fresh pot of coffee.

Once he hit the bridge leaving the Isle, she checked her texts. The first was from Bob.

> *Halted work in the square due to lightning.*
> *Still on schedule.*

The second was from the payroll company.

> *Deposit received. Checks cut today.*

Relieved, she glanced at Rafe's profile. Her lie of omission was another problem for another time. As she texted Bob, her phone rang and she answered.

"Are you back?" Samantha said.

"On our way. We found my King's Grants."

"Wonderful! And the vial?"

"Not yet. But we have an idea where to look. We'll be home within the hour."

"No prob. Mr. Delacroix stopped by to drop off copies of the original plans for the Habersham gardens. I think he was looking for your renditions."

"They're not done yet." She'd barely started. "Where are you?"

"At the shop, waiting to meet the bride we'd canceled. She sounded desperate, so I told her she could come at six. When I get married, please don't let me lose my mind."

"I promise." Juliet put the phone on speaker so Rafe could hear. "Is Pete with you?"

"No. Pete got the job at the gym and is teaching his first Krav Maga class at six thirty. I'm fine alone. It's just a bridal consultation."

Rafe frowned. "Make sure Nate or Calum or Detective Garza is with you."

Samantha snorted. "I can handle a bridal consultation."

"I'm not asking," Rafe said.

Samantha's sigh sounded like an eyeroll. "Alright."

After she hung up, another text came through.

> *Give me my Romeo. And when I shall die,*
> *take him and cut him out in little stars, and*
> *he will make the face of Heaven so fine that*
> *all the world will be in love with night.*

"Why are you quoting Shakespeare?"

She'd read it aloud? "It's a text." She threw her phone in her purse. "From the same man who's been texting me Shakespearean verses since you left."

"What were these texts about?"

"You. I received a few the first years you were away, and then after your arrest in St. Petersburg, your extradition, your trial and sentencing to Leavenworth."

Rafe glanced at her. "That's how you knew where to send the divorce papers."

"Yes."

"And you never asked the sender for his ID?"

"I did. But he refused. And I was afraid if I annoyed him, he'd stop texting me." She turned her daddy's gold ring on her thumb. "He was my only link to you."

"Even though you hated me?"

"I couldn't let you go." She reached over to rub the back of his neck. "The texts never felt threatening."

"Arragon probably sent them. He has a protective streak when it comes to women, and he never approved of my joining the Prince. The deepest scars on my back are from his blows in the Gauntlet."

"Arragon wanted you to come back to me?"

"I believe so, yes."

"But you didn't."

"I couldn't."

She sighed. "I wish I understood."

"So do I, sweetheart." The rain started again, and Rafe turned on the wipers. "So do I."

Was it possible to be sad and joyful at the same time? Juliet was his everything. His heartbeat. His peace. His reason for breathing. That he was here with her, *had been with her*, was a miracle.

Last night had been about forbidden passion. Today was about clinging to the moments they had left. He'd been through every scenario in his head. No matter how he looked at it, there was no option in which he stayed with her. The Prince would never let him out of his tithe regardless of whether he won or lost this contest with Balthasar.

Holding the wheel with one hand, he pinched the bridge of his nose. His sinuses felt full, and his eyes burned. He had no idea how much time they had because once he found the vial, he'd leave. And if the vial was in Gabriel, that would be tonight. He was driving toward his own doom.

"You're mulling," she said softly.

He watched the palm trees bend in the rising wind. "Not mulling. Remembering our wedding day. You were so beautiful."

She wrinkled her nose. "I wore a white sundress. Nothing special."

He smiled at the memory. "You carried a bouquet of gardenias, roses, and lavender. You wore your hair in a complicated knot with your grandmother's silver hair combs."

"And your mother's sapphire bracelet."

"Something blue." When she dropped her arm, he asked, "What's wrong?"

"Are you disappointed?"

He tightened his wheel hand and put the other on her thigh. "No. The fact that you survived on your own, after what Kells Torridan did to you, speaks to your strength."

"I took my clothes off for money." She stated it plainly, as if daring him to call her out on her actions. As if making sure he understood all that she'd done.

"I killed men for less. Sometimes brutally. After hunting and emotionally torturing them." He squeezed her leg. "Nothing you did could come close to the horror I became."

"When you left on your mission, after your momma's funeral, did you know you weren't coming back?"

"No." His voice cracked. "I couldn't wait to return to you. I was considering not reenlisting. I dreamt of returning to the Isle, rebuilding the manor, and living there with our children. I didn't tell you because I was worried you were slipping away from me. When we were together, even though I knew you needed me, you'd disappear into yourself."

"I was protecting my heart. You were gone so often, it was easier to keep you at a distance so the next time you went away it wouldn't be so hard." She paused. "What changed your mind?"

He turned the wipers on high and returned his other hand to the wheel. The blur was making it hard to drive. "I was planning our life together, and then Colin disappeared. When I went undercover to find him, I found Arragon and other warriors who were combat-tested, battle-hardened, broken by war. Highly trained men made whole by their commitment to the Fianna. They were men I understood. Men who craved self-discipline and penance. And…"

"And?"

"I suspected that my mother's death wasn't an accident."

"How? Why?"

"It was something in the way Arragon spoke about her death. That was the first time Arragon mentioned you might be in danger as well."

Rafe felt the heat of her gaze. Finally, she said, "Did you ever consider that Arragon found *you*? That maybe, because of Sebastian, Arragon was waiting for you?"

"No." Rafe had never considered that. But maybe he should.

"The Fianna are masters at mind games." She rubbed his neck again and whispered, "Maybe you weren't the recruit. Maybe you were the mission."

CHAPTER 39

FORTY-FIVE MINUTES LATER, RAFE PARKED BEHIND JULIET'S store. Neither one had spoken since her insight, but she'd sat next to him, her thigh against his. It wasn't the same as being in bed but better than nothing.

After she ditched her jacket and traded her boots for her sandals, she left to open the shop's back door. He sat with her words working their way through his heart and head. Could she be right? Had he been the hunted instead of the hunter? Had the past eight years, even his mother's death, been part of some larger game? The only problem was he'd no headspace with which to deal with that right now. He needed to stay focused. He had to win.

He tossed his jacket into the back seat and met her at the door. He went in first, ready to pull his weapon, while she turned on the workroom lights.

He led the way into the main store. "It's almost seven. Where's Samantha?"

"It was a short consultation. Maybe she's with Pete."

Rafe scanned the area while she flipped on the over-heads. He checked behind the counter and saw architectural plans next to the cash register.

She sorted them. "These are the drawings Mr. Delacroix dropped off."

He shoved the weapon in his waistband and knelt before the angel. Gabriel stood on a two-foot-tall block and was similar in stature to Raphael. Gabriel held a lily in one hand, and a trumpet lay at his feet.

"Do you need my help?"

"No." Using his weight as leverage, he shimmied the statue out of the corner. "Flashlight?"

She handed one over.

He knelt and traced the carvings until he felt the indentation and the metal pin. He pressed it, and a door opened. He reached in to find…nothing. "It's not here."

How could it not be there? He'd been so sure. *Unless…*

"What?" She tried to squeeze next to him, but he stood and tucked her into his arms. St. John's church bells rang seven times.

Her phone buzzed. He reached into her pocket and handed it to her.

"Samantha's with Pete," Juliet said, reading the text. "After his class, they're celebrating his new job and will meet us later."

"Two things have gone well today," Rafe said wryly. "Has to be a record."

She laid her phone down and cupped his face. "We'll find the vial. Give it to the Prince. And figure out a way to live happily ever after. Maybe we can even use the vial as leverage."

They couldn't, but he nodded anyway.

Another text, this time on Rafe's phone. She read it and said, "Calum wants to know why we're late for dinner."

She texted a response before pressing her lips against Rafe's. "Don't worry. We have friends helping us. A detective. Two Green Berets. The richest man in the South. And Arragon."

Arragon wasn't even close to being a friend.

She gripped his T-shirt. "We're not alone in this."

Rafe kissed her softly, then not so much. His lips trailed along hers, devouring her sweetness. How could he leave her again? When he raised his head, he said. "We need to shower and change. Your apartment or mine?"

"I'll grab some clothes and we'll go to yours." Taking his hand, she shot him a sexy smile. "Your shower holds two."

∽

Juliet unlocked the door to Calum's apartment and threw the keys on the table nearby. The cold air was tinged with jasmine. Breathing deeply, she laid her dress on the couch with the zippered suit bags from Antoine's Tailoring.

Rafe stood in the doorway.

"What's wrong?" She held out her hand. "Don't you want—"

"I *want*." The way he said it, with his voice two octaves lower, made her smile. "I just…wish this day wouldn't end."

She took his fingers to tug him in. The door slammed shut. "We found my grants, we'll find your vial."

He let go of her hand. "Juliet—"

"No worries. No sadness. No regrets." As she spoke, she unraveled her braid. "We'll solve this if we work together." She shook out her long hair.

His eyes narrowed, and his nostrils flared. His intake of breath raised his shoulders.

She crossed her arms, took the edges of her T-shirt, and pulled it over her head. She tossed it to the ground.

He swallowed.

Lowering her eyelids, she unbuttoned her jeans.

"Juliet…" Now he sounded like he smoked three packs a day.

"No talking." She unzipped her jeans and slipped them off her hips. Once she kicked them away, all she wore were her white lace panties and bra.

Rafe's stance shifted as if he was about to fall over. With

two fingers, she traced the lace waistband of her panties before trailing up to the lace framing her breasts.

Rafe's chest jackhammered, moving in and out so fast he sounded like he was hyperventilating.

She bit her lower lip. He *was* hyperventilating. Slowly, she reached behind.

"We're going to be late."

"Calum won't mind." As her bra floated to the ground, she let her gaze wander. From the desperate intensity in his brown eyes, to his wide chest with the muscles cutting through the cotton T-shirt, to his flat stomach and tapered hips, ending at the obvious reaction to her teasing. She licked her lips, and his erection jumped behind the zipper of his jeans, the outline proving how much he'd missed her. Her hands reached for her remaining garment. The lace slid over her hips and down her legs, and she kicked the panties away.

The AC compressor kicked in with a loud hum and a rush of cold air. Her nipples hardened instantly, and Rafe fisted his hands at his sides. "You're killing me."

She chuckled while her fingers brushed over her nipples, tightening them even more. "I want you to love me."

He closed his eyes, and she could've sworn his eyelashes were wet. "Forever and always, sweetheart."

Forever and always. She took his hand and walked him to the bathroom. He followed, keeping his eyes closed. She turned on the two showerheads and, when the temperature was perfect, concentrated on him again. She'd been ready to undress him, but when she turned, he stood fully naked, fully aroused, fully focused on her. His brown gaze was so dark and intense she wondered if he could see into her heart.

And what would he find? For all of her sadness and anger over the past eight years, all of the grieving and throwing things and pretending she hated him, all of her heart closing in to protect herself, there was a truth she'd been unable to admit to until now. She loved him. Without rancor or regret. Without pride or humiliation getting in the way. She couldn't pinpoint the exact moment when it'd happened, but sometime within the past few days she'd not only forgiven him, she'd fallen in love with him all over again.

Only this time her feelings weren't tied to the young bride or the wronged wife she'd once been. Her feelings came from deep inside the woman she was meant to be. A woman who could take care of herself but who knew when to rely on others. A woman who would sacrifice anything, including her own life, for love.

She tugged his hand again. "Come on."

Once they were in the shower, he still made no move to touch her. It was as if he was afraid that if he did, he'd shatter, take her as forcefully as he could without hurting her, and send her flying into a million pieces of glittering light. Then it would be over, and the day would end. Maybe he was as afraid of having to leave her as she was to have him leave. Except she was no longer the frightened girl who'd let Nate interrogate her. She was no longer the person who'd endured days of endless light and nights of endless darkness while struggling with questions she couldn't answer.

She'd become a woman who'd fight for those she loved, fight for her husband, fight for her future. And she'd figure out a way to break Rafe's tithe to the Prince even though she still wasn't sure what that meant.

Rafe leaned his head back under the water and ran his hand over his shorn hair. He'd closed his eyes again, and being a woman of opportunity, she took advantage. She poured shower gel into her hands and ran her hands over his body. She started with his neck, his shoulders, feeling his sharply defined chest muscles.

He opened his eyes. While her showerhead soaked her hair and body, she soaped up his torso and made sure her hands didn't miss an inch of skin. The ocean breeze body wash filled the room with a scent resembling sunscreen and lemonade. It reminded her of lazy summer days spent in her canoe and picnicking in her back meadow. Sometimes they'd fall asleep in the sun holding hands.

She slid her hands down his thighs, and then his legs, touching all of him—except for one very male, very insistent part demanding attention. *That* she'd leave for last. Blinking against the warm water, she saw that his eyes were closed again and he'd stretched out his arms. One palm pressed against the tile wall, the other against the glass door. He was like a tension rod holding himself up.

"Rafe? Will you turn around?"

He opened his eyes, his lips stretched tightly over his teeth. His only sound was a long hiss.

She gripped his hips and pressed her breasts against his chest while the water rushed over them. His erection was the only thing separating them. His hard length cut into her stomach, but she'd something to do first. "Please."

Slowly he turned, placing his hands against the wall and door again. This time, she started at the bottom, soaping and washing the backs of his calves and thighs. The light hair flattened beneath the streams of water. She had not realized the previous night how hard his butt was, even though she'd not only grabbed it while he'd pounded into her, she'd apparently dug in her nails and left scrape marks. "I'm sorry if I hurt you last night."

He shifted his head so she could see his profile. "You could never hurt me."

She wasn't so sure about that but didn't want to argue. Not now that her hands had wiped all the soap off his backside. Her next stop was his arms. His body arched as she trailed her hands over his biceps. The bandages on his left arm had gotten wet and would have to be changed, while his other arm tensed as she ran her hands down it. When she was done, he exhaled as if he'd been holding his breath.

When most everything on his body had been attended to, she slowly traced her fingers along the horrific scars on his back. The water and soap ran down in irregular rivulets, not unlike the random tidal estuaries that cut through her property. The diverted water ended at the small of his back. And that's where she placed the first kiss.

Rafe's inhale jacked up his shoulders, but he let his head hang low. He looked exhausted, defeated, discouraged, and lost.

She stood on her toes and, starting at his neck, began to kiss each scar. She lost count but didn't stop until she sank to her knees and her lips returned to his lower back. His body trembled as she kissed every wound he'd received over the past eight years. His butt muscles contracted, and the veins in his arms bulged. Yet he let her do whatever she wanted. "Turn around."

He let one hand fall, and it disappeared in front of him. "That's not a great idea."

"Please."

He faced her, holding his erection. Slowly, he began to move his hand up and down until she stopped him. Taking over, she slipped his erection into her mouth. She sucked and pulled, her fingers holding the weight of his balls. Her tongue swirled around the top and trailed the length. Rafe groaned and panted, and she increased the pressure and speed until he grabbed her shoulders. "Juliet."

She released him and looked up. His wet hair outlining his skull, as well as the absolute resolve in his eyes, made him appear even more dangerous. "Yes?"

"Stand."

She stood, but before she could throw her arms around his neck, he spun her to face the wall. His arms wrapped around her waist, holding her close.

"*I love you.*" His whisper was half prayer, half demand.

"I love you, too."

He growled against her neck. One hand left her waist to reach between her legs. Intense pleasure shot through her, and she arched her back, using one arm to reach up and hold onto his neck. He tightened his hold, his fingers moving to a rhythm that made her cry out.

"I need you so damn much." He nipped her neck, and she tried to press herself even closer to him. "I'm sorry."

She tilted her head to see his hooded eyes. "For what?"

"For this." Using both hands, he lifted her hips and drove into her. He filled her completely, and she inhaled sharply. He paused to adjust his arm around her waist while the other braced himself against the tile above her head. She pressed her palms against the wet wall and forced her hips against his.

"*Juliet.*" The warm water was a cleansing prayer, her whispered name a sanctifying grace.

She craved more of his strength and size, finally understanding that not only had her outwardly successful life without him been empty and alone, her complete acceptance of his demanding body was a gift to him in return.

Although she was on her toes, she moved her hips to increase the tempo and meet his need. His mouth trailed along her neck, and tiny little bite marks sent shivers down her spine. "Please, Rafe. *Harder.*"

"*Daaaaaaaaaaaamn.*" He reached down again, his caressing fingers meeting his own punishing pace.

She cried out as the pressure built. Her knees weakened first, and then her legs, until she found herself suspended by his strength alone. As he slammed into her, contractions started low, and she pressed her head back against his shoulder. One of his hands buried in her sex, the other clasped around her breasts holding her tight against his chest. She felt his thunderous heartbeat, heard his labored gasps, and used the last of her strength to tighten her muscles around his thick length. Every nerve ending exploded, leaving her hanging in an electrified field of pleasure. Like the night before, he'd taken everything from her and returned it tenfold.

Rafe suddenly pulled out, leaving her bereft and empty. His erratic breathing almost hid his next words. "Hold on."

Rafe spun her around, lifted her by the waist, and drove into her again.

He was a damn brute. And, at that moment of being buried inside the woman he loved, with her breasts crushed against his chest, there was nothing he could do about it.

The moment she contracted around his cock, he pushed her against the wall and forced her legs to loop around his hips. The water burned his supersensitive skin. The roar in his mind obliterated everything except for her cries begging for more.

He hoped he wasn't hurting her with his punishing pace, but the driving need to make her his took over. His balls tightened painfully, and his fingers gripped her thighs. Since this might be the last time he'd ever make love to her, he was determined to force every ounce of pleasure out of her. He'd use his fingers, his tongue, his cock—whatever it took to prove to her that she was his *everything*. That for as long as the stars hung in the sky, he'd love her.

"*Rafe!*"

He closed his eyes and gave in to the sensation of being buried deeply in her tight sex, the constriction in his balls, the heat scorching the rest of his body. His mind told him to wait, drag out the pleasure even more, but his body had other ideas. He held her against the wall, and on the third stroke, his world exploded.

It took three more deep drives to make her scream and empty himself completely inside her. A fourth to lengthen his time with her. A fifth to make the point that he was a part of her as much as she was a part of him. Both equal in their relationship as husband and wife.

She collapsed against him, trusting him to hold her up.

He carried her to the bedroom and laid her in the bed. He went back to turn off the shower and returned with a towel. Once he gathered her wet hair with the terrycloth, he got into the bed, making sure her still-damp body lay on top of his, her head tucked beneath his chin.

His heart beat erratically, his nerve endings sparked, and his cock lay against his stomach, half hard. It was as if that part of him, while exhausted, was making a valiant effort just in case she needed him again.

"I've never been so happy." Her breath tickled his chest.

"Neither have I." Which, of course, meant they were doomed. Fate loved irony and hated him. When life was about to turn in his favor, he could always count on that vengeful bitch to fuck it up.

"It's raining."

He heard rain on the roof, the rumbles of distant thunder. A storm had approached without them even realizing. "It's almost over."

"Your voice," she said in a sleepy voice. "You're mulling."

He kissed her head. "We can't fall asleep. We have to go to Calum's."

She yawned and closed her eyes. "Just a few minutes."

How could he deny her that? This was the last time he'd ever hold her in bed, feel her soft skin against his hard body. He squeezed the bridge of his nose and blinked away the burning in his eyes. How had he ended up here again? On the verge of having the life he'd always dreamed about, yet having to walk away?

Because Gabriel hadn't been empty. He'd been *emptied*.

Which meant Balthasar had won.

And it was almost time for Rafe to leave.

CHAPTER 40

JULIET LED RAFE UP THE STEPS OF CALUM'S MANSION. "We're late."

He wrapped an arm around her shoulders. "Showering with you was worth it."

Heat worked its way up her neck and cheeks. Their lovemaking had been unbelievably erotic and powerfully cathartic. They'd offered everything they had to each other, with the unspoken promise to protect each other's hearts. She'd feel better if they could find that vial and figure out a way to get Rafe out of his tithe. But they'd found her grants, and she was sure they'd solve the rest. "I hope Calum doesn't yell at us."

"Maybe me, but never you." Rafe chuckled under his breath and rang the bell. "I hope this place isn't still haunted."

The red Greek Revival house with white columns was considered the city's most haunted home. "Samantha is convinced a ghost felt her up here."

The door opened, and Calum's butler/chauffeur, Ivers, ushered them in.

"Good evening, Miss Capel. Mr. Montfort is recuperating in the drawing room."

"Thank you." Juliet moved in while Rafe placed the duffel in the marble foyer. The low thud filled the spacious area marked off with red marble columns, a crystal chandelier, and two authentic Roman statues.

"It's good to see you again, Ivers," Rafe said.

"You as well, sir."

Juliet touched Ivers's hand. "Thank you for driving Miss Munro and Mr. Walker out to the Isle today."

A flush traveled up Ivers's neck. "My pleasure, Miss."

"You're late." Calum appeared with a glass of scotch. He wore gray wool pants, a black shirt, and a burgundy silk tie. He kissed her on the cheek. "Philip is resting while we wait for the others."

Juliet was glad she'd changed into a black linen dress and black patent-leather sandals and tied her hair into a high ponytail. Calum liked his guests to look good.

"We were delayed." She took Calum's arm, and he led her to the drawing room. "How's Philip?"

"In pain but hiding it." Calum tapped her arm. "Since the greatest fear of most men is to be shamed in front of other men, he's determined to act strong."

Like Rafe, who wore black trousers with a black long-sleeved shirt molded to his sculpted chest. He had a gun in the holster on his leg and hers in the coat he carried. With his smooth gait and the way he studied every detail, he oozed confidence and controlled violence. When he caught her stare, he winked, and she turned quickly.

Yes, she could see how Philip wouldn't want to show weakness around his brother.

Calum opened double doors, and she went into her favorite room of the fourteen-thousand-square-foot house. Although it had a walk-in fireplace, two couches, four arm chairs, and Aubusson carpets, it felt cozy.

When she saw Philip on the couch, dressed but covered in a blanket, she sat on the coffee table across from him. "I'm glad you're out of the hospital."

Rafe gripped Philip's shoulder. "How're you feeling?"

Philip's eyes darkened. "It's a scratch."

"You were gouged," Rafe said.

"I'm fine."

"Where's Pops?" she asked, hoping to break the tension between the brothers.

Philip shrugged. "Pops left."

She wasn't surprised. She picked up Philip's sketch pad and noticed a stack of architectural plans. "Are you working on Prideaux House?"

"I am. Mr. Delacroix said he dropped off plans at your store. He's anxious to start."

Calum handed Philip a glass of sparkling water. "Miss Nell's devastated by Miss Beatrice's death and won't sign the papers to sell the mansion."

"Speaking of papers," Rafe said, "we're late because we found Juliet's King's Grants."

"Really?" Calum quirked an eyebrow. "Where?"

She told them the story, leaving out the snake. "I have the grants. Once Rafe signs my deeds, I'll sell the land. And since Carina paid me, I made payroll."

"When did that happen?" Calum handed her a glass of red wine, which she placed on the coffee table. After the previous night, she was hesitant to drink anything.

"This afternoon."

"Hmmm." Calum took out his phone and started texting.

Philip adjusted himself on the couch. "Things are working out."

"Not sure about that," Calum murmured while his fingers worked the keyboard.

"Me neither." Rafe stood by the fireplace with one arm on the mantel, the other holding his glass. "Selling your land is a terrible idea."

Calum picked up his glass to clink Rafe's. "To not selling Juliet's land."

"Hear, hear." Rafe drank his water while Calum finished his scotch in one gulp.

She ignored them.

"You've no vision," Philip said to the other men. "Selling that land will give Juliet freedom to do whatever she wants wherever she wants."

She stood. "I'm going to pay off my loan, and I may travel. To Venice."

Rafe coughed so hard he put down his glass. Then his cell buzzed. Once he'd read the text, he came over and kissed her hand. "I need to leave. I'll be back soon."

"I'll walk you out," Calum said.

She exhaled and forced herself to act normal. Except the silence filled the space until Philip grabbed an engineering drawing of the Prideaux House gardens.

"See this?" Philip pointed to arches and supports. "The underground pipes? And the rectangular basin beneath the fountain? It's a cistern."

She gasped and took the plans. "That means more water features. A fish pond on the side of the house. A waterfall behind the parterre. A fountain in front of the cascading stairs. It could rival the water gardens at the Calhoun Mansion in Charleston." She hugged the drawing against her chest. "It's wonderful news."

"What are we celebrating?" Calum returned, but his smile seemed tighter than before.

She smiled at him. "The cistern under the Prideaux House."

Calum poured another scotch. "Most are caved in or filled with debris."

"Don't be a pessimist," she said.

Philip picked up his phone and texted like a Calum clone. "I'm not sure Calum trusts Delacroix being in his city."

"I don't know him well enough to trust him."

"Everything'll work out," she said. "We found my grants, we'll find Rafe's…thing."

"Hopefully before anyone else gets hurt." Philip laid his phone on the table, face down. "When Rafe leaves, so will the violence."

"That's not fair." Nate walked into the room with Ivers. He wore jeans and a black T-shirt with a biker jacket. He'd pulled back his long hair, and the circles around his eyes looked like someone had gouged them out with an ice-cream scoop and shoved them back in.

"Mr. Walker has arrived." Ivers spoke, turned, and left.

Nate held out his hand to Philip. "I'm Nate Walker."

Philip shook. "Calum told me about you and Pete."

"Really?" Nate sent a questioning glare toward Calum. "I can't imagine what he said."

"Only that you're helping Juliet and Rafe find something." Philip tilted his head. "What did you mean by my comment not being fair?"

Nate laid his jacket on a chair and stood by the fireplace. "People assume soldiers thrive on violence, when the truth is we're the biggest peaceniks. It's not in our best interests to encourage wars since we're the ones who have to fight. Our goal is to be so strong and intimidating, people will think twice about starting anything."

"You don't know Rafe," Philip said. "He's been at odds with everyone his entire life."

"I trained Rafe. Served with him on an A-team. He never sought out fights for violence's sake. He just doesn't back down when threatened. What you see as a character flaw, I see as fearlessness."

"My brother went AWOL. From *your* unit. How can you defend him?"

"Sometimes men do the wrong thing for the right reason. And when that happens, they should be given the chance to make things right."

Ivers appeared. "Dinner is served."

Behind Ivers, a woman in pink scrubs held a tray of pills and bandages.

"Ivers," Calum said, "will you escort Juliet and Nate? Philip and I will follow."

"Yes, sir."

She took Nate's arm and whispered, "Thank you for defending Rafe."

Nate squeezed her hand. "I was defending myself."

∽

Rafe stopped outside John Sinclair's law office, Arragon next to him.

Rafe had been right when he'd seen Gabriel's empty chamber. Balthasar had found the vial first. As much as that pissed Rafe off, he'd been shocked when Arragon told him about Balthasar ditching the Prince and joining the team who'd seduced Escalus away.

"It's time," Arragon said.

When Rafe had gotten the text demanding this meet and greet, it'd almost killed him to leave Juliet behind, not knowing if he'd ever see her again.

"I know." The night stole the words from Rafe's throat.

Even if he'd been set up, was the victim instead of the recruit, it didn't matter. He was a Fianna warrior. If he grabbed Juliet and ran to the ends of the world, they'd be hunted and killed. Why had he thought he could see Juliet and leave without out consequence? Because he was an arrogant bastard.

Arragon crossed his arms, his leather jacket squeaking with the stretching across his wide shoulders. "The choice is true."

"Is it? I'm leaving the woman I love, breaking both of our hearts. Again."

"Solemn vows are not made lightly. Between husband and wife. Knight and lord. But a man can only serve one master. 'Twas known when you tithed."

Except Rafe hadn't understood back then. Arragon had tried to explain, but Rafe thought he could infiltrate the Fianna, find Colin, learn more about his momma's death, and get out. "I have to choose between the woman I love and a vow I made under duress years ago."

"If you'd listened then, you wouldn't be here now."

Arragon had always reminded him of Kells Torridan. "An elegant *I told you so*."

"Balthasar has taken Samantha Barclay. He murdered Lady Habersham and the Fair Sally. Now he's working with the same villain Escalus chose over the Prince. How many others must be sacrificed for your love?"

Arragon's logic didn't make this easier. The moment Rafe had seen Gabriel's empty chamber, he should've called the Prince. But Juliet had been so alluring, dragging him to the shower, to his bed. While he might've been able to resist, he hadn't wanted to. It was his last time in her arms, burying himself in her body, and he wasn't strong enough to give that up. "Have you been sending Juliet texts about me?"

"No." Arragon glanced at his watch. "And Escalus— then Balthasar—was responsible for Juliet's vandalism. Not the Prince."

"Did you desecrate the cathedral?"

"No. 'Twas Balthasar." Arragon sighed. "Balthasar hoped fear would drive you and Lady Juliet apart. He destroyed the lilies and left the verses. Afterward, I lit the candles and incense as reparations to the sacred space and offered prayers for the event to bring you together."

Rafe remembered kissing her for the first time that night and how he ended up sleeping with her in his arms. "Thank you," he said as another truth slapped him out of his self-centered haze. "Escalus killed Eugene, Legare, and Gerald." At Arragon's nod, Rafe added, "But you left those verses after finding their bodies. For me."

Arragon looked up at the full moon pushing its way through the cloud cover. "To bring you comfort. And maybe hope."

"For God's sake, why?"

"After your extradition, we knew you'd return to us in time. But a man can only lose so much. The Prince used your grief over your mother's death to force you to join, making you believe the Fianna was involved, and he regrets that. The Prince wanted you to know we still considered you brother, albeit a wayward one."

That didn't leave Rafe with the warm tinglies. "Why didn't you assassinate Escalus before he killed them?"

"We didn't understand the depth of Escalus's treachery until Gerald Capel's death."

"Do you know who killed my momma with a misericord?"

"The villain who lured Balthasar and Escalus is suspect but has not been confirmed." Arragon clasped Rafe's shoulder. "Once you return, the Prince will give you permission to find her murderer and avenge her death however you see fit."

Seeking vengeance on behalf of his momma might temporarily deflect the pain of leaving Juliet. "When I walk away tonight, I'm leaving hope behind."

Arragon bowed his head. "As you wish."

Rafe swallowed, except his spit tasted bitter. Like regret mixed with sorrow. "What happens after I sign the deeds?"

"You may say farewell to the Lady Juliet. Although it might be easier to disappear."

"I can't do that to her again. I couldn't live with myself."
He touched his lips. That would mean his kiss on her hand
would be the last one he'd ever give her.

"Lady Juliet is uncommonly strong. She'll survive."

"Surviving is not living. You taught me that."

"'Tis for the best. The Prince has assured me you'll not
face the Gauntlet if you come back willingly."

"Why? I failed."

"Losing your love will be punishment enough."

Punishment? Arragon had no concept of the word.

Arragon waved to the darkness behind him. "Your
brothers are waiting."

A street lamp cast a glow around a twenty-foot area. In
the shadows, Rafe counted six warriors. There were probably more. One warrior waited across the street, one on top
of a truck, another in the entrance next door. Two stood
on nearby roofs.

Arragon whistled, and the warriors moved simultane-
ously. They hit their chests with their fists and bowed
their heads.

Rafe closed his eyes. There'd been so many deaths, so
much destruction, maybe it was time for him to go home.
Just not the home he yearned for.

He opened his eyes and entered the law office. Like the
Band-Aid analogy, the sooner he did this, the sooner he
could work through the pain. Although the queasiness in
his stomach and the sharp ache in his heart warned him this
pain would last his lifetime.

CHAPTER 41

CALUM'S HOUSE IS ENORMOUS. NATE COULD FIT SIX PLATOON bivouacs in the foyer.

He held Juliet's arm and followed Ivers into the dining room. "What does Philip know?"

"You and Pete are helping us find something. And that we found the King's Grants."

"Did you find the vial?"

"No. And Rafe is on an errand. He'll return soon. What about Garza?"

"Late. There's a lot going on with this heroin." After seating Juliet next to him, Nate waited for Ivers to leave. His head felt foggy, but his vision was clear. Despite the REM hangover, he was glad he'd set that alarm. If he hadn't, he'd probably still be passed out in the club. The new pills *were* more powerful than Deke's. Next time he'd cut them.

He hated the fact that he was counting the hours until his next one.

"Have you talked to Kells?" Juliet drank from a glass of water that had already been poured. "Is there an update on your men?"

Minutes later, after Nate told her about his conversation with Luke, Calum and Philip appeared.

Calum sat at the head of the table. "Everyone alive?"

"Obviously." Juliet took another drink of water.

Nate knew he'd upset her. But he wanted her to know what was going on with the men in his unit. She'd known most of them. And protecting information wasn't as important as rebuilding her trust.

Philip sat next to Juliet as Pete stormed in. With his dark eyes flashing, wearing a black tank, combat pants, and boots, his badass looked painted on his face. "Samantha is missing."

Juliet rose. "She's having dinner with you."

"She never met me. She's not at the store. And she's not answering her phone." Pete glared at Nate. "Where were you? I texted you. You were supposed to stay with her until I finished work."

"I never got it." Nate stood as that numb feeling in his hands came back. He'd not gotten it because he'd turned off his phone.

"Detective Garza has arrived," Ivers said as Garza pushed past.

Calum threw down his napkin. "What's wrong?"

"I'm taking Montfort in for questioning." Garza paused at the end of the table. "Rafe is a suspect in a murder at the Savannah Preservation Office."

Nate gripped the edge of the table, all thoughts gone except one. *Sarah.* "*Who?*"

"A research assistant who was working late. The SPO's archivist found her. The woman was killed with a misericord and left in the fountain. The archivist is fine, just shaken up, as we can all imagine."

Nate sat down again because his legs would no longer hold him up. A light-headed feeling nauseated him, and he realized he'd been holding his breath. He gripped a glass of water with both hands and forced himself to breathe normally before he started hyperventilating.

"*Fuuuuuuck,*" Pete said.

Garza moved toward Juliet. "Where's Rafe? My chief

has taken his head out of the heroin crisis long enough to threaten me with a suspension if I don't figure this mess out."

"I don't—"

"Rafe's not here," Calum said. "But we have another problem. Samantha is missing."

Garza zeroed in on Pete, who was pouring a glass of water with trembly hands. "When did you last talk to her?"

"Around five. I left her at Juliet's store and went to my first Krav Maga class."

Just about the time Nate was taking a pill and shutting down his phone. Because he was such a class act. "Could Balthasar have taken her? Maybe to his safe house?"

"Who's Balthasar?" Philip asked. "And why would he take Samantha to a safe house?"

Calum started texting. "Philip, why don't you lie down while we clear this up?"

"No," Philip said. "I'm not going anywhere until I know where my brother is."

Juliet put a hand on Garza's arm. "How is Rafe involved?"

"We have a witness who saw Rafe leaving the SPO around the time the woman was killed."

"Ridiculous," Juliet said.

Nate drank his water, wishing it was scotch. He agreed with Juliet's take. This entire situation was ridiculous. *Green Berets. Lilies. Pirates. Murder.* Maybe he was losing it like Kells and the other men suspected.

Garza slammed his hand on the table. "I need to see Rafe."

"Why?" Rafe came into the dining room and, because missiles seek heat, headed right for Juliet. He held her tightly, one hand against her head, the other around her waist.

"They think you murdered an assistant at the preservation office," Calum said. "And Samantha is missing."

Rafe stroked Juliet's back. "Balthasar has Samantha. She's safe. For now."

The room hushed, and Juliet left his embrace. "How do you know?"

"Arragon told me."

"You saw him?" Calum asked.

Rafe nodded. "Arragon texted me, and I met him."

Garza rubbed his chin with his fist. "Arragon texted you on your new burner phone?"

Rafe raised a *You're surprised?* eyebrow. "Balthasar also has the vial."

Juliet closed her eyes and leaned against Rafe's chest again.

Finally, news Nate could work with. "We can get it from him. Right?"

"It's too late." Rafe ran his thumb up and down Juliet's spine. "Because the really bad news is that Balthasar is now working for the same man Escalus worked for."

Juliet opened her eyes. "The man hiding behind Beaumont, Barclay, and Bray?"

Rafe tucked a hair behind her ear. "Yes."

"It's not too late," Pete said. "We find Balthasar, save Samantha, and get the vial."

Rafe lowered his head to Juliet's neck as if he'd already been defeated.

But Nate wasn't ready to give up. "Maybe," he added with the most hope he'd had in days, "we'll find out more about this law firm and how it relates to our doomed Afghan operation."

Calum picked up his phone and started texting. Again. "Sounds like a plan."

"Except," Garza said, "a witness swears Rafe was near the SPO at the time of the murder."

"Don't speak, Rafe," Calum said while his fingers moved across the keypad.

"Who's the witness?" Juliet asked Garza.

"Someone who claims to have been beaten up by Rafe a few nights ago. A man named Deke."

Juliet followed Philip, Rafe, Garza, and Calum into the police station. Nate and Pete were on their way. Since Rafe had agreed to go with Garza, he wasn't handcuffed. It also meant that as soon as they reached the bullpen, he was sent to lineup.

She followed the men upstairs. Both floors of the station held groups standing around chalkboards and maps of the city. There were also lots of people in handcuffs while officers in blue yelled into cell phones.

"There are three task forces going on at the same time." Garza found a chair for Philip. "Two for the explosion and one for the heroin."

Philip held an arm against his abdomen and lowered himself slowly. She'd tried to talk him out of coming, but he'd insisted.

Calum studied the room with his hands on his hips. A Caesar surveying the chaos in his dying empire. "Is there someplace we could speak privately?"

Garza pointed to a room a few feet away. "We're next on the list."

She placed her handbag on the desk. "I don't understand why I can't be with Rafe."

"Because he's a suspect." Garza picked up a clipboard from his desk and started flipping through it.

"How long will this take?" Philip said. "There's a witness."

"Do you want your brother to be guilty?"

"No. But it's odd that he left us to meet Arragon and we've no idea where."

"Where is he?" Deke's nasally voice came from behind. "I wanna see the son of a bitch who killed that woman."

She froze. The short, bleached hair and purplish bruises covering Deke's face made a good disguise. As did the missing front tooth and bandaged ear. She'd not seen him after Rafe's attack, but now that she realized how badly Deke had been beaten, she was grateful.

Garza took Deke by the upper arm and threw him into a chair near Philip. "Shut up."

"Screw you," Deke spat. "I'm a witness, not a suspect." He saw her and blew her a kiss.

She slapped him across the face.

"Whoa." Garza pulled her away.

She'd already told Garza everything that had happened at the club on Monday night, but right now, without Samantha to corroborate, it was her word against Deke's.

"This is the guy who attacked you?" Garza asked.

"Yes."

Deke flapped his arm in the white sling. "Montfort tried to kill me."

"Because you were trying to rape me," she said.

"Prove it."

"Excuse me?" Philip struggled to stand. "What do you mean he tried to rape you?"

"I, uh…"

"She worked for me." Deke leaned back, leer firmly affixed. "As one of my whores."

Juliet launched herself at Deke, but Calum grabbed her waist. "Not here. Not now."

Philip kicked Deke's chair. "What the hell is going on?"

Deke licked his lips. "Your brother's wife is a stripper at Rage of Angels."

"She stopped that a year ago."

"Then why don't you ask her what she was doing there Monday night?"

Philip's eyes widened, and he stared at her. "That's how you were going to pay the loan?"

"I—"

"Detective," Calum ordered, "we need a private room. Now."

"Peterson?" An officer ran over, and Garza pointed at Deke. "Take Hammond down for the lineup."

"I'm going with him," Philip said. "I want to prove to you all what a mistake it'd be to let Rafe back into our lives."

Once Peterson left with Deke and Philip, Garza banged on the nearest door. "Time's up."

It swung open, and two cops came out, one chewing gum, the other holding a notebook.

"I need the room." Garza nodded toward Calum, and the detectives left with a guy in handcuffs.

When the door shut, she sat. She wanted to lay her head on the table and cry, but she had to be strong for Samantha's and Rafe's sakes. "Why aren't you arresting Deke for attempted rape?"

Garza took his notebook out of his jacket and threw it on the table. "I believe you, but we've no other witnesses here. You didn't file a report when it happened."

"You saw the bruises on my face at the cathedral. You asked me about them."

"You told me they were nothing."

Why hadn't she said something when she'd had the

chance? Because she'd wanted to fix this on her own. "What'll happen now?"

Calum cleared his throat. "Deke will ID Rafe in the lineup."

Garza nodded. "If Deke ID's Rafe, I have to arrest him."

She shook her head. "No—"

"I can't *not* follow procedures," Garza said. "It'll do Rafe more harm than good if I screw up this investigation."

Calum touched her shoulder. "Rafe is more concerned about you than about himself."

"Nate and Pete were there the night of my attack," Juliet reminded Garza.

"According to Deke, they were also involved. Don't forget we're here because of a woman's murder, not what happened to you."

"Deke is using that fight to prove Rafe has a violent streak."

"I know about Rafe's violent streak. I saw it out on the Isle. You were there too."

"You've no evidence to hold Rafe," Calum said. "Just Deke's circumstantial bullshit."

"Unfortunately, we do." Garza left the room for a second and then came back with two evidence bags. One held the journal she'd read this morning. The other looked like a ticket and receipt. "We also have a murder weapon found at the scene that we're dusting for prints."

She pointed to the bag with Rafe's journal. "You searched his apartment?"

"No," Calum said. "They searched *my* apartment. I'm assuming you had a warrant?"

"Yes," Garza said.

"How?" she asked. "Don't you need probable cause?"

"I had it when Deke gave us this." Garza handed the

second bag to Calum. "It's a bus ticket stub from Kansas to Georgia. The receipt is for Rafe's personal items from Leavenworth. It includes a journal identical to Escalus's."

"Which you lost," she reminded him.

Calum held up the ticket and receipt bag. "How'd you get this?"

"Deke. He said they fell out of Rafe's jacket the night Rafe beat him up."

"There's no chain of evidence, and a prison list isn't enough for a search warrant."

"Judge thought otherwise."

"Why are you doing this?" she asked Garza. "I thought you were helping us!"

"I can't ignore evidence, and I can't play favorites. A journal similar to Escalus's, with the same numbering system, was found in Rafe's bag. A misericord was discovered near the body."

Calum threw down the receipt bag. "Who leaves a murder weapon at the scene?" He snapped his fingers. "I know. The murderer who wants to frame someone else."

A knock sounded before Pete and Nate came in.

Pete knelt in front of her. "Have you heard from Samantha?"

"No." Juliet took Pete's hands and squeezed. "We'll find her."

Nate crossed his arms and stared at Garza. "Where's Rafe?"

"Lineup."

"This is bullshit," Nate said. "What the hell was Deke doing at the SPO anyway?"

Garza picked up his notebook to read. "After getting fired on Monday night, Deke went to a friend's house to recuperate. He was taking a walk when he found the body."

"It's nonsense," she said. "Deke changed his appearance so he could get around town without being seen."

"Deke's appearance isn't the issue," Garza said.

Juliet's head ached, and she rubbed her forehead. "You said Sarah found the body?"

Garza read his notes again. "According to Deke, he was walking by when he heard a Miss Sarah Munro scream. When he entered the courtyard, he saw Miss Munro near the body in the fountain and ran inside the SPO to call 911. The archivist corroborated."

"But Sarah didn't see anything?" Nate asked.

"No." Garza flipped through his notes again. "Although, after the police arrived, she discovered a book was stolen. *The Chronicle or Discourse of Virginia.*"

"Oh, fuck this," Nate snarled. "That was the book Sarah showed me today. The one with maps similar to Juliet's."

After Nate explained what Sarah had said about the book and the map, Calum glared at Garza. "Is it possible the murder was a diversion in order to steal the book?"

"Or that Sarah was the intended target?" Nate asked. "I've met the assistant. She also has long brown hair. In the dark, it would be easy to mistake one for the other."

"They're all possibilities," Garza said. "But that doesn't exonerate Rafe. I have a weapon and a witness."

"They're setting Rafe up." Juliet hated the desperate whine in her voice.

"All I see," Garza said, "is Rafe's disregard for the rule of law."

"What about Juliet's map?" Pete asked. "If that book was stolen, her map might have something to do with it."

Nate bowed his head. "I don't have the map."

"Why not?" Pete asked.

"I traded it to Balthasar for some pills. With Deke out of the picture, I was desperate."

The air stilled. Or maybe it felt that way because she'd stopped breathing.

Pete clenched his fists and spoke with short, clipped words. "Is that why you weren't with Samantha at the store this afternoon? Because you were stoned?"

Nate's green eyes had shifted into the hazel zone, the scar on his cheek darkening into a charcoal line. It was the face of apology. Of regret. "Yes."

Juliet wanted to scream at Nate, but it wouldn't do any good. His demons were as daunting as Rafe's. There was nothing to do except save Rafe so they could save Samantha.

In her calmest voice, she asked, "When can I see Rafe?"

"Soon." Another knock had Garza opening the door to talk to an officer. They stood outside, but she heard the conversation. "Sir, Deke Hammond ID'd Rafe Montfort as the killer. We have confirmation of Montfort's fingerprints on that sword thing, so we've put him in a holding cell in the older part of the station. We didn't want to mix him in with general lockup. And Detective Elliot wanted me to let you know that he was contacted by the Third MP CID at Hunter Army Air Field."

"What the hell for?" Garza said. "Montfort's not in the army anymore."

"They're looking for two Green Berets, one awaiting a military trial. They know the men worked at Rage of Angels and that they were at the restaurant last night during the explosion. The MPs already searched the club and that skeevy motel. They're on their way here next. To talk to you."

"Thank you, Peterson." Garza shut the door and leaned against it, his arms crossed. "Why are MPs looking for you two?"

"No idea." Nate ran his hands over his head while Pete began to pace the room.

"It seems to me," Calum said in a calm voice, "that if we don't regain control of this situation, Balthasar may win. And the stakes aren't whether or not Rafe returns to the Fianna while Pete and Nate go to prison. It's about saving Samantha and stopping Balthasar from selling that vial to this mysterious man-behind-the-law-firm."

"Great," Garza said. "Why don't I tell my chief about Anne Capel and her poison? The ancient order of assassins who bow before they kill. And a lily that may or may not cause global epidemics. Oh, that's right, because he'll fire me for being crazy, and then we'll both be executed by the Fianna."

"Join the club," Nate said dryly.

"Sarcasm isn't helping," Calum said.

Pete sank into a chair, head bowed, and Juliet took his hand. "They've no reason to arrest you."

Pete gave her a sad smile. "They don't need one."

Calum checked his watch. "I'll take Juliet to see Rafe while I work on his release."

"For murder?" Garza exhaled with bullet-train force. "Rafe won't get bail."

"Not true." Calum put the phone in his jacket pocket. "While I'm helping Rafe, Nate and Pete need to hide. Since the MPs have searched the club, go there. If the streets are dicey, take a tunnel. They all eventually lead to the club."

"Okaaaaay," Pete said with an exaggerated head tilt. "How do we find these tunnels?"

Calum's aristocratic laser stare could cut concrete. "Have you seen my graffiti symbol? The skeleton hand holding the cutlass with the words *sans pitié* written below?"

They nodded.

"When you see the tag, you'll know there's an entrance to a usable tunnel nearby."

She'd always wondered about that. "Your sigil is part of a secret tunnel system?"

"Yes. But be careful. Many are still partially blocked, some have rats, and Samantha believes they're haunted." Calum kissed Juliet on the cheek. "Now let's get Rafe out of jail."

CHAPTER 42

NATE FOLLOWED PETE OUT OF THE INTERROGATION ROOM. When they hit the landing at the top of the stairs, he stopped. A police officer was escorting Sarah around the corner.

"I know what I saw," Sarah told the officer, who was talking on his cell. Her hair was braided over one shoulder. She carried her straw bag and walked with a determined stride.

Pete was almost downstairs, unaware Nate's heart was skipping beats. "Sarah?"

She blinked. "Nate?"

"I heard what happened." He touched her arm, and then dropped his hand. "Are you okay?"

"I wasn't hurt." She looked away, and he noticed the tear tracks on her cheeks. He wanted to trace them with his thumbs, but he knew she'd back away. "This is my fault, Nate. I'd asked my assistant to do some research for me. I had no idea she was staying late."

"This isn't your fault." Nate hated seeing her so sad and really hated the fact that she was blaming herself. "I'm sorry."

She raised her chin. "My dad was a police chief in Boston, so unfortunately, I'm used to things like this. I'd just hoped Savannah was safer."

"Nate?" Pete yelled from the bottom of the steps. "We gotta go, man."

The tic above Nate's eye acted up. "I couldn't help but overhear. What did you see?"

"You'd never believe me."

A noise distracted him. Two fully armed MPs entered the station.

"That's odd," she said. "What do you think they want?"

Nate took her elbow and led her into an alcove, hiding them. "What did you see?"

She pressed her smaller hands against his chest. "What are you doing?"

Could she hear what she did to his heart rate? Did she care?

"Nate?" Pete ran up the stairs, his face hard and angular. "Time to go. Now."

"Please, Sarah. *Tell me.*"

The MPs were coming, and Sarah's officer was still distracted.

Her breasts moved faster as her breath shortened. "In the shadows, I saw a man bow."

Nate kissed her. He couldn't help himself. He pressed his lips against hers and, after a moment, her lips softened. The scent of gardenias hit him, and his body reacted with rocket-fueled power and thrust.

Pete grabbed Nate's arm, said, "Excuse me, ma'am," to Sarah, and pulled Nate away.

The MPs were on the landing, talking to Sarah's officer. Pete dragged him down the hall while Nate looked back. Sarah stood where he'd left her, watching him. His last view was of MPs running in his direction.

He slammed the door and took off his belt. His raging erection would make sure his pants didn't fall off his ass.

Pete was halfway down the staircase. "Nate!"

Nate used his belt to tie the door handle to the fire extinguisher case and double-timed the stairs. When they hit the station's back alley, his eardrums rang from the alarms. The night air filled his lungs, and he found his bike next to Pete's motorcycle.

After Pete roared away, Nate pedaled fast until he turned a corner, hit a puddle, and wiped out. Since neither he nor the bike were broken, he walked it to the end of the flooded alley. When the road was clear, he hopped on again until he turned another corner and saw the MPs beneath a street lamp.

Nate pressed himself against the wall. The MPs knelt with their backs together, hands on their heads. Two other men wearing jackets over hoodies stood near the kneeling cops, and Nate saw a third man, similarly dressed, across the street. Someone whistled, and the three hooded men hit their chests and bowed at the waist.

Holy. Shit.

The two men guarding the MPs each pulled something out of their pockets. Nate was too far away to be sure, but it looked like syringes. A moment later, the warrior across the street tossed a smoke grenade. The MPs dropped to the ground, the air filled with white phosphorus, and Nate took off. Ten minutes later, he hit the club. He hated leaving the MPs with three Fianna warriors, but it wasn't Nate's fight.

Pete was waiting inside the back door. He'd rolled the motorcycle into the kitchen and Nate left his bike next to it. Then he went through the club, making sure the other doors were locked as well. Once satisfied the perimeter was secure, they met in the security office. The power worked, and this room had no windows to the outside.

Pete's hands-on-his-hips routine reminded him of Kells. "Where've you been?"

"Backtracking." Nate secured the door, and then plugged in his cell phone. "The MPs ran into three Fianna warriors."

Pete hit him. A right hook caught Nate's chin, and he fell to the side. A deep throb invaded his jaw. "What the hell?"

"For leaving Samantha alone and letting her get

kidnapped." Pete struck Nate's stomach. Nate blocked the hit but missed the left hook that took out his nose. "That's for trading the map for pills." Then Pete hit Nate in the solar plexus, and the breath left his body. "That's for kissing the woman. What the *fuck* is wrong with you?"

Nate stumbled to the couch and touched his nose. Bruised, not broken. "I'm trying to fix this."

"How? By letting Samantha get kidnapped? By kissing random women? There are lots of things against us, and we don't need people thinking you're a sexual predator."

"It was a kiss."

"While being chased by MPs and trying to save our men?" Pete ran his hands over his head and paced the room. "Not only was that too damn close, your fighting skills suck. You're a Green Beret. You used to be able to kill with a Post-it note. Now look at you. Hopped up on migraine drugs and painkillers. You can't drive. You're soft, and it's affected your executive functioning. Your last few decisions—including kissing that woman—suck ass."

"Her name is Sarah. And I fight every day."

"How many times have you won? Or are all those bruises a fashion statement?"

"Who wins or loses isn't important." The whole point was to rile up the aggression to tamp down the seizures.

"Forget it." Pete threw himself on the couch next to Nate, one hand over his eyes. "When this is over, I'm reteaching you basic self-defense and Krav Maga. You and your self-hatred should be able to handle that."

Nate gave the sigh of failure. It killed him that Pete was right. Nate's choices lately had been poor. Still, he didn't need lessons in street fighting or self-defense. A refresher, maybe. But basic lessons were bullshit.

"What do we do now, Nate? We have to save Samantha."

Nate grabbed his cell still attached to the power cord and dialed Luke. No answer.

A second later, Luke texted.

> *Can't talk. MPs here for us & looking for you & Pete.*

Nate nudged Pete so he could read along.

> *Why?*
> *To lock us in Bragg's preconfinement facility for own safety until trials. MPs worried we'll take off.*

"Fucking nightmare," Pete muttered.

No kidding.

> *When?*
> *Tonight. You're on your own. Don't get caught. Counting on you two. Last hope.*

"Shit." Pete's elbows dug into his legs, his hands holding his head. "Now what?"

"We prioritize."

"Which is first for you? Getting high, losing my girlfriend, or screwing the archivist? I've heard about historians. Quiet on the outside, wild—"

"Don't talk about Sarah that way."

Pete shook his head. "So, almighty XO, what's the plan?"

Nate didn't laugh. He hadn't been an executive officer since his court-martial. That wound still bled. "We need a map of the city and a pen."

"What for?"

Nate went to the desk. "We have to find Balthasar's safe house to snag the map and retrieve the vial. We'll use them as leverage to get Samantha back."

"Balthasar could have them with him. And we don't even know if Balthasar wants to give Samantha back. There's no ransom. All we have is Montfort's word that Balthasar has her."

"I wouldn't carry the map and vial around. They're too valuable. I doubt many things, but not Rafe's take. If Balthasar has her, he has his reasons."

"What about Montfort? He needs the vial too."

"Finders keepers." Nate rummaged through another drawer. He'd seen a tourist map and…success. He laid it on the desk and smoothed it with his fist. Now he needed a pen. "Garza and I checked out five properties earlier today—all of them near Calum's sigil but still duds. If we can figure out where the tunnels run, we may be able to locate Balthasar's safe house. Those tunnels would be perfect for running a covert op in the middle of a city. Maybe even hiding a kidnapped woman."

Pete leaned his ass against the table and watched. "Secret tunnels. Hunting a Fianna warrior. Stealing his map. Rescuing the girl. It's a doomed plan with no chance of working."

"Our favorite kind."

"Now you sound like Jack Keeley. You remember. Your best friend rotting in prison."

"Sarcasm noted." Nate found a black marker and tried to remember the properties Calum had marked earlier in the day. "We can't sit while our CO and the rest of the unit join Jack in prison. Now, mark every place you've seen Calum's graffiti."

Pete X'd the club's alley. "I can't believe we're going to save the girl."

"And our men"—Nate pointed to Iron Rack's gym—"with a black Sharpie and a Gray Line Trolley tourist map."

"Hooah, Brother. Hoo-*fucking*-ah."

CHAPTER 43

RAFE SAT IN THE CELL, HEAD BOWED, STUDYING THE PHOTO of his momma helping Juliet with her veil. He smoothed the paper that'd gotten wrinkled from spending days in his back pocket. His momma's smile sent an ache into his heart.

He wasn't surprised Deke had picked him out of the lineup or that his fingerprints had been found on the sword. The same sword he'd taken from Balthasar that night in the alley. Both situations were Rafe's fault because he couldn't control his temper. Arragon was right. Rafe, not Balthasar, was the one soaked in self-righteous anger who couldn't accept that his past mistakes were beyond redemption.

Rafe slid the photo into his pocket. He'd already taken off the blue ribbon and shoved it into his boot. He heard footsteps but didn't get up. His brothers would be coming for him, and when they did, there'd be noise. Until then, he'd wallow. Because once he was back with the Fianna, selfish emotions were forbidden. Warriors were beaten for less.

"Rafe?"

Juliet's voice hit him like a grenade to the chest, and he raised his head. She dropped her purse and clung to the bars, the skirt of her black dress rising as she pressed herself against the steel. Her brown eyes seemed too large; her lips quivered. She'd taken down her hair, and curls fell over her shoulders, almost to her waist. Red blotches on her cheeks offered proof of tears.

He stood and inhaled sharply. A bad move since the faint

scent of lavender almost drove him to his knees. Arragon was right about this as well. Seeing her would be harder than leaving her. "What are you doing here?"

She reached a hand into the cage. "Calum is getting a judge to free you."

"Where is he? I need to talk to him."

She glanced down the hallway, and her hair covered her bare shoulders. "He'll be here soon." When she turned back, her breasts pressed against the bars, as if she could dissolve the steel by sheer will. "Philip is coming too."

"What were those alarms about?" Rafe thought they might be Arragon's signal, but when they stopped, he was still imprisoned.

"Two MPs from Hunter Army Airfield showed up to take Nate and Pete away."

Now that was an interesting setback. Rafe gave in to his baser instincts and moved against the bars. He covered her hands with his. "Why?"

"I don't know. They're in hiding."

"Are you sure the MPs didn't find them?"

"Yes. Detective Garza told us the MPs were attacked a few blocks from here. They were drugged, their bodies dumped near the ER. They're in the hospital now but aren't talking."

Now why would Arragon protect Nate and Pete?

Rafe gripped her hands. "Any word on Samantha?"

Juliet shook her head, and a tear traced the curve of her cheek. "There's something else. Someone jumped my lawyer John Sinclair behind his office. He's unconscious."

Shit. Rafe closed his eyes and leaned his forehead against the metal. How many had to get hurt in this war between him and Balthasar?

"A detective is checking the security cameras."

Rafe opened his eyes and swallowed. "Arragon disabled them before we met John."

"Why would Arragon meet with John tonight?"

"Arragon was my witness when I signed the deeds."

She reached through the bars to touch his face, and he closed his eyes. "Why would you do that now?"

Because he was leaving her and wanted to make sure she could take care of herself. "You're going to need them."

Calum's voice carried throughout the cellblock. "I want his door open now. I need to talk to my client. And Mr. Montfort wants to see his brother."

An officer followed Calum and Philip with his keys out. "Where's your paperwork?"

"Have you seen the station?" Calum said. "It's chaos."

The officer blinked.

Calum found his wallet and took out a hundred-dollar bill. "Will this work?"

The officer took it and handed Calum the keys. "Ten minutes."

"Twenty."

The man's gaze lingered on Juliet's shoulders long enough for Rafe to consider reaching through the bars and strangling the corrupt cop.

"Twenty. No more."

Once the cop left, Calum opened the door. Juliet rushed into Rafe's arms, and he held her closer than he'd known was possible for a man to hold a woman.

"Juliet?" Calum tapped her on the shoulder. "I need to talk to Rafe alone. Can you and Philip wait down the hall? Once I'm done, he's all yours."

She kissed Rafe and let Philip lead her away.

Calum snapped his fingers in front of Rafe's face. "You heard about John?"

"Yes. I went there earlier to sign the deeds over to Juliet, but I didn't hurt him."

"Why? I thought we were on the same side when it came to her selling her land."

"Because I'm returning to the Fianna."

Calum raised his eyebrows into a perfect arch and tilted his head. "Excuse me?"

"I'm leaving tonight and never coming back."

"*Okaaaay.*" Calum scrubbed the back of his neck with one hand. "You mean you're leaving with Juliet."

"I lost, Calum. Balthasar has Samantha and the vial."

"Weren't they going to kill you or torture you or something?"

"If I return to the brotherhood tonight, all punishments will be lifted."

"What about Juliet?"

"I'm going alone."

Calum dropped his hands to his hips in full-on lecture mode. "No. We can still fight. We'll hunt Balthasar, save Samantha, retrieve the vial. Nate, Pete, and Garza can help us."

"Nate and Pete are wanted men. Garza has already bent his moral convictions. I won't ask him to break them. And I don't want you getting any deeper involved with this. Saving Samantha and the vial is now the Fianna's responsibility—if the Prince acts."

"What the hell does that mean?"

Rafe stared at his friend. "If they take out Balthasar, there'll be collateral damage."

Calum backed up, his eyes stone-cold blue. "You'd let Samantha die?"

"I've no choice."

"This will kill Juliet." Calum's breaths sounded short and labored. "And you? How will you survive without her?"

"Not well." Understatement of the millennium.

"I called in a lot of favors to get you free. I did it to save you *and* Juliet. To save the best friends I've ever had. It can't end this way."

Rafe grasped Calum's shoulder. "This second chance has been the greatest gift anyone's ever given me. I'll never forget it."

"Will we ever see you again?"

"No. It won't be allowed."

Calum swallowed and looked away. "This will destroy her."

"Which is why I need you to promise to look out for her, to protect her. When she's hurt, she retreats into herself. Refuses help and goes to extremes to prove her independence and worthiness. Don't let her do anything self-destructive."

Calum's hand covered his. "I promise to keep her safe. To make sure she never wants for anything."

"Thank you."

Calum wiped his cheek with his sleeve and jacked up his shoulders. "What do you want me to do about the judge?"

"Don't worry about it. When the time is right, my brothers will come for me."

"And Juliet? Do you want to see her? To say goodbye?"

No. "Yes."

Juliet and Philip sat in the waiting room near an emergency exit. She checked the clock. Twelve minutes left. "Who are you texting?"

Philip hit send. "Just business."

"Oh." She stared at the gray floor, wishing she could stop time, when the back of her neck tingled. She scanned the room until she saw a dark-skinned man leaning against the wall, staring at the cell block door.

How did I not notice him before?

He almost rivaled Rafe in height and width. His motorcycle jacket emphasized his upper body. Black leathers encased muscular thighs and trim waist, and a black beanie covered his head. His crossed arms exposed a tattoo on one wrist, a leather cuff on the other. From his aggressive eyebrows to his steel-toed boots, his hard angles reeked of strength and force. He reminded her of Rafe.

Since Philip was engrossed in another text, she peeked again. Only this time the man stared at her. His dark eyes slashed and burned as they trailed across her body.

Her toes curled, and she wiped her hands on her skirt.

The lights hummed and blacked out for a moment. When they came back on, the man had disappeared and Calum stood in front of her.

She stood. "May I see him now?"

"Yes." Calum handed her the keys. "But he'll only see you and Philip together."

Philip pressed a hand against her lower back. "How much time?"

"Seven minutes. When you're done, meet me at the car."

She ran into the cell block and down the hallway. Since this was the older part of the station, Rafe was the only one incarcerated down here. When she got to Rafe's cell, she opened it with the keys, dropped her purse, and flung herself into his embrace. His warmth soothed her ragged edges and helped her breathe.

"I need to talk to both of you," Rafe said softly.

Philip came in, arms crossed, scowl engraved. "You're leaving again, aren't you?"

"That's ridiculous." She shifted to glare at Philip. "Why would you say such a thing?"

"Because it's the truth."

Those words hadn't come from Philip. They'd come from Rafe.

His arms dropped, and he stepped away. The brown eyes she loved held a hardness she'd never seen. His granite jaw could cut diamonds. Everything about him shifted to cold and hard. No humor. No winks. No teasing smiles. He'd also rolled up the sleeves of his shirt exposing the tattooed names on his right forearm. And the ribbon on his left wrist? Gone. As if it had never been there. "I've been lying to you."

Philip scoffed. "We're supposed to be surprised?"

She focused on the dark swirls in Rafe's gaze. "About what?"

"My deal with the Prince. Whether or not I found the vial, I always had to return. I was never staying with you."

"You were never staying with me?" She repeated the words just to hear them properly. "How long have you known that?"

"Since that first moment in Liberty Square."

"You sought me out. I'm the one who ran away."

"I needed you to find the vial. I couldn't do it without you."

"And what happened between us earlier tonight?" She didn't care that Philip was listening to this. To his credit, Philip put a hand on her shoulder to keep her steady.

Rafe looked away. "Two adults seeking comfort."

She put her hands on his chest. The heat coming off his body seared her. His muscles contracted, and his heart rate had to be ten times normal. "It was more than that. I can *feel* it."

He gripped her wrists and pushed her away. "I'm leaving. For good this time."

Her eyes burned, and her face felt tender and hot. He crossed his arms and sighed as if tired of the whole thing. "Philip, tell Pops thanks for the car. I gave the keys to Calum."

She heard Philip swallow before saying, "Okay."

"I still don't understand," she said. "Your tattoos— they're not real." She forced herself to look at his arm. Despite the time spent in his bed, washing his body, making love to him, she'd shied away from reading his right arm. But now, she didn't. Without his permission or approval, she pushed his sleeve up his massive arm. He didn't stop her. In fact, he moved it up higher until he revealed the bicep she couldn't encircle with two hands.

In perfect script, names had been inked in a circular pattern from wrist to shoulder. She lost count after sixty, but traced each one with her finger. And he let her.

"The names are true?" Philip's voice sounded breathy, tortured.

She threw Rafe's arm away and backed up.

"Why wouldn't they be?"

"I'd just hoped..." Philip paused because Rafe went to the cot, grabbed a manila envelope, and put it in Juliet's bag on the floor. "What are you doing?"

"Those are the deeds to Capel land." Rafe then said to Philip, "Take Juliet and get out of here. ASAP."

She tore her attention from Rafe and turned to Philip. He'd shoved his hands in his pants pockets and stared at the ground. His shoulders heaved and then slumped. For the first time she realized that Rafe's betrayal—then and now—hadn't just affected her. It'd torn apart his family. He hadn't only abandoned her. He'd left his younger brother who'd always adored him and the father who disapproved of yet loved him.

She stared at Rafe's arm again, remembering everything

she'd learned about Fianna warriors and their tithes to the Prince. Rafe's tattoos weren't real. Not just because she wanted that to be true but because the idea of the tattoos had, for years, kept her from trying to find him. The idea of the tattoos had been a perfect ploy to break them up and set Rafe free.

"No." The word came as an order instead of a response. "You're not doing this. I'm not letting you sacrifice yourself for me again. We're going to figure this out together. And if you won't help me, I'll get Nate, Pete, Calum, and Garza to help me."

"Juliet—"

She held up her hand. "I'm going to find the Prince and tell him we're not playing these games anymore. You've given them eight years of your life. You've paid your tithe."

"What are you talking about?" Philip's stare bounced between her and Rafe. "Who is the Prince, and what the hell is a tithe?"

She didn't answer because Rafe's jaw moved from the force of his molars grinding themselves down.

"Don't do this, Juliet." Rafe's voice dropped, and he grabbed both her arms. "You can't negotiate with them. It's too dangerous."

"I don't need your protection or your permission." She broke out of his grip and pressed one hand against his heart. "I need *you*. And if you won't fight for yourself, then I will."

The lights flickered again. When the regular lights didn't return, the backup generator kicked in with a loud grunting noise followed by red emergency lights.

"Time's up," the officer said from outside the cell. "Another storm's come through, messing with the power. Gotta lock him back up."

She reached for her purse. "Don't worry, Rafe. I'll take care of everything."

Rafe moved forward until the guard blocked his way. "Stay away from the Prince. You'll make everything worse."

"Things can't get any worse." She slung her purse handle over her shoulder and pulled on Philip's arm. "Let's go. I'll explain it all outside."

Once she and Philip left the cell, Rafe called out, "Don't do this, Juliet. *Please.*"

As hard as it was to ignore him and not look back, she had a goal. She was going to extricate Rafe from the Prince. She just had to figure out how.

At the cell block door, she ran into the dark-skinned, leather-clad man, who said, "*Je suis désolé, madame,*" and kept going.

Once they were back in the waiting room, alarms blared and the red emergency lights blinked.

Philip shouted over the blaring sounds, "Let's get out of here."

The red flashes blinded her as they left through the emergency exit. Drizzle glistened on the asphalt, and by the time she reached the sidewalk, her hair and dress were soggy. Officers ran into the building, and she heard shouts.

She hiked her purse higher onto her shoulder. It now held her grants and her deeds. The two things she once thought she wanted more than anything.

"Come on." Philip hustled her across the street until they found a covered storefront. Fire trucks raced by, and smoke rose above the riverfront a few blocks away. Sirens whirred in the night air. Helicopters hovered overhead.

A dark SUV came around the corner as two men ran out from an alley next to the police station. The first man shoved the second into the car. The driver pulled away before the door shut, tires squealing.

A black car pulled up in front of Juliet and Philip, and the back door opened.

Philip took her arm. "The sooner we get away from this mess, the sooner we can get on with our lives."

She slid across the leather seat, except Calum wasn't there. This wasn't Calum's car.

"What are you—" Philip's voice ended with a thump. A man in a hoodie punched Philip in the stomach. He fell onto his knees, and the man kicked him. His head hit the curb.

"No!" She scrambled out, but the man pushed his way in and leered.

Deke.

She kicked him. He slapped her across the face, throwing her against the door frame. Her vision faded, and pain radiated from her cheek to her ear.

"Go!" Deke ordered the driver. "Balthasar is waiting."

"Straight. Savage."

She scrambled for the handle, and the locks *clicked*. Through the window, she saw Calum get out of his car across the street and run toward her. But the driver of her vehicle gunned the engine.

The SUV must've made a U-turn because it came roaring down the street. A black van came from the other direction and swerved, forcing the SUV to the side of the road.

"Drive!" Deke's hot hand moved up her thigh, and she spat at him. He slapped her again. "Bitch!"

The car sped away. She couldn't see the SUV or Calum because Deke had captured both of her wrists in one hand. He shifted over her, his black cross hanging off his neck. His garlic-tainted breath burned as he hissed, "*Finally.*"

The car halted suddenly, brakes squealing, throwing her and Deke onto the floor. She hit her head and slipped into blackness.

CHAPTER 44

NATE AND PETE LEFT THE CLUB. INSTEAD OF AFTER-STORM coolness, the humidity was cranked to 100 percent. They were loaded with water and weapons, ready to search for the safe house.

Nate paused. "Do you hear sirens?"

"Yes." Pete faced the river. "I smell smoke."

Nate's phone buzzed with a message from Calum. Nate's heart kicked like a pistol being cocked. Then he ran back inside the club, yanking Pete's arm along the way. "Do we have a first aid kit?"

"Yes. I think someone who worked here was an army medic or something. There's a combat medic kit in the kitchen closet."

Ten minutes later, they had the stainless-steel kitchen work table cleared and the windows covered with cardboard and duct tape so they could turn on the lights.

Pete checked his watch. "They should be here by now."

Nate went to the back door as a black Bentley drove into the alley with its lights off. Garza jumped out of the driver's seat.

Nate ran to help Garza and Calum with Philip. His shirt was sticky, and his hands were covered with blood.

"I don't know how much blood he's lost," Garza said.

Hopefully Philip wouldn't need a transfusion. They made it to the kitchen and laid him on the counter. Pete was laying out first aid supplies.

"Nate, I need hot water and clean cloths." Pete nodded

toward the bottle of industrial soap and a box of latex gloves near the sink. "Everyone washes hands and puts on gloves."

Nate came back to the table with the water and dish towels that still smelled like bleach. For as disgusting as the club was, the kitchen was surprisingly clean. "What happened?"

"I'll tell you what fucking happened." Garza held Philip's shoulders down on the table while Pete cut away Philip's blood-soaked shirt. "The Fianna set two diversions, attacked your MPs, and broke Rafe out of jail."

"That's what happened to you," Calum said while washing his hands. "I was almost run over by Balthasar's guys."

"Wait." Nate glanced up. "Balthasar has guys?"

"Yep. At least two."

"I didn't see any guys." Garza washed up, put on a pair of gloves, and went back to securing Philip. "By the time I got outside, I found Calum trying to carry Philip."

"Shit." Pete began to clean up Philip's stomach and muttered, "*Shit*," again.

"Is it bad?" Philip asked.

"Some of your sutures ripped. And you have a goose egg on your head. If I can stitch you up and stop the bleeding, you'll only have to worry about infection and pain and maybe a concussion."

"I'm good with that."

"Nate," Pete said. "I need a suture kit. It's in the bottom of the first aid box."

Nate opened the suture kit for Pete while Calum took out his phone and started texting.

"What are you doing?" Nate asked Calum.

"Fixing this."

"It's my fault," Philip groaned from the table.

"Nate!" Pete ordered. "Any pain meds in that case?"

"Tramadol pills and lidocaine cream."

"No narcotics." Philip struggled to sit until Garza pressed him down again. "I can't help her if I'm drugged."

While Nate cleaned Philip's wound, Pete laid out the tools he needed to stitch up Philip. "What do you mean by it being your fault?"

Calum's shoulders sloped over the phone. "Balthasar has Juliet."

"And I helped get her kidnapped," Philip said.

Nate took Philip's jaw and stared into his eyes. "Juliet is *where*?"

"With Deke."

"With Balthasar," Calum corrected.

Pete stopped sewing. "Why would she be with either?"

"Because," Philip said, "I was taking her to someone who wanted to buy her property. Now that Rafe's left her again, I wanted her to be free."

"This whole thing is a damn soap opera," Garza said.

"What about that SUV?" Philip said. "It tried to stop the car, but then a van forced it off the road."

"I don't know. I thought…" Calum opened a water bottle he found in the fridge and took a long drink. "Doesn't matter now."

Garza sighed. "Rafe is gone. Juliet is kidnapped. And we've no idea where she is."

"She's probably with Samantha," Pete said. "We just need to find where Balthasar's taken them. Except we have no idea where he's been hiding. Although we do have a map we were hoping to try out."

Nate handed Pete more gauze. "Arragon might know."

Garza snorted. "Arragon isn't helpful. Even if we knew how to contact him."

"We don't need to contact Arragon," Calum said. "Rafe is with Arragon."

"Does Rafe know about Juliet?" Philip asked.

Calum held up his phone, showing his text. "He does now."

∽

Rafe braced himself against the seat as the SUV slammed to a stop. The cops had barricaded the entrance to the interstate. It was the eighth roadblock they'd encountered.

Good.

He'd seen Deke take Juliet. Even worse, Rafe had ID'd Eddie Marigny as the driver before that van forced them off the road. And that's when everything fell into place. Deke was taking Juliet to Balthasar. "Ditch me here. I'll find Juliet and meet you wherever you want."

"No." Arragon, next to him, leaned forward to speak to Orsino, who held a death grip on the wheel. "Is there another way, Brother?"

Orsino glanced back, his long blond hair and pale-blue eyes betraying his Nordic ancestry. "There may be recourse along the river."

Rafe tapped his foot. "Balthasar took Juliet. You saw it. Let me find her and Samantha, and I swear I'll return after I kill him."

Orsino drove the car into an alley. "Lady Juliet is not your concern."

"I'm not talking to you."

"Rudeness is beneath you, Romeo." Arragon clucked his tongue. An annoying habit Rafe hadn't missed.

"She's my wife."

Orsino caught his gaze in the rearview mirror. "You have no wife."

Rafe's heart contracted, and his breathing shortened. "Balthasar knows the only way to get me is through her.

It's the same leverage game the Prince has been using for eight years."

Arragon checked his watch. "Lennox has been instructed to find the rogue Balthasar and retrieve the vial. If possible, Lennox will retrieve the two women."

"The deal was I return and Juliet lives. If she doesn't, I don't. That's how leverage works. When the thing a man desires is gone, you no longer control the man."

Orsino stopped the car near Nate's motel. Red and blue lights flashed in the distance. The entire lower river area had been blocked off too. "'Tis an impasse."

"Because the cops have the city on lockdown. Something you should've thought about before setting those diversions."

Arragon started texting.

Rafe grabbed the phone. "You're not getting out of town with me in the car."

Arragon held out his hand. "Return it."

Orsino shifted to stare at them both.

"No." Rafe dialed. "I need to speak with the Prince. And since you took my cell phone, I'll use yours."

"Orsino, find us a refuge."

Rafe put the phone on speaker. "Head to Liberty Square, between Montgomery and West President Street. It's under construction."

The Prince picked up after two rings. "Yes, Arragon?"

"'Tis Romeo. Balthasar has Juliet and the vial. I want to go after him and the men he's now working with. I need to save her."

"No."

"I have information. Something that affects your youngest brother. In exchange, I want to find Juliet. When I know she's safe, I'll return with Arragon."

After a long pause, the Prince said, "I'll hear you out, and then consider your request."

Arragon raised an eyebrow, and Orsino frowned in the rearview mirror.

It was more than Rafe had expected. "Balthasar is selling the vial through a law firm in New Orleans. Beaumont, Barclay, and Bray."

Arragon murmured, "An unscrupulous group of villains."

"Indeed," Orsino added.

"I know," the Prince said.

"The night of Nate Walker's operation in Afghanistan, Nate's in-theater commander made a call while Nate's two A-teams were being ambushed. Instead of helping Nate and Jack's teams, the commander called this law firm. And that night every team member's wife received one of Juliet's lilies."

"What does this have to do with my brother?"

"Juliet's lily, the vial, Nate's ambush—they're related to one plan. Weaponizing a poison derived from Juliet's lily. And there's one man who's patient enough to do something so complicated and cunning. One man with a connection to Juliet, her lily, and a Special Forces unit. One man who hates Colonel Kells Torridan more than you."

"I hold no hatred for Torridan. And *that man* you speak of is dead."

"What if your brother didn't kill him? What if *that man* is alive and playing all of us?"

"It's not possible—"

"If I can prove *that man* lives, then your brother could be freed from prison. But I need to do this alone—without the brotherhood." Rafe clenched the phone until he was sure he'd break it. "I give you my word. I'll come back once I save Juliet and prove your brother's innocence. Technically, I'm still a free agent until I return."

Arragon shook his head. "'Tis a false hope, Romeo."

Rafe ignored the lack of support. "Balthasar isn't working alone anymore. This is larger than Kells Torridan's A-teams."

"Arragon?" the Prince asked.

"'Tis true, my lord. Balthasar isn't alone."

Orsino pulled into Liberty Square and parked between a dump truck and a bulldozer. When he turned off the car, the only light came from the silent phone.

"What say you, my lord?" Maybe switching to formal language would help.

"You've twenty-four hours. But you will return, Romeo. Do you understand?"

"That you'll kill everyone I love? Got it." Rafe tossed the phone to Arragon. "I need a gun, my cell, and any other weapons you can spare."

Arragon exhaled loudly while Orsino handed him a nine-mil, two loaded mags, and a knife.

After loading up, Rafe asked Arragon, "Do you know the Prioleau Plantation on the Isle of Hope?"

"Aye."

"In twenty-four hours, I'll meet you near the tomb of Noble Jones. You shouldn't have trouble getting out of town by then."

Arragon took Rafe's cell from his back pocket and handed it to Rafe. He had a string of texts from Calum to which he responded Meet you at the club in ten minutes.

Orsino unlocked the door, and Rafe got out. He was about to close the door when Arragon said, "And if Balthasar has killed your joy?"

Rafe pressed his gun against his hip. Then he pounded

the top of the car with his other fist. Arragon would know this wasn't a threat. It was a promise. "This day's black fate on more days doth depend. This but begins the woe others must end."

❧

Rafe met Nate at the club. Rafe had run from Liberty Square, but adrenaline hammered in his veins, and he was barely out of breath. "How's Philip?"

"Stable."

Rafe pushed open the door to the kitchen. Philip lay on the table. Calum sat on a counter, his shirt stained with blood. Pete had dark circles under his eyes, and Garza leaned his ass against the sink.

Rafe beelined for his brother. "What happened?"

"It's my fault." Philip struggled to sit, and Rafe helped him.

"Yes, it is." Calum hopped off. Strange since Rafe couldn't remember Calum ever *hopping off* anything. "Philip set up a meeting for Juliet to meet with a buyer for her land, and then Deke and Eddie took her."

Rafe kept a hand on Philip's shoulder to keep him steady. "I saw that part."

"Did you see the part where Eddie attacked Philip and I was almost run over?" Calum held up one hand. "Pete stitched Philip up, and, although I'm in pain, I'm told I'll be fine."

Philip's body shook from his erratic breathing, and Rafe asked, "Are you okay?"

"Yes." Philip straightened his shoulders until his face crumpled.

Rafe nodded to Garza, who helped lay Philip back down. "You need to rest."

"I need to find Juliet."

"Do you have any idea where Deke took her?"

"We were supposed to meet Delacroix at Prideaux House." Philip pressed a hand against his side. "Delacroix wants to buy her land."

"Holy shit." Nate yanked off his gloves and pulled something out of his back pocket.

A tourist map?

"Did you know about this?" Rafe asked Calum.

Calum scowled. "No."

Nate smoothed the paper on the table. He'd marked black X's in the historic district.

"Why would Delacroix want to buy Juliet's land?" Garza asked.

Philip spoke in short bursts. "For hunting. A getaway. On the Isle."

"Who the hell is Delacroix?" Rafe asked.

"The second-richest man in town." Calum took two pills Pete handed him and downed them with a bottle of water. "Didn't you meet him the night of the explosion?"

"No." Juliet had talked about him, but they'd never met. "Where does Delacroix come from? Why is he in town?"

"Shit, shit, shit," Nate muttered, staring at the damn map.

"Delacroix arrived almost a year ago," Calum said. "Started buying property. Even got the Habersham sisters to recommend him for the preservation society."

"Delacroix knows the city," Rafe said.

Nate raised his head. "We met at the gym and have been daily fighting partners."

Pete scoffed while cleaning up blood-soaked towels. "Delacroix knows your strengths and weaknesses?"

Nate sighed. "Yes."

Rafe clasped his hands behind his neck and paced. "Dammit, Nate."

"Delacroix also gave a lot of money to the police," Garza added.

"Delacroix bought connections." Rafe fought to keep the exasperation out of his voice. "A rich man comes to town around the time Juliet's problems started. The same time our family members and a detective were murdered. This man befriends Nate, one of the strongest men in the city. Supports local cops. Endears himself to the gatekeepers of Savannah's upper crust. And no one thought that was odd?"

Calum put down the water bottle. "I checked Delacroix's background. His father is from Lyon, his mother from Louisville. They made their money in textiles and railroads. He went to Oxford and speaks six languages."

Rafe paused his pacing. "Calum? Where does Delacroix bank?"

"RM Financial."

"That's strange," Philip said. "That's the bank that bought Juliet's business loan."

"*Fuck*." Rafe pulled out his gun and dropped the magazine. He needed to reassure himself he was fully loaded with a round in the chamber.

"I don't understand," Garza said.

Nate pointed to one X on the map. Prideaux House. "This is Balthasar's safe house."

"Clarification would be nice," Calum added. "Before you start shooting things."

They didn't have time, and Rafe didn't have the patience. "Nate, load up every weapon and flashlight we can find."

"I brought the duffel bag," Calum said. "With the guns."

"Good." Rafe helped Philip sit up again. Rafe wasn't leaving Philip behind. "Garza, figure out a way to drive us across those police barricades."

Garza helped Pete wipe down the table. "Where are we going?"

"Prideaux House. Then, if the women aren't there, the Isle. Calum, call Sheriff Boudreaux and have him grab every armed man he can—except for the Marignys—and meet us at Pops's house. Just in case."

Calum, Pete, Garza, and Philip asked at the same time, "Why?"

Rafe shared a long look with Nate. "Because it's likely that Balthasar has taken Juliet to the manor to find the other vial."

CHAPTER 45

NATE STOOD TO THE SIDE IN POPS'S TRAILER. IT'D BEEN A HARD trip out here. Not because they'd raided the Prideaux House attic and found Balthasar's safe house, along with a nice stack of the same C-4 used in the previous night's explosion and no women. Or because Garza lied to get them across the barricades. It'd been hard because Nate felt responsible for this clusterfuck. Every action he'd taken had made everything worse, and he still had no way to save his men.

Rafe stood in front of a table in Pops's trailer with tidal charts, a hand-drawn sketch of the Isle, and architectural drawings of the manor. Philip sat nearby; his face was drawn and pale, and his breathing sounded short and choppy. Garza and Pete stood with arms crossed, frowns affixed. Calum leaned against the door jamb leading to the kitchen, controlling his world through text.

"What's the situation?" Jimmy Boudreaux came in with Pops, Grady, and Tommy.

Rafe got to the point. "Balthasar, a dangerous man, has kidnapped Juliet and another woman, Samantha. I believe he, with armed men, is holding them at Capel Manor."

"Are you sure?" Jimmy asked.

"Mostly sure," Rafe responded. "Balthasar's safe house was empty, and it's the only place he would've taken them that makes sense."

"Why take her at all?" Tommy asked.

Rafe pressed his fists on the table. "Juliet's lily is a poisonous flower brought over from Italy in 1645 and used by pirates to control the population. Technically, it's a biological agent that could be weaponized. But only from the original source, which is why Gerald went crazy eradicating it. It's also why Gerald, along with Eugene and Legare, were murdered. They were protecting the secret of the lily."

Jimmy scoffed. "This is insane."

"It's true." Grady glanced at Pops, who nodded. "I helped Gerald hunt that lily until his death. Now Pops helps me."

"And now," Rafe continued, "someone's figured out that there are two vials containing a poison and an antidote made from the lily. *This someone* has one vial. And Balthasar, who's now working for *this someone*, has taken Juliet to find the other."

The men of the Isle murmured, scratching their heads, before Pops said, "What do you want us to do, Son?"

"Divide into four groups. One goes by johnboats down the Black River, toward Crab Creek, and hikes in from the south. The second will take Tommy's boat and come in through the back meadow and cross Oyster Creek, using smaller estuaries to make it to the manor. The third group will canoe along Snake Creek and protect the east perimeter. I'll head through the cemetery, hitting the back of the house.

"I want a soldier and guide on each team. Nate and Grady will lead the first. Pete and Pops will go with Tommy on his boat. Garza and Jimmy will take the third route."

"I'm going too," Philip said.

"No," Pops said.

Philip started to get up, when Rafe put a hand on his shoulder. "Stay here with Calum to monitor the SAT phone. It's the only comm we'll have out there."

Philip glanced at Calum, who was *still* texting, and then nodded.

Rafe went back to the hand-drawn map and used a chess piece to mark the manor. "Balthasar is probably holding the women here. Deke and Eddie Marigny are working for him, along with two armed guards. Our three teams will advance from the front and sides. I'll get into the manor and set up in the upper bedroom, facing the front lawn. I've got my father-in-law's sniper rifle with a thermal scope. I'll lay down cover fire while your teams take out the guards and storm the house."

Nate studied the property again. Swamp and forest cut apart by estuaries. "How will you be able to tell us from the bad guys?"

"Infrared glow tape," Tommy said. "We use it on our shirts for night paintball."

"Works for me," Pete said. "Weapons?"

Jimmy said, "My brother and I have four handguns and two bolt action rifles with scopes. Pops has two shotguns, a .22, and two Remington bolt action rifles. Gerald left us three big game rifles and two double-barreled shotguns. Everyone gets a thermal scope."

"And plenty of ammo," Pops added.

Garza crossed his arms. "Who's going with you, Rafe?"

"I'm going alone through the cemetery. I move faster on my own and can walk those woods blindfolded."

Murmurs rose up until Rafe said, "Our Isle—and our women—are under siege. What happens tonight will affect our future, and we'll be judged by those who come after us. We have to win. If we don't, we deserve to die."

～

Where am I?

Juliet lay in the dark on a hard surface. Her first deep breath burned her nose. It smelled like death in a bathroom. She moved until her bare feet hit a wall. Someone had removed her sandals? So she wouldn't run away? Her head ached and she tasted blood. Then she remembered the car and...*Deke*.

She rolled over and threw up. After a minute or an hour, she struggled to her feet. She ran her hands over herself. Her body felt liked she'd been thrown in a dryer with rocks, and she had a lump on her forehead. But other than not having shoes nothing seemed...wrong. *Thank God*.

She heard male voices and inched in their direction. When she found a door, it opened into a foyer lit by flashlights held by two men—Deke and Eddie Marigny—facing two other men. One sat on the stairs with only his legs visible, the other on a folding stool with a briefcase on his lap. This second man wore a black suit and shirt, leather shoes, and thin tie.

It was dark, and rain puddled on the floor. She was in her manor, and the men stood between her and the only usable exit.

"Sir?" A man in black combat pants stood in the front doorway, a rifle in his arms.

"What's the ETA on the helo?" the man on the stairs asked.

"An hour. Possibly less." The soldier left.

She turned her daddy's gold ring on her thumb. There was no point in running. She'd no weapons or shoes. Armed men patrolled her property. She had to go on the offensive. "What are you doing in my home?"

Deke, Eddie, and the undertaker shifted their lights to her. She lifted her arm until they dropped the beams.

Deke smiled. "I was just suggesting one of us should kiss you awake."

She fisted her hands and raised her chin. "Try it, and you won't eat for a week."

Eddie laughed. "Just like her daddy. Mean. As. Shit. But I'll hold her down for you. Always wanted to tame that bitch."

The undertaker coughed. "It's time to proceed."

Deke and Eddie shone their beams on the man who came off the stairs. When he faced her, he hit his chest with a fist and bowed. "I am Balthasar."

Except he wasn't. The hair on her arms raised, and words stuck in her throat. He'd replaced his Italian suit with black combat pants, T-shirt, and boots. Delacroix *was* Balthasar.

How was that possible? How had she not suspected?

Because, she thought ruefully, she'd needed the money and had been determined to save her business on her own.

"I apologize, my lady. 'Tis an awful thing to lie to a beautiful woman."

She pressed the heels of her hands into her eyes. She'd made such a mess of things. "What do you want from me?"

"What I've always wanted. To destroy Romeo."

She opened her eyes and reached for a baluster. "Rafe has returned to the Fianna. You've nothing to fear from him."

"I've never feared Romeo. I just want to see him destroyed."

"By killing me?"

"I'm not going to kill you." Balthasar's smile reeked of condescension. "Show her," he said to the undertaker.

The undertaker took a box out of his briefcase and handed it to her. It was made of polished oak, and yew tree carvings decorated the top. She lifted the brass clasp and opened the box. A crystal vial lay nestled within the velvet interior, which had been designed to hold *two* vials.

Balthasar took the box, snapped it shut, and gave it back to the undertaker. "It was in the statue of Gabriel. Hidden in your shop the entire time."

"Are you sure whatever's in that vial is still viable?" She wiped her hands on her dress. "It's three hundred years old."

"I am."

"Get to the good part, B." Eddie's light wobbled. "The *good* part."

"I already know," she said. "You're selling the vial. So why do you need me?"

"You know what's in that vial?"

"Some kind of poison or biological agent that's probably evaporated by now."

"The poison derived from Anne's Lament, the real name of your lily, is suspended in oil from the yew tree. I'm confident the contents are intact."

"Yew tree oil is poisonous and volatile."

"It's stable enough," the undertaker said. "Ancient Celts used it to coat the ends of their arrows. If the arrow didn't kill quickly, the poison would kill slowly."

They were all crazy. "What do I have to do with this?"

"I need the land where your lily grows."

"It's not cultivated," the undertaker said. "It's important to say it's *not cultivated*."

"My lily hasn't been seen on my land since I was a child."

Balthasar waved his arm. "It grows wild in the back meadow and the cemetery."

The undertaker opened his briefcase again and pulled out the King's Grants and signed copies of her deeds. He laid them on top of the case and took a pen out of his jacket. "Your grants have three stipulations that must have been maintained to remain valid. First, the lily known as Anne's Lament may never be *cultivated* on the properties." He lowered his glasses and stared at Balthasar. "While there's anecdotal evidence of wild lilies, there's been no cultivation."

She frowned at him. "The second stipulation?"

"The property must never, at any time, have been out of the hands of the Capel family—male or female. According to my law firm's research—"

"You're a lawyer?" Why was she not surprised?

"I specialize in real estate and contract law." The lawyer adjusted his glasses. "At no time has the land passed out of your family's hands."

"My father put Rafe's name on the deeds."

"Within a trust. And your ex-husband could never have sold without your signature. Therefore, it's still within the legal framework of the stipulation."

"And the third?"

"A Capel must live on the land at all times."

She smiled at Balthasar. "I haven't lived here since I got married, and my father's been gone almost a year."

Balthasar smiled back. "You make money from tours and Boudreaux's restaurant. You pay taxes, receive rent, and reimburse Grady Mercer to maintain docks and roads."

"I don't pay much. Have you seen the docks and roads?"

The lawyer coughed. "The condition of the property is sufficient."

She paced the room, avoiding the puddles, her bare feet feeling the give of the rotted wood beneath. "You sell the vial to the buyer, but how does he get the land?"

Balthasar nodded. "He understands the stipulations and is willing to lease the property."

"From me?"

"From both of us."

She stared at the lawyer. "What kind of contract law?"

"Marriage and family."

She laughed. She couldn't help it. "I'm supposed to marry Balthasar so he can lease the property to your client?"

The lawyer nodded.

She faced Balthasar directly. "Why not let the buyer reengineer the poison in a lab?"

"He needs the vial's contents *and* a constant supply of live lilies. Unfortunately for you, your lily only grows on this Isle. Something about phosphates and a rare bird."

"How do you know that?"

"My buyer's been stealing wild lilies for years to propagate and replicate the poison, with little luck."

Deke laughed. "Haven't you been paying attention? People are dropping like flies on horse shit all over town. The heroin and street pills giving people seizures? It's a trial run from lilies Escalus stole nine months ago."

"Nine months ago?" She swallowed, and her throat burned. "That's when Eugene Wilkins died in my back meadow."

Eddie smiled. "Got in Escalus's way. As did Legare and your daddy. Oh, and apparently your mother-in-law as well. Although that wasn't a Fianna kill. You can thank Balthasar's new boss for that one."

The floor wobbled. Or maybe it was her legs. "You expect me to marry you and then let you sell that vial and my lily to a monster who'll turn it into a weapon? The same monster who killed my mother-in-law?"

"Yes." Balthasar nodded to Deke, who left the room. Now they were down to two flashlights. "And once we have a child, I'll kill you."

This was so insane. She paced the uneven floor, fisting and unfisting her hands. "There's no way I could disappear without people noticing."

"Your husband left you. The scandal when people learn you've been stripping because you're broke will destroy your business. Calum and Philip will understand if you go to Europe."

"I have friends."

"Walker and White Horse? When their unit goes to trial, they won't remember you."

"People will notice if we're living out here." Grady, at least.

"We won't. We'll collect tourist dollars, pay taxes, and let Grady keep up the land. We'll return to New Orleans, and the law firm will handle the rest."

"I won't go with you."

Deke reappeared and laid something wrapped in a blanket on the floor. "This should keep the bitch in line for you."

Samantha. Juliet knelt. Samantha's eyes were closed, but her breathing was steady and her pulse strong. "What did you do to her?"

"What I was told." Deke licked his lips. "I wanted to do more."

"Touch her again, and I'll beat you with a shovel until you cry like a baby."

"Bring it, *Jade.*"

Balthasar placed a hand on her shoulder, and she shrugged him off. It was only then that she saw his misericord. "If you don't agree to come with me tonight, I'll kill her."

"You'll have no leverage. You can't lease the land without me, and you can't kill me."

"After Samantha, I'll kill Philip. Calum. Pops."

"Once Rafe finds out, you'll be sorry you ever spoke my name."

"He's returned to the Prince. You'll never see him again."

"Face it, Jade," Deke sneered. "You're alone. No one to help. No way out."

"Then why bring me out here if we're just leaving town?"

Balthasar pointed to the undertaker. "That box holds two vials, and one of the windows shows Anne holding two vials. That means one is missing. You're going to help me find it."

"Why would I do that?"

"Supposedly, one drop of the poison is enough to kill. There's enough to spare if I give one drop to Samantha."

Now Juliet understood. The other vial was the antidote.

CHAPTER 46

AN HOUR LATER, RAFE MADE IT TO THE BACK OF THE MANOR. As suspected, the SAT phone didn't work this far in.

He'd run the entire way with Gerald's sniper rifle strapped to his back, a nine-mil in his waistband, a knife in his boot, and a machete on his hip. He appreciated the cooler night air clearing his head. It was always this way before killing a man. He needed time and space to process the horror of who he was and what he had to do.

The full moon hid behind storm clouds, and he whistled low. No answer.

Since he couldn't cross the thickets or jump the mud flats, he found the tree near Juliet's balcony and climbed. When he landed on the balcony, it swayed beneath his weight. He knelt on one knee, a hand pressed to the floor. The shaking timber felt like a giant exhale, as if the manor was relieved to see him.

Holding his breath, he slipped into the hallway, avoiding rotted floorboards. He didn't hear any unusual sounds, but he knew she was here. He could feel it.

When he reached the balcony over the foyer, he saw Deke standing near Samantha. An armed man guarded the front door. Another stood on the porch. Rafe retreated to the front bedroom. After taking off his T-shirt to clear away broken glass on the front-facing window, he set up his position. He was locked, loaded, and ready.

Balthasar gripped Juliet's arm and pulled her around the

dining room. Her feet stung from tiny cuts and splinters, her head ached, and her lips were cracked. "Where is it?"

Balthasar yanked her arm. Pain shot from her shoulder to her wrist. "I don't know."

He threw her to the ground, and she skinned her knees.

Eddie used a flashlight to illuminate the stained-glass windows. "Freaky."

Balthasar dragged her to the window with Anne handing the box of two vials to the men. "Where. Is. It."

"I don't know."

He slapped her, and her ears rang. "Look harder."

"It's too dark."

Balthasar motioned to Eddie, who dropped the light to the lower part of the window.

She remembered the vials and the warrior, but she didn't remember Anne's depiction. In this window, unlike the others, Anne wore a Roman-style dress with her hair in ringlets. Two trees stood in the background, each sending out vines that wrapped around Anne's bare feet and ankles as well as her bare arms from her shoulder to her wrists.

Juliet touched the glass oak leaves entwining Anne's feet. The leaves around her arm were from a yew tree. Similar to the leaves carved on the mantel. The newel posts.

And drawn on her map.

Daddy, she spoke silently and turned his ring on her thumb. *Help me.* Studying the band, she realized the worn engravings weren't words. They were oak leaves.

"Sir." An armed man appeared, his rifle cradled. "ETA fifteen minutes."

Balthasar yanked her hair again. "Ten minutes or Samantha dies."

"I don't need ten minutes," she said confidently. "It's upstairs."

ᔥ

Nate whistled low, and Pete responded from the other side of the open field. The house sat three hundred yards on his left on a small hill. Rafe had been right about how hard the trip would be and wrong about the number of armed men. Two protected the house while three more walked the perimeter between the woods and the lawn.

Although it was dark, it would be foolish to cross the area without cover. Even more so if the full moon appeared. Nate whistled again. No response. Garza's team hadn't arrived.

Nate adjusted the rifle against his shoulder and felt for his nine-mil at his side. He hated having no comms and borrowed weapons. He would've given anything for a shoulder-mounted grenade launcher and decent ear radios.

Grady knelt next to him. An owl hooted near the house. "Ain't no owls sounding off this time of year. If they ain't breedin', they ain't hootin'."

"Huh." Nate used binoculars to scan the house. So much harder without night vision. "Watch the upper floor, toward the left end." Flashes of light, like a punch of a laser pointer, shone in short dashes and dots. Morse code. "Run. Cover. Oorah."

Grady chuckled.

"Grady? Were you a Marine?"

It was too dark to see a smile, but Nate heard the pride as Grady said, "Task Force Ripper. Me, Pops, and Gerald. We signed up together and fought together."

Operation Desert Storm. Diversionary battle in Kuwait along the Persian Gulf while the main Marine force attacked from behind. A hundred-hour blood bath.

"Guard's coming," Grady whispered. "And the moon's coming out."

The armed man passed ten feet in front of them. The moonlight showed the man all in black with no insignia or markings and heavy body armor. Private security all the way.

Once the guard was out of sight, Grady took off and Nate followed. They moved quickly and silently until a guard appeared on Nate's left. A shot ripped through the night, taking out the soldier. *Thank you, Rafe.*

Grady stopped suddenly. "Mud pits."

A river of mud surrounded the house. One of the perimeter guards yelled behind Nate, and he turned just as Rafe's sniper bullet took the second guard down.

"Cover me." Grady dragged the dead body over and shoved it into the mud. Crosswise. "Come on!"

The mud was thick and the body dense, so they were able to make it with a leap at the end. Nate had done a lot of things in his years as a Special Forces soldier, but he'd never crossed a human bridge. This wasn't something he needed to remember.

The third perimeter guard fired, and another sniper shot dropped him. Nate kept running, he and Grady jumping over the body. Grady headed toward a window while Nate met Pete in the bushes below the porch. Pete was breathing heavily and shouldering his weapon. Pops was hunkered down with a pistol between his hands, his gaze on the open area behind them.

They'd all changed into combat pants and T-shirts covered in infrared tape before this adventure. Except for Pops. He wore his overalls.

"Where are Garza and the sheriff?" Nate asked.

"Not here yet," Pete said. "We found the boat Balthasar and his goons used. Tommy's protecting our ride home and disabling theirs."

Grady appeared, out of breath. "Two guards in the

manor, along with Eddie Marigny and some guy with a broken nose and bandaged ear."

"Deke." Nate really hoped never to see that guy again. "Juliet?"

"No sign. But there's a woman lying on the floor. Blond hair. Unconscious."

"Samantha." Pete raised his head to check out the situation.

"What's that?" Pops lifted his face to the night sky.

Nate shut down his own breathing to listen. It took a moment, but then he heard the air rustle. "You gotta be kidding me."

"Fuck," Pete whispered. "Who ordered a helo?"

"Pete and Pops, cover us." Nate checked the rifle's load. "Grady and I'll go in."

Nate led Grady up the steps to the porch. It was clear. Through the window Nate saw Samantha on the ground with Deke crouched over her, a gun in his hand. Time to roll.

CHAPTER 47

JULIET LED BALTHASAR INTO HER DADDY'S BEDROOM. WITH
Balthasar's light guiding her, she stayed near the wall and
prayed her plan would work. "In there." She pointed to
the closet on the other side of the room. "A metal box in
the floor."

Balthasar wrapped her hair around his hand and dragged
her with him. Her bare feet scrambled against the floorboards until he threw her against the wall next to the closet.
The floor groaned, and she inched away.

Gun shots reverberated, and the manor trembled.

Eddie ran in, shoulders shaking. He stopped in front of
the closet. "We got company."

Balthasar took out his gun. "Romeo?"

"Don't see him. At least two guys coming across the
field."

Balthasar fixed the barrel on Juliet. "Where is it?"

"Underneath the floorboards, but I can't lift it. That's
why it's still there."

Balthasar pushed Eddie to his knees. "Find it."

"It's a heavy metal box." Thank goodness for the *girl
card*. "I'll hold the light."

More gunfire exploded, and Balthasar went into the hall.
Eddie gave her the flashlight, and she intentionally pointed
the beam up.

"I can't see a thing," Eddie said.

"Left side, toward the back. Feel for a loose board."

"I need more light."

She shifted. "Go in farther."

"I—" A loud creaking was followed by a ripping sound. "No!" Eddie fell to the first floor, and a cloud of dirt and debris blew through the opening. "Help me! Please!"

She stood just as Balthasar backhanded her. She slid across the floor and hit the door jamb. Balthasar stalked her, his weapon pointed. Her head pounded, and she tasted blood.

"Bitch!" He grabbed her arm, forced her into the hallway, and threw her down the stairs. She rolled, trying to keep her arms tucked in, and used her feet to stop herself at the bottom.

Despite her dizziness and aching body, she used the banister to pull herself up, only to see Nate and Grady on their knees with hard eyes and determined jaws. Two soldiers held a gun to each of their heads while Deke pointed his at the still-unconscious Samantha.

The lawyer sat in his chair, licking his lips as if he needed popcorn.

"Nate?" She took a step until Deke pointed his gun at her. "What are you doing here?"

"I know, right?" Deke snickered. "Nate walking and talking? I mean, after all the poisoned dope he's been taking, I'm surprised he's not toe-tagged by now."

She pressed her arm against a sore rib. "You've been poisoning Nate?"

Deke snorted. "Nate's been poisoned off and on since Afghanistan. Easy to do since he's been too blinded by self-pity to notice those pills he's been taking were laced with the same stuff as the zombie heroin."

The shock in Nate's wide-open eyes had to be mirrored in her own.

Balthasar came up behind her. "Where are the rest of Walker's men?"

"This is it. The Indian got shot outside." Deke nodded toward Eddie's sobbing coming from the kitchen. "What about that racket?"

Balthasar left the room. She made eye contact with Nate, who blinked twice. She knew that meant *don't move*. She swallowed, wanting to throw herself at Deke. A pointless move that would get them all killed. A moment later, a gunshot rang out, and Eddie's cries stopped.

Balthasar came back and stood in front of Nate. Balthasar's legs were spread, one hand fisted, the other holding the gun. "Where's Romeo?"

Nate spat. "Rafe left with the Fianna earlier tonight. Warriors broke him out of jail."

Rafe was gone, and she was too late. All of their lives were now her responsibility.

Balthasar spun around, grabbed her shoulders, and lifted her until her chest hit his. "If you don't tell me, one of your friends will die."

A loud roar sounded, and bright lights appeared. A helicopter was landing in front of the manor. By the time she realized what was happening, Balthasar held the misericord to her neck. "Show me. Now."

"Don't do it, Juliet," Nate urged. "Don't give it to him."

"If I give it to you and come with you, will you let them go?"

"He won't," Grady said. "He'll kill us the minute you get in that bird."

"I promise," Balthasar said. "They go free once I have both vials and you leave with me."

She nodded.

"Dammit," Nate's voice rang out. "Don't fucking do it."

The noise and wind from the helicopter whipped around

the house. More shots ripped through the night. "I need something to cut the finial off the staircase's newel post. The one carved with oak leaves."

Balthasar smiled. When he headed for the stairs, she threw herself onto the lawyer. His bag skittered across the floor, and she rolled toward it. Balthasar reached for her legs, but it was too late. She'd gotten the box and taken out the vial. Before he could stop her, she yanked the cork and threw back the liquid. It was cold and burned her throat on the way down.

Another set of shots reverberated, and a screeching sound filled the air. Lights spun, and a loud whirring came closer and closer. In the noise and chaos, she barely heard Nate screaming "No!" or Balthasar calling her vicious names.

Her body felt heavy, and her limbs became paralyzed.

"*Juliet!*" Rafe stood at the top of the stairs, holding an enormous gun. She'd never seen him like this before. In black combat pants and boots, no shirt, tattoos littering his arms, and the blue ribbon.

But it was the look in his eyes that shattered her heart into a million pieces. A huge push of air blew through the room, and something crashed into the other side of the house. The shock wave swept dust and sharp debris into a mini tornado. She tried to turn her head, except she couldn't move.

The chaos gave Nate a chance to elbow his guard, take his gun, and kill him before turning the weapon on Deke. Grady ducked and rolled until he came up behind his soldier and ran a knife across his neck. Her lungs slowed down, and she began to choke. But she kept her gaze on Rafe running down the stairs and launching himself at Balthasar. Both men hit the ground at the same time everything went gray.

∽

Rafe threw himself on top of Balthasar with a roar and a knife. He'd dropped the guns and machete out of a pure rage to rip Balthasar's throat with his bare hands. The personal was always physical.

They landed at the bottom of the stairs, and Rafe dug his boot against the riser for leverage. But Balthasar was hopped up on desperation. They both knew the truth. Even though the Prince would hunt Balthasar down for leaving the Fianna, if Juliet died, Rafe would torture Balthasar until he begged for death.

Balthasar grunted and tossed Rafe off. He rolled away and landed on one knee. When Balthasar stood, Rafe attacked. The knife sliced Balthasar's abdomen, but it wasn't deep enough to do damage. Balthasar grunted and swung a roundhouse kick into Rafe's gut. He fell to his knees, breathing hard, still clutching the knife.

Off to the side, he saw Juliet's body lying lifeless and pale. Was she breathing?

"Nate! Check on Juliet." Rafe stood, trying not to favor his left side. He didn't want to give Balthasar any indication that his ribs felt like they'd been snapped.

Balthasar circled him, holding his own knife. The whirring sounds from the helo rotors ceased, which meant it'd crashed and died in the conservatory. That's what happens when a sniper kills the pilot and hits the tail rotor. Hopefully the whole thing wouldn't drain fuel, build up vapor, and ignite.

"'Tis foolish, this game we play," Balthasar said.

"You should've thought about that before you betrayed the Prince."

"The perfect Romeo. The favored son. Always listened to, never berated. How I hated you." Balthasar charged and nailed Rafe into the wall. Balthasar's elbows in Rafe's chest forced the breath from his crushed lungs.

Rafe drove the knife toward Balthasar's neck until he deflected it with his arm. The knife skidded across the floor. The entire house shook as if the manor was saying *enough*.

"I never wanted the favor." Rafe spat out blood. "From the moment I tithed, all I wanted was out."

Balthasar opened both arms, his lips twisted. "Why join us, Brother?"

"I wasn't given a fucking choice." Rafe swung, his fist hitting Balthasar's jaw. Pain shot from his knuckles through his shoulder.

Balthasar backhanded Rafe, and he fell against the wall. Pieces of the ceiling rained on them, and he used the distraction to dive for the knife. He rolled and swung up just as Balthasar came down. The knife caught Balthasar in the spleen, and he fell onto his knees. He roared and lunged, catching Rafe's legs. They both hit the ground hard, and Rafe freed a leg to kick Balthasar in the face.

Balthasar grabbed Rafe's wrist. "You'll never win, Romeo. The Prince is wrong about the lily. It's too late. Remiel has everything he needs to destroy you all."

Rafe spat in Balthasar's face and pulled out his nine-mil. "Shut the fuck up."

Balthasar went for the gun. Rafe fired into Balthasar's chest. The close-range shot deafened the room, and the stench of burning flesh made Rafe gag. Balthasar's eyes widened, his head tilted, his mouth opened. An unspoken scream stuck in an impossible question: Romeo had beaten him?

Balthasar fell, his breath stuttering while his hand covered the bleeding hole.

Rafe didn't wait for death. Juliet and Samantha were gone, as were Grady and Nate.

An explosion from the conservatory sent a gust of hot air spiked with splinters and pieces of metal through the foyer.

The man with the briefcase lay beneath a roof beam, his round, lifeless eyes matching his open lips.

Rafe covered his face and turned to leave when Nate ran back in. He found the machete on the stairs and began chopping at a carved finial. "Are these oak leaves?"

"No idea." The room filled with a darker smoke, confirming fears of a fire. "We have to leave."

"Help me!" Nate dropped the machete and tried to twist off the finial. "Don't break it."

"Break what?"

"Twist, dammit!"

They both coughed, and smoke obscured the few flashlights that had lit the room. Rafe grabbed the finial with Nate and twisted. After two good tugs, they screwed it off. It was hollow inside.

Nate tossed it and headed for the other one.

"We have to leave." Smoke rolled down the stairs and was creeping out of the dining room. Another eardrum-shattering explosion hit, and the second floor lost what was left of the roof.

"Turn!" Nate's face, covered in soot and blood, wore a fierceness Rafe had never seen before.

He used the last of his strength and turned. It took four turns with the strength of two men, but the finial came off. Inside the hollow area was a small vial.

"Grab that briefcase." Nate cradled the finial and ran out.

Rafe found the briefcase near the door and followed. The hot handle burned his hand, and he clutched it to his chest. Outside in the night air, he coughed and doubled over. His lungs felt like they'd been scorched, and his watery eyes blinded him. He stumbled down the stairs, barely aware of Garza taking the case and Pete holding him up. Together, they ran from the blazing house. Somehow they got Rafe over the mud pits, but then he stopped near Pops and Jimmy. Samantha was now in Pete's arms, and he held her close.

Samantha was awake and alive, thank God.

A few feet away, Arragon held Juliet in his arms. Her eyes were open; her head and arms hung down, unmoving. Her bare legs were covered in soot and blood, her long hair a tangled mess. Her chest was still. No undulations. No coughs. No breaths.

Rafe fell to his knees. His mind broken into a million *no no no nos*.

"Lay her down!" Nate threw away the finial. "Open her airway."

Pete and Garza laid her out while Arragon stretched her head back. Nate uncorked the vial and held it to her lips.

Samantha sat on the other side and held her hand. "How do we know—"

"We don't." Nate tilted the bottle. Some liquid rolled down the side of her mouth, and Nate gently wiped it away with the edge of his filthy T-shirt. Then he checked her pupils with a small flashlight Pops had given him. "Pete, when I say, start CPR. And don't you fucking stop until she's breathing again."

Rafe crawled over to her and took Arragon's place. But his former trainer didn't go far. Arragon sat next to Samantha and closed his hand over both of the women's. Pops stood nearby, his mouth moving in a silent prayer.

"I know you," Samantha's weak voice came out husky. "You came into the shop yesterday and bought all of Abigail Casey's prints."

Arragon bowed his head. "Aye."

"Pete?" Nate used a flashlight to check her pupils again. "Now."

Pete took over with chest compressions while Nate kept time.

"Talk to her, Rafe," Nate commanded. "Tell her she can't leave."

"She's—"

"She's not, Pops. She's stuck in a seizure-like paralysis, and there's still a chance. Talk to her, Rafe."

Rafe lay next to her in the opposite direction, head to head but with his body out of the way. He coughed, and it felt like his lungs broke apart in his chest. He'd inhaled too much smoke and couldn't even give his own breath to save her. "Please, sweetheart. Fight. Harder than you ever have before."

Pete continued with the compressions and breaths while Nate counted. Now Pops, Garza, Grady, and the Boudreaux boys surrounded them. All breathing heavily, offering her the air she couldn't find.

"Come on, Juliet," Nate demanded, "don't you die on us."

Pete stopped to wipe his brow, and Nate counted under his breath while he checked her eyes again. "On the count of three, start the compressions again."

"But—"

"Do it."

A fireball blew off the top of the house, and a rush of hot air drove over them. The trees and bushes close to the house started to burn as well.

"Should we call someone?" Garza asked.

"No one to call," Jimmy said. "Besides, the mud is a natural fire break."

"Pete," Nate ordered. "Compressions. Now."

Arragon and Samantha moved so Garza could kneel on Juliet's other side and place his hands on her chest. "I'll compress, you blow."

Once Nate started the count again, Rafe whispered, "Come back to me."

Sweat beaded her forehead, and her pulse barely blipped.

"Are you sure about this?" Garza asked Nate.

"I was reading about Anne's poison. It causes a seizure-like paralysis throughout the body that eventually reaches the lungs and heart. We gave her the antidote, and now we have to get her heart pumping."

"That antidote was over three hundred years old," Samantha said.

Arragon took Samantha's hand and kissed the palm. "Fair lady, if the poison worked, so will the cure."

"If that was the cure," Pete said softly.

"If you're not going to help"—Nate flicked the light and checked her pupils for the third time—"shut the hell up. On the count of three, we start again."

CHAPTER 48

COME BACK TO ME.

Juliet blinked. It felt like rubbing sandpaper over her eyes, but she did it again because she could. She felt trapped in her own body, barely seeing, her arms and legs immobile, but aware of life around her and able to breathe.

Come back to me, Juliet.

She heard the voice in her mind, her name ending in a soft drawl instead of a hard consonant. Her skin felt hot and clammy, and she heard the crackling of fire.

Breathe.

The new voice was harsher, more insistent.

Just. One. Breath.

She did.

Just. One. More.

She inhaled and started to gag until someone lifted her shoulders. She still couldn't control her extremities, and her lungs felt like they'd been crushed. She swallowed and tasted ash. Someone held a water bottle up to her mouth because she couldn't move her head or lips.

"Will she be okay?" Samantha's voice felt like cool water running over river stones.

"I hope so," Nate said.

Suddenly she was airborne, held in strong arms against a bare chest with a powerful heartbeat. She wanted to wrap her arms around his neck, but her body ignored her mind.

"We can get her out with Tommy's boat," Jimmy said. "Then take her to the hospital."

"How are we going to explain a three-hundred-year-old poison?" Pete asked.

"I have a physician. He'll be discreet." The new voice had a French tinge. "I'll send him to Mr. Prioleau's house."

"Will you take care of this?" Rafe asked.

"Yes," the Frenchman said. "By dawn, the manor will be ash, and no one will know what happened here tonight."

"Rafe?" Jimmy said. "There's a helo and at least six dead men. I'm not sure—"

"Trust me," Rafe said. "Arragon can handle this."

"Agreed," Garza said. "Last time there was a fire out here, no one bothered to report it until it was almost out. With all the chaos going on in the city, I'm sure the same will happen tonight. We'll get everyone back to where they belong, and this will all be forgotten."

"You're sure Arragon can do this alone?" Pops asked.

"Arragon won't be alone." Rafe adjusted her in his arms, and she sighed against his warm skin. "And I doubt there are any official flight records for that bird."

"Still, it'll be taken care of," Arragon said. "And Romeo, the time has changed. Tomorrow. Noble Jones's tomb. Noon."

Rafe sighed, and she felt the shift in his heartbeat.

"Who are all those men?" Nate asked.

"There have to be at least twenty," Pete said. "And they're armed."

Pops coughed again. "Men of the Isle. They're here to help. Although they're late."

"Pops, Grady, and I will take care of this," Jimmy said. "We'll assure them the fire is controlled and there's nothing they can do."

"Thank you," Rafe said. "Tell them I appreciate it."

"I will."

"Let's go," Nate said. "Let's get your woman home."

Around five a.m. Nate came out of the kitchen of Calum's mansion and met Garza in the foyer. Together, they headed up the stairs for the second-floor sitting room. A nurse had covered Nate's burned arms with a salve and gauze, and the pain meds were finally working.

When they went in, they found Calum at the window staring out into the dark street below. Arms crossed, shoulders hunched.

"How are they?" Garza asked.

"Samantha has been checked out and is asleep in one of the guest rooms," Calum said. "Doc Bennett is with Juliet now."

Philip sat in a club chair, his feet up on an ottoman and blanket over his legs.

Pete lay on the couch, one booted foot hanging off the arm rest. He had a bandage on his forehead and an arm in a sling. He'd showered and put on sweats and a black tank. "Will Arragon's doc keep his mouth shut?"

"For an exorbitant fee that I'm paying," Calum said. "What happened at the police station?"

Garza shrugged. "I spoke with Jimmy Boudreaux. No one called in the fire or the helo. The manor burned to the ground, and there's no evidence that anything happened other than a lightning strike. As long as no one sends out investigators, that is."

"Will they?" Nate asked.

"No. I checked in at the station. I told my chief about the terrorist's safe house and led the raid. I just left my partner there. It's enough to keep everyone busy and not ask questions about what else I was doing tonight. I'll write up my reports tomorrow."

"You're sure we got all the 'other' evidence out of Delacroix's place?" Philip asked.

"Yes. They found the C-4 but nothing else that will lead them to Montfort, the Fianna, or Nate's unit."

Ivers came in carrying a tray with bottles of water and hot coffee.

Calum opened a bottle and drank deeply. "The charges against Rafe for that SPO murder?"

"Since the witness and the evidence have disappeared—thanks to Arragon—they've no reason to bring him back in. I'll write up a report letting him off. Rafe should probably stay away from cops for a while."

"Did anyone else break out when the power failed?" Pete asked.

"A few. The added confusion buys us time." Garza opened his own bottle and finished it in four swallows.

"Good." Calum went back to his position near the window.

Rafe came in and took one of the coffees. He'd been rebandaged and had added a few more to his collection, including one around his right hand. "Thank you, Ivers."

Philip struggled to get up until Calum pushed him back down. Pete swung his legs around and sat forward, his arms on his thighs.

"How is she?" Nate and Calum asked together.

"Breathing on her own. Her vital signs look good. Her heart rate and pulse are normal. The doctor took blood samples, and we'll have to wait for the results. Hopefully there's no permanent liver, kidney, or neurological damage."

Nate sat on the arm of a club chair. "How long?"

"A few days, hopefully."

Garza exhaled like it was the first time he'd taken a breath all night. "Can someone tell me what the hell happened?"

"I'm still not sure how Mr. Delacroix became Balthasar," Philip said.

Rafe ran a hand over his head. Like everyone else, he'd showered and put on clean clothes—in his case, a pair of low-slung jeans and a black T-shirt. "A year ago, Balthasar and Escalus were sent here by the Prince to make inroads into Savannah society. An undercover, in-plain-sight kind of operation. It's a plan only used for long-term missions, and this mission was to find Anne Capel's vials. Somewhere along the way, Escalus betrayed the Prince and started working for a man in New Orleans, promising to sell him the vials once they were found. When Escalus died, Balthasar went rogue as well and agreed to sell this man the vials and access to Juliet's land."

Nate reached for Ivers's tray and took a coffee. "When I was in the manor, Deke told me Balthasar had the helo to pick up him, Juliet, and that creepy lawyer. They were going to take Juliet to New Orleans where Balthasar was going to marry her and lease the land back to this man. With the vials and access to the lilies, this man would then develop some kind of biological agent he could market as street heroin or some other kind of illegal drug."

Garza hissed low. "My chief says we've seen the worst of this heroin epidemic. The dealers and the dead are drying up. We're almost back to pre-crazy numbers."

"Which means this man may be out of his practice batch." Nate paused. "There's something else. Deke mentioned someone's been poisoning me since Afghanistan. Lacing the Z-pam I've been taking to control my seizures."

"Dammit," Pete said. "I told you—"

"Pete," Rafe said quietly. "There's enough blame to go around."

"Did you tell the doctor?" Calum asked.

"Yes. He took some blood samples and gave me another

prescription." Nate stared at Pete. "A real prescription to help the headaches."

"There's something I don't understand." Philip threw off his blanket. "Why not cultivate the lily somewhere else?"

"According to Deke, who was quite the chitchatter," Nate said, "this man has tried that and failed. Because Juliet's lily is a hybrid, it doesn't propagate well. It needs specific growing conditions including well-draining soil with a high level of naturally occurring phosphates. Deke also mentioned a rare bird that sows flower seeds in its droppings."

"Balthasar was going to take her to New Orleans and keep her hidden?" Philip said.

"The man Balthasar was working for has money," Rafe said. "It wouldn't take much to keep her a prisoner."

"Dudes." Pete flung himself back against the couch and covered his eyes with his good arm. "When these women wake up, I'm teaching them how to defend themselves. This is ridiculous."

Garza asked, "And the lawyer?"

"Dead," Rafe said.

"After you beat the shit out of Balthasar," Nate said.

"And laid down sniper fire," Pete said. "Well done."

"Sorry we missed that," Garza said. "We got stuck in that god-awful river. How did Juliet end up drinking the poison?"

"She was the key to everything," Rafe said. "Without her, Balthasar had nothing to sell to the man in New Orleans and the land would end up with the federal government."

"Balthasar also needed Juliet to help him find the second vial," Nate added.

"Good God," Philip said softly. "She sacrificed herself to save the rest of us."

"She was relying on us to save her," Nate said. "She knew where the other vial was and was hoping one of us would find it and save her before it was too late."

Too bad he and Grady had gotten caught trying to rescue the women. Maybe Pete was right. Maybe Nate needed remedial street-fighting training.

As far as the poisoning info went, he simply wasn't in the right headspace to deal with that yet. Hopefully his blood work would come back normal and the new meds would help.

Rafe gripped Nate's shoulder. "Thank you."

Nate covered Rafe's hand with his own.

"How'd you figure it out?" Calum asked Nate.

"According to Sarah, Juliet's map had yew and oak leaves drawn along the edges. When Juliet told Balthasar to cut off the finial with oak leaves, I realized one was carved with yew leaves, the other with oak. I knew from my reading that yew was poisonous, so I figured oak carried the antidote. I just wasn't sure which finial was oak until I cut them off."

They all laughed low.

"But," Nate continued, "I checked online, and oak trees have anti-poison properties."

"Wow," Garza said as he ran his hands over his head. "Just…wow."

Calum coughed, probably to hide his shiny eyes. "What does this man in New Orleans have to do with Nate and Pete?"

"All I know," Rafe said, "is the man in New Orleans orchestrated the ambush of Nate's A-teams in Afghanistan. A low-level arms dealer named Remiel L. Marigny."

Pete coughed on his own spit. "That fucker is *dead*."

"I know the guy who killed him," Nate said. "He's in prison with my men."

Rafe opened a bottle of water and, before he left the room, said, "Remiel Lucien Marigny isn't dead. And he's coming for you two next."

CHAPTER 49

JULIET WOKE UP IN THE DARK TO A BUZZING SOUND. HER head was on a pillow, and a blanket covered her. She wore a nightgown Calum must've gotten for her and had an IV in her arm. Snoring told her Rafe was asleep nearby. She lay in a furnished bedroom hooked up to a monitor keeping track of her heart rate and pulse. Through the window, a pinkish cast told her it was almost dawn.

The buzzing sounded again, and she shifted. A man stood at the end of her bed. Tall with dark skin and a piercing gaze that cut through the shadows. She pushed herself up, ignoring the dinging from the machine. "You're Arragon?"

He hit his chest with a fist and bowed his head. "Aye, my lady."

She heard the buzzing for a third time, and a light flickered in his other hand. "You have my cell phone."

"You've been receiving texts from a warrior."

"I've received them off and on since Rafe left eight years ago." She coughed and reached for the water next to her bed. Her throat felt like it had been scraped out. "I sent him one earlier tonight, asking for help, thinking they were from you."

"They're not."

Arragon handed her the phone.

> *A glooming peace this morning with it brings. The sun, for sorrow, will not show his head. Go hence, to have more talk of these sad things.*

"They're from the warrior you met as children."

"Sebastian? I don't understand."

"Sebastian was once the Prince of our brotherhood until he failed to find Anne's Lament. After a contest in the Gauntlet, another warrior—our current Prince—took his place."

"What happened to Sebastian?"

"He was allowed to leave the Fianna and find a new life."

"A new life that included watching me." She coughed. "I thought no one left the Fianna alive?"

"One of the few perks of being the Prince." Arragon sat on the edge of her bed, and the mattress sagged. "Did Sebastian ask Romeo to swear loyalty to him?"

"Yes." She wiped her cheeks with her hands. "Why has Sebastian been texting me?"

"To protect you. You're the beloved of two men who swore him loyalty. 'Tis his privilege to protect you."

Two men? She rested her head against the headboard. "My daddy?"

"Your father understood the part the Capel family and the Fianna has played over the centuries to protect the secret of the lily."

"Sebastian tried to kill us."

"His intent was to scare, never hurt."

She ran her hands over her head, her fingers catching in the tangled curls. Arragon's explanation made sense. Her father's paranoid fears had been true, and she'd dismissed him as crazy. "I wish I'd known."

"Your father wanted you to find your own life and not be bound to the land."

Except she'd been a terrible daughter who'd ended up condemning the man she loved to a life he'd never wanted. "The Fianna took Rafe instead."

"Yes." Arragon leaned forward, his forearms resting on his thighs. "Because of Rafe's oath to Sebastian, I was tasked with Romeo's recruitment."

"Now that I know, I can fix this. I can take over where my father left off. You don't need Rafe anymore."

"It's too late."

She grabbed Arragon's arm. Hard muscles tensed beneath the leather jacket. "There must be a way. *Please*. Help me find it."

He kissed the back of her hand and stood. "Only healing the past can save the future."

"I don't know what that means. *Please*." She glanced at Rafe's prone body on the small couch. The fact that he hadn't woken up proved how exhausted he was. "Help me save him."

"What you did last night took great courage. You sacrificed yourself to defeat Balthasar."

"I did it to save those I love."

"You will be rewarded." Arragon started to leave, his walk even more graceful and elegant than Rafe's.

"Wait." She hated herself for asking, was ashamed for having doubts, but she needed the answer. "Rafe's tattoos. Are they real?"

Arragon looked back. "That's not the question you should ask."

Now he sounded like Rafe. "Then what should I ask?"

"Have you read Romeo's journal?"

She shrugged. "What I could."

"Did you notice the numbers on each page?"

"Yes." She sat up higher. "What do they mean?"

"The numbers on the right are an accounting of every man he's killed."

"Oh." She hadn't expected that. That number had

been over three hundred. "The other one was over four thousand."

"As of today, five thousand one hundred and fifteen." Arragon picked something up from the dresser and laid it on her bed. *Hume's History of England*. Then he opened the door and glanced back. "The number of days Romeo has loved you."

Rafe stretched and fell off the love seat. Considering his aches from forcing his large frame on the tiny couch, he should've slept on the floor. Sunlight streamed into the room, and he checked his watch. Nine a.m. Three hours left.

Juliet lay on her side, hands beneath her cheek. The IV dripped, and the monitors hummed. The doctor had assured him she'd be fine. But he wanted to see her blood work. Hopefully, the Prince would allow it.

After using the attached bathroom, he found his leather jacket on a dressing chair. His journal and misericord lay beneath. *Arragon*. Rafe stowed the sword and book in the jacket pocket and left the blue ribbon on her pillow. Leaving her yesterday had destroyed him. Today? He'd walk away hollow and empty. A situation he dreaded, since the only things that filled those holes were aggression and violence. His throat tightened. He'd trade anything to leave the Fianna, but he had no leverage. The only thing the Prince wanted was Rafe's return.

He pressed his lips against hers. More a brushing than a kiss. He traced her bare shoulder with his thumb. He'd had no choice but to come home after Leavenworth, but if he'd known this was the hell destined for him, he would've stayed in the shadows. It killed him to admit that Escalus had been right. Rafe never should've sought her out. He'd fallen in love with her all over again.

Rafe slipped his gun in his back waistband and turned to find Philip blocking the doorway.

"You're leaving?"

Rafe led his brother into the hall and closed the door. "I don't want to. I have to."

"I don't understand. You're stronger than all of them put together."

"I'm not, Little Brother. I can fight a lot of things, but I can't go up against the people who want me back."

"You mean the Fianna? Calum told me."

"He shouldn't have."

"I know they threatened Juliet." Philip crossed his arms and stared at Rafe's boots. "And all the others you love. That's why you're running again."

"Not running, returning. There's a difference."

"It destroyed Pops the first time you left. When you went AWOL and disappeared. He never got over it. We both know what it did to Juliet."

Rafe didn't want to argue. He had things to do before he met Arragon. "Philip—"

"It destroyed me as well." Instead of jealousy and resentment, Philip's eyes shone with unshed tears.

"I didn't know."

"You were my big brother. The one who looked out for me. Protected me." Philip wiped his cheek with his sleeve. "When you left, I was all alone. I needed you, and you were gone. Then so was she."

Rafe pulled Philip in for a hug. He'd failed so many people in his life, so many he loved. "I'm sorry."

Philip whispered, "Is it true that Momma was murdered?"

"Yes." Rafe pressed his cheek against his brother's head. "Juliet told me a few hours ago that Momma was killed by Remiel Marigny. I promise he'll pay for her death."

Philip pulled away and nodded. "We'll be fine. Calum and I will watch over Juliet, if she'll let us."

"And Pops."

"And Pops." Philip headed for the stairs. "Calum is eating breakfast. I'm sure he'll want to see you."

"I doubt that," Rafe said, falling into step next to Philip. "Calum must regret freeing me." And buying all those clothes.

Philip stopped halfway down, one hand on the rail, the other on Rafe's arm. "Calum didn't get you out of prison. Carina told me she couldn't pull off a pardon."

Rafe's heart revved into a punishing rhythm. If Calum hadn't gotten him out, who had?

Rafe hopped over the rail and double-timed it into the dining room. Calum sat at the head of the table, in a tan seersucker suit and green bow tie, reading the *Financial Times* and drinking coffee. The silver serving dishes on the gleaming table shone in the morning light.

"Did you know?" Rafe demanded.

Calum folded the paper into fourths and smoothed it out with his hand, laying his phone on top. Then he took a sip of coffee. "That you're running away again? Yes."

"I'm not—" Rafe exhaled and leaned on the table. "Did you know Carina didn't get me out of prison?"

"That's absurd."

"Not according to your twin."

Calum picked up his phone and texted. "It's a misunderstanding."

Philip poured coffee and sat at the table. He lowered himself slowly, favoring his side.

"Did the doctor check you out last night?" Rafe been so focused on Juliet that he'd given the others little thought. So much for becoming a better man.

Philip nodded. "Pete did a great job. No ruptures or infections yet. The doctor did give me a more powerful antibiotic, though. And I'm supposed to rest."

"Good." Rafe drummed his fingers while Calum texted again. "What does Carina say?"

Calum laid his napkin next to his plate and stood. "We have a problem."

"*Fuck*."

"If you didn't free Rafe," Philip asked, "who did?"

"I don't know," Calum said. "But a favor like this always requires repayment."

Philip coughed. "What are you going to do?"

Rafe ran his hands over his head. "Return to the Prince. Deal with this later."

"Could it be Remiel Marigny?" Philip asked. "Or Colonel Torridan?"

"No idea. All I know is I have less than three hours before leaving my family. Forever."

Calum came around and gripped Rafe's shoulder. "How can I help?"

He wanted to wake Juliet, but he wouldn't do that to her. She needed to rest, and he wasn't sure he could walk away if she were awake. "I have legal things to work out."

"Philip, please tell Ivers to bring fresh coffee into my study." Calum straightened his jacket and led the way. "If Juliet wakes, tell her Rafe is gone."

CHAPTER 50

Nate paused outside Juliet's bedroom. He'd slept for five hours without nightmares. Had to be a record.

Calum had offered them guest rooms, and although Nate hadn't gotten a full night's worth, he'd make it work. He had things to do, including but not limited to figuring out who'd poisoned him and why.

He reached for the medal around his neck that wasn't there anymore and felt for the handkerchief in his back pocket. Early this morning, Ivers had brought Nate's and Pete's very few possessions from the motel to the mansion. A favor Nate was grateful for.

Later today he and Pete would make a plan, but for now he knocked on Juliet's door.

He didn't hear anything and went in anyway. Calum had put her in a bedroom with floor-to-ceiling windows overlooking the river and a king-size four-poster bed. An armoire and dresser dwarfed the hospital equipment. Nate had expected to see Rafe sleeping on the sofa near the windows or on the floor.

But Juliet was alone, sitting up, and reading a large book. "Hey."

Nate took one of the throws from the couch and draped it around her shoulders. "I wasn't sure if you were awake."

"I just woke." She adjusted the blanket. "Would you pour me some water?"

He found the pitcher on the bedside table and handed her a glass. "Where's Rafe?"

She pushed back her hair, which hung down to her waist. Despite the bruises on her face, she had more color in her cheeks than he'd seen in days. "I don't know."

Nate sat on the edge of the bed and studied his boots. Although he'd changed into clean clothes, his boots still carried mud and other things from the night. "I'm sorry."

She put the glass down. "I am too."

He faced her direct gaze. "You've nothing to be sorry for."

"If I'd not been so angry, so stubborn—"

"None of this is your fault." He took her hand. "We won. You defeated Balthasar."

"What about Samantha?" Juliet nodded to his arms. "And that?"

"Samantha is with Pete right now, and the doctor says she'll be fine. They're both probably still asleep." Nate held up his arms soaked in a mint-smelling salve and covered in gauze. "I'm okay." Not really. The burns felt like someone was power-sanding his skin. "The doctor even gave me new anti-seizure meds."

"And your headaches?"

"Not great. Not debilitating. A win all around."

"I don't believe you." She squeezed his hand. "You were poisoned."

"And the doc is checking out my blood." He covered her hand with his other one. "I'll be okay."

"There's more to it—"

"Juliet." He smiled. "Don't worry about me." He didn't want anyone worrying about him, especially the one person he'd hurt the most.

She gave him a half smile and sank deeper into her pillow. "Thank you for saving me."

"Rafe is the one who took down Balthasar."

"I kind of remember that. But not much after. It was like being frozen in my body, aware but not really."

"I know the feeling." Nate told her everything that happened after she blacked out, about Balthasar, and about the arms dealer in New Orleans.

"Nate, there's still so much we don't know about how my lily is connected to your unit and the horrible things that happened to you. If I hadn't held on to all that fear, if I'd allowed myself to trust others, we might have found the answers sooner. Before the trials tomorrow."

"There won't be trials for the rest of the unit. I just spoke with Kells. A secret congressional committee decided to end our careers instead of having a trial with classified black ops intel exposed."

She pressed a hand against her chest, her eyes widening. "You were discharged?"

"The men already in prison who were in the theater of battle—including myself—were dishonorably discharged after we were rescued and sentenced. The others back at the command post, including Pete, were dishonorably discharged last night and told to leave Fort Bragg within hours. The men in prison will stay there. Kells's team is now…on their own."

"But we have some answers. We can track down Remiel Marigny in New Orleans. Half his family lives on the Isle and poaches on my land."

"Marigny is supposed to be dead, and no one's going to believe a story about a Puritan woman and her poison having anything to do with my unit."

"What are your men going to do?"

Nate clasped his fingers behind his neck, appreciating the stretch in his arm muscles. "They're coming to Savannah. According to Rafe, this city where Balthasar and Escalus set up an elaborate undercover operation has to be important. So Kells has decided to move the men discharged last night to Savannah. We'll set up a command post here and work to clear our names and get the rest of our men out of prison."

"Where will you live?"

"Still working on that. But if Balthasar can con his way into Savannah society, we can too. It's not quite noon. That gives me and Pete the day to figure this out."

She sat up higher, and a blue ribbon fell off her pillow. Nate handed it to her while her gaze darted to the empty couch. "What time is it?"

"Eleven."

She wrapped and unwrapped the ribbon around her hand. "Have you seen Rafe?"

"Not since he came back in to watch over you a few hours ago."

She threw off the blankets and struggled with her IV.

"What are you doing?"

"You said you were sorry, right? Which means you want to make it up to me."

"I guess." Nate didn't like where this was going.

"I need you to come with me to Prioleau Plantation."

"Why?"

"If I can save Rafe, I may be able to help your men as well. Oh, and we can't tell Calum. He'll freak."

"Calum isn't here anyway. Ivers said he left half an hour ago."

"And Philip?"

"Resting." Nate moved the monitor and helped her out of bed. She wore a white nightgown that was too sheer and short for his comfort. "Do you have clothes here?"

"Ask Ivers. I'm sure he'll find something for me." Her legs wobbled, and Nate caught her before she fell.

"Juliet—"

"I'm fine." She brushed away his hand and used the bedpost to steady herself. "Just don't tell anyone. Promise?"

"Sure." Because why the hell not. "But I can't drive, and neither can you."

She pulled out her IV and shut down the machine. "We'll ask Ivers."

"Super."

She took his hand and forced him to meet her gaze. "Being able to drive does not make the man."

"Not helping, Juliet."

Now she cupped his face in her palms. "One thing I've learned this week is we can't live in the wreckage of the past *and* the wreckage of the future. We have to be present to each moment as it comes." He frowned, and she laughed. "I have a good plan. I promise."

He didn't believe her, but he had nothing left to lose. "Where are we going?"

"To talk to the Prince."

༄

Rafe and Calum paused near the tabby ruins of the original Prioleau Plantation house on the Isle of Hope. It was noon. He breathed deeply to release the tension in his chest. How could he be back in the same position he'd been in eight years before?

"You sure about this?" Calum wiped his brow with a handkerchief. It had to be almost a hundred degrees in the sun. "You can go into hiding. I have properties, contacts—"

"No. The Fianna will find me and hurt you." A whistle came from the left. "Come on."

"You want me to come with you?"

"I need a witness."

"Wonderful."

Rafe led the way through the woods to the tomb. The small peninsula was surrounded by a river on one side and gnarled mangrove trees on the other two. The hundred-acre marsh lay beyond the estuary, owned by the Prioleau family but ruled by white egrets and alligators. They entered the clearing and stopped. Arragon wasn't alone.

When Rafe got within arm's length, he hit his chest with his fist and bowed his head. "A warrior returns."

Arragon cleared his throat. "Welcome home, Romeo."

Rafe raised his head and met the brown eyes of the Prince, who'd changed little in eight years. Wide-shouldered, slim-hipped, with a hard face cut with angles. His pressed trousers and silk shirt only emphasized his physique. While he was better dressed, he was as strong and muscular as his warriors.

"Romeo," the Prince said quietly. "You came."

"I promised. But why are you here?"

"You killed Balthasar."

"I did."

"Yet you lost the vials."

"True." Rafe motioned to Calum, who held up a brief-case. "I did retrieve the briefcase of the lawyer Remiel Marigny hired. There's information in there you'll find interesting."

Arragon took the briefcase while the Prince asked, "And your wife's King's Grants?"

"I have them in a protected safe," Calum said. "Along with her deeds. She is the sole owner of Capel land."

"No one, not even Remiel Marigny, can get to the land," Rafe added.

"Unless she decides to make it so," Arragon said.

"Juliet won't," Calum said.

"I'm so glad there are men willing to speak for me."

Juliet's voice rang out, and all four men turned to see her emerge from the woods, with Nate and Orsino behind her.

Rafe held his breath as she strode forward. She wore a pair of cargo pants that hugged her hips and sat low on her slim waist. Her black T-shirt stretched across her breasts, the color highlighting her pale skin and the bruises and scrapes on her face and arms. She'd plaited her hair into a complicated braid that hung over one shoulder.

Her gaze held grim determination and courage.

"How do you do?" She held out her hand to the Prince. "I'm Juliet Capel."

The Prince kissed the back of her hand. "A pleasure."

"I'm here to make a deal," she said. "I want you to let Rafe go. In return, he and I will continue my father's work. We'll protect the secret of the lily and destroy it wherever it grows."

"Your father did that on his own," the Prince said. "We had no formal agreement."

"That's not true. The Capel family has had a long history with the Fianna, a fact you know. And years ago my father made a deal with Sebastian. You might remember him. He was the Prince before you."

The Prince's nostrils flared. "I don't deal with civilians, Miss Capel."

Rafe glared in frustration at his wife. "What are you doing?"

"Saving you." She took her phone out of her pocket and held it up to the Prince. "See these texts? I thought they were from Balthasar, but they're from Sebastian. He's been protecting me since you forced Rafe to join you. Now I want Rafe to come home with me."

"Romeo tithed to me. He belongs to me."

"Yet you believe a man cannot serve two masters. You knew that if I came looking for Rafe, he'd choose me instead of you. That's why you made him tattoo those names on his arms. So *I'd* give him up, *I'd* let him go."

The Prince crossed his arms over his chest. "All warriors give up their world when they join. It's voluntary."

"Except neither one of those things is true in Rafe's case. He was married to me in a sacred ceremony, and he'd promised fealty to a Prince when he was sixteen. When you used his grief over his momma's death to blackmail him into giving me up, you never asked him to forswear Sebastian."

The Prince's eyes narrowed. "When Sebastian lost, his fealties transferred to me."

"Not true." She spoke simply, without anger or reproach. "I read *Hume's*. A warrior is given the choice to offer his oath to the new Prince. You forced Rafe to join, tortured him by threatening me and my family. Yet did he ever offer to serve you *instead* of Sebastian?"

Orsino snarled. "This is absurd, my lord."

"She speaks true," Arragon said.

"'Tis a play on words," Orsino said. "A play on meanings."

"Yet"—Calum came into the circle, his gaze on the Prince—"legally, she has a point."

The Prince moved until he was a breath away from Juliet. "Are you willing to take over the contract between the Capel family and the Fianna? Do you know the cost?"

"I am," Juliet said. "And I do."

"It means never selling the land. Never moving away. Always preparing for another attack like last night's."

"I understand."

"I'll be with her, my lord." Rafe moved next to her. "If you'll allow it."

"They won't be alone." Calum nodded at Nate. "They have friends and family to help."

"And you, Major Walker?" The Prince shifted his

attention to Nate. "What about your men? What are you willing to do for them?"

"Anything," Nate said.

"I heard about the discharges and that Colonel Torridan is moving his civilian operation to Savannah. Do you have any idea what your unit is getting themselves into?"

"We'll figure it out."

The Prince laughed. "With what? You and your men have no money. No power. No influence. Just the clothes on your back and whatever weapons you can scrounge."

"Nate won't be alone," Juliet said. "He'll have me, Rafe, Detective Garza, and Calum."

Orsino scoffed. "You're naive and unprepared."

"But we can fight," Nate said. "I'd take Juliet, Rafe, and Calum over a dozen Fianna warriors."

"Which brings me to my next request." She raised her chin. "While Rafe and I rebuild our home on the Isle and protect my lily, Nate and his men will move into Prideaux House, which Balthasar was purchasing with Fianna money. I want you to give it to Kells so his men can live there."

"I'm impressed with your courage, Miss Capel. But I don't own Prideaux House. It was purchased by another party."

Calum coughed. "As of yesterday, I own the house and a few other new properties. I'm sure I can work something out with Colonel Torridan."

"It's settled then," she said. "You let Rafe go and allow Colonel Torridan and his men to live in the city undisturbed. Your warriors leave town, and you keep your issues with Remiel Marigny away from us."

"I'll agree to letting Rafe stay with you to protect the land—"

"My lord!" Orsino stepped forward until the Prince held up a hand.

"But Rafe will always be a Fianna warrior." The Prince stared at Rafe. "You will heed when I call. Regardless of the situation."

Since it was the best Rafe could hope for, he squeezed her hand. "Aye, my lord. And my accounts?"

"You'll have access to all that was yours by this afternoon."

Rafe bowed his head. "Thank you."

The Prince added, "Major Walker, while you help your men, you must keep Romeo's truth. You know what happens to those who speak?"

"I do," Nate said. "Do you know if Remiel is the one who set up my men? Or why?"

"I can confirm the former, not the latter. That, I'm afraid, is up to you and your men to figure out. I suggest you do so before his next move." The Prince paused. "As tempting as it may be to tell Kells Torridan who I am, I expect you'll keep my identity secret. Or all of these agreements here today"—he waved to Rafe and Juliet—"will be forfeit. As will your life."

Nate crossed his arms over his chest. "Yes, sir."

Juliet looked at Nate. "Maybe we shouldn't tell Detective Garza about all this."

"On the contrary," the Prince said. "To withhold truth puts him in even greater danger. But the same rules apply to him. Those who speak, die."

"One more thing." She wrinkled her nose. "RM Financial. The bank that bought my business loan. I know you own it, and I don't appreciate you using my business as a pawn in whatever games you're playing."

"I do apologize," the Prince said. "It was a desperate move on my part."

"Thank you." She blew a stray hair out of her eyes. "As a businesswoman, I respect that you also have a business to run. But I want to renegotiate my loan and expect better terms on collateral and interest rates. And I'm *not* paying closing costs on a loan I didn't initiate."

The Prince nodded, yet Rafe was sure he was holding back a laugh. Although it was hard to tell since Rafe had never seen the Prince smile.

"We're agreed?" she asked the Prince.

"Yes, Juliet of the Lily."

She let out a breath as if she'd been holding it for days. "Good."

"You may live on your land in whatever peace you can find." The Prince took something out of his pocket and handed it to her. Rafe's gold wedding band he'd given up the night he'd tithed. "Romeo is yours."

She smiled as the Prince left with Orsino following behind.

"May we speak alone?" Arragon asked Rafe.

Rafe kissed her quickly before meeting Arragon near the river's edge. "Do you think the Prince will uphold this decision?"

"For now. As long as Walker keeps his peace. But you must be prepared to return whenever the Prince requests."

Rafe gripped a tree branch over his head and stared across the river. "It's more than I'd ever hoped for."

Arragon frowned at birds skimming the water. "I've been duplicitous. I, too, have two masters."

"Your wife died years ago."

"Not my wife." Arragon handed him an envelope.

Rafe took out a document printed on official White House letterhead. Rafe inhaled so hard he felt light-headed. "I received a presidential pardon? How'd that happen?"

"I serve two Princes. Although if the current found out about the former—"

"I understand." Arragon still worked for Sebastian. "Does the Prince know about my pardon?"

"No. And he cannot. The world must believe that Calum and Carina Prioleau released you from prison." Arragon clapped him on the back. "Do you have Escalus's cell phone?"

"The Prince's technologically advanced phone that can't be hacked?" Rafe exhaled. "Yes." It was probably still in the Impala's glove box. "Although I'm taking down those cameras with the cell phone feed that Escalus put up to watch my wife."

Arragon nodded. "For now that phone will be our mode of contact. Remember, your business with Colonel Torridan must stay separate. He cannot know you still work for either Prince."

"Kells Torridan isn't stupid, and Nate knows."

"It's your job to make sure Major Walker doesn't speak."

"Got it." Rafe shoved the envelope into his jacket pocket. "One more thing. Escalus—"

"Is on his way home."

Good. For some reason, that mattered.

"Now go kiss your wife, Romeo. She's waiting."

Rafe walked back to Juliet, Calum, and Nate to find them speaking in hushed tones. When he coughed, Juliet spun around and jumped into his arms. He closed his eyes while breathing in her lavender scent. He wanted to kiss her senseless, but since they had an audience, he settled for a few soft kisses.

"Shit." Nate held up his phone. "Colonel Torridan arrived in town with five men a few minutes ago. They're with Pete at the motel."

"Not to worry," Calum said. "Have them meet us at Iron Rack's at three p.m." He took Juliet's hand and pulled her out of Rafe's embrace. "Juliet told me her plan, and we have things to do to make it work. I need both of you focused. Time enough later for nookie."

"Nookie?" She punched Calum in the shoulder. "You wanted us back together."

"After things are settled." Calum took her arm and led her back to the cars. "Then you can get married again and make me as many godchildren as you want."

Rafe and Nate followed.

From Nate's downcast gaze and slumped shoulders, Rafe knew something else was bothering Nate. "What?"

Nate reached for his neck and then shrugged. "The murder at the SPO. Garza believes that woman was murdered for that book, which he still hasn't recovered."

"Garza's working on it."

Nate stopped walking. "What if Balthasar made a mistake? What if Sarah had been the real target and he hit the assistant by accident?"

"That's a hell of an *if*." Rafe started moving again, and Nate fell into step next to him. "But if it'll help your stress level, we'll watch over her. Alright?"

"Thanks." Nate checked his phone again, and Rafe was glad to see a smile on Nate's face. "Once you hear Juliet's plan and my men realize they can't live in Savannah without dealing with you, you're going to be one suffering soldier. I'm going to enjoy every minute."

Just another form of penance, and Rafe was good with those. "If it means I can stay here with her, I'll do anything."

"Including help Colonel Torridan? The man who ordered me to torture your wife?"

"Yes, Brother. Even that." Rafe clapped him on the back. "Let's hurry up and save your men. I have other plans tonight."

CHAPTER 51

LATER THAT DAY, AFTER EATING LUNCH, RESTING IN CALUM'S mansion while the doctor checked her over again, and arguing about moving her things into Calum's apartment or vice versa, Juliet followed Rafe into Iron Rack's Gym. She wasn't feeling great but definitely better.

She wasn't sure what she'd expected from this place since she'd never been, but she was surprised by the UNDER NEW MANAGEMENT sign on the front door. "Calum moves fast."

Rafe's hand rested on her lower back, and he whispered, "When we're done—"

"No." She glanced up at him, laughing. "Not until our wedding night."

"We waited the first time." He frowned. "I don't think—"

She kissed him hard. He tasted like peppermint and fresh air. He held her close enough for her to feel his arousal pressed against her lower stomach.

Calum's voice rang out. "Enough of that."

She put her head against Rafe's chest, loving the steady beat of his heart until she sneezed twice and wrinkled her nose. "Calum, this place smells like feet."

"Not for long." Calum stood in front of the check-in desk, texting.

Philip sat in a metal chair nearby, a set of plans on his lap. "In less than two weeks, everything will be up to code, including the HVAC system."

Nate and Garza came out from the locker room and met them in front. Nate's nose looked swollen, and his arms were still bandaged, while Garza needed serious concealer to hide the dark circles below his eyes.

"Pete is with Kells and the other men," Nate said. "Juliet's idea might work."

"It *will* work," she said. "And Prideaux House?"

"We're done clearing the three rooms in the attic," Garza said. "This morning we boxed up everything we could find. I'll have an officer take down the police tape around the building."

"Kells and his men can live in the rooms above the gym for a few weeks," Philip said. "After that, the basic renovations on Prideaux House will be finished and they can move in. It won't be beautiful, but they'll have cold running water and a generator."

"You're sure you're on board with all of this?" Rafe asked Garza. "It means covering for Nate's men and protecting me for however long this takes."

Garza crossed his arms. "If my choice is between telling my chief about the Fianna or keeping quiet and helping Nate and Pete however I can, I gotta go with the latter. There's too much at stake."

"We're agreed, then?" She looked at each man directly. "We tell no one about who Nate and his men are, no one mentions the Fianna, and we keep to the story that Calum and Carina got Rafe out of prison."

"Will Carina go for that?" Philip asked.

Calum nodded. "She agreed as long as her party goes on as planned on Sunday."

Juliet tucked a hair behind her ear. "The fountain is finished. Bob and his team will complete the planting today, and I'll inspect it when we're done here. The privacy fence comes down on Sunday morning with plenty of time for the event coordinator to set up for the party."

"What about Miss Beatrice's funeral?" Philip asked Calum.

"Monday afternoon at St. John the Baptist Cathedral. Juliet, Miss Nell asked you to handle the flowers."

"I'd be honored," she said.

"Also," Calum said, texting again, "Miss Nell is living with me temporarily. After the funeral, she's moving to Charleston to live with a cousin. I was hoping you and Rafe could oversee the movers while they pack up Habersham mansion."

"Of course." Juliet took Rafe's hand and squeezed. "It'll be strange to have no Habersham sisters in the city."

"Indeed." Calum put his phone down. "That leaves one more thing. And that thing will be Tuesday. I expect all the men here to be there in tuxedos."

"For the record," Nate said, "I don't have a uniform or a tux."

"I'll supply the dress clothes. Six p.m. St. Mary of Sorrows on the Isle of Grace."

"What's going on?" Garza asked.

Calum smiled at Juliet. "A wedding."

Rafe kissed her hand, and all the men clapped, including Philip.

Rafe held out his hand. Philip shook once and looked up at his brother with eyes both sad and happy. "Maybe we can be a family again."

"I hope so too."

Philip looked at Calum. "If you don't mind, I'm going to go back to the mansion to rest."

"Good idea." Calum found his phone and texted. "Ivers will pick you up in a minute."

"Thank you." Philip stood and nodded to the other men in the room. "I'll be working on the renovations. Tell Pete that if he thinks of anything else he wants in the gym to let me know."

Once Philip left, Calum leaned against the counter and crossed one foot over the other. "This plan of Juliet's is *faaaaantastic.*"

"Not so sure about that." Pete came out of the locker room. His face had stitches and scratches, and one arm was in a sling. "I tried my best, but this"—he waved a hand around the worn-out gym with the crazy pirate decor— "can't be shoved into the comfort zone."

"Let me talk to them," she said.

Pete laughed. "If they see Rafe, there'll be blood."

"Working with Rafe isn't an option. And neither is my plan." She marched to the men's locker room, and then stopped to look at the group behind her. "Are you coming?"

Pete stared at Rafe. "Blood. Bath."

"Can't be that bad," Garza said.

Rafe laughed. "Colonel Torridan is one of the deadliest SF commanders ever in the U.S. Army."

"And," Calum said, leading the way, "prior to Torridan's wife divorcing him, two of his teams were ambushed, dragged to a POW camp, and sent to prison. Then he got fired."

Rafe stared at Nate until he said, "I guess if Juliet's brave enough to go in there, so am I."

Kells shoved the envelope, scrawled with the name *Juliet*, into his rucksack and moved into the center of the locker room. He was still trying to figure out how he and his men had ended up in a rundown gym decked out with Jolly Roger flags and cutlasses on the walls that smelled like ass. To say the last forty-five hours were the worst of his life would be an understatement. First his men had been sent to a holding cell at Fort Bragg. For their own protection, until the trials began. Then they'd learned there'd be no trials. Just dishonorable discharges for all of his men not already in prison.

Kells studied the remaining five soldiers in front of him. The other five had already taken off. "You all have the option of leaving like the others. Go back to your families, figure out the rest of your life."

"To live in hiding?" Vane straddled a bench and ran his hands over his long brown hair. "In disgrace?"

Although Vane had recently shaved his beard, he'd yet to cut his hair and kept it tied back at the base of his neck. Now that they were in a garrison, Kells should probably have all of his men clean-shaven and buzz-cut. Then again, they were a voluntary, civilian group of men who'd been fucked by their superiors. So maybe the army's grooming standards didn't matter.

Kells raised one eyebrow and responded to the sneer in Vane's voice. "Versus living in a pirate-themed gym with no money, weapons, or contacts while we figure out what to do next."

"Then what?" Cain sat in a folding chair, his arms draped over his thighs. The geometric tats on his arms trembled beneath the force of his self-control, which was iffy on a good day. Especially if his wife Charlotte wasn't around. "The world thinks we fucked up."

"The world knows nothing about it," Zack said from his dark corner. The tattooed, dark-haired Cajun always kept to the shadows. "It's all black ops classified bullshit."

"You're okay with this?" Ty leaned against a locker and scowled at Zack. Ty's all-American blond crew cut appearance was at odds with Zack's bleakness. "Being thought of as trash? Thrown away?"

"No," Zack said. "But someone set us up. First Nate's

team, and then Jack's. If this plan works, we may be able to pick the next battle. And we might win."

"I agree with Zack," Vane said. "We establish a CP here in Savannah. Regroup. Figure out how to redeem ourselves."

"Luke?" Kells asked his youngest team member. "I can't even buy you a laptop. You okay staying, fighting, proving our innocence?"

"Sure." Luke leaned his chair back and clasped his fingers on his stomach. His high-and-tight jet-black haircut was at odds with his wry smile and blue, almond-shaped eyes. Of all the men in the unit, he'd always been the most upbeat. "I don't have anyplace else to go, and none of you knows how to snake an Ethernet cable or open your email. I'm kinda the lynchpin to this whole plan. Without me, you're all screwed."

Laughter shook the room, and Kells was able to do the regular inhale/exhale thing. It felt like he'd been holding his breath for a year. No, since Nate and Jack's teams had been taken. Everything changed that night. His command. His career. His men. His marriage.

Although, in some way, Kells's discharge last night had been a relief. He'd not been looking forward to the trials. They'd found little evidence that the teams had been set up and nothing to support his claim that the men who'd stayed behind at the CP were innocent.

Now that they were out and didn't have to deal with the stress of being under investigation, they had time to sort through what had happened and decide what to do next. Since the doomed Afghan op, Kells had been reacting. Now he could plan and move forward. He tried not to think about the fact that they had no income, no health insurance, and no weapons.

The locker room door opened, and he blew out a breath. He had a few things to discuss with Nate, including where they were going to live. A moment later, Kells's hands were fisted and the blood pounded with enough force to rip open his veins.

Juliet Montfort stood near the door. Nate had told Kells to expect Juliet, but Kells hadn't expected Rafe right behind her. Two other men Kells didn't recognize were there as well. The room went silent, and his men formed a half-circle behind him. Nate had mentioned that they didn't know the truth about Rafe's leaving the unit. Except Kells didn't care. He'd never forgive Rafe. Deserting an A-team was, in Kells's humble opinion, grounds for a firing squad.

It wasn't Rafe's frown that bothered Kells. It was Juliet's brown gaze. He remembered what he'd ordered Nate to do. And Kells wasn't sorry. "What do you want?"

She raised her chin. "I'm not here to accept your apology."

"You're not going to get one."

She crossed her arms. "I have a deal to make. Take it or leave it, I don't care. But it's the only one you'll get."

"Why are you making this offer?"

"For Nate's and Pete's sakes." She nodded at Cain. "For Charlotte. And Abigail. I understand Liam is still in prison with Jack and the other men and can't protect her."

Cain inhaled until he grew almost two inches, his chest wider than two pairs of the lockers behind him. "I can still protect my wife."

"I'm not just talking about protecting," she said. "I'm talking about ending the threat."

"We don't know who we're fighting," Zack said.

"But we do." Juliet waved to the men behind her. "And we're here to help."

"How?" Ty asked.

"By giving you a place to live that's unobtrusive. By providing you jobs and an identity in the world. By offering information in return for help."

Kells considered her hard jaw and direct gaze. She wasn't lying, and she wasn't afraid. "What's your offer?"

"First, you stay here in the gym until Prideaux House is ready. Second, the gym is under new management but will still be known as Iron Rack's."

Pete came forward, hands settled on his hips. He'd traded his combat pants and T-shirt for gym clothes. He'd even taken out his lip piercings. "We're going to reopen, keeping it the hard-core workout place it already is. Except for one thing. We're going to offer self-defense classes—Krav Maga and other things—for men and women. It's come to my attention recently"—he glanced at Nate and then Juliet—"that we need refreshers in self-defense and basic street fighting. I'm going to retrain you all and turn some of you into instructors. It'll give us income."

Nate got in on the convo, saying, "As well as a place to channel our aggression. There's a fighting ring."

"You want us to run a self-defense school?" Zack said. "Here? In this dump?"

The smartly dressed man in a beige seersucker suit with a complicated silk-tie knot came forward. "As the owner of said *dump*, I'd like to add that the gym is undergoing a renovation. Not too much, since I think you'd want to keep the regular daytime clientele."

"Yeah?" Cain said. "And who the hell are you?"

Juliet put her hand on the man's shoulder. "Calum Prioleau is the man who owns the gym, the mansion where you'll be moving to when it's ready, and the club."

"What club?" Kells asked.

"The one Rafe will manage," she said. "The one where your men will take turns working security."

"Bouncers and gym rats?" Vane laughed until he coughed. "You're kidding, right?"

"No," she said. "Like Pete said, these jobs will give you money and help reestablish your identity in the civilian world. They're the perfect cover. You can work during the day or at night at the club and still have time for your mission."

"We're not working with Montfort," Kells said.

"Then you can leave," she said.

"Give us one reason why we should trust Montfort," Cain said.

"I'll give you two," she said with her hands on her hips. "Nate and Pete have spent the last week working and fighting by his side, and they trust him. Second, you're going to need information. And the club is the best place to find it."

"Sounds like you've figured all this out," Kells said.

"I have." She nodded toward the tall Hispanic man in a lightweight jacket, jeans, tie, and holster. Clearly a cop. "Detective Garza understands your situation and is willing to protect you while you figure out what to do next."

"Why the hell would he do that?" Zack asked.

"Because, gentlemen," Garza said in a hard-edged voice with a Jersey accent, "in the past twenty-four hours, I've met your enemy's minions. And they're as badass as they come."

"There's something else about the property," Juliet said. "There are tunnels between this place, the mansion, and the club. They're not all clear, especially the ones leading to the mansion, but I'm sure you and your men won't mind helping with that."

Kells finally looked at Rafe. His brown eyes glowed with

resentment. Maybe even hatred. "What do you have to do with all of this?"

"I'm just the man who, with the help of a few friends, defeated my enemy and learned the name of yours."

"You know who set us up in Afghanistan?" Luke said.

"I do."

"And?" Kells asked.

"Do you agree to Juliet's terms or not?"

Kells studied his soldiers. Although he'd been their CO for years, this had to be a joint decision. Once they made it, there was no turning back. "What do you say?"

One by one, his men—including Nate and Pete—nodded. So Kells looked at Juliet. "You have our answer. We agree. We'll run the gym, live in the mansion, work at the club—"

"And clear the tunnels," Calum added.

"Yes. Clear the tunnels." Whatever that meant.

Montfort took Juliet's hand and, on the exhale, said, "Remiel Marigny."

"Bullshit," Zack said. "He's dead."

"Even if he wasn't," Cain said, "he's a low-level player. A hack gun runner."

"I've never heard of him," Luke said.

Vane rolled his eyes while Ty sat on a bench and gave them all the stink eye.

"Colonel?" Juliet prompted. "Do you believe us?"

Kells exhaled and wished he could sleep for the next forty years. "Unfortunately, I do."

"You can't be serious," Zack said. "This is—"

"True." Kells spoke directly to Juliet. "We accept your offer."

She nodded. "We'll leave you with Nate and Pete to get settled."

"One more thing." This time Kells looked directly at Montfort. "Is the Fianna in any way involved with our mission? Past or present?"

"No. But if you see a man bow"—Rafe looked at each man in the room—"run."

CHAPTER 52

RAFE SAT ON THE COUCH IN HIS APARTMENT TO TIE HIS BLACK shoes, frustrated as hell.

When Calum appeared in a tuxedo carrying a florist box, Rafe ripped the lace out. "These don't work."

"They're not combat boots. You do that before you put them on, not after."

Rafe tugged the shoes off and tossed one to Calum while he searched for the other lace in the clothing bags littering the floor. It'd been a long few days helping, from the sidelines, Nate and his men get settled. Then there'd been Carina's birthday party, where they'd celebrated with champagne near a stunning Pegasus fountain, and Miss Beatrice's funeral, where they'd cried. Rafe even spent time with Philip, who'd asked if they could celebrate Thanksgiving with Pops.

Calum finished lacing the first shoe and threw it back at Rafe. "I went to great trouble to buy you new clothes, including the tuxedo you're wearing, and you can't hang them up?"

Rafe slipped on the shoe and tied the laces. "I told you I didn't want them."

"I told you you'd need them." Calum laced the second shoe. "Hurry up. Ivers is double-parked, and we can't leave your bride waiting."

With one shoe on, one off, Rafe went into the bedroom to get both rings. On his dresser, he found them in the folded blue ribbon next to the photo of Juliet and his momma. He'd wanted to buy new bands, but Juliet still had hers and had insisted on using their original ones. "Did you bring the other ring?"

"Yes," Calum said.

Rafe came out, and Calum held up the diamond-and-sapphire engagement ring in one hand, the florist box in the other.

Rafe put on his second shoe, slipped on his jacket, and pinned the gardenia-and-lavender boutonniere to it. Calum would hold the rings until they were needed. "Let's meet my bride."

Juliet tightened the belt of her silk robe and paced the rectory/sheriff's office. Her high-heeled sandals clicked on the pine floor. When Samantha came in with two bouquets of white roses, gardenias, and lavender, Juliet asked, "What's the time?"

"Don't worry." Samantha laid the bouquets on Jimmy's desk and adjusted her strapless seersucker dress. Her hair, like Juliet's, had been braided and twisted into a bun. It was too humid to wear their hair down. "We have thirty minutes."

"I don't have a dress."

"Miss Nell promised it would be delivered on time."

After the ceremony, Miss Nell was leaving for Charleston. "What if she's forgotten—"

Samantha held up her hand. "Let's go through the checklist. Something blue?"

Juliet showed off her mother-in-law's sapphire-and-diamond bracelet. "My silver hair combs are old. And my dress will be new."

"This will do for borrowed." Samantha took a small box out of her handbag.

Juliet opened it and found a silver heart locket engraved with delicate scrollwork. "It's beautiful."

"It was my grandmother's. You have your hair combs. I have my locket."

"Are you sure?"

Samantha took the necklace and stood behind Juliet to clasp it around her neck. "I'd be honored if you'd wear it."

Juliet held the heart and looked back at her friend. "Thank you. After everything that's happened, I'm surprised you're even talking to me."

Samantha kissed her cheek. "I'm okay. I have you and Pete. I might even count Rafe, Calum, Garza, and Philip as friends. For the first time, I have a family, and I'm grateful. I want today to be everything you've ever dreamed of."

Juliet's eyes blurred, and she hugged Samantha.

"But," Samantha said, pulling away and wiping her eyes, "if any of them disappoint us, they're going down. Now that Pete is training us in Krav Maga, no one's safe."

Juliet laughed and found her compact to fix her makeup. "Agreed."

A knock sounded, and Samantha opened the door to allow Miss Nell in. Today she wore a light-pink silk Chanel suit with a strand of diamonds. She held a long box with a veil on top. "I hope Juliet's not fretting."

"A little." Samantha took the box and laid it on a table against the wall.

Miss Nell placed the veil next to the bouquets on the desk. "Juliet, remember the dress you found in your daddy's trunk?"

"The one belonging to my mother?"

"Miss Beatrice and I sent it to the most wonderful couturier in Charleston who specializes in updating vintage gowns." Miss Nell opened the box and with Samantha's help unwrapped the tissue around the dress. "You'll have to meet her when you come visit me. She couldn't save much of your mother's original gown, but she was able to use the lace."

Samantha and Miss Nell helped Juliet into the white silk gazar strapless slip with a chapel train. The white silk gossamer dress floated over her head with her mother's Chantilly lace forming the scoop bodice and delicate cap sleeves. The lace-trimmed skirt and train were fuller and longer than the dress, giving the gown an ethereal look. When Samantha used Juliet's silver combs to attach the veil trimmed with the same lace, Juliet felt like a bride.

Miss Nell kissed Juliet on the cheek while Samantha handed her a bouquet. "Ready?"

"Always and forever."

～

Rafe inhaled the smell of orange oil and flowers. The white church with eight rows of pews had been polished and decorated with gardenias, roses, and lavender. The sun streaming through the stained-glass windows cast the room in an otherworldly light.

He stood in front of the church with Calum and Father Quinn. He was surprised to see some of the Isle's residents there, including Grady, Miss Mamie, CJ, and Tommy Boudreaux. Nate, Pete, Garza, and even Bob, all in tuxedoes courtesy of Calum, sat in the front left row. Jimmy Boudreaux and Philip sat on the right side with Miss Nell and Carina.

Rafe was shocked Carina had come. But he wasn't about to question the woman who'd agreed to keep the truth of his pardon a secret.

He whispered to Calum, "You knew this would work out, didn't you? That's why you ordered me a tux."

"Yes." Calum clasped his shoulder. "Here they come."

Samantha led the way. Once she stopped at the steps to the altar, everyone stood. Juliet didn't need an entrance hymn. When she walked through the church doors on Pops's arm, her smile made the angels sing. Rafe's heart got tangled up in his chest. He could barely breathe, and there was no way he could speak. He'd have to nod his way through his vows.

Once she took his hand, though, he found his courage and his voice.

The woman he'd adored his entire life stood in front of him. She'd forgiven him. Believed in him. Loved him. When he slipped on her wedding band, followed by the new engagement ring, she met his gaze. Her eyes had filled, and he almost missed her soft "I do."

The back of his throat burned, and he had to be prompted—twice—to kiss his bride. When he lifted his head, the room thundered with claps and cheers. Juliet wiped her cheeks with trembling fingers and took his arm to face their guests. They were surrounded by the people they loved. They were no longer alone. They had friends, family, a new beginning.

EPILOGUE

AFTER PHOTOS AND WELL WISHES, JULIET PULLED RAFE onto the dance floor at Boudreaux's. The band was playing her favorite Creole waltz, and she needed his arms around her.

"You were right," he said against her hair. "About waiting. It's going to be...intense."

Her smile hid the fact that her lower stomach was clenched in knots. They were spending the next week in Charleston at the Mills House, the same hotel where they'd had their first honeymoon.

He kissed her nose and then twirled her before bringing her back in for the slow waltz. "When can we leave?"

"Soon." She laughed while her veil and dress surrounded them like spun sugar. Her bare feet barely touched the ground. "Look at how many people are here."

Almost every family from the Isle had shown up at Boudreaux's with food and coolers filled with sweet tea and beer. All of them had offered congratulations and, in their own way, forgiveness and acceptance. They were no longer outsiders within their own home.

"Except for the Marignys," he said. "They didn't have the guts to show."

"They wouldn't have come anyway. Anytime everyone's here at Boudreaux's, they're poaching on my land."

He chuckled, and his chest rumbled beneath her cheek.

"I'm serious," she said. "The Tobans, Mercers, Prioleaus—they all came. And when they heard we were rebuilding the manor, they offered to help. I didn't have the heart to tell them we don't have the money right now."

"Actually, we have the money."

She pulled back to meet his gaze. "What do you mean?"

"I worked for the Prince for five years before prison. While I wasn't allowed to give money away, I was allowed to will it. I saved, invested, and named you my beneficiary. After my arrest, I assumed the Prince confiscated my accounts. Apparently not."

"Accounts? As in more than one?"

"As in many, with lots of zeroes."

She stopped dancing and took both of his hands in hers. "Why didn't you tell me?"

"There hasn't been time, and I wanted to sign the paperwork. Calum reviewed it, and everything that once was mine is now ours." Rafe took her face in both hands and kissed her softly. When he was done and her head was spinning, he whispered, "My home is with you. Wherever you are, that's where I'll be. Besides, you made an agreement with the Prince, and you're stuck on the Isle."

She punched him in the arm, except it probably hurt her more than him. "My daddy always told me to stay away from men who bow."

He laughed. "Too late for regrets."

"We haven't made love yet."

"Soon, that's all we'll be doing." This time he kissed her properly, and she was vaguely aware of clapping.

His lips left hers to trace her cheek. "I've loved you for five thousand one hundred and nineteen days." His words broke apart as if there wasn't room in his voice for all the laughter and happiness. "There aren't enough stars in the sky to match the *I love you*s in my heart."

His words healed those wounded places hidden inside

and offered her a life she thought she'd never have. Because of him, the future—their family—was theirs to build.

"I love you, Rafe Montfort." She threw her arms around his neck and whispered, "I just don't know what I'm going to do with you."

"Love me." He swung her up in his arms, his eyes narrowing as his lips met hers. "As I love you."

"Forever and always, my love." Her veil caught the breeze and swirled around them, leaving them in their own private world. "Forever and always."

ACKNOWLEDGMENTS

The problem with a debut book, especially a long one like this, is that there are so many people to thank. Then there's the added issue of order and rank. Is the last one more important than the first? Or vice versa? So in the interest of fairness, the following list is random. Kind of.

First, I want to thank my extraordinary agents, Deidre Knight and Kristy Hunter. Your confidence and support made this all possible. I have no idea where I'd be without you both, but definitely not here, with a book in my hand and my name on the cover. Thank you! Thank you! Thank you!

Unfortunately, there aren't enough thank you-type words in the English language to describe how grateful I am to my editor at Sourcebooks, Deb Werksman. I handed her a massive manuscript with multiple plotlines and she guided me with patience and the most amazing feedback until we ended up with a book we both loved. This story exists because of your brilliance!

The rest of the Sourcebooks staff rocks as well. Thank you Susie Benton, Laura Costello, Rachel Gilmer, Stefani Sloma, Stephany Daniel, Beth Sochacki, and Emily Chiarelli for all of your help with my newbie questions. I'd like to say that I won't have any more, but I don't think that's true. So I'm also thanking you in advance and apologizing in case I've forgotten someone.

And OMG! The Sourcebooks art department! Thank you so much for the awesome cover. I still can't stop looking at it!

I'd like to thank my sister-in-law Kieran Kramer, who stepped off the writing cliff first and told me it was safe to jump. Then there are my critique partners, Karen Johnston, Christine Glover, Juliette Sobanet, and Mary Lenaburg, who read this manuscript in so many versions and so many times that I will be forever in their debt. I am truly grateful!

I'm so lucky to have my amazing RWA Golden Heart sisters and brother, as well as the Washington, DC, Romance Writers, who've held my hand for all these years and never let go. I love you guys!

A huge thanks to my brother-in-law and Charleston, SC, lawyer Bill Hanahan (William Ogier Hanahan III, Esquire) whose family stories inspired the historical aspects of this series and whose knowledge of obscure Southern seventeenth-century real estate law and the history of King's Grants saved this book.

A girl is nothing without her friends, and I'm lucky to have Jean Anspaugh, Shannon McGrail, and Jackie Iodice by my side, and Zoe Gwennap in my heart.

Sandals South Coast Resort in Jamaica. I started this book on the French beach, where the bar staff kept me hydrated, the lifeguards kept me safe, and the concierge reminded me to wear sunscreen. Thank you for providing such a wonderful place to relax and dream.

No acknowledgment is complete without mentioning family. So I'm raising my glass in an Irish toast to:

My mother and Rooster, my sister and her husband, my mother-in-law and father-in-law, along with my husband's enormous family, who stood by me during the *Great Rejection Years* with love and support. You all are more awesome than words can convey.

My father, who may not be here on earth, but is with me always.

My twins, who made me a mother when everyone told me it would never happen. You've filled my life with laughter and given it meaning. I will always be here for you.

My husband, whose heroic qualities and unconditional love taught me to believe in romance and made me a better woman. I will always love you.

My one-eyed rescue dog, whose constant need for attention made me a more patient person. I will always feed you.

Finally, to my readers. This book's journey took seven and a half years from idea to shelf, along with an army of people who believed in it. This book, and the ones to come, are absolute proof that dreams do come true. Just don't ever, ever, *ever* give up.

ABOUT THE AUTHOR

Sharon Wray is a librarian/archivist who studied dress design in the couture houses of Paris and now writes stories of adventure, suspense, and love. She lives in Virginia with her superhero husband, teenage twins, and Donut the one-eyed dog.

SEARCH AND RESCUE

In the Rockies, lives depend on the
Search & Rescue brotherhood. But this far
off the map, secrets can be murder.

By Katie Ruggle

Hold Your Breath

Louise "Lou" Sparks is a hurricane—a
walking disaster. And with her, ice
diving captain Callum Cook has never
felt more alive...even if keeping her
safe may just kill him.

Fan the Flames

Firefighter and Motorcycle Club
member Ian Walsh rides the line
between the good guys and the bad.
But if a killer has his way, Ian will
take the fall for a murder he didn't
commit...and lose the woman he's
always loved.

Gone Too Deep

George Halloway is a mystery. Tall. Dark. Intense. But city girl Ellie Price will need him by her side if she wants to find her father…and live to tell the tale.

In Safe Hands

Deputy Sheriff Chris Jennings has always been a hero to agoraphobe Daisy Little, but one wrong move ended their future before it could begin. Now he'll do whatever it takes to keep her safe—even if that means turning against one of his own.

For more Katie Ruggle, visit:

sourcebooks.com

SURVIVE THE NIGHT

Third in the thrilling Rocky Mountain K9 Unit series.

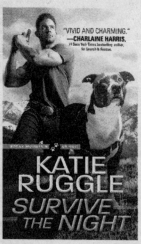

K9 Officer Otto Gunnersen has always had a soft spot for anyone in need—but for all his big heart, he's never been in love. Until he meets Sarah Clifton

All Sarah wants is to escape, but there's no outrunning her past. Her power-mad brother would hunt her to the ends of the earth...but he'd never expect her to fight back. With Otto by her side, Sarah's finally ready to face whatever comes her way.

"Vivid and charming."

—Charlaine Harris, #1 *New York Times* **Bestselling Author**

For more Katie Ruggle, visit:
sourcebooks.com

FATAL DREAMS

Suspense and action abound in this gripping paranormal romance series by Golden Heart finalist author Abbie Roads.

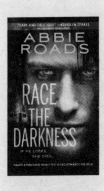

Race the Darkness

Her voice haunts his thoughts; her whispers fill his days. But when he discovers the woman of his dreams is real, he'll race the clock to save her before she's lost to him forever.

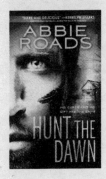

Hunt the Dawn

When Lathan Montgomery's hunt for a serial killer leads him to a woman whose nightmares provide very real clues, he'll have to keep her out of harm's way if their relationship has any hope of survival.

For more Abbie Roads, visit:
sourcebooks.com

BLACK KNIGHTS INC.

These elite ex-military operatives are as unique and tough as their custom-made Harleys.

By Julie Ann Walker, *New York Times* and *USA Today* Bestselling Author

Too Hard to Handle

Dan "The Man" Currington is hot on the trail of a rogue CIA agent when he runs into old flame and former Secret Service Agent Penni DePaul. Now Dan's number one priority is keeping her safe—at all costs.

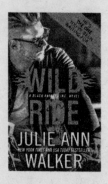

Wild Ride

Former Navy SEAL Ethan "Ozzie" Sykes is the hero everyone's been waiting for. When he's stuck distracting reporter Samantha Tate, he quickly loses his desire to keep her at bay...

Fuel for Fire

Spitfire CIA agent Chelsea Duvall has always had a thing for bossy, brooding covert operative Dagan Zoelner. It's just as well that he's never given her a second look, since she carries a combustible secret about his past that threatens to torch their lives…

Hot Pursuit

Former SAS officer and BKI operator Christian Watson has fought for his life before. Doing it with the beautiful, bossy former CIA operative Emily Scott in tow is another matter entirely.

"Her best yet… This razor-sharp, sensual, and intriguing tale will get hearts pounding."

—Publishers Weekly, Starred Review for Wild Ride

For more Julie Ann Walker, visit:
sourcebooks.com